The Golden Anklet

By the same Author

'Julie'
A captivating novel

'With Rucksack and Bus Pass'
Walking the Thames Path

'Roots in Three Counties'
Family history

'A Touch of Autumn Gold'
A novel for the young in heart

The

BEVERLEY HANSFORD

Matador
9 Priory Business Park,
Wistow Road, Kibworth Beauchamp,
Leicestershire. LE8 0RX
Tel: 0116 279 2299
Email: books@troubador.co.uk
Web: www.troubador.co.uk/matador
Twitter: @matadorbooks

ISBN 978 1784624 675

British Library Cataloguing in Publication Data.
A catalogue record for this book is available from the British Library.

Printed and bound in the UK by TJ International, Padstow, Cornwall
Typeset in 11pt Bembo by Troubador Publishing Ltd, Leicester, UK

Matador is an imprint of Troubador Publishing Ltd

This book is dedicated
To all those people like Jane
who seek the truth
and have to brave challenges
along the way.

Chapter 1

Tim Bostock felt the rear wheels of his taxi slide slightly as he made the sharp turn into Station Road. He scolded himself; he should have remembered that this part of the road could be slippery at certain times, and tonight there was already an inch of fresh snow on the road.

He gave a quick glance at the interior mirror to see if his passenger had noticed anything, but she still sat quietly with her briefcase resting on her knees. 'Will you take me to the railway station? I want to get the train back to London,' had been her request at the start of the journey, but since then she had been quiet, seemingly not wanting to engage in conversation, though she had responded politely and in a pleasant manner to the occasional comment he had made during the short ride.

It had been her remark about wishing to get back to London that had made him hurry. He knew the last train to London from Tatting Green was around 11.30pm, and the clock on the dashboard was fast approaching that time. He had not intended to do another journey this evening. He was tired after being up since four this morning, but when the phone call had come through from Angus Pike, Tim knew he could not refuse. Angus Pike was an artist who lived in the nearby village of Tatting Green. He had a reputation among the other residents of the village for being both rude and irritable, but for Tim he was a good customer. Hardly a week went by without a request to take him somewhere, usually to the station. On top of that there were the frequent calls to transport various young women to and from the station, all models the artist appeared to employ to pose for his paintings. At first Tim

1

had assumed his current passenger must be one of them, but he had quickly changed his mind: she was too smartly dressed, in a neat, dark business suit and high heels. On top of that the briefcase she carried didn't fit in; perhaps she was a solicitor or something similar, he wondered.

Tim pulled up outside the station entrance. 'Here we are,' he announced.

His passenger immediately sprang into action and quickly opened her door. She stepped out and came round to his window. Tim lowered it.

'How much do I owe you?' she asked.

'Five pounds, please,' he replied.

She rummaged in her purse, produced a five-pound note and some small change and handed it to him. 'Thank you very much,' she said, with a pleasant smile.

'Thank you.' He was prompted to add, 'I think I hear the train now.'

'Oh, no! I don't want to miss it. Good night. Thank you.'

And with those few words she was gone, hurrying towards the wicket gate that opened onto a path leading down to the station platform.

'Good night,' Tim called after her and then closed his window. He watched her disappear from view and then waited a few minutes. He wanted to be sure she caught the train. Tatting Green was a lonely station these days. Few trains stopped there and most of the station's business was at peak times, serving commuters travelling the twenty-five-mile journey to and from London, but many people preferred to drive to the town of Tatting Cross three miles away, where there was a better train service. Tatting Green had only really come into existence when the railway line had been built, due to the insistence of the family who resided in nearby Tatting Hall. If the railway company wanted to buy some of their land for a railway line, then the railway company would have to provide a station for the family and villagers to use, and thus Tatting Green had come into being. The station had been quite busy in its first years, particularly after Tatting Hall was sold and a golf course was built on the land. Now all the golfers preferred to use their cars, so Tatting Green railway station had seen better days.

Satisfied that his mysterious late-night passenger was safely on the train, Tim put the taxi into gear and slowly drove off. Now for home, a hot drink and then bed, he thought.

But Tim Bostock was wrong. His passenger had not caught the train. As she hurried down to the platform, conscious that the train was already standing in the station, a stiletto failed to get a grip on the icy surface. Her foot slipped, she tried to keep her balance, but she ended up sitting on the path; one shoe had come off and her briefcase had fallen from her grasp. She recovered quickly; grabbing the briefcase and stuffing her foot into her shoe, she continued as best she could down the slope. Just as she reached the level security of the platform, the train revved its engines and started to move.

'Oh, no!' Her exclamation was almost a wail of despair.

She watched helplessly as the lights of the train disappeared from view. The driver had not seen her desperate waving and the train had not dropped off any passengers. She was alone on the station platform.

Resigned to the fact that she had missed the train, she considered her options. Initially she considered hurrying back up the slope to see if the taxi was still there, but she thought that by now it would have gone. She turned to the small building that served as a waiting room and tiny ticket office. There was a timetable on the wall, but it was behind glass, and condensation and the poor light made it impossible to read. She peered into the tiny waiting room, but it was unlit and had an odd smell about it. Still, it was some sort of shelter, and she stood in the open doorway trying to decide what to do next. The snow was falling in quite large flakes now. Several times she had to brush them out of her hair. On top of that she shivered in her inadequate covering. The pleasantly warm March morning had prompted her to leave her coat at home. Now she regretted the decision. The sunshine had soon disappeared, to be replaced by dark clouds, and by about teatime the snow had started to fall. It was winter having a last fling.

The sound of another train roused her from her thoughts. However, it was going in the other direction. She watched it stop on the opposite platform, wait a minute or two and then start to move out of the station. At first she thought no passengers had alighted, but then she realised that there were two, a man and a teenage girl. Both were walking over the bridge that connected the two platforms. The girl passed her quickly, almost running, with only a brief glance in her direction, but the man walked at a more leisurely pace.

She seized the opportunity and darted out in front of him. 'Excuse me, do you know if there is another train to London tonight?' Her voice had an anxious note to it.

The man quickly recovered from the surprise of her sudden appearance. He stopped and glanced at his watch. 'No. The last train will have gone.' He sounded concerned.

'Oh, no! That must have been the one I just missed.' In almost the same breath she asked, 'Is there a taxi I can get somewhere?'

He responded immediately. The next instant he had his mobile phone in his hand. 'I've got the number for the local taxi. I can try it for you,' he suggested, and without waiting for her to reply he selected the number. He waited, the phone to his ear. After a minute or so he turned to her and spoke again. 'Unfortunately, shut down for the night. Not available until tomorrow morning.'

She received the news glumly. 'I expect that's the one who brought me here. He said it was going to be his last run of the evening.' The remark was almost made to herself.

Another thought struck her. 'Is there a hotel nearby?' she asked hopefully.

He thought for a few seconds. 'Yes. There is one, but it's about two miles away.' He studied her to see how she would respond to this news.

She replied immediately. 'Can you point me in the right direction? I'll walk there.'

He admired her determination, but a glance at the high-heeled shoes that peeped out below her trousers highlighted the problems she would have. She must be cold as well, without a coat. He thought for a few seconds. He had to offer some sort of assistance.

'Can I help? I only live about a quarter of a mile away and I've got a car. I can run you there quite quickly.'

She was taken by surprise. Getting into a car with a strange man late at night was not without some concerns, but he did seem quite genuine.

'But that's putting you to a lot of trouble,' she protested mildly.

He smiled at her. 'I don't like to see people stuck.'

She thought quickly. It was her only option. The prospect of walking two miles in the snow was not inviting. She had to take a chance – just for once.

'It would be most helpful, if you don't mind.'

'Great. Let's go, then.'

They retreated up the path from the station platform. She took the opportunity to study her benefactor. He was much younger than she had first thought. Now that he was closer to her she could see that he could not be much older than her own age of 27.

After a few minutes' silence, he asked, 'So what brings you to Tatting Green?'

'Oh, I had to interview Angus Pike, the artist. Do you know him?' She turned to him as she spoke.

He smiled. 'I don't know him personally, but I've seen him around. He's quite a character and he has a reputation for being a bit eccentric.'

'I had to interview him for a magazine I work for. We're doing a feature on him.' As she finished volunteering this last information she suddenly halted and turned to him. She held out her hand. 'By the way, I'm Jane Carroll.'

His response was immediate. He grasped her hand firmly and smiled again. 'Bob Harker,' he replied.

They crossed over the small car park to the road.

'Have you always lived in Tatting Green?' asked Jane.

He shook his head. 'Only since my divorce three years ago. I wanted somewhere to live and I knew the couple who were selling the house I live in now, so I bought it from them.'

'It's always nice to know the person you buy a house— Oops!' Jane's reply was cut short as her foot slipped on the snow-covered road. She almost fell again.

'Can you manage? It is a bit slippery.'

'Umm…' Jane stopped walking. She looked down at the ground and then slipped off first one shoe and then the other. Standing barefoot, she made a face at the sudden cold.

Bob watched her with curiosity. 'I say, are you sure you'll be all right? Your feet will be freezing cold.' His voice was full of concern.

Jane gave a little laugh. 'Well, I may get cold feet or chilblains, but hopefully I won't break an ankle or a leg,' she replied breezily, adding for good measure, 'I've been on my bottom once already this evening.'

They continued walking and chatting. As they neared some houses, Bob announced, 'Here we are. This is me.'

Jane followed the wave of his hand and spied a pair of semi-detached houses, each with a short drive off the road.

Bob turned into the drive of the first house. 'I'll just get my car keys,' he announced.

Jane waited on the drive while he went into the house. While he was unlocking the garage door, she dusted the snow off her feet and slipped on her shoes again, glad of their comfort.

Bob reversed the small car out and waited for her to get in.

As they moved off, it was Jane who spoke first. 'I really am most grateful to you for helping me out.'

He turned to her and grinned for a second. 'Well, Tatting Green station waiting room is hardly the Ritz.'

'At least it's stopped snowing now,' observed Jane, as they drove along the country road, the car headlights illuminating the fallen snow.

'The weather forecast is for it to do that,' replied Bob, 'and clearing by the morning.'

She gave a little laugh. 'Well, at least that's something to look forward to. The cold snap certainly caught me out. If I'd known it was going to suddenly get colder, I'd have worn something warmer.' She glanced down at her clothes.

Bob smiled and nodded. He had almost been taken in by the sunny morning himself, but as things turned out he had been glad he had worn his trusty anorak. He had felt a bit sorry for Jane as they walked to his house. She had looked really cold. The thought prompted him to turn up the heater. 'I'm afraid my car is a bit old and the heater doesn't work very well,' he observed.

'I wish I'd used my car now,' lamented Jane. 'I could have been tucked up in bed by now.'

'Where do you live?' asked Bob.

'Near the river, at Kew,' she replied.

He was just about to point out that driving that distance might have been difficult this evening, but they had now reached the main road and the hotel neon sign was already in sight.

'Here we are. This is the place I had in mind,' he announced.

'It looks super.' Jane felt relieved at the sight of the hotel.

Bob stopped the car almost at the hotel entrance. He kept the engine running. 'I'll just wait to make sure you get a room OK.'

'Thanks a million. I'll be back in a jiffy,' and with that Jane got out of the car.

Bob watched her disappear into the hotel lobby. He was intrigued by his newly found companion. She was quite attractive with her slim figure and clear complexion. He liked her practical approach to everything as well. He had felt obliged to help her, in spite of the fact that normally he wouldn't have taken his old car out in snowy conditions. The way she had dealt with walking on the slippery road surface had surprised him. Many women of his acquaintance would have merely whinged, but she had suffered discomfort to solve the problem. He wondered whether she was married. She wasn't wearing a wedding ring, but in this day and age that meant nothing.

His pondering was broken by her reappearance. She was looking a bit glum. 'The hotel is completely full. They've got a conference on or something,' she announced as she opened the passenger door and looked in at him.

Bob received the news in silence. He thought for a moment. 'There is another place in the village – a sort of bed and breakfast place.' He spoke slowly as if he were still thinking. In the same breath and with a voice engaging more vigour, he suggested, 'I could take you there.' He looked at her enquiringly.

'Oh, please. Would you do that?' She was already slipping back into her seat and clipping on her seat belt.

Bob nodded his assent. 'I'll take you there. It's not far.'

They returned the way they had come, their conversation limited, Jane concerned that she was putting her saviour to a lot of trouble, and Bob concentrating on his driving. The road was quite drivable but it demanded care.

As they passed Bob's house, Jane voiced her concern. 'I feel I'm putting you to a great deal of inconvenience. I'm beginning to feel quite bad about it.'

'It's not every night I get to play knight gallant.' He laughed.

Jane made no reply. She wondered if there was a hidden meaning in his remark. Perhaps not, she thought.

Within a few minutes Bob had stopped the car outside a large house with a bed and breakfast sign in the front garden. A quick glance told them all they wanted to know. A second notice was displayed: 'No Vacancies'.

The shock of this created a few moments' silence between them. It was Jane who spoke first. 'Oh, no!' she exclaimed, looking at Bob, who appeared to be deep in thought.

Suddenly he turned to her. 'I can provide you with a bed for the night,' he announced.

Chapter 2

For a few seconds Jane felt stunned. Bob's suggestion had created the worst possible scenario for her. It was a fear that had been at the back of her mind since she had first accepted his assistance, but desperation had forced her to put it aside. He had appeared quite genuine, anxious to help her and not the sort of man who would take advantage of the situation. Now, however, she was faced with a problem: how to extract herself from an awkward predicament. She hastened to find suitable words to use – kind but firm.

She turned to him and forced a brief smile. 'Well, thank you for the offer, but I'm not really a one-night-stand girl.'

As soon as she observed his reaction she knew she had made a terrible mistake. His face coloured slightly and he struggled to get his words out. 'Look, I'm terribly sorry… I didn't mean it that way… It's just… Well, it's just that I live on my own and I have a spare room you can use.' He paused for a second and then he added a bit miserably, 'You can even lock the bedroom door.'

It was Jane's turn to be embarrassed. She had got it all wrong. Somehow she had to try to rectify an awkward state of affairs. She placed her hand gently on his arm. 'I'm so sorry. I really am. I got your suggestion completely wrong, but you know a girl has to be careful.' She spoke more softly. 'And if your offer of a room for the night is still there, I'll be pleased to accept it, providing there are no strings attached.'

Bob recovered quickly at her words. He smiled at her. 'That's fine. Sorry I didn't phrase my invitation better,' he offered, as he put the car into gear and they moved off again.

For a couple of minutes there was silence between them. It was broken by Bob. 'Just for the record, I'm not a one-night-stand guy either. I like to get to know women before I invite them into my bed.' He spoke without looking at her.

Jane was a bit taken aback by the remark, but given the circumstances she felt that she deserved it. After all, men had feelings as well.

It was a case of responding gracefully. 'I know what you mean. Thank you for telling me,' was her reply.

It was only a short time before Bob drove the car into his driveway and parked neatly in front of the garage. They both got out, and Bob ushered Jane into the house, turning on the light as they entered.

Jane looked around her with interest. They were in a small hall, empty except for a coat rack and a side table with a telephone.

Bob dropped his rucksack on the floor and took off his anorak and hung it up. This short interlude gave Jane an opportunity to study her companion more closely. He was quite nice-looking, really, she thought, perhaps an inch or two taller than she was, even though she was wearing high heels, and he had a mop of sandy hair that was quite attractive.

Her brief scrutiny was interrupted by Bob speaking to her again. 'Come into the kitchen,' he invited. 'It'll be warmer in there.'

Jane followed him into a fairly large bright and cheery room.

'Do sit down,' he said.

She chose a convenient chair close to the kitchen table. She felt a bit awkward.

Bob started to fill a kettle. He turned to her, hesitating. 'I usually make myself a drink – cocoa or something like that. Will you join me?'

'I'd love to. Cocoa would be fine,' enthused Jane. She still felt cold, and the thought of a hot drink to warm up was inviting.

Bob clicked the kettle on to boil as he announced, 'I'll just quickly get your room ready. Can I leave you for two minutes?'

'Off course you can. I'm fine.' Jane smiled at him as he rushed past her.

She sat alone in the kitchen. She could hear some movement upstairs and wondered what sort of accommodation she would have for the night. She glanced at her watch. It was already past midnight. She still felt a bit bad about misinterpreting Bob's suggestion and she hoped he hadn't taken offence. He did seem quite nice and really rather handsome. With his slim build and pleasant smile, he would be eyed up by many women as a potential partner.

The click of the kettle turning itself off ended her musing. She wondered if she should try to start making their drinks, but at that moment Bob reappeared. He grinned at her. 'That's done. Now for the cocoa.'

'Can I help?' She was anxious to do something instead of just sitting there and being waited on.

He shook his head. 'No. You're a guest,' he replied, smiling. He was busy for a few minutes making the cocoa, pausing once to enquire whether she took sugar – which she did not. He placed the two mugs on the table and slipped into one of the chairs opposite her.

Jane clasped her hands around the mug, enjoying the heat. 'You appear to live very well and be well organised,' she said, looking at him and then around the neat and tidy kitchen.

He smiled. 'That's really down to Mrs McGinty. She came originally to do some cleaning for me, but now she does everything: washing, the lot. She even tells me when I need a new toothbrush.' He ended with a little laugh.

'It's nice to have somebody like that,' Jane agreed politely.

They chatted over the cocoa, beginning to feel a bit more relaxed with each other.

'What do you do for a living, Bob?' Jane asked the question she had been pondering since they met.

'I'm a photographer,' he replied, looking at her as if enquiring how she would receive the announcement.

11

'That's interesting.' She looked at him encouragingly, inviting more details.

He continued. 'I do a lot of magazine work and I also have an interest in a studio in London. I'm usually there several days a week. I also have a photo stock library.' He thought for a second. 'I do a bit of writing as well.'

'Gosh, that's quite a lot!' Jane exclaimed, smiling at him.

'It keeps me busy and a roof over my head,' he replied. His remark was accompanied with one of his grins. He took another drink of his cocoa and studied his guest. He was keen to know more about her. 'What about you? What exactly do you do?' He looked at her enquiringly.

She responded immediately. 'Do you know '*Discerning Woman* magazine?' she asked.

Bob nodded. He remembered that it was an upmarket glossy publication for women.

Jane continued. 'I've worked for it for about three years now. I'm the features editor. We're just a small team.'

'I think you used one of my photos once,' he remarked thoughtfully, trying to remember what the photo was about.

'That's quite possible. We do use photo libraries from time to time.'

'And you interviewed Angus Pike.' He chuckled.

His remark prompted a smile from Jane. 'Just by accident, really. My colleague Amy, who was going to do the interview, rang in sick, so the task fell into the lap of yours truly. That's how I came to be completely unprepared for this weather.' She glanced down at her business suit.

'How did you get on with him?' asked Bob. 'He's got quite a reputation for being unsociable.'

Jane made a face. 'An awful person to deal with,' she announced. She sipped her cocoa. 'Trying to get his co-operation in the first place was quite difficult. We were at it for twelve months. Then when he finally agreed, he kept changing the date.'

'But you made it in the end,' Bob interjected.

She nodded. 'But not without some aggravation. First of all the appointment was supposed to be for two in the afternoon, then when I rang up to confirm, he wanted to make it six-thirty this evening, so I had to come straight from the office.'

'What was he like to interview?' Bob asked.

'We didn't get off to a good start. When I arrived his housekeeper let me in and took me into his studio, where he was still working. He had a model posing for him. He just told me to go and sit down and be quiet until he had finished.'

'Whew. That was some greeting,' Bob sympathised.

'I know. I had to share a settee with a large, smelly dog. I must have sat there for over an hour and he hardly said a word.'

'What happened then?' By now Bob was completely intrigued.

Jane smiled as she recollected her interview. 'That's the odd part,' she explained. 'When he had finished working, he became quite friendly. He wanted to show me some of his paintings and then he insisted on me staying to supper. That's when he talked about himself a bit and allowed me to take some notes.'

She was silent for a few minutes, drinking her cocoa and recalling her time with the eccentric artist. She remembered his appearance, dressed in a dirty pullover and paint-spattered jeans. His mass of grey hair and untidy beard, together with sandals and no socks, had added to his air of eccentricity. In his studio there had been paint everywhere and she had been worried about getting it on her clothes. Her recollections were interrupted by Bob, who was eager to know more about Angus Pike.

'You don't see a lot of his work in this country.'

Jane shook her head. 'No. I think he fell out with the art world here ages ago. He sells most of his paintings abroad, particularly in America. I think he makes quite a lot of money. Some of his work is specially commissioned.'

'His paintings are rather erotic, aren't they?' Bob asked, draining the last of his cocoa.

Jane grinned at him. 'That's right. A lot of them have a fantasy

13

theme and feature women in some predicament, usually without clothes. He had a nude model posing for him this afternoon.'

Bob smiled as she finished speaking. 'I know. I've seen some of his paintings,' he commented. 'But you got your interview in the end.'

'Absolutely. I'm really pleased with myself over that. It's a scoop, because he has flatly refused in the past to be interviewed by the media.'

'You must have charmed him.'

Jane paused for a few seconds, then she casually remarked, with a slight smile, 'He ended up by asking me to model for him.'

'Will you?'

She shook her head. 'I said I'd think about it.' She added with a grin, 'I won't say no until after the article is published.'

Bob laughed. 'Good for you.'

His remark prompted another smile from Jane.

There were a few seconds' silence between them. Bob was becoming attracted to his guest. He still wondered whether she was married. She was surely in some sort of relationship, particularly as she was clearly well into her twenties. He plucked up courage to ask the question that had been at the top of his agenda since they had started chatting. 'Are you married, Jane?'

She shook her head. 'I was. I lost my husband three years ago in a plane crash.'

A wave of sadness appeared to come over her, and Bob immediately regretted asking the question. 'I'm so sorry,' he said. 'That's a raw deal.' He felt in the circumstances that his reply was a bit inadequate.

Jane appeared to want to elaborate. She gazed down at the table for an instant, as if deep in thought, and then continued. 'I was completely devastated at the time. We were very much in love and had only been married two and a half years.'

Bob was about to say something, but she changed the subject. She glanced up at the clock on the wall and then at her watch. She turned to him with that smile again. 'It's lovely chatting, but it's

14

morning already and I have to be at work by nine. If you don't mind, I think I'll turn in now.'

Bob jumped up immediately. 'Of course. I'll show you your room. It's all ready.'

He led the way into the hall. Jane noticed that he had changed into house shoes. She slipped off her own shoes before following him up the stairs.

On the tiny landing, Bob threw open a door, turned on the light and stood aside to let her pass. 'Here we are,' he announced.

Jane was impressed. The bedroom was small and simply furnished, but it had a homely feel. What took her immediate interest were the articles neatly placed on the single bed. A clean white towel and what looked like a pair of pyjamas were placed side by side. On top of the towel was a new toothbrush in its wrapper.

Immediately she turned to Bob. 'Gosh, what room service!' She gave a little laugh as she spoke, but then became more serious. 'But I feel I'm putting you to such a lot of extra work.'

He shook his head. 'Not at all. My sister Cissy comes to stay with me from time to time and the pyjamas are hers. She's about your size, and I'm sure she won't mind you borrowing them. And Mrs McGinty will do the necessary afterwards.'

'I really appreciate your kindness. Thank you very much for all your help.' Jane really meant what she said.

'It's been my pleasure. What time would you like a call?' he asked, adding, 'I'm usually up and about early.'

'So am I,' replied Jane. 'And I'll have to catch quite an early train.'

'If I don't hear you about by seven, I'll give you a knock,' he offered.

'Marvellous. And thank you again.' She held out her hand.

Bob grasped it and, with 'Good night and sleep well,' he turned to leave her.

'Good night,' Jane called after him from the landing as he retreated down the stairs.

She went back into the bedroom. She picked up the pyjamas

and shook them out. They looked as if they might be a bit big, but so what? It was better than sleeping in underwear. She smiled to herself, thinking of Bob's care and attention to her. He would make a good catch for someone, she thought. She wondered what had caused his divorce. Perhaps he would tell her.

Her thoughts turned to more practical matters. She could hear Bob pottering downstairs in the kitchen. She took the opportunity. Grabbing the towel and the toothbrush she dived into the bathroom across the landing. Five minutes later she was back in the bedroom. She closed the door and then silently turned the key in the lock. It just gave her that extra feeling of security.

She undressed quickly and put on the pyjamas. She had been mistaken with her first appraisal of them. They were not as big as she had at first thought, and they fitted her reasonably well. What a nice gesture on Bob's part to let her use them.

She turned out the bedside light. She heard Bob come up the stairs and go into the bathroom. For a few seconds she lay back in bed and went over the events of what was now the previous day. First Amy ringing in sick, making her obliged to do the interview with Angus Pike, with the subsequent delays. Achieving her goal, and then missing the last train. If Bob hadn't turned up, where would she have spent the night? Before she reached an answer she was asleep.

Chapter 3

The first spots of rain were starting to fall as Jane emerged from the Underground station. She hesitated for an instant, debating whether she should extract her umbrella from her bag, but quickly dismissed the idea. The *Discerning Woman* offices were no more than three or four minutes' brisk walk away.

She hurried along. She was already running late due to delays on her train. The rain became heavier towards the end of her walk and she was glad to reach her destination. She pushed open the heavy door and climbed the stairs to the first floor. Margaret, the receptionist, was already seated at her desk.

'Good morning, Margaret,' Jane greeted her cheerfully.

Margaret looked a bit glum. Her reply was equally flat.

'Good morning, Jane.' She looked at Jane for a second and then added in a subdued voice, 'Queen Bee's back. She's been asking for you already.'

Jane grinned. 'Thanks for the tip. I'll make myself a coffee and go and see her.'

Margaret said nothing. Jane smiled to herself. She was aware of how some of her colleagues viewed the magazine's editor-in-chief. Brisk and domineering, Annette Burrows had a tendency to ruffle a few feathers from time to time. 'Queen Bee' was the name the staff called her behind her back.

Jane made her way to her tiny office, passing Amy as she went. Jane had hardly greeted her before Amy burst out, 'Queen Bee's got the draft of the Angus Pike article. It was the first thing she asked me for. I had to give it to her.' She looked anxiously at Jane.

Jane reassured her. 'Don't worry. I'll go and see her in a minute.'

17

She felt a bit sorry for her younger colleague, who, though quite capable, appeared to be easily intimidated by Annette. In her first few months in the job, Jane had also experienced Annette's interference, but she had quickly established a working relationship with her and ignored her brusque, overbearing manner. It usually fell to Jane to keep an eye on things while Annette was out of the office or on holiday.

Five minutes later, coffee in hand, Jane was at her desk. Being late for work had upset her plans for the start of the day. With Annette returning from holiday that morning, she had intended to be in the office extra early so that she could have everything ready for the inevitable discussion with her. Now she knew she was fighting time until the summons came.

Her assumption was correct. She had only taken a few sips of her coffee before the buzzer on the internal telephone sounded. She picked up the receiver and gave her usual answer: 'Jane.'

'Ah, good morning, Jane. You are there. Can we get together?'

Jane answered as cheerfully as she could. 'Good morning, Annette. Yes, of course. Now, if you like.'

'Excellent.' Annette put the phone down. She was not accustomed to wasting words.

Jane sighed. She would have liked more time to get everything together, but in the circumstances she would do the best she could. Collecting as much of the paperwork as she thought she would need, coffee in hand, she made her way up to the next floor.

She hesitated before the slightly open door marked 'Annette Burrows B.A. Editor-in-Chief'. She could hear her boss talking on the phone. She waited until she heard her finish the call, and then she pushed open the door and entered.

'Good morning again. Did you have a nice holiday?' She deliberately tried to sound cheerful as she sat down on the chair opposite Annette.

Annette shuffled some papers on the desk before looking up and giving Jane her attention and answer.

'Weather was awful. What's been happening while I've been

away?' It was almost as if the reply and question were all part of the same thing.

Jane smiled inwardly. That was typical of Annette. Rarely did she speak about her private life and activities. All the staff knew was that she lived in Greenwich with two dogs and a henpecked partner for company. She had told Jane before leaving that she was going to Cornwall, but that had been all. Jane took her time and started to relate the fortnight's activities, answering Annette's questions as she went along.

Suddenly, Annette interrupted her. 'I've got the draft here of the Angus Pike article.' She picked up the paperwork from the side of her desk and placed it in front of herself. She scrutinised it for a few seconds before looking at Jane again. 'It looks quite good. Of course there are one or two things that could be altered.'

That was inevitable, Jane thought. She had been down this road many times, but all she said in reply was, 'That's just the draft, based on my interview with him.'

'When did you see him?'

'The week before last.'

'How did the meeting go?'

Jane hesitated before answering, recalling her meeting with the artist. She chose her words carefully. 'Hmm. A bit difficult at first, but in the end he was quite agreeable. I got everything we wanted.'

'What about photos? What have we got?'

'At first he didn't want any pictures at all, but in the end I managed to get four from him and the go-ahead to use them.'

Jane extracted the photos from her file and placed them on the desk in front of Annette. 'I thought we might use this one of him just under the header, and at least two of the others among the text,' she suggested.

Annette studied the images for a few seconds and then stared straight at Jane, a look of reproach and horror on her face. Jane waited for the comments she knew were bound to follow.

'We can't use these in our magazine. They're almost

19

pornographic.' These seemed to be her final words on the subject.

Jane already had an answer ready. 'I think they may be OK among the text, and they won't be that big,' she suggested confidently.

Annette shook her head. 'I don't like them. Can't you ask him for something else?' she demanded.

Remembering the struggle she had had to obtain the pictures, Jane was not enthusiastic about the suggestion. 'It was quite difficult getting these. I don't think he would be very cooperative,' she replied.

Annette thought for a few seconds. Suddenly she snapped into action. 'Give me his phone number,' she demanded. 'I'll contact him and get something different.'

'Of course.' Jane searched in her file for the artist's number and scribbled it on the desk pad. She and Amy had discussed the images in detail and agreed that all except the one of the artist were explicit, to say the least. Each was a photograph of a painting that featured one or more pretty young women suffering some sort of ordeal or indignity. The fact that all the subjects were fully or nearly naked added to their erotic nature. Jane and Amy had deliberated over the pictures and in the end had decided that they would use them. After all, this was an article about the celebrated artist, and this was the sort of painting he created. At the same time they had both anticipated problems with Annette.

Jane handed the phone number to Annette, who gave it a cursory look and then placed it in the top drawer of her desk. She turned to Jane again, at the same time glancing at the clock on the wall. 'We'll have a meeting later on about the Pike feature,' she announced. 'What else have you got for me?'

Jane sighed to herself. It was quite clear that she and Amy were held up on the feature until Annette had contacted Angus Pike. She knew that the exercise was doomed from the start. Annette's overbearing manner and the artist's irritability were certain to clash head-on. She just hoped that the editor-in-chief's interference didn't blow things apart after all her efforts.

Jane's report on the happenings in the office during Annette's absence lasted over an hour, but at last Annette looked at the wall clock again and announced that she was going to be late for an appointment. It was a signal that the meeting was over. Jane gathered her files together, picked up her mug and took her leave. As she passed by Amy's desk on the way back to her office, Amy looked up enquiringly.

'We're going to have a meeting later on with Annette about the Angus Pike feature,' Jane replied to the silent question.

'What about the pictures?' Amy asked in a hushed voice.

Jane leaned towards her. 'Annette's going to phone him to see if she can get something different,' she replied. She added almost to herself, 'I just hope she doesn't ruin everything.'

'Oh, no!' wailed Amy.

Jane grinned at her colleague as she offered a few words of reassurance. 'I expect we'll end up using the ones we have.'

Amy made a face and grabbed her mug from the desk. 'I'm going to make myself some tea,' she announced, getting up from her chair. 'Do you want one?'

'Please.' Jane handed Amy her mug and then, glancing at her watch, announced, 'And I'd better get on with some work. I've got some calls to make first.'

She retreated to the privacy of her tiny office. Dumping the files on the end of the desk, she picked up her notepad ready to start work. First, though, it had to be those phone calls, and one in particular. She reached into her bag and took out a business card: *Bob Harker – Freelance Photographer.*

Holding the card brought back memories of the night she had spent at his house. He had been so sweet to her. Goodness knows where she would have ended up if he hadn't rescued her.

Despite her initial anxiety about sleeping in a strange man's house, she had experienced a restful night. She had woken up early and waited until she heard Bob in the bathroom and then his footsteps going downstairs. After a few seconds she had dived into the bathroom.

Back in the bedroom, she had been fully dressed except for her shoes when she heard Bob coming back up the stairs. A second later there had been a tap at her door followed by Bob's voice: 'Are you awake? I've brought you some tea.'

'Hang on a second.' She put down the pyjamas she was folding and hurried to the door. She flung it wide open. Bob stood there, a steaming mug of tea in one hand. 'Good morning. Did you sleep well?' he asked, smiling.

'Good morning. I had a marvellous sleep, thank you.' Smiling broadly, she glanced at the mug of tea. 'And such room service. Fantastic.'

Bob grinned at her and turned the mug round so that she could grasp the handle. 'I guessed no sugar and not too much milk,' he announced.

Jane took the mug. 'Super. Just what I need.'

'It's just coming up to seven. I thought you might like some breakfast before you go for the train.'

'Oh, yes, please.'

'Fine. I'll get that going. Toast and marmalade OK?'

'Great. I'll be right down.' She turned to go back into the bedroom.

'The snow's gone,' Bob called as he went down the stairs.

'That's fantastic,' she called back.

Bob had insisted on driving her to the station. One of the last things she had done before leaving his house had been to pick up one of his business cards from the holder next to the telephone. Even then she had considered inviting him out to lunch one day as a sort of thank you, but with Annette being away she had had to put the thought on the back burner. Now that Annette was back there was no reason why she should not carry out her plan. She wanted to meet him again and find out a bit more about him. A lunch date would give her the opportunity.

She had just dialled his number when Amy pushed open the door and put a mug of tea on her desk. Jane put up her hand to thank her. The phone rang for a long time, and she was just about to put the receiver down when there was an answer.

'Bob Harker.'

Jane felt a bit excited. 'Bob, it's Jane, your unexpected guest. Remember me?'

'Of course I do. How are you?'

'I'm fine. I was wondering when you'll next be in London.'

'Actually, I'll be there tomorrow.'

There was a note of expectation in his voice. Jane felt her strategy was working. 'Could an appreciative guest take you out to lunch?' she enquired hopefully.

'I'd like that very much,' he replied enthusiastically. 'Where shall we meet?'

Jane thought quickly. She hadn't worked out the details, but the choice of venue was relatively easy. 'Do you know The Green Man in Elbon Street?' she asked.

There was a pause on the other end of the telephone.

'I know Elbon Street, but not The Green Man – but I'm sure I can find it OK,' he added quickly. 'What time?'

'Twelve-ish? It'll be quieter then.'

'Great. I'll look forward to that.'

'Terrific. I'll see you tomorrow, then. I'd better get on with some work now.' As she replied, Jane glanced at her watch.

'Me too. Bye for now.'

'Bye.'

Mission completed, she sat thinking for a few seconds. She was rather pleased with her strategy and planning. The thought of meeting up with Bob again was appealing.

Chapter 4

Bob was looking forward to meeting Jane again. It was something he had been thinking about a great deal, ever since the morning when he had delivered her to Tatting Green station. He had kicked himself afterwards for not arranging at the time to see her again, but he had hesitated in the rush of things, and the opportunity had been lost. He had planned to try to contact her at work, but her phone call the previous day had changed everything.

He walked along Elbon Street and found The Green Man easily. It was a pleasant-looking pub with tables and chairs on the pavement, though the current cool weather did not encourage lingering outside for any length of time. He entered the building. It had a bright and cheery atmosphere. He glanced at his watch and then around the room. It was coming up to midday and he wondered if he was a bit early. Then he saw Jane. She was sitting at a table in a corner looking at a menu card. He hurried over to her and she spied him almost at the same time. She jumped up, smiling cheerfully.

'Bob, it's lovely to see you again.' She grasped his hand and offered her cheek.

'It's great to see you again, Jane.' He smiled at her politely.

Jane dropped back into her chair, and as he sat down opposite her she handed him the menu. 'Now, this is all going to be on me. Just a small thank you for rescuing a little girl lost in the snow.' She laughed.

'Hey, I should pay for something,' he protested, grinning.

She shook her head and feigned an astonished look. 'Absolutely not. Goodness knows what would have happened to me if you hadn't come along that night.' She looked at him for an instant and chuckled. 'I can see the headlines in the newspaper: "Unknown female found frozen to death at Tatting Green station".'

Bob shared her mirth and was about to reply when she took control again. 'What would you like to eat? I am going to have a glass of apple juice and a tuna salad.'

A quick glance at the menu, and Bob made up his mind quickly. 'I'll have the same to eat, but I'll have half a pint of lager.'

'Right. I'll only be a minute,' she replied promptly. Grabbing the menu, she was off to the bar to order before he could protest.

He watched her walk away, taking confident steps in her high heels. She was wearing a figure-hugging business suit, which suited her trim figure, he observed. Her cheek had been soft and warm when he bent to kiss her, and there had been a faint scent of perfume about her. She was, he thought, a very attractive woman.

Jane returned and placed the drinks on the table. 'They'll bring the food over to us,' she said.

She held her glass aloft. 'Cheers.'

'Cheers,' Bob seconded. Then he enquired, 'Do you often come here?'

'Just occasionally. It's a nice place to bring anybody, and the food and service are very good.' As an afterthought she added, smiling, 'And it's not far from my office.'

'How is life at the office? How did the Angus Pike article go?'

'Life's been pretty busy, work-wise. My boss, Annette, has been on holiday and when she's away lots of things get dumped on my desk.' She hesitated for a second. 'As to the Angus Pike thing, Annette, who has the final say, didn't like the pictures I had.'

Bob nodded sympathetically. 'So what's going to happen now?' he asked.

'She's going to phone him and ask for something different. I just hope she doesn't upset things.'

Bob thought for a moment. 'I doubt it.' He smiled. 'But she'll most likely find that any other pictures of his work will be pretty similar.'

They continued chatting about Jane's job until the arrival of their meal enabled Bob to steer the conversation in the direction he desired. He was keen to know more about Jane's private life away from the office. 'So what do you do in your spare time?' he asked.

Jane smiled. She thought for a second and then replied, thinking as she spoke, 'Well, I go swimming sometimes, I play a bit of tennis in the summer; I like to go jogging or walking along the river close to where I live. Weekends? Well, there's always shopping to do and occasionally I visit friends. Other than that, I lead a very quiet life.' She ended with a little laugh.

'What about nightlife?'

She smiled again. 'Oh, just the occasional theatre visit or a film.' She felt that she had to add, 'Most nights I'm tucked up in bed with a good book by half past ten.'

'What about family? Do you have any brothers or sisters?' Bob was determined to know more about his companion.

Jane shook her head. 'I'm an only child and an orphan,' she replied.

'That's a hard start to life,' he remarked sympathetically.

Jane nodded. She sipped her drink. 'It was. I was in an orphanage until I was thirteen and then I went to live with a middle-aged couple in Bristol.' She paused for a second, seemingly deep in thought, and then she went on. 'They were so kind to me. They treated me almost like their own daughter. I think that was the first love I experienced from anybody.'

'How long were you with them?'

'Until I left school. I knew a girl from the orphanage who went on to university and I was determined to do the same. I worked very hard to get there.'

Bob was pleased he had asked his questions. He was beginning to get a different impression of Jane. By the sound of it she had had a bit of a raw deal from life, but oddly enough she appeared to remain quite cheerful, though he had noticed the sadness that had crept in briefly when she mentioned the orphanage. Gosh. That was a bit different from his early life surrounded by family and friends.

He would have liked to ask her more, but she butted in breezily, 'Hey, I've been talking all about me. Tell me a bit about you.'

'You're quite right,' he replied with a grin. 'Sorry about the interrogation.'

Jane swallowed a mouthful of food and then rushed in, almost apologising. 'No, no. It's quite all right – really.'

'What would you like to know about me?' asked Bob.

'Were you born in the Tatting Green area?' Jane asked.

Bob shook his head. 'No. I was born and brought up in Kent – Canterbury. I did the usual sort of things – grammar school and then university.'

'And then you became a photographer?'

Bob nodded. He dealt with a mouthful of food before answering. 'Yes, but not straight away. I studied fine art at first, but then decided that I was better at photography.'

'Tell me about your studio.'

'My business partner, Jeff, does most of the work there. I just help out. We do quite a lot of commercial work for advertising and that sort of thing. We get quite busy at times.'

'You mentioned magazine work once,' Jane observed. This was, of course, of particular interest to her.

'Yes, we do that as well.' Bob must have interpreted her thinking, because he suddenly suggested, 'I could show you some of the work we've done in that area.'

'That would be really most interesting.' Jane was hoping there might be an invitation in the offing there and then, but Bob switched the conversation back to her.

'Are you into photography?' he asked.

She looked amused. 'I have a good camera, but it's wasted on me. I just take snap photos. Graham, my husband, liked photography. He was really good at it, much better than me.'

'What did he do for a living?'

27

'He worked in the Foreign Office. He was quite high up. Even I never knew exactly what he did – it was all hush-hush. He travelled quite a bit; that's how he got killed. He was coming back from Russia, and the plane crashed on takeoff.'

She was silent for a few seconds, looking down at her plate and playing idly with her salad with her fork. For an instant she seemed to be deep in thought – remembering.

'I'm sorry.' Bob felt his reply was a bit inadequate.

His response prompted Jane into the present again. She looked up at him. 'There were survivors and I kept hoping Graham would be among them, but it was not to be.'

'That's a pretty awful thing to happen to anybody.'

She nodded. She continued speaking, almost as if she were thinking aloud. 'I was devastated for a while. I couldn't sleep or eat. Graham's parents and his sister were wonderful. They really supported me. My workplace was good as well, letting me have as much time off as I felt I needed.'

'Is that where you're working now?'

She nodded again. 'Yes. I'd just started there.'

'That was unfortunate.'

'It was, but I managed to pull myself together fairly quickly. Work was my therapy.'

Bob nodded and gave a slight smile. 'A bit like me when I was going through the divorce,' he said.

'What happened?' she asked gently. It was a subject she had been anxious to know more about but hadn't liked to broach. Now was the opportunity. She tackled her meal again as she waited for Bob to answer.

It was his turn to be reflective. He sipped his drink. 'I met Janice when she had just finished at drama school. She was mad keen to be an actress and came to the studio where I was working, to have some publicity photos taken. We were attracted to each other and things carried on from there.'

He paused for a second, taking another mouthful of lager. 'We were married quite quickly and had a flat in Islington. Things seemed to be all right between us at first, but it was pretty clear after a while that we didn't really have much in common. We'd been married about two years when Janice came home one evening and told me she'd fallen in love with someone else and wanted a divorce.'

'Gosh, so sudden. Just like that?' Jane remarked, surprised.

He smiled. 'I think that was the bit that got to me.'

Bob's last comment stirred more memories in Jane. 'I suppose it does happen to quite a lot of people,' she said. 'You meet someone, get married and think that's it – this is forever. And then suddenly something happens and your world falls apart.'

Bob nodded in agreement. He had long got over his divorce, but he could see that for Jane memories still came to the surface now and then. He decided to tactfully change the subject and at the same time ask the question that was uppermost in his mind: 'Are you in a relationship with anybody now?'

Jane gave a slight smile. 'No. I've been taken out a few times since... since Graham, but nothing serious.' She looked at him. 'How about you?'

Bob shook his head. 'Nothing ongoing,' he replied. He grinned. 'I've been working lots of evenings – I suppose, like you, to take my mind off things.'

Jane nodded. 'It helps,' she said.

Suddenly she thought of something else. 'You said you did a bit of writing. What are you writing about?'

'Oh, it's a book on photography,' he replied.

'That's interesting.' She paused. 'I'd like to write a novel.'

'Why don't you?' he enthused. 'You could be good at it.'

Jane thought for a moment. 'Perhaps,' she replied. She stared down at her plate for an instant, as if thinking, and then she suddenly looked up at Bob, her face full of questioning. 'But there's something I want to do first. I feel it's important.'

Her statement raised Bob's curiosity. 'What is it you'd like to do?' he asked.

Jane sipped the last of her drink. She thought for a second, and then started to speak slowly, as if voicing her thoughts. 'Well…' She hesitated for a few moments. 'Well, it's just that I know nothing about my background. I know that my parents both died and that I was put in an orphanage when I was quite young, but that's about all.' She looked at Bob, seeking his reaction.

He was about to reply, but suddenly she spoke again. 'I've been thinking about it for years, but it's something I now feel I have to do,' she burst out.

Bob seemed to be thinking for a moment. 'How much do you know?' he asked. 'For example, do you have a birth certificate?'

Jane warmed to his apparent interest. 'Yes, I do,' she exclaimed, adding, 'The orphanage gave it to my foster parents when I left there, and then they gave it to me.'

'That should tell you your parents' names and where you were born.'

'Yes, it does. It states that my parents were James and Sarah Carroll and that I was born in a village in Gloucestershire. I've looked the village up on the map. It's quite a small place.'

'That's a good start. Does the certificate give your father's profession?'

She nodded. 'Yes, it does. Apparently he was a farmer.'

'That's good. It should also give your mother's maiden name. What you want to do now is find your parents' wedding details.'

Jane responded immediately. 'There's a couple in the flat below me. They're both retired. Gerald is into family history, and he said he'd help me. Apparently there's a place somewhere in Islington where you can do searches.'

Bob smiled. 'The Family Records Centre,* he replied immediately. 'I've been there.'

'Gosh. You are knowledgeable!' exclaimed Jane.

He knew he would have to elaborate. 'At one point Janice wanted to look into her family history and we made several visits

---

* The Family Record Centre closed in 2008

30

there. It can be a laborious task searching. You have to look through books full of names until you find the right one.'

'How do you know you've got the right one?'

'If you're looking for a marriage, by cross-referring the two names. You search for the bride or groom and then when you think you have the right person, you look for the second name in the same place on the same date.'

'Phew. As simple as that,' remarked Jane.

Bob smiled again. 'It does take a bit of time,' he said.

'Hmm.' Jane was thinking. 'I'll have to go along there one Saturday,' she said, almost to herself.

Bob saw his opportunity and dived in. 'I could give you a hand,' he suggested hopefully.

Jane was elated. 'Would you really? That would be super.' She couldn't help adding, 'I'll look forward to that.'

Things were going better than Bob could have hoped. 'I'll have a look at my diary when I get back to work,' he said. 'I'll give you a ring and we'll make a date.'

'That's fantastic,' replied Jane. 'I'm free most Saturdays.'

Bob was about to make a further comment, when Jane suddenly looked at her watch. 'Gosh!' she exclaimed anxiously. 'How the time flies! It's lovely chatting, but I'll have to get back to the office so that somebody else can go to lunch. We take our lunch breaks in turn,' she elaborated.

Her action and words prompted Bob to glance at his own watch. 'I must go too. I've got an appointment at two.' He made a move to get up from his chair, following Jane's lead.

Outside the pub they paused, regarding each other for a second. Bob held out his hand. 'Thanks for the lunch and the chat,' he said. He sounded as if he really meant it.

Jane grasped his hand. Once again she offered him her cheek. 'It's been lovely seeing you again. I've really enjoyed it.'

'We'll have to do it again soon,' suggested Bob.

'Fantastic. I'll look forward to it. Now, I must dash.' She released his hand.

'Me too. Bye for now.'

'Bye,' echoed Jane as they parted.

He watched her hurry away. At one point she looked back and gave him a wave. He waved back and then turned to walk in the opposite direction.

Jane hastened back to the office. She had enjoyed her lunch break, and meeting Bob again had lived up to all her expectations. She hoped he would keep to his word and ring her. She would have liked to make a firm date there and then, but she was anxious not to appear pushy. Now she would have to wait and see what transpired. She just hoped he would contact her again soon.

Chapter 5

Jane walked home from the railway station, a spring in her step. The grey and gloomy sky of earlier in the day had cleared and it was now a fine and rather warm June evening. As she turned into the quiet road where her apartment was situated, her thoughts were still at the office. *Discerning Woman* was doing quite well at present and this was largely as a result of the exclusive features that had appeared recently in its pages. The Angus Pike interview had been popular with readers and had started the cycle off. As Jane had hoped, Annette's efforts to secure different pictures had met with little change from the artist. It was rumoured in the office that he had issued a 'take it or leave it' ultimatum, with the result that Annette had caved in and allowed Jane and Amy to do what they wanted with the photographs they had. Of course, now that the article had proved to be a success, Annette was strutting about as if all the credit were due to her. However, that did not stop Jane and Amy feeling extremely pleased with themselves.

Jane was feeling particular happy with life. Not only were things going well at work, but in her private life things had changed too, now that she had a new focus – Bob. It was almost three months since they had first met. Now hardly a week elapsed when they did not have some sort of contact with each other. They would chat on the phone regularly or meet up for a pub lunch during the week. On top of that Bob had been as good as his word. One afternoon Jane had taken a few hours off work and accepted his invitation to visit his studio. She had been surprised to find that it was not very far from her office. The studio was light and airy, and bigger than she had expected. After a cup of coffee with Bob's partner, Jeff, they had spent some time looking at the type of work the two photographers carried out at the studio. Jane had been impressed and thought that perhaps there might be other occasions when the studio could be of use to *Discerning Woman* magazine.

While they were looking at some of the photographs that adorned the walls of the studio, Jane had stopped in front of a beautifully composed picture of a naked kneeling woman. She turned to Bob. 'Do you do nude photography here?' she asked, a bit surprised.

Bob gave a slight smile. 'Occasionally,' he replied. 'Mostly for actresses or models who hope a nude photograph will impress a producer or an agency.'

The photograph stirred memories for Jane. 'Graham took a really good... picture of me once.' She could have bitten her tongue. She had been going to say 'nude', but at the last moment she decided that this wasn't the sort of information she wanted to share, at least not yet. The incident had occurred early in her marriage and she had willingly consented to her husband's suggestion that he photograph her naked, provided that, as she had put it, it would be 'tasteful'. She had kept the photograph among her treasures as a memento.

Bob had an idea what Jane had been going to say, but he pretended not to notice and tactfully drew her attention to the next photograph, a head-and-shoulders portrait.

Jane had enjoyed the visit to the studio, but the highlight of her new friendship with Bob had been their visit to the Family Records Centre and a search for her parents' marriage record. Bob had been busy for a few Saturdays, but eventually the long-awaited day had come. They had arrived at the Family Records Centre late in the morning to find it packed with researchers. With the records listed in large books, and four books to a year, it had taken the two of them ages to find what looked like the entry for Jane's father, and then a match with the bride. Bob worked at one end of the table, fighting for space with other researchers, while Jane occupied the other. It was Jane who discovered the right entry.

'I've found it!' she shouted aloud in her excitement, much to the surprise – and some disapproval – of the other researchers; but nothing could stop the emotion she felt at long last, knowing a little bit more about her roots.

She filled in a form to order a copy of the marriage certificate, and waited excitedly for it to arrive.

A few days later she had just been leaving for work when the post came. There was no mistaking the large brown envelope with her handwriting on it. She tore open the envelope there and then and looked at its contents. Hands shaking and heart thumping, she read the document. It clearly showed that the marriage of James Carroll and Sarah Andrews had taken place at the parish church of Great Wishington, Gloucestershire. The pre-marriage addresses of the bride and the groom were in the same village. James's occupation was given as 'farmer'.

Jane felt quite overwhelmed. Not only had the document she had just received confirmed her parents' details, but she now had definite information about her roots. After years of mystery and unanswered questions about her past, she now felt like a different person. Not only that, but she now felt that she had the foundations to explore the history of her family in more detail.

Jane was relieved to leave the hot and dusty pavement and walk up the drive to her apartment block, which was surrounded by lawns and contained eighteen apartments. As she let herself into the building and entered the hall space, the lift doors opened and Margot, one of her neighbours, emerged with her pug dog.

'Hi, Margot,' was Jane's greeting.

'Hello, Jane. It's very warm, isn't it? I wasn't going to go out, but Sam wanted to have his evening walk.'

'Yes, it is rather hot,' Jane agreed.

Margot was a retired civil servant and lived with her sister and Sam in the apartment opposite Jane's. 'Do you want the lift?' she asked, holding the doors open.

Jane declined. 'I usually walk up,' she explained.

Margot was slightly aghast. 'I've never done that,' she revealed.

Jane smiled. 'It keeps me fit,' she replied cheerfully.

Margot made a face, muttered something about Jane being energetic, and went on her way, leaving Jane climbing the first flight of stairs. It was Jane's habit to walk up to the third and top floor of the block, where her apartment was situated, and she saw no problem in the exercise, though she had to admit she was both younger and slimmer than Margot.

She let herself into her apartment. She dumped her briefcase in the corridor and kicked off her shoes before walking into the lounge. The evening sunshine was streaming in, making the room hot. She quickly opened two of the windows to let in a bit of air. The thought of a cool shower was inviting after her journey home in the hot and stuffy train, and she quickly disappeared into the bathroom. A few minutes later she was enjoying the tepid water.

Refreshed after her shower, she slipped into the bathrobe that hung on the bathroom door. She wasn't going anywhere this evening, and the robe, which she had treated herself to the previous week, was cool and comfortable. She went into the tiny kitchen, trying to decide what to have to eat. A boiled egg seemed to be an easy option. She busied herself for a few minutes preparing the simple meal, and after setting the egg and the kettle to boil she wandered back into the lounge. Her parents' marriage certificate still lay on the coffee table where she had left it. She picked it up and for the hundredth time studied its content. The thrill was still there. But this was only a start. She wanted to find out more about her ancestry. Her excitement had already prompted her to show the certificate to Gerald, her neighbour. He had been very interested and had written down the details and told her he would see what else he could find out. Bob had also promised to help her again.

The thought of Bob completely switched Jane's thinking from family history to a more personal level. Over the past few weeks she had been increasingly aware that she was very attracted to Bob. They had not discussed their relationship, but she could tell that Bob felt the same way about her. Their meetings had become more

36

frequent and, it seemed, eagerly looked forward to by both of them. Now when they met she offered her lips to him instead of a cheek, and of late their kissing had become more passionate. On the last occasion, when she had kissed him goodbye, his hands had lingered on her back, waiting to explore. She guessed that under Bob's quiet and calm exterior a fire smouldered that with prompting would burst into flames of passion. At the same time she could not completely ignore the craving and demands of her own body. She knew that sooner or later their relationship would transcend to the next stage. She had already given a lot of thought to that eventuality, and for the first time since her marriage she had ensured that she was protected. She had never taken chances, unlike some of her friends at university, trusting to luck after a one-night stand. If she and Bob were to become more intimate, then she would make sure that she was prepared both mentally and physically.

It was the sound of the kettle clicking itself off that brought an end to her musing. She went back into the kitchen and finished preparing her food. Usually she cooked her main meal of the day in the evening, but today she had been out to lunch and had had a full meal. It did not take long for her to eat, and she was just about to wash up the egg-cup, plate and mug she had used, when the front doorbell rang. This was unusual. She didn't know many of the other people in the apartment block and this was definitely an internal caller, because the outside door to the apartment was secure and entry could only be obtained with the cooperation of one of the residents. She hurried to the door and peered through the spyhole. Gerald stood there holding some papers. It was clear to Jane that he would only be calling on her if he wanted to see her about her family history. That was the only thing they had in common. Her excitement rising, she opened the door.

'Ah, Jane. I just wanted—' Gerald suddenly halted. He appeared almost flustered for a second, and then he burst out, 'Oh, I can see that I have called at an inopportune moment. Perhaps I can come back some other time.' As he spoke he was staring at Jane's undress.

It was Jane's turn to be embarrassed. In her excited anticipation

37

she had almost forgotten she was wearing her bathrobe without a bra. Pulling it more tightly around herself, she recovered quickly. 'No, Gerald. It's quite all right, really. Do come in – that is, if you don't mind me being dressed like this.'

Gerald hesitated. 'Well, if you're sure it's not an inconvenient time.'

Jane opened the door fully and stepped aside to let him enter.

'I'm not going out or anything. It's just that it's so warm this evening that I dressed like this for comfort.' She smiled cheerfully at him as a way of encouragement.

'Yes. It is rather warm.' Gerald somewhat reluctantly stepped into the hall.

Jane closed the door. 'Come into the lounge,' she invited, leading the way.

She was sorry she had obviously embarrassed poor Gerald. He and Anna were such good neighbours and both were quite sweeties, really. Gerald had been so taken aback at her dress; she guessed that he had rarely, if ever, seen a young woman in a shortie bathrobe. He and Anna were very much of the old school. Even on a warm evening he wore a collar and tie and a tightly buttoned-up waistcoat. Jane did not know a great deal about her neighbours, but Anna had once told her that Gerald was a clockmaker and that they had kept a jewellery shop.

Walking ahead of Gerald, Jane could feel his eyes looking at her legs and bare feet. As they entered the lounge, she indicated the papers Gerald was carrying. 'I see you have some documents with you. Have you found something out about my family?'

It was a good ploy. Once onto his favourite subject Gerald seemed more at ease. He immediately brightened up. 'Yes. I have something quite interesting here,' he announced, looking for somewhere to display his papers.

Jane grabbed her parents' marriage certificate from the coffee table. 'Put them here,' she suggested. 'And do please sit down.'

Beaming, Gerald spread out the documents and perched on the edge of the settee. Jane sat opposite, all her interest centred on the papers, once again pulling her robe tightly around her body. She waited eagerly for Gerald to explain.

'I have looked at the census for 1901 and I think I have picked up your family living in Great Wishington.' He handed Jane a computer printout.

Jane studied the document in silence for a few seconds, trying to take in the information it contained. It was clearly the details of a family, collected on census day. Her reaction was one of excitement.

'Gosh, this is fantastic!' She hesitated, absorbing the details, and then continued, reading aloud. 'John Carroll… farmer, and only one son – another John, also a farmer, age 18. All the rest of the children are girls… three of them.' She looked up at Gerald. 'So you think this must be my family?' she asked.

Gerald nodded. 'I would think that the son aged 18 will most likely be your great-grandfather.'

'Phew.' Jane was staggered. 'That's a major step forward.'

Gerald smiled at her. 'It's another piece of the puzzle,' he agreed.

Jane suddenly thought of something. 'How often do the censuses occur?' she asked.

'Every ten years since 1841,' Gerald replied immediately, adding as an afterthought, 'except for 1941.'

'Can we go forward… to the 1911 census?'

Gerald shook his head. 'The 1911 isn't available yet. They only release them to the public after a hundred years.'

'Hmm…' Jane thought for a minute. 'So what should I do next?'

'Well, now you have the names of your grandparents, you need to obtain their marriage certificate. That way you will know that you have the right people.'

'How far can I go back?' Jane enquired, still scrutinising both her parents' marriage certificate and the census details.

'Until 1837 with official records, but for events before that date you can look at parish records,' Gerald replied.

'Parish records?'

Gerald smiled again. 'Records kept by the churches,' he explained, adding for extra measure, 'Every church keeps records of baptisms, deaths and marriages conducted in the parish.'

Jane thought for a second. 'So will I have to go to the Family Records Centre again to search and order more certificates?' she asked, looking at him for confirmation.

He nodded. 'Yes. You can do that, or you can get a computer program with all the records, but you'll have to buy that.'

Jane's response to this suggestion was immediate and enthusiastic. 'I think I'd like to do that,' she replied, recalling the hustle and bustle and the time-consuming exercise of her recent visit to the Family Records Centre.

'I can give you all the details of a good one to use,' Gerald offered.

'Oh, that would be super.'

Gerald promised to drop the information into her letter box and then they continued chatting for a few minutes, Jane asking more questions and Gerald answering, clearly enjoying being able to talk to somebody else with an interest in family history. However, it was he who brought the conversation to an end. Suddenly, he glanced at the clock on the wall and leapt to his feet.

'Oh dear! I must go now – Anna wants me to watch a television programme with her.'

Jane jumped up as well, exclaiming as she did so, 'Yes, of course. You must do that. And thank you for all your help.'

'Oh, I enjoy doing it.'

Jane knew it was true. According to Anna, Gerald's main focus in retirement was family history, and not only his own family but those of other people as well. Privately, Jane had already decided that if her own research became too complicated, or time became a problem, she would ask him to continue with the task.

As she ushered him through the front door, Gerald suddenly stopped and turned to her, as if he had just thought of something. 'Of course, it might be interesting to make a visit to Great Wishington. You can often pick up snippets of local information that way. Churchyards can be interesting and can yield clues as well,' he added, looking at Jane as if to determine how she would receive his suggestion.

Jane was enthusiastic. 'That's a fantastic idea. Great Wishington isn't a million miles away.'

'Do let me know how you get on. Goodbye for now.' With a beaming smile, he headed towards his own apartment.

'Bye, Gerald, and thank you again.'

'It's a pleasure.'

'Greetings to Anna,' Jane called after him.

He half turned and put his hand up as he disappeared from view.

She closed the door and went back into the lounge. Once again she took up the documents and looked at them, but her thoughts were elsewhere.

The beginning of an idea was starting to form.

Chapter 6

It was almost an hour since Gerald had left. Jane was reclining on the lounge sofa, still musing about his visit and occasionally picking up and scrutinising the census details he had given her. She felt that her family history had taken another jump forward, and had already decided that she would take up Gerald's suggestion to purchase the family history program for her computer and search still further. She would ask him to help her set it up for her. She was quite conversant with computers, but she knew he would enjoy doing that for her.

Another idea was now taking prominence in her thinking. Gerald's last remark had stimulated a further plan. She would make a visit to Great Wishington and ask Bob to go with her. The more she thought about the idea, the more attractive it became to her. She had already decided that she would phone Bob this evening and perhaps arrange another meeting. The idea of inviting him down to her apartment one Saturday and then going out for an evening meal had been appealing, but now that was paling in comparison to the thought of a visit to Great Wishington.

She glanced casually at her watch and then at the clock on the wall. It was just after eight. Bob should be home by now. She knew that he often worked late in London and was not home much earlier, but now would be a good time. She jumped up and went into the hall. Extracting her address book from her briefcase, she glanced at Bob's number as she dialled. Perched on the edge of the chair, she waited for him to answer. She listened as the phone continued to ring. Disappointment clouded over her. Bob couldn't have arrived home, or he was out somewhere. She was about to put the phone down when suddenly there was a response.

'Bob Harker.'

Jane was overjoyed. 'Bob, it's Jane. I thought you were out. I was just about to ring off.'

'I just got back. I heard the phone ringing as I opened the front door. I'm glad I caught you. Anyway, how are you? It's great to hear from you again.'

Jane could hardly contain her excitement. 'I'm fine, but I've got lots to tell you.'

'OK, fire away.'

'Well, I've received the marriage certificate we ordered and it confirms everything. My parents were James and Sarah Carroll and they were married in a place called Great Wishington. Also, Gerald – that's my neighbour who is an expert on family history – has been looking at the census and discovered some Carrolls living in the same place at the time of the 1901 census. So it looks as if the family roots could be there.'

She paused for an instant to let Bob absorb her news. His response was immediate and enthusiastic. 'That's fantastic! Tell me more.'

Jane was eager to continue. 'I'm going to get a program for my computer. Then I'll be able to do some research at home and not have to go to the Family Records Centre each time, though I suppose I'll have to go there to order any certificates I need…' She was almost thinking aloud.

Bob butted in. 'You can order those online as well,' he advised.

'Oh, that would be helpful – and time saving.' She chuckled. She paused for an instant before launching her big idea. 'Bob, I've been doing some thinking. Gerald thinks it might be a good idea to make a visit to Great Wishington and try and pick up some local information about my family. What do you think?'

'It sounds a great idea.'

She hesitated. 'Would you come with me?' she asked hopefully.

'Of course I will. When are you thinking of going?'

Bob's obvious enthusiasm took Jane off-track for a second, but she recovered quickly. 'It would have to be a Saturday. What about next weekend?'

It was Bob's turn to hesitate. He spoke slowly. He was obviously thinking. 'I'm working next Saturday morning, until about one. That's a bit late. How about the Saturday after? I'm free then.'

Jane was a bit disappointed it couldn't be sooner, but she was determined not to show it. 'That would be fine. We could start early then.'

Bob hesitated again. When he replied, he was clearly concerned. 'Hmm... There's just one minor problem. I'm a bit worried about taking my old car on such a long trip. It's getting a bit long in the tooth now. Perhaps I could hire a car for the day. It would—'

Jane butted in. 'That's not a problem. We can take my car. It needs a long run.'

'That would be great, if you don't mind using it.' Bob was his normal self again.

'Of course not. I'll come up to you early and you can help me with some of the driving. I'm insured for any driver.' Jane was beginning to take to the idea.

What Bob said next caught her unprepared. 'I've just had a thought...' He paused. 'It might be an idea to stay overnight somewhere.'

Jane's surprise at his suggestion made her reply sound vague. 'I suppose we could do that,' she said.

Bob took control. 'We can talk about it nearer the time.' His tone was firm and final.

'I'll give you a ring next week and we can finalise our arrangements then,' Jane suggested, trying to put more enthusiasm into her voice.

'That sounds to be the best idea.'

Jane suddenly thought of something else and changed the subject. 'Bob, you've only just come home and I'm hogging your time. You must want to have something to eat.'

She could hear a bit of a laugh at the other end of the telephone.

'That will be welcome,' he said, 'but I enjoy talking to you as well.'

'That's sweet of you, but I'll let you get on now and talk to you again.'

'I'll look forward to that.' He sounded as if he really meant it.

'Super. I'm looking forward to the trip to Great Wishington, but I'll say goodbye now. Talk to you again soon.'

'Great. Bye for now. Thanks for ringing and giving me the news.'

'Bye for now.' Jane replaced the handset.

She went back into the lounge and resumed her relaxing position on the sofa. She felt quite pleased with everything. Her search for her roots was well under way and Bob's response to her suggestion to visit Great Wishington had been positive and full of enthusiasm. She was excited about the prospect of their visit.

Suddenly a horrible thought struck her. Suppose Bob had got the wrong impression from her response to his suggestion that they stop somewhere overnight... She now realised that her reaction could have been off-putting. Her reply had been stimulated by the suddenness of the invitation and the fact that she had assumed they would discuss the arrangements for the weekend nearer the time. Now on reflection she knew that she had most likely given Bob the impression that she wasn't interested in deepening their relationship.

In reality nothing could have been further from the truth. She knew that she was prepared for such an eventuality and considered that it was only a matter of time before they became more intimate. She sensed that Bob felt the same, but there was hesitation in his approach to things – hesitation she had initiated on their first meeting. He had been very sweet to her on that first evening, accepting her statement that she was not up for one-night events. She could hardly blame him for respecting rules she had made up. She knew that many men would have taken the opportunity that evening and tried to get her into bed within a short time.

45

Somehow she had felt safe with Bob, but now she realised that her initial explanation that she was not free with her favours was no doubt working against her.

Permissiveness had not been something she had indulged in at any time. She had lost her virginity while she had been at university. She had met a fellow student, and a relationship had developed between them. One night he had taken her back to his room and she had allowed intercourse to take place, believing in her naive way that they were in love. When she learned later that her lover had other women in line and she actually witnessed him with another student, she had been hurt and upset. She had also learnt the hard way that intercourse was not the emotional encounter for men that it was for women. The experience had taught her to be on guard in her approach to men and their desires, and then she had met Graham. With him she had enjoyed an adventurous and positive sexual relationship. Since losing him, she could have had several intimate relationships, but she had declined to do so, partly out of loyalty to Graham and partly simply because she recognised that the opportunities offered weren't what she was looking for.

With Bob it was different. In him she recognised many of Graham's qualities. It gave her the encouragement and the confidence to want to break her own boundaries. Having reached this point, she did not want anything to mar their blossoming relationship. The more she pondered the evening's phone call to Bob, the more concerned she became.

She got up from the sofa, deep in thought; the glimmer of a solution was beginning to emerge. She wandered over to the window, staring out but, absorbed in her thoughts, taking in little of the view.

Suddenly she snapped into action, at the same time talking aloud to herself. 'Jane, my girl, it's time to show where you stand.'

She grabbed her mobile, which was lying on the table. Her hands trembling a little, she retrieved Bob's number. Sometimes, she thought, a girl just has to take the lead.

The phone seemed to ring for a long time.

46

'Bob Harker.' The answer came suddenly.

'Bob, it's me again – Jane.'

'Hello. I didn't expect to talk to you again so soon.'

'Well, I just had an idea—' She stopped short. A thought suddenly struck her. 'Bob, I haven't interrupted your meal, have I?'

She could hear a chuckle at the other end of the line. 'Just finished. I've got a mug of tea in my other hand, so don't worry if you hear me slurp from time to time. But do carry on with what you were going to say.'

'I've been thinking…' She hesitated. Might as well come straight out with it, she thought. She changed tack. 'What are you doing this weekend? I mean, after you finish work on Saturday.'

There was a pause at the other end. Bob was obviously thinking. Then he responded. 'Nothing, really. Might have to do a bit of shopping, some paperwork perhaps.'

This was the opening, Jane thought. 'Would you like to come and visit me here?'

She didn't have to wait long. Bob's reply was almost instantaneous. 'I'd love to. I could get down to you by early evening.'

'That would be super. We can go out for a meal. I know a lovely place. I'll book a table.'

'Sounds great. I'll look forward to that.'

So far, so good. Now for the difficult bit. This was new territory for Jane. There was an anxious element in her voice as she spoke. 'And, Bob, you can stay over if you'd like to.'

She waited anxiously for his reply.

'That sounds a great idea. I'll pack my overnight gear.'

It was a relieved Jane who answered. 'Oh, that's super. I'm going to look forward to Saturday.' The relief prompted her to add a bit of humour. 'But there's just one thing…' She hesitated deliberately. 'Unfortunately, my spare bedroom hasn't got a lock on the door.' She was being mischievous, and she knew it.

Bob clearly got the message. He gave a little laugh. 'OK. It's no problem,' he said.

It was Jane who changed the subject. 'Will you come by car, or train?' she asked, resuming a more serious tone.

'Train, I think. I don't trust my old banger on long trips. I really must get some better transport.'

'That's fine. There's a good train service. Can I give you directions to find me?'

'That would be useful. Hang on a second — I think my pen's run out. I'll just fetch another one.'

Jane waited until Bob was ready and then gave detailed instructions for getting to her apartment.

When she had finished, Bob remarked, 'Terrific. I should be able to find you now. I guess I'll be with you around five. Would that be OK?'

'That would be super. I'm really looking forward to it.'

They continued the conversation for a few minutes and then Jane tactfully suggested that Bob might want to relax after his long day. After they had said their goodbyes, she settled back down on the sofa. She was pleased with how well everything had gone, and now all she had to do was to make the final arrangements for Saturday. She already had a plan. On the floor below her lived Mario, who ran a really nice restaurant overlooking the river. She had taken guests there on several occasions. Very often she encountered Mario when she went to work, but tomorrow if she failed to see him early she would call at the restaurant on her way home. She knew how to handle Mario, who tended to be a bit of a flirt with attractive women, and she would persuade him to let her book one of the prestige tables. When Saturday came, she would spend the day making everything ready.

Chapter 7

Jane was looking forward to the trip to Great Wishington immensely, partly because her revised thinking had worked out so well. Originally it had been her intention to invite Bob over for a visit that particular weekend, but when the option to visit Great Wishington had come up it had taken precedence. Then her concern and spontaneity had resulted in both events being planned.

Her preparations for the first weekend had not gone quite to schedule. She had intended to set to and clean her apartment on the Friday evening, but she was late home from work and then as she opened her front door she discovered a note from Gerald asking whether he could have another look at her parents' marriage certificate. After a quick bite to eat, she made her way to Gerald and Anna's apartment with her documents. That was the end of her plans for the evening.

Anna invited Jane to come in and have a coffee, and the three of them spent a leisurely time chatting. After that, Gerald insisted that she come into his 'workroom', as he termed it, so that he could show her the program he thought she should buy for her computer. They left Anna in the lounge watching television while they went into the second bedroom, where Gerald worked.

Before showing Jane the program, he scrutinised her parents' marriage certificate. 'I just wanted to see who the witnesses to the wedding were,' he explained. 'Witnesses can often provide valuable clues in family history,' he announced, looking up at a wondering Jane.

'In what way?' Jane asked.

Gerald went into great detail about family histories he had researched where the name of a witness had resolved a question.

While Gerald copied down the information he needed from her certificate, Jane's attention was focused on his workroom. It was full of shelves crammed with books and files, all, as far as she could see, dealing with family history. Clearly for Gerald the subject was no passing phase.

When Gerald showed her the computer program he thought might be suitable for her, Jane was excited and intrigued. Here on the tiny screen in front of her were records similar to the big books she and Bob had looked through at the Family Records Centre.

'You mean you can view all the birth, marriage and death records on a computer just like this?' she asked in amazement.

Gerald smiled. 'Absolutely,' he replied. 'Provided you buy the right program, you will also have the census records. Census records are a keystone in family history,' he added.

He then suggested that he help Jane download and set up the program over the weekend, and she tactfully said she was doing something else. The event was duly postponed until the following week.

The evening was well advanced when at last Jane indicated that she had to go. After saying goodnight to Gerald and Anna, she retreated to her own apartment. Once there she realised that any cleaning that evening was out. It was already close to ten o'clock.

Jane was late up on the Saturday morning. She woke from a sound sleep to realise that it was close to half past seven, half an hour past her normal rising time. At the same time she suddenly remembered that she had an appointment at the hairdresser's at eight-thirty. After a quick shower and a rushed breakfast she managed her appointment in time. When she left the hairdresser's, there was some weekly shopping to do. It was while she was passing the shop where a few weeks previously she had bought her new bathrobe that she had an idea. She went into the shop and was pleased to see they still had stocks of the same item. She hurriedly searched through the rack. Bob was about the same build as Graham had been. A medium size should fit perfectly. 'Why not?' she thought. She took the robe to the till and left the shop with her purchase in a bag.

Back home she set to and did the weekly cleaning. Lunch was just a cup of coffee and a cheese sandwich. While she was finishing her coffee she wandered, mug in hand, into her second bedroom. Everything was ready for Bob's visit. A clean white bath towel lay on the bed, and beside it Jane's latest purchase, the white bathrobe, with the labels removed. She hoped Bob wouldn't mind a robe the same dazzling white as her own, but she didn't think he would.

By two-thirty she had retreated into the bathroom and was enjoying a relaxing bath. After that, all she had to do was finish getting ready. She had already decided on the dress she would wear. She had bought it for a friend's wedding a year or so previously and it would suit the evening just fine. It was in a blue floral material and had a deep vee neck, and she had the necklace with the deep blue stone to go with it.

When she took out the shoes that matched the dress, she was a bit dismayed to discover that they looked decidedly shabby. She had worn them frequently and the heels were scuffed from driving in them. Suddenly she had an idea. Rummaging in the bottom of her wardrobe, she pulled out a shoebox and took out a pair of shoes, scrutinising them carefully before dropping them on the floor at her feet and trying them on. She hadn't worn them for years, but they fitted perfectly. They were medium-heeled mules with thin, soft brown leather straps. Skimpy, but enchanting to look at. She held them against the dress and that made up her mind. They would be perfect for the evening, and she had a soft brown leather shoulder bag that would go with them. Now she just had to get changed and wait for Bob to arrive.

It was just after half past five when Bob stepped off the train at Kew Gardens. Though he had travelled through London, the journey had been good, without any hold-ups, and he was slightly earlier than he had intended to be. He had phoned Jane a few

51

evenings before to confirm their arrangements and she had told him that she had booked a table at the restaurant for seven o'clock. He had intended to get to Kew around six, and he hoped he wasn't too early for her. The last thing he wanted to do was arrive when she was getting ready.

He pulled from his pocket the crumpled bit of paper on which he had scribbled Jane's directions. The walk was easy to follow and he soon arrived in the tree-lined road where Jane's apartment was located. It was a very nice area and decidedly a bit upmarket, and it reflected the air of affluence that sometimes surrounded Jane. Despite being an orphan and having had a tough upbringing, she appeared now to have a comfortable lifestyle.

He walked up to the front door and pressed the buzzer next to the label marked 'J CARROLL'. Jane's voice answered almost immediately.

'Hello.'

'Jane, it's Bob. I've found you.'

'Come on up. I'm all ready.' There was an element of excitement in her voice.

There was the unmistakable sound of the door catch being released, and Bob pushed the door open and stepped into the entrance hall. He scorned the lift and walked slowly up the carpeted stairs to the top floor. Jane was waiting at the open door. She was beautifully dressed, but shoeless.

'Bob, it's lovely to see you. Welcome to my home.'

She offered her lips for a kiss and then stepped aside, holding the door wide open.

Bob entered the apartment. He glanced down at Jane's feet and then at his own. 'I've got some house shoes somewhere,' he said, lowering the weekend bag he carried over his shoulder to the floor.

His comment and glance downwards prompted Jane to blush slightly. 'Oh, Bob, I'm sorry. You don't mind me being like this, do you? It's a habit of mine to walk about in the flat without shoes.'

Bob grinned at her. 'I don't mind one bit. I do the same quite often at home.'

Jane took control. 'Put your bag in here and then come into the lounge and relax.' As she spoke she was already making for the spare bedroom and pushing open the door.

Bob deposited his bag and opened it to take out his comfortable shoes. He glanced quickly around the room, noting the items set out on the bed, and then he joined Jane in the lounge. She was already seated on one of the settees.

'What about some refreshment?' she asked, smiling breezily. 'Tea, coffee, a cold drink?'

Bob thought for a second. It was a warm evening. 'I'd love a cold drink,' he replied.

Jane immediately jumped up. 'Orange or apple juice?'

'Apple would be nice,' he replied, smiling at her.

She disappeared in the direction of the kitchen. Bob watched her go. She was, he thought, looking very attractive this evening. The figure-hugging dress she was wearing suited her, and for the first time since he had known her she was allowing her light brown hair to fall around her shoulders instead of wearing it pinned up in a practical fashion. It made her look even more feminine, he thought. He had also been pleased to see when she greeted him at the door that she was showing her legs for the first time in his company – legs that were quite shapely. Her appearance made him glad he had taken more care with his own outfit, exchanging his usual jeans for a pair of smarter cotton trousers and adding a lightweight jacket. He had even remembered to put a spare shirt and tie in his bag, just in case they were needed.

He was looking around the room as he heard Jane returning. It was pleasant, light and airy, enhanced by the white decoration enlivened with a spot of colour here and there. The window opened up onto a balcony, and in the faint evening breeze the curtains moved slowly. His eyes had just fixed on a photograph when Jane returned carrying a tray with two glasses of juice.

'My wedding photograph,' she remarked, her eyes following his.

She offered him a glass of juice from the tray. 'We got married in the village where Graham's parents live. They have this beautiful manor house in Oxfordshire. It's a fabulous place. I still go to see them from time to time.'

'Did you have a honeymoon?' Bob asked. He was interested in Jane's life.

Jane put the tray on the coffee table and, taking her own glass, she sat down opposite Bob as she replied to his question. 'Yes, we did. We had a marvellous time in Venice.' She paused for a second, thinking, holding her glass with both hands, then continued. 'We always enjoyed our holidays together, because Graham was away from me so much due to his job.'

Bob was about to respond, but she continued almost immediately. 'Graham was very good for me, because he took me out of myself. We did things together I'd never have dreamed of doing alone. We used to do quite mad things.'

She took a sip of her drink. It gave Bob the opportunity to ask another question. He was becoming quite fascinated by Jane's revelations. 'That sounds interesting. What sort of things?' he asked.

Jane gave a little smile. 'We went bungee jumping once. I screamed all the way down.' she burst into laughter.

'Good for you!' Bob joined in her mirth.

He suddenly noticed a second wedding photograph. It intrigued him. Whilst the first photograph depicted a formal wedding group, with Jane and her husband surrounded by family, this one featured just the two of them. Graham had Jane in his arms and, though she was in her wedding dress, she was barefoot.

Jane watched Bob's interest in the photograph. When he turned to her, she was smiling as she answered his silent query. 'That was taken on our first wedding anniversary.'

She guessed that he would not be satisfied with her simple explanation. His enquiring look confirmed it. She usually had the photograph out of sight when she had guests, but somehow she didn't mind Bob seeing it, or elaborating on her first explanation.

'Graham and I decided that each year we would confirm our marriage vows in a different way. I had this mad idea that I wanted to be married barefoot on a beach somewhere, so we packed my wedding dress in a suitcase and off we went to Florida.'

'It looks as if everything went well. You look very happy.' Bob felt he had to say it.

Jane nodded. 'It was fabulous. Every bit as good as I wanted it to be.'

Bob was captivated by Jane's revelations. This was a side of her he had not encountered before. He rather liked it and was eager to learn more.

'What about the second anniversary?' he asked. 'What did you do then?'

Jane looked at him and made a face. The conversation was going further then she had intended, but so what? Why shouldn't Bob know about her past?

'Do you really want to know?' she asked, knowing perfectly well that he would say yes.

Bob grinned at her. 'Of course,' he replied.

She made another face at him and then continued. 'Graham arranged everything and kept it as a big secret. All I knew was we were going to America and I didn't need my wedding dress. We arrived at the airport and then had to drive quite a few miles to a place up in the mountains.'

She paused for a second, looking at Bob.

'What happened then?' he prompted.

Jane felt she wanted to finish quickly. She had never talked to anybody about this experience before. She continued, studying Bob's reaction all the time.

'Within a few minutes of our arrival, the penny dropped...' She hesitated, but Bob's enquiring look made her complete the sentence. 'It was a naturist settlement.'

Bob was surprised and amused. 'You mean everybody was... naked?'

She nodded. For a few seconds she avoided his look of surprise and spoke more slowly. 'Absolutely. Or most of them. I was furious with Graham and refused there and then to do what he had in mind.'

'You mean a nude ceremony?'

Jane blushed slightly. 'Yes,' she replied simply.

Bob felt great compassion for her. She was relating to him something most women would have kept to themselves, unless they were extroverts. Jane certainly wasn't one, and he could see that she had been reluctant to disclose this experience. He had practically forced her to tell him. He spoke more softly. 'Tell me what happened then.'

Jane suddenly brightened up and became more cheerful. 'Well, I was grumpy all evening, but everybody was so kind and friendly that by the time we went to bed I was beginning to soften. The next morning I woke up and thought, why not? Nobody knows me here and none of our friends need to know. I'm going to do it.'

'So you went through with it?'

Jane nodded. 'I did. Two of the women helped me get ready.'

'Were you completely naked?'

Jane gave him a coy grin and hesitated before continuing. 'I just had a tiny apron of flowers and that's all. I had a flower in my hair and a garland of flowers round my neck.'

'Was Graham the same?' asked Bob.

'More or less,' she replied, with a slight smile.

'What about the actual ceremony? How did you cope?'

Jane's expression took on a serious note. She thought for a few seconds before answering. 'That's the odd thing. There were three other couples getting married. We were second. The fact that everybody else looked the same made all the difference. After the first appearance I became quite relaxed about the whole thing.'

She suddenly laughed quite breezily. 'In fact, the main concern I had was that I could feel that the soles of my feet were almost burning on the hot surface we stood on for the ceremony.'

Bob joined her laughter. 'I hope the parson was fully dressed,' he said.

Jane gave an amused smile. 'He was,' she replied. 'He was really quite sweet and afterwards everybody had a fabulous celebration

56

party. There must have been sixty or seventy people there, all in their birthday suits.'

'I hope you've got a photograph,' Bob butted in.

Jane gave him a fake disapproving scowl. 'Yes, I have, and I'm not showing it to you.'

Bob laughed. 'Spoilsport!' he joked.

Jane's response was to hurl a cushion at him.

As he recovered, Bob observed that Jane now had a more serious look about her. He was about to say something, but she spoke first.

'So you see, I am not the demure little office girl you first thought I was.'

She waited for his reaction.

He smiled at her. 'I never thought you were,' he replied, 'but now you've told me that, I'm even more fond of you.'

Jane pretended to be surprised. 'What? I don't think you're nice to know. You're supposed to be shocked and disapproving.'

'Sorry.' Bob grinned at her as another cushion was thrown at him.

As they recovered from their interlude of play, Bob looked at Jane again. 'You have a very nice apartment,' he commented, looking around the room.

She nodded, serious again. 'Yes, I like it very much. It's nice and spacious.' She paused for an instant, and then added, as if to answer an unvoiced question, 'Graham left me very well provided for.' She looked at Bob, waiting for his response.

He sensed immediately that remembering her loss was still painful for her. 'Did you move here when you got married?' he asked.

Jane shook her head. 'We had a house in Richmond. I couldn't bear to go on living there after Graham died, so I sold up and moved here.' And then, grinning cheerfully, she remarked, 'I'm nearer work now.' She gave a little laugh.

Bob glanced down at the marriage certificate, which was still lying on the coffee table. 'May I have a look?' he asked.

'Oh, please do.' Jane grabbed the piece of paper and handed it to him.

As Bob studied the document, Jane suddenly remembered something. 'Gerald had a look at it and he seemed to think I might have a relative somewhere.' She pointed to the certificate. 'Look at the name of the witness. Susan Carroll.'

'Could be your father's sister,' Bob commented, still engrossed in the document.

'You mean I could have an aunt somewhere?' There was an element of excitement in Jane's voice.

'That could well be,' Bob replied, looking at her again.

'But why have I never heard from her?' Jane was puzzled.

'Perhaps a family feud or something,' Bob suggested. Then he added, smiling, 'That's family history.'

Jane was thinking as she replied to his remark. 'You know, I'm really looking forward to our visit to Great Wishington. I really want to find out more about my family.'

'I'm looking forward to it as well,' said Bob.

Jane looked at him for a second. It was time to nail her colours to the mast. 'And, Bob, I'm quite happy to stay overnight somewhere.' Now I've said it, she thought.

Bob was smiling at her. His growing affection for her became plain to see. 'So am I,' he said simply.

Chapter 8

Jane stifled a yawn as she drove her car through the early-morning traffic. A whole week had passed. Now she was on her way to pick up Bob, and together they would drive down to Great Wishington. At long last she hoped she would find some more information about her parents. Only last evening Gerald had popped in to help her install the family history program on her laptop, and he had appeared to be almost as excited as she was over the next day's visit. 'It's only a small village and it's not impossible that you could meet somebody who knew your family,' he had enthused. The very thought had made Jane determined to exploit every aspect of the visit.

Her excitement for the day ahead meant that she had woken up much too early. By six o'clock she had showered and breakfasted. By half past six she had been ready to go, dressed in a white blouse and blue casual trousers. Somehow it was much too early, but she could stand the waiting no longer. With her family history file under her arm and her weekend case in her hand, she made her way to the parking lot at the rear of the apartments. After placing the suitcase in the boot of her car, she slid into the driving seat. She had the usual rummage to find one of the shoes she used for driving and eventually discovered it under the passenger seat. Slipping the shoes on only took a second, and after clicking her seat belt in place she turned the ignition key. The BMW burst into life. Slowly she drove out onto the road. The petrol gauge showed only half full, so she pulled into a convenient 24-hour petrol station and filled up. Then she was on her way towards Kew Bridge and the M4.

It had been quite a hard week. Amy had been on holiday and that had meant extra work for Jane to get through. This had required her to stay late on two evenings. On top of that, Annette had been particularly difficult to handle at times. In spite of everything, Jane had sailed through the week, fired up with a new wave of contentment, inspired by the thought that her family history was at long last under way and by an awareness that her relationship with Bob was deepening. The events of the previous weekend had firmly cemented in place how they felt about each other. For the first time since losing Graham Jane had found someone she could relate to. In Bob she found many of the qualities that had so attracted her to Graham and stimulated the short bliss of her marriage to him. She now knew that Bob felt the same about her, and that made her heart sing and put her on top of the world.

As she cruised along the unusually quiet motorway, the events of the weekend came back to her. She had had a wonderful time with Bob. Her arrangements for dinner could not have been better. Her charm had obviously worked on Mario, who had greeted them on arrival at the restaurant with his usual exuberance and led them to a secluded table in the window. They had lingered a long time over the meal, chatting and discovering more about each other, relaxed by the bottle of wine they had shared. The evening was well advanced when they took their leave of Mario and his team and walked hand in hand slowly back to the apartment, content in each other's company. The warm summer evening encouraged them to take much longer over what was normally a ten-minute walk.

It was close to ten when they arrived back at Jane's apartment and slowly climbed the stairs. Jane fumbled in her bag for the keys and opened the door.

'Here we are. Home again,' she announced softly, entering the apartment first and holding the door open for Bob.

He followed her inside and slowly closed the door.

'Home, sweet home,' he agreed and gave a little chuckle.

Jane lifted one foot and removed the shoe. She performed the same procedure with the other one. Standing barefoot and holding her shoes, she turned to Bob.

'How about a nightcap? Cocoa all right?' Her suggestion was accompanied with an enquiring look.

'Sounds a great idea. I'm all for it.'

'I'll make some. You go into the lounge and relax. And, Bob... ' She hesitated. The next bit was more difficult. She plucked up courage, perhaps encouraged by the two glasses of wine she had drunk earlier, and continued. 'If you want to get a bit more comfy, you can change into my present for you. Have you seen it?' She studied him. Her look was a combination of anxiety and amusement.

Bob looked at her for a second and then suddenly put his arm round her and drew her towards him. He could smell her perfume as he kissed her.

'I did see it. Thank you very much. I'll put it on right away.' He looked at her, smiling.

'I'm going to get out of this dress as well,' Jane almost squealed, and with a quick peck on his lips she broke away and headed for her bedroom. 'See you in a minute.'

In the privacy of the bedroom she quickly disrobed. It took only a minute to slip on her bathrobe, take a glance in the mirror and then add an extra dab of scent. As she turned to leave, she looked at the double bed and then discreetly turned back the duvet, before making her way to the kitchen.

Bob was already seated on the sofa when she returned to the lounge with two mugs of cocoa. She was pleased to see that he had changed into the bathrobe she had bought – and, thank goodness, he had opted for bare feet. Nothing was more off-putting than a man who insisted on wearing socks in such a situation. She set the mugs down on the coffee table and sat down beside him. He was scanning through the issue of *Discerning Woman* that had been lying on a side table. It contained the article on Angus Pike.

'It looks quite good,' he remarked, hardly glancing up from the magazine.

'Yes. Amy and I were quite pleased with it,' Jane replied. She took a sip of cocoa.

'Did you lose many readers?' asked Bob, as he picked up his mug. He turned to her and smiled.

Jane shook her head. 'On the contrary, our sales went up nearly ten per cent.' She smiled at Bob and then as an afterthought added, 'but we did get a couple of letters complaining that the standard of the magazine was going down.'

Bob laughed. 'You're bound to get that from somebody,' he said. He glanced at the article again. 'He certainly paints erotic pictures,' he observed.

Jane joined him to look at the feature. Both paintings featured practically naked subjects. One depicted a young woman kneeling on the floor of what appeared to be a prison cell, being observed by two evil-looking men. The other picture was reminiscent of the Perseus and Andromeda legend, with a young woman chained to a rock, apparently awaiting a fate worse than death.

'Most of his paintings are like that. He showed me a book of them when I visited him,' remarked Jane.

'Have you thought any more about posing for him?' Bob asked suddenly, looking at Jane. It was a question he had wanted to ask her for some time.

Jane feigned a disapproving look. 'No,' she replied simply. Suddenly she gave a little shy smile and added, 'I can think of better things to do in my birthday suit.'

Bob leaned towards her. 'I wonder what you have in mind,' he said softly.

'I could show you,' Jane whispered, as their lips touched.

They both realised that it was the point of no return. The next instant they were locked in an embrace. They were oblivious to the magazine dropping onto the floor as they kissed and allowed their hands to start wandering over each other's bodies to experience pleasures previously denied.

How long they kissed and embraced each other neither could tell, but suddenly Jane eased away from Bob and raised herself from the sofa. She took his hand and pulled him to his feet as he followed her urging. Their arms encircling each other, Jane led the way to her bedroom. Two mugs of unfinished cocoa remained on the coffee table.

Jane's recollection of the weekend's events was interrupted suddenly as she realised that her exit point from the motorway was looming up. She carefully circled the roundabout to ensure she took the correct road towards Tatting Green. She drove through several villages that were stirring into life, and in no time at all she found herself passing the hotel where Bob had taken her on the first evening they had met. She remembered the shock of the night porter's statement, 'Sorry, we're full.' Bob had been so kind and caring that evening, and in the more recent weeks of their developing relationship she had been concerned that her remark about not being a 'one-night-stand girl' had hindered their progress. When she reached the stage of being content to allow intimacy to take place, she had become more and more worried about this. She was well aware that she had manipulated events the previous weekend, and in a way it was completely out of character for her, but at the same time she had felt it was necessary. Suddenly the turn-off for Tatting Green appeared, and within a few minutes she recognised Bob's house and turned into the drive.

It was at that point that she realised that she was extremely early. Both the car clock and her watch showed that it was only half past seven, a full half-hour before the time she had said she would arrive. On top of that, Bob's sitting-room curtains were still closed. Suppose he wasn't up yet? She began to feel embarrassed about being so early. She decided to wait in the car until some sort of activity showed in Bob's house. With a bit of luck he wouldn't have heard her car arrive. She slipped off her driving shoes, replaced them with her sandals and settled down to wait.

She was wrong. Bob had been up for quite some time and was

ready for her. His weekend bag was carefully packed and stood in the hall adjacent to the front door. He had been busy in his bedroom, when he thought he heard a sound. It prompted him to go and look out of the front bedroom window and down at the drive, where he saw the deep blue roof of a car. He hurried downstairs and opened the front door. Jane saw him immediately and waved. The next instant she was getting out of the car.

She turned to him anxiously. 'Bob, I'm dreadfully sorry. I woke up miles too early and miscalculated how long it would take me.'

The next instant he embraced her. 'It's fine. I'm all ready and it's great you're here early.' He kissed her several times.

As they drew apart he still had his arm round her waist. He smiled at her. 'Come on in. I'll make you a coffee.'

He led her by the hand towards the front door. As she pressed the remote car lock with her free hand, she exclaimed, 'Oh, a coffee would be marvellous. Perhaps keep me from falling asleep.' She laughed.

Once inside the house, Bob ushered her into the kitchen. Being there brought back memories for Jane. She remembered that first evening she had met Bob. Even then she had been attracted to him, but now, a few months on, their relationship was on a completely different basis.

'Black or white?' Bob asked, clicking the kettle into life.

Jane was already seated at the table. She stifled a yawn. 'Black, please.'

Bob produced the coffee and sat down opposite her. 'What's your week been like?' he asked.

They chatted about the week's events. Their telephone conversation finalising the arrangements for the weekend had been brief because it had been on the evening when Gerald had been with Jane sorting out the family history program on her computer.

It was Bob who brought the conversation to a close. 'Shall we get under way?' he asked politely.

Jane immediately jumped up. 'Oh, yes, please. I'm feeling quite excited. I can't wait to get to Great Wishington.'

Five minutes later Bob was locking the front door and Jane was unlocking the car.

'Would you like to drive?' she asked hopefully.

Bob grinned at her. 'I was hoping you might ask me,' he quipped. He had been looking forward to driving Jane's car.

Jane handed him the key and slipped into the passenger seat. She was glad he was going to do some of the driving. She stifled another yawn. 'The coffee hasn't kicked in yet,' she laughed.

Half an hour later they were cruising along the M4. They had been chatting non-stop since starting the journey, but gradually Jane's comments and replies became more spaced out, and then she became quiet. Bob glanced at her. Her head was cushioned against the headrest and she was asleep.

Bob smiled. He guessed that being up early and her tiredness had finally overcome her excitement. He was quite excited himself and was genuinely looking forward to helping her discover her roots. He was also enjoying driving her car. The BMW was comfortable and purred along the motorway. The brief driving experience so far had already persuaded him to buy a more up-to-date car for his own use. He looked at Jane again. She was turned slightly towards him. One of the top buttons on her blouse had come undone and the gap exposed the swell of her breasts. Out of politeness he quickly focused on the road ahead again, but the glimpse had stirred memories of the previous weekend. He knew that their relationship was now on a different basis. When a man and a woman had shared intimacy, their feelings towards each other altered. They shared secrets no others had access to. A bond had been established between them that was unique.

He knew that in a way Jane had engineered what had happened between them, but he admired her for it. She had done it with finesse and style. He had thought it might happen during the weekend. For weeks now when he had touched her, his body had demanded more, but she had beaten him to action. When Jane had tactfully instigated their union he had been a ready participant. In her bedroom they had kissed passionately, their hands no longer limited by decorum. He had peeled back her bathrobe, exposing her body, and she had willingly done the same with his, her hands caressing his chest. His fingers had found the clip of her bra, and a second later his hands were caressing her breasts. Bathrobes abandoned on the floor, he had led her to the bed. Their lovemaking had been controlled but passionate. Eventually Jane had uttered a little cry, and the fruits of his own labour had burst forth a second later. Afterwards, they had fallen asleep in each other's arms.

Bob had awoken to hear a voice talking to him. Jane stood at the foot of the bed, fresh from her shower, dressed in her bathrobe and holding two mugs of steaming tea in her hands.

'Room service,' she had laughed.

They had chatted over the tea and then breakfasted on the balcony that adjoined Jane's lounge, enjoying the early morning sun. Afterwards they had walked hand in hand along the river. After a pub lunch, Bob had had to leave. This time their parting had been slightly different from on previous occasions: now there was the promise of even better things to come.

It was Jane waking up with a jerk that brought Bob's thoughts back to the present. She struggled to get herself together, glancing here and there.

'Gosh,' she said. 'I must have nodded off. Have I been asleep long?'

Bob smiled at her. 'Only about half an hour,' he replied, slowing down for the traffic that was now building up ahead of them.

'I'm awfully sorry.' Jane's embarrassment was steadily growing.

Bob laughed. 'Don't worry about it,' he said.

'Where are we?' Jane looked around, at the same time retrieving a sandal that had come off and wandered under her seat.

'Not far from where we have to leave the motorway,' observed Bob.

'And I've let you do all the driving,' she commented, making a face.

Bob smiled. 'I've really enjoyed driving a decent car. I think it's finally convinced me to update my banger.'

Jane continued more quietly. 'I bought this one just after I lost Graham and moved into the apartment. It doesn't get a lot of use really – just the occasional pleasure trip or one for work now and then.'

'It's a nice car to drive,' Bob commented.

Soon afterwards, they left the motorway and continued their journey on minor roads. Jane was getting more and more excited. When she caught sight of a signpost pointing to Lower Wishington, she almost shouted her surprise. 'Look! We must be getting close.'

'A couple of miles yet.' Bob turned and grinned at her. Her excitement was beginning to extend to him.

It seemed no time at all before they were entering Great Wishington. Bob slowed the car down as they followed the road curving down into the village, where houses and cottages surrounded a tree-lined village green. They passed The Poachers, a large pub bedecked with ivy and hanging baskets of flowers. A sign announced 'Dinners. Lunches and Accommodation'. Bob was the first to notice it.

'Somewhere for lunch,' he suggested, nodding towards the pub. He added as an afterthought, 'Or to stay the night.'

Jane followed his gaze. 'Absolutely,' she murmured, and then her excitement burst through. 'Oh, isn't it picturesque? I think I quite like being from here already!' she exclaimed, looking around her.

Before Bob could reply, she had a question. 'Where shall we start?' she asked eagerly.

Bob had already seen a spire above the trees. He pointed it out with a wave of his hand. 'Look, that must be the church. The best thing is to have a look in the churchyard. Your parents should be buried there. It might give us a clue.'

'That would be fantastic.'

A minute later they arrived at the church, a majestic building standing against a backdrop of trees populated by noisy crows. Bob parked alongside the stone wall surrounding the churchyard and switched off the engine. Jane was the first to jump out, her family history file under her arm. She made her way immediately to the lychgate leading to the church.

Together they walked down to the church entrance, paused for a minute to look into the porch with its various notices, and then followed the path round the church into the graveyard at the rear. Except for the crows, who kept up a constant chatter, it was quiet and peaceful there in the bright morning sunshine. They walked slowly, glancing at each gravestone as they went.

'What we want to do is to try and locate your parents' graves first,' suggested Bob, continuing to scrutinise the gravestones.

'That's what I thought,' agreed Jane, 'but these ones are much too old.'

'Good morning.'

Neither had noticed the stranger walking up the path. They turned to see a portly, rosy-cheeked gentleman dressed in black beaming at them. He wore glasses from behind which a pair of twinkling eyes observed the two visitors.

Jane and Bob returned his greeting. The man paused in his slow gait. He looked at them curiously.

'Are you looking at anything particular, or just visiting our lovely old church?' He was clearly interested in seeing two strangers in the churchyard.

Jane quickly explained. 'I'm looking for my parents' graves,' she replied, adding for good measure, 'I think I was born here.'

'Ah, then I may be able to help. I'm the verger here.' He smiled kindly at them.

The thought that she might be able to find someone who remembered her parents prompted Jane to ask a question. 'Have you been here long?' she enquired.

'Thirty-two years this month,' the verger replied proudly.

Jane's heart gave a leap. Here was somebody who could well have known her father and her mother.

'Perhaps you were acquainted with my parents,' she said hopefully.

The verger beamed at her once again. 'What name would it be?' he asked pleasantly.

'Carroll,' Jane replied. 'I'm Jane Carroll.'

The smile faded from the verger's face. He took on a puzzled expression. 'I think there must be some mistake,' he said.

He studied Jane for a few seconds and then spoke again more softly.

'Jane Carroll died as a baby and is buried in this churchyard.'

Chapter 9

There was a stunned silence between the three of them, Jane looking puzzled, Bob trying to think of something more to ask, and the verger scrutinising them both closely for a response.

It was Jane who recovered first. 'But... but...'she stammered. 'I'm Jane Carroll. I have my birth certificate here.'

She hurriedly extracted the document from the file she was carrying and showed it to the verger. He peered at it through his glasses, studying the contents, while Jane and Bob stood silently watching and waiting.

At last the verger handed the certificate back to Jane. 'It appears to be genuine,' he remarked, still serious. Suddenly he turned to walk away. 'Please come with me,' he invited.

Jane and Bob followed him in silence to a different part of the churchyard. Eventually he stopped in front of a grave close to the path. He pointed to the headstone and stood back politely for Jane and Bob so that they could read the inscription.

The engraving was quite clear. *Sarah Carroll, aged 26 and her daughter Jane Eleanor Carroll, aged 6 months. Tragically died together January 3rd 1978. Also James Carroll, loving husband and father, died November 6th 1978, aged 34.*

There was another silence between the three. Jane struggled to comprehend what she was reading. 'But I don't understand,' she protested. 'I have this certificate and I've always been Jane Carroll – all my life.'

'I think there has been some mistake somewhere,' the verger said kindly.

'Perhaps there's another family called Carroll,' suggested Jane hopefully.

The verger shook his head. 'There was only one family in the village named Carroll and they only had one child.' After pausing for a second, he continued. 'I knew the family quite well. James Carroll was an active member of the church. One of the bell-ringers, in fact.'

'Can you tell us what happened to them?' Bob asked softly.

The verger nodded. 'Yes. Sarah and her daughter perished in a house fire. The neighbours and the fire brigade were unable to save them. It was a tragedy that shook the whole village.'

'And James Carroll?' asked Bob.

The verger hesitated, remembering, before replying. 'James took things very badly. He committed suicide a few months later.'

'Thank you,' said Bob.

Jane was shattered. Her dreams and hopes for the day were fading fast. She looked first at Bob and then at the verger. 'But I don't understand. Why have I got this certificate, and why am I called Jane Carroll?'

'Have you no family who might be able to help?' the verger asked softly.

Jane shook her head. 'I was brought up in an orphanage,' she replied miserably.

'Perhaps we need to ask a few questions there,' suggested Bob.

The verger's beaming smile returned. 'I think that would be an excellent idea,' he agreed.

Jane was silent. Her world had collapsed around her.

The verger glanced at his watch. 'If I might be excused… Unfortunately, I am late for an appointment. However…' he fumbled in his pocket and produced what looked like a small printed notice. 'My name and telephone number are on here. Do please contact me if you feel I can be of any further assistance.' He handed Jane the piece of paper.

'Thank you,' Jane replied simply, still shocked by what she had just learnt.

'Thank you very much,' echoed Bob.

With a cheerful 'Goodbye' the verger hurried on his way.

71

Jane and Bob stood looking at the gravestone for several minutes. At last Jane turned to Bob.

'Oh, Bob, I wanted so much to find something out about my past today. Now it's all a mess.'

Bob could see that the information she had just received had affected her badly. She was the picture of misery. His heart went out to her. Somehow he had to help her.

'We'll sort things out. I'm sure we can. There's just been a mistake somewhere.' He spoke softly as a way of comfort.

Jane said nothing.

He spoke again. 'Perhaps for the record, we'd better make a note of the details from the gravestone.'

Again Jane did not reply, but she bent down and, taking a piece of paper and a pen from her file, copied down the information. When she had finished and stood up again, she was close to tears.

'I'm a person without any name, an impostor. I don't even know who I am. I—' She burst into tears.

Bob took her in his arms. She buried her face in his jacket. 'I'm a nobody,' she sobbed.

Bob gently massaged her back. 'It's all right, it's all right,' he said soothingly. 'Don't worry. We'll get to the bottom of things, I promise you.'

He held her close for several minutes. A woman passed them and, though she looked as if she wanted to say something, she made no comment and went on her way.

Jane eventually eased herself away from Bob. Her face was stained with tears.

'I must look a mess' she said miserably.

'Don't worry about it now. Let's go and have some lunch; then you can clean up and we can talk things over,' Bob suggested soothingly. He put his arm around her and gently led her back to the car.

As Jane sank into the passenger seat, another thought struck her. 'I don't even own this car. The person who owns it is dead,' she remarked miserably. 'And my apartment,' she added glumly.

Bob clicked his seatbelt on. He placed his hand gently on Jane's arm. 'It's most likely a simple mix-up on paperwork. You'll see,' he replied confidently.

'I hope you're right,' murmured Jane.

They retreated to The Poachers, where they ordered two ploughman's lunches at the bar before Jane sped away to the ladies' room to clean up. The pub was not very busy and Bob selected a quiet table in a corner. When Jane returned she was looking a bit brighter.

'I must look a bit better now,' she remarked with a forced little smile.

'You look beautiful any time,' Bob replied with a grin.

His comment caught Jane by surprise. He was not prone to amorous remarks.

'As a kid I was an ugly duckling,' she remarked.

'The ugly duckling grew up to be a swan,' he responded.

The lighter tone of their conversation did not last long. Jane took a sip of her apple juice and looked at Bob intently.

'Bob, what do you think we can do now?' she asked, her face a mass of worry and concern.

Bob considered for a few moments. 'It seems to me that we have to go backwards to when you were born,' he replied thoughtfully.

'But how?' Jane asked glumly.

'Your neighbour – Gerald, is it? – sounds very knowledgeable. He might have some ideas.'

For the first time a glimmer of hope appeared to Jane. 'Of course! Gerald is a mine of information on family history research. I'm sure he could help.'

Ever since they had left the churchyard, Bob had been thinking things over. He could see how what they had learnt that morning had upset Jane. It was bad enough being an orphan, but to suddenly discover that you were not who you thought you were must be a big load to carry. He voiced the thought that was now uppermost in his mind.

'I've been thinking. Do you want to cancel our idea to stop over tonight?' He studied Jane's face for her reaction. It was what he had expected. She looked at him for a second. He could see that she was still quite miserable.

'Can we go home?' she asked sadly.

Bob nodded. 'We'll go straight back to your place and talk things over.'

Bob's acceptance of how she felt made Jane feel even more despondent. Secretly she had been looking forward to her 'night of sin', perhaps because it was a bit out of character for her. She had even purchased a pretty nightdress for the occasion. Now everything had blown apart. She looked at Bob again and voiced her dejection. 'I'm spoiling things for both of us, aren't I?'

Bob smiled at her. He placed his hand on hers. 'No, you're not. There's always another time.'

The drive back to London was a very low-key affair. Bob drove some of the way, and then, after a stop for a break at a motorway service station, Jane took over, explaining that she wanted to concentrate on something to take her mind off family history.

She had rung Gerald from her mobile phone while Bob was driving. When she had finished she had turned to Bob. 'Aren't they sweet? Anna and Gerald want us to go round for a cup of tea as soon as we get back.'

Bob was enthusiastic. 'A good idea. I'll look forward to a cuppa.' Then he asked, 'How did Gerald respond to your news?'

'He wants us to take all the paperwork we have round so that he can have another look for any clues.'

It was late afternoon when Jane pulled into the parking space she had left with such high hopes early that morning. Now she was returning in a completely different frame of mind. They got out of the car, removed their weekend luggage from the boot and walked in silence to Jane's apartment. Jane once again carried her family history file under her arm.

Thirty minutes later they were seated in Anna and Gerald's

lounge; Anna was plying them with tea and cake, and Gerald was casting his eye over Jane's documents once more.

'What do you think?' It was Jane who spoke.

Gerald looked up. 'This is most interesting,' he observed.

'But what do you think I should do now?' Jane insisted. Her concern made her add, 'At present I haven't even got a name.'

Gerald put the document he was reading down and reached for his cup. 'I have never come across a situation like this before,' he replied. He sipped his tea before continuing. 'What we have to do is work from the material we have at present. Where did you get this?' He indicated the certificate that was lying on the settee beside him.

'It was given to me by the couple I lived with after I left the orphanage,' Jane explained.

'They were most likely given it by the orphanage,' he replied.

'I suppose so,' Jane responded glumly. Memories of her time at the orphanage were not happy ones.

'What about the couple you lived with after you left the orphanage? Would they know anything?' It was Anna who asked the question, looking at Jane.

Jane shook her head. 'Derek died suddenly while I was at university, and Mabel died about five years ago,' she replied.

It was Bob who spoke next. 'It seems to me that the big question is, where did the orphanage get the birth certificate from?'

Gerald nodded. 'Precisely,' he agreed. He turned to Jane. 'I think you will need to visit the orphanage and find what information they have.'

Jane nodded, but she did not reply immediately. Suddenly another more serious thought struck her. 'But at the moment I don't have a name. Everything about me is false. I'm using the name of a dead person. That must be a crime.' She looked anxiously around at her audience.

Gerald chuckled. 'Put that way it most likely is,' he replied. He looked at Jane and smiled. 'But as you have used that name ever since you can remember, I should think another few weeks will make no difference.'

'Just think, you might come from a famous family,' chipped in Anna.

'I just want to know who I am,' Jane responded, taking a sip of her tea.

'I think we need to get in touch with the orphanage. They must have records of who placed you there,' said Bob.

Jane looked at him. The thought of returning to her childhood home was not a pleasant one, but she was heartened to hear Bob indicate that he included himself in the undertaking. 'I have the address and telephone number,' she remarked, almost to herself.

'I think you should contact them and see what you can find out,' said Gerald, helping himself to another slice of cake.

Jane pondered the suggestion for a second.

It was Bob who broke the silence. 'Can you remember anything about your life before the orphanage?' he asked her.

She shook her head. 'Very little. I was so young.' She thought for a few seconds, playing with the spoon in her saucer. 'I remember being taken there by this lady and being left there. I remember I cried a good deal.'

'You don't know who the lady was?' Bob persisted.

Jane shook her head. 'No,' she replied.

'We'll contact the orphanage and see what they have on you,' Bob replied cheerfully, adding for good measure, 'I'm sure you'll find it's all just a simple mistake.'

His words cheered Jane up. Her three companions were so positive that it seemed stupid of her to be so downcast. After all, Gerald was helping her and Bob was being very supportive. Anna was doing her best to make everything appear light-hearted. The most sensible thing for her to do would be to phone the orphanage. She would do that next week.

A sudden thought interrupted her planning. She turned to Bob with an agitated expression. 'We forgot to ask the verger about the witnesses on the wedding certificate,' she exclaimed.

'I guess it was in the shock of everything,' replied Bob.

'That could be an important clue,' observed Gerald.

76

Jane became concerned again. She thought for a moment. 'I'd better ring the verger next week as well,' she remarked with a sigh.

'Do it now. Use our telephone.' Gerald had already jumped up. 'I'm anxious to know the answer,' he added, smiling broadly at Jane.

Jane was a bit reluctant to telephone the verger there and then, but she picked up the certificate and followed Gerald into his study. When he returned to the lounge, Jane sat at his desk and produced the printed church notice the verger had given her. With it in front of her she picked up the phone and dialled the number.

A male voice answered. 'Hello.'

Jane glanced at her information. 'Hello. Is that Bernard Thornton?'

'It is indeed. How can I help?'

Encouraged by the friendly response, she responded quickly. 'I'm Jane Carroll. We met in the churchyard this morning.'

'We did indeed.'

Jane hesitated for a second, searching for the right words. 'I was wondering if you might be able to help me.'

'I'll do my very best. What can I do for you?' Bernard replied.

Jane plunged in. 'It's just that I have what I thought was my parents' wedding certificate and there are the names of two witnesses on it. I was wondering if you might know them.'

'What are the names?' asked Bernard.

'John Harvey and Susan Carroll.'

There was a pause before Bernard replied. 'John Harvey was a farm worker. I think he later joined the army.'

'And Susan Carroll?' Jane interjected.

'She would be James Carroll's older sister. She had left the village some years earlier.'

'Do you know where she went?'

There was another short pause, and then Bernard said, 'I think she worked at an orphanage somewhere.'

This bit of news intrigued Jane. Could it be the same orphanage she had lived in? Perhaps not, but it was certainly worth a try. 'Do you know where the orphanage was?' she asked, eagerly.

'I'm afraid not. The information was only village hearsay.'

'Oh, I see.' Jane struggled to contain her disappointment. She was trying to come up with another question to ask, when the verger broke into her thoughts.

'Is there anything else I can help you with?' he asked.

Jane responded quickly. 'No. I won't take up any more of your time. You've been very helpful.'

'It's been my pleasure. If I can be of further assistance, do please contact me again.'

'Thank you. I will. Goodbye for now.'

'Goodbye.'

Jane replaced the telephone and, gathering up her papers, returned to the lounge, where Bob, Gerald and Anna greeted her with questioning eyes.

'What did you find out?' asked Bob.

Jane resumed her seat and picked up her mug of tea again. She took a sip and then related the content of her conversation with the verger.

'I think there is an answer here somewhere.' It was Gerald who responded first to Jane's account. He had the marriage certificate in his hand again and was scrutinising it. He looked up at Jane and Bob and spoke again. 'I think there could be a clue with this sister of James Carroll. It's also interesting that she is alleged to have worked at an orphanage and you were in an orphanage.' His last sentence was directed at Jane.

'Do you think it might be the same one I was brought up in?' Jane asked. The idea had been bugging her ever since the verger had mentioned it.

Gerald smiled at her. 'The golden rule in family history is not to disregard any information you find, even if it doesn't seem useful.' He took a pause and then added confidently, 'We need to find out a bit more about Susan Carroll.'

'Do you think she could hold the answer?' asked Bob.

'It's not impossible,' replied Gerald, draining the last of his tea.

'Perhaps she's your mother!' exclaimed Anna, who had been listening intently to the conversation.

'Well, at least then I'd know who I am,' replied Jane.

The conversation continued for a little while, with various theories being brought up and discussed. Then Jane and Bob took their leave, a move Jane welcomed. She felt drained by the day's events and now just wanted to spend some time quietly with Bob. Once back in her own apartment the full impact of her situation hit her. She was a person without a name. Everything she possessed was in the name of a dead person. She turned to Bob, her face full of questions and anxiety.

'Bob, we will find out who I am, won't we?'

Bob sensed her distress. He could see the trace of a tear in her eye. Gently he took her in his arms and she nestled against him.

'Of course we will. I'll help you. We'll get to the bottom of everything.'

'Do you really think so?' Jane had burrowed her face into his shoulder.

He stroked her hair. 'Yes, I do,' he replied softly. 'We may find that the whole thing is easier to sort out than you think.'

'I do hope so,' Jane replied, almost to herself.

Bob held her for several minutes, gently caressing her hair and back.

'Stay with me tonight,' she murmured.

His reply was to kiss her gently on the lips.

Chapter 10

Jane was glad it was Friday evening and pleased she was on the way home. It had not been an easy week. Almost seven days had passed since the revealing events in Great Wishington, and in that time hardly an hour passed when the question did not come into her thinking: who was she? Again and again she asked herself, but for the present there was no answer and she was forced to accept her false identity.

The week at work had been particularly heavy and at times stressful. Margaret, who normally answered the telephone, was on holiday, and this meant that the task had to be shared out among the rest of the staff. On some days Annette seemed to receive a continuous stream of telephone calls, and this was a constant disruption to them all. However, the biggest headache was that Annette had suddenly decided to change the timing of a special feature and have it appear in the issue of the magazine currently being prepared, instead of a later one. This had meant extra work for Jane and Amy, and on two evenings both of them had worked late. To make matters worse, Annette had been particularly difficult at times, and as usual it had fallen to Jane to smooth matters over with the rest of the staff affected.

Even her telephone call to the orphanage had not gone well. After several aborted attempts due to interruptions, she had at last managed to dial the number and wait for an answer.

'Goodmanton Children's Home.' The male voice was a trifle abrupt.

'May I speak to the matron?' asked Jane, as pleasantly as possible.

'We don't have a matron any more. What is the nature of your enquiry?'

The reply was uninviting, but Jane was not going to be ruffled. She took a deep breath before answering. 'My name is Jane Carroll and I was an orphan at Goodmanton for about ten years. I would like some information about my admission details.'

'You need to speak to the manager. Hold on, please.'

Jane waited for what seemed an incredibly long time before a voice answered.

'Laura Brompton. Can I help you?'

Jane introduced herself again and explained the reason for her telephone call.

There was a pause at the other end, then a curt reply. 'We cannot give you any details over the telephone. You will have to attend in person and bring some form of identification with you.'

Jane took another deep breath. The response from the manager was hardly encouraging, but she was determined to persevere. 'When can I come?' she asked. 'I live in London. Can it be on a Saturday?'

She felt sure she heard a sigh at the other end of the telephone.

'The only time I can see you is ten o'clock this coming Saturday morning.'

Jane thought quickly. She was not sure Bob was free this Saturday, and on top of that Goodmanton was near Bristol. It would mean a dreadfully early start, but she had to do it.

'I would like to come along at that time,' she replied.

'Very well. What was the name again?'

'Carroll. Jane Carroll.'

'I will make a note and expect you on Saturday. Goodbye.'

'Thank you. Goodbye.'

As Jane spoke she heard the click of a disconnection at the other end of the line.

'Hmm,' she murmured. The call had been brief, but at least she had an appointment.

That evening she rang Bob. His reaction was heartening. 'That's great news!' he exclaimed.

'Can you come with me?' Jane asked hopefully.

81

'I'd like to...' There was a slight hesitation in Bob's reply, as if he was thinking. He continued. 'It's just that I'm supposed to be doing a job at the studio this Saturday morning. I'm pretty sure Jeff will do it, but I'll have to check. Give me five minutes.'

Exactly four minutes later he was back. 'No problem. Jeff's quite happy to take over.'

'Oh, that's marvellous! But I feel that I'm putting everybody to a lot of trouble.' Nevertheless, Jane was pleased that Bob could come with her. She felt happier about things after hearing his next sentence.

'Don't worry about it. I think Jeff likes to work Saturday mornings. If he's at home his wife finds him jobs to do.' Bob laughed as he finished speaking. He thought of something else to say to reassure Jane. 'I'm going to cover for him on Monday so that he can have that day off instead of Saturday.'

'Oh, that's super. I'm so glad you can come.'

Jane was beginning to look forward to the trip now. Then she remembered something. 'We'll have to leave quite early. The appointment is at ten.'

'No problem. Pick me up at seven. You can have a sleep in the car.'

Jane couldn't think of a suitable reply to Bob's flippant suggestion and after a few more pleasantries they said goodbye, with the anticipation of meeting on Saturday.

They were relaxed with each other now and humour had become part of their repertoire. Jane was also increasingly aware that she was growing steadily quite fond of Bob. She felt in tune with him and he had the quiet knack of being a tremendous support to her. The previous weekend it had been his supportive attitude that had lifted her out of her misery. When she had eventually lain, curled up in bed, with Bob's arms encircling her, she had rediscovered a feeling of comfort and contentment. Not since her brief marriage had she felt that way.

It was arriving outside the front door of her apartment block that stirred Jane out of her evaluation of the week's events. Knowing that Bob would most likely stay over on Saturday night had prompted her to pop into the supermarket after leaving the train and buy some essentials and extra food. Now she found her load heavy, and on top of that one of the plastic carrier bags was in danger of losing a handle. She was glad to arrive at her destination without mishap. It was now past seven and she was tired, and with all that she was carrying she considered taking the lift, but she decided to stick to her usual routine and climb the stairs to her apartment.

As she opened the door of her apartment and stooped to pick up two letters from the mat, she noticed the piece of paper that lay with them. She picked it up and read it.

Dear Jane,
I have some more information for you. Can I see you urgently?
Regards,
Gerald

Jane thought for a few seconds. It had been a hard day and she just wanted to relax, but she knew it must be something important for Gerald to have left the note. Perhaps it would be better to go and see him immediately rather than waiting until later. She placed her bags in the kitchen, then made her way downstairs to Gerald and Anna's apartment and rang the doorbell.

It was Anna who opened the door. 'Jane! Come along in,' was her greeting. 'Gerald's got some news for you,' she announced as she ushered Jane into their lounge.

Gerald was sitting on the settee. He greeted Jane as she entered.

Jane sank gratefully onto the settee beside him. 'Hello, Gerald. You've found some more information?' she enquired.

Before Gerald could answer, Anna butted in. 'Jane, would you like a drink? Tea or coffee?'

Jane smiled at her. 'A cup of tea would be welcome,' she replied.

Anna looked at her with concern. 'Have you had anything to eat, young woman?' she asked.

The mention of food reminded Jane how hungry she was. 'A long time ago,' she replied in rather a matter-of-fact way, eager to know what Gerald had for her.

'And what was that?' Anna asked, with a pretence of sternness.

'Just a roll for lunch,' Jane answered awkwardly, remembering that she had eaten it at her desk hours previously.

'Goodness gracious! You young girls starve yourselves. Let me get you some food. Cheese on toast OK?' Anna was in her element.

'Oh, no. Please don't go to such trouble. I can easily get something later,' protested Jane.

'Give in gracefully.' Gerald was watching everything with amusement. Almost under his breath he added, 'I always do.'

Jane laughed. She didn't mind Anna's faked bossiness one bit and she was really hungry. 'That would be marvellous.'

With a grin and a wink, and pleased with her victory, Anna disappeared into the kitchen.

Jane could not contain her curiosity any longer. Turning to Gerald, she asked eagerly, 'I know you must have found out something. I can't wait.'

Gerald was immediately focused. 'Ah, now this is interesting,' he remarked, leafing through the papers on the table in front of him. He extracted a handful of documents. 'I've being doing some more research into the Carrolls,' he said, 'in particular Susan Carroll, the witness on your parents' marriage certificate.'

He handed Jane a piece of paper. 'Susan Carroll was married,' he announced.

Reading the document brought an exclamation of surprise from Jane's lips. 'Susan Marshall?' She looked at Gerald. 'The matron at Goodmanton while I was there was Mrs Marshall!' she exclaimed excitedly.

'I've found out more as well,' said Gerald, reaching for another piece of paper. 'James Carroll, your alleged father, had three other sisters: Elizabeth and Evelyn' – he handed Jane the piece of paper – 'and a third sister, who died as a baby.'

Jane studied the piece of paper, absorbing the information it contained. Her earlier excitement had dissipated. She turned to Gerald. 'I wonder if the verger knows anything about these two sisters,' she said.

'It's possible,' Gerald observed thoughtfully.

'I was in such as state of shock at the time, that I never thought about asking about any other members of the family,' Jane said solemnly.

'Understandable, in the circumstances. I—'

He was interrupted by Anna's entry into the room. She carried a tray, which she put down on the table in front of Jane. 'Now eat that right away,' she demanded, taking a seat opposite Jane.

Jane regarded the tray. A plateful of toasted cheese on bread, with tomatoes on top, together with a small pot of tea, a tiny jug of milk, a little bowl of sugar, and a cup and saucer. There was even a serviette. As soon as she saw the food, she realised how hungry she was.

'Oh, Anna, you're spoiling me. Thank you.' Jane felt quite overwhelmed. She was not used to this kind of attention.

'Nonsense. Eat it all up. You're far too thin. Anyway, I don't want you fainting on me for lack of food,' retorted Anna, at the same time grinning cheerfully.

Jane just smiled and started to pour herself a cup of tea. She knew Anna was enjoying pretending to be stern with her and treating her almost like a little girl. She accepted the role gracefully.

'Gerald's been finding out a great deal more about my family,' she announced to Anna, bringing her into the conversation and at the same time starting to munch a piece of toasted cheese.

'Yes, he told me,' Anna responded proudly. 'Perhaps you're the daughter of one of those sisters,' she chipped in.

Jane thought for a second before answering. 'Yes, but if that was the case, why do I have the birth certificate of a dead child belonging to another sister?' she asked, looking at Anna and Gerald in turn.

It was Gerald who spoke next. 'You're going to the orphanage tomorrow. Find out as much as you can. These places have admission records. You could find that it's a simple administrative error.'

'I'll try and do that,' Jane replied thoughtfully.

Suddenly, once again, panic started to cloud her thoughts. 'But everything about me would be wrong,' she said. 'My name, my documents… Everything.' She appealed to Gerald.

'Oh, these things can be sorted out,' he reassured her.

'Yes, but how?' She still needed convincing. The thought of what might be before her was overwhelming.

Gerald gave a little smile before replying. 'It may not be as difficult as you think at this stage. You just officially change your name,' he explained.

'I think your parents might be somebody famous.' Anna could not help adding her thoughts.

'Oh, I hope not. Getting used to a new name would be bad enough without having to deal with famous parents into the bargain,' Jane replied with a grin. Anna's light-hearted approach to things and Gerald's wise counsel had relaxed her again a little.

For the next ten minutes their conversation was of more general matters. Gerald gave her one or two extra snippets of advice about what to ask the next day, and Anna wanted to know what time she was leaving in the morning and whether Bob would be going with her.

Jane finished her meal, asked Anna if she could do the washing up – an offer firmly rebutted – and then, after thanking both of them for their efforts on her behalf, retreated upstairs to her apartment.

Once there, she realised how tired she was. She retrieved the shopping bags from the kitchen floor where she had dumped them, and put the contents away. She collected together all the things she needed to take with her the next day and put them carefully, all ready, on the hall table. One important thing remained to be done: she had to ring Bob and confirm the arrangements for the morning.

Bob must have been close to the phone, because he answered after the first couple of rings.

'Hello.'

'Bob, it's me.'

There was a chuckle at the other end of the phone.

'Hello, me. Are you all ready for tomorrow?'

Thinking of the next day made Jane serious. 'I'm looking forward to it, but I'm also a bit apprehensive about what we might find out. I saw Gerald this evening, and I've lots to tell you, but I'm really tired now, so I'm afraid it'll have to wait until the morning.' With Bob, she felt that she could express how she actually felt.

Bob was intrigued, but he could hear the tiredness as well as the concern in Jane's voice. 'Don't worry about it,' he replied. 'We'll deal with everything as it comes.'

Bob's calm approach and his continued support reassured Jane. She changed the subject to deal with practical matters. 'Will it be OK, then, if I pick you up at about seven? That should give us plenty of time.'

As usual, Bob was fully compliant. 'That'll be fine. I'll be ready.'

'Great. I'm going to bed soon, as I'll have to get up at five,' Jane announced.

Bob's next suggestion was quite unexpected. 'Just one more thing,' he said. 'When we come back, how would you like to stay over with me here? There's a delightful pub we can walk to for a meal.'

Jane quickly got over her surprise. 'I'd love to,' she chipped in eagerly, adding mischievously, 'I won't lock the bedroom door this time.'

'I've taken the lock off,' Bob replied.

'Oh, how awful! What is a poor innocent girl to do?' Jane wailed in mock anguish, latching onto his humour.

'Accept the situation gracefully, my dear.'

'How can you even think of such a thing, let alone suggest it?' replied Jane, continuing in the same light-hearted vein.

The patter might have gone on longer, but Jane suddenly switched to more mundane matters. 'Bob, it's lovely talking to you, but I'd better finish, because this little girl has got to get up early in the morning and I want to tackle my hair before I go.'

Bob took the hint. 'Fine. I'll expect you in the morning around seven. I'll do the driving and you can have a snooze.'

Jane laughed. 'I most likely will, but bye for now. See you in the morning.'

'Bye. Sleep well.' And with that Bob was gone.

Jane thought carefully as she put the phone down. If she was going to spend the night away, she had better do some packing. She flew into the bedroom, pulled out her weekend bag and started flinging things onto the bed. If Bob was taking her out for a meal, she would need something different from the blouse and trousers she would be wearing during the day. Dress after dress was taken out of the wardrobe and scrutinised before she finally settled on a blue summer one with dainty shoulder straps. But which shoes should she wear with it? She had a pair of high-heeled white court shoes with a bow on the front, but Bob had said something about walking to the pub… She looked at a pair of white pumps that she thought might come in handy. In the end both pairs went into a weekend suitcase. Her usual bag would be far too small for all the things she ended up wanting to take. The last item that went into the case was the pretty nightdress she had purchased for the previous weekend. With a sigh of relief she closed the lid and carried the case into the hall. A glance at the clock showed her that she had taken far longer than she had intended and that her plans for an early night had gone sadly awry, but she was determined to make an effort and be attractively dressed for the occasion. She would fix her hair in the morning.

Ten minutes later she had retreated to the comfort of her bed. Tomorrow was a new day and hopefully she might at long last solve the mystery of her past.

Chapter 11

The alarm clock jerked Jane out of sleep. She groped instinctively for the switch to silence the noise. Pulling the eiderdown from her face she glanced at the bedside clock. It was just after half past four. She lay there for a minute and then became conscious of another sound. It was the noise of raindrops falling on her bedroom window. Flinging back the eiderdown she tiptoed to the window and drew back the curtains to look out. It was a dismal scene, with rain falling steadily. The thought of driving any distance was not appealing to her; she hated driving in the rain, but it had to be done and Bob would share it with her.

She took her time showering, and washing and styling her hair. When she emerged from the bathroom and put on her watch she was alarmed to see that almost an hour had gone by. She dressed quickly and then there was just time for a quick breakfast of tea and muesli. It was close to six when she collected all her things and finally locked the door behind her. It was still raining as she walked to the car and she was glad she had put on her trusty red plastic raincoat. Thank goodness the petrol tank was already quite full, so she would have no need to stop on the way to Bob's house. She quickly put her luggage in the boot and slipped into the driving seat, glad to be out of the rain. While the car was warming up and the windows were clearing she had the usual search to retrieve her driving shoes from under the seat where she had flung them. Once she had changed into them, she was on her way.

Bob was also up early. He had one or two jobs to do before his guest arrived. His plan to spend some time the previous evening on the task had been thwarted. It had been one of his days in the studio, and he had worked late. On the way home he had stopped at the supermarket to buy some extra food and essentials for Jane's visit. He had only just arrived home when she phoned. He had been over the moon when she readily accepted his invitation to stay Saturday night at his house. Now he was anxious to have everything looking nice before she arrived.

His original plan to tidy up a bit the evening before had been abandoned in preference to getting up early and whisking through in the morning. Not that there was a lot to do. Mrs McGinty kept his house spick and span and he was generally a tidy person. However, he changed the bed, using the fresh linen Mrs McGinty had washed and placed in the airing cupboard, and tidied up the bedroom in general. The lounge rarely got in a mess, because he didn't spend a lot of time in there. It was the kitchen that required the most attention. A few dishes to wash up, and the worktops to tidy. He even cleared the kitchen table. He was just finishing a quick breakfast when Jane arrived. He opened the front door to see her sitting with the car door open, changing her driving shoes for her white casuals.

She looked up as he appeared. 'Hi!' she called out as she got out of the car.

Bob grabbed the golf umbrella he kept in the hall and sheltered beneath it as he went to meet her.

Jane turned to greet him and offered her lips for a kiss. Bob's free hand encircled her and held her as he kissed her.

'Good morning,' he said. 'Mmm... You smell nice today.' Her perfume was faint but tantalising.

Jane looked at him with a smile. 'Do you like it? It's new. I thought I'd try it out.'

Bob grinned at her. He always liked her perfume. 'It's great. I like it. But you always smell delicious.'

Jane pretended to be serious. 'Well, a female has to try and lure a male into her net somehow.'

Bob was about to reply and perhaps continue their titillating humour, but Jane disentangled herself. She looked up at the sky and made a face. 'I didn't expect it to rain,' she said solemnly as she slammed the car door.

'It's going to be fine by midday,' replied Bob, holding the umbrella over her.

'Thank goodness,' she remarked. Then she exclaimed excitedly, 'I've got so much to tell you! Oh, and I've got a bag of goodies in the boot for us.' She was already moving towards the back of the car, ignoring the rain and the umbrella.

For the next minute or so she was busy removing her bits and pieces from the boot including a plastic bag that bore the name of the supermarket. With a bag in one hand and the umbrella in the other, Bob led the way into the house. As they walked, Jane turned and clicked the remote locking device for the car. Once inside the house, she dumped her bag on the floor and flung her arms around Bob.

'Now I can kiss you without embarrassing your neighbours!' she exclaimed.

Bob lingered over kissing her. He ran his hand over her hair, which fell softly to her shoulders instead of the pinned-up practical style she wore for work.

'Hey. I spent ages doing my hair this morning,' Jane said reproachfully.

Bob laughed. 'All the more reason for me to handle it,' he replied, nevertheless taking the hint and directing the offending hand to her back. 'Come into the kitchen and I'll make you a coffee,' he invited, suddenly releasing her and making a move in the direction of the kitchen.

'Oh, that would be great. Just what I could do with.' Jane followed him into the kitchen and sat down at the table.

'What time did you get up?' Bob asked, busy filling the kettle.

Jane made a face. 'The middle of the night,' she replied, adding by way of explanation, 'Half past four.'

'Gosh, you must be tired out.'

Jane laughed. 'I'll survive.' Then a thought struck her. 'But I must tell you what's happened,' she insisted.

Over coffee she updated Bob on everything that had happened during the week, keeping the best bit until the end: the new information Gerald had discovered.

Bob listened intently. When she had finished, he thought for a second and then commented thoughtfully, 'So you could have some aunts somewhere around.'

'Absolutely. That's what I was thinking,' replied Jane. Then, almost thinking aloud, she added, 'That is if I *am* Jane Carroll.'

'Yes, but even if you aren't, James Carroll's two sisters, if they are still alive, should have some information about why you have been living under that name,' Bob pointed out.

'But how would we find them?' asked Jane.

'Well, let's start with the orphanage, today. They must know something there.' Bob's approach to the problem was quite upbeat.

Jane gave a little sigh. 'I suppose you're right,' she observed, but there was an air of sadness about her reply.

Bob studied her for a second. He could see that she was going over in her mind the events of the previous week, and on top of that he knew that the thought of visiting the institution where she had spent her early years was depressing for her, despite her cheerful countenance.

'Don't worry. We'll get everything sorted out,' he assured her.

Jane smiled at him. 'I do hope so. Thank you for your reassurance. I know I'm jolly lucky to have both you and Gerald taking such an interest in my hidden past.'

'That guy Gerald is a useful chap to have around,' commented Bob.

Jane nodded. 'I know. He's an absolutely authority on family history. Anna says he's been at it for years and years.'

'Good for him and us,' remarked Bob with a grin.

Their conversation continued for another ten minutes or so as they finished their coffee, Jane chatting and Bob responding and adding a comment here and there. It was Bob stealing a quick look at the clock on the wall that prompted Jane to look at her watch.

'Hey, we'd better get going, or we'll be late!' she exclaimed.

Bob was already on his feet.

'This is it. We're almost there.' Those were Jane's words as she read the sign advising motorists to drive slowly through the village of Goodmanton.

Bob, who was enjoying driving the BMW, gave her a quick glance. 'Whereabouts is the orphanage?' he enquired.

'It's not far now,' Jane responded quickly. Then, as another familiar landmark appeared, she exclaimed almost excitedly, 'That's the bus stop where we older girls used to catch the bus to school! The orphanage is coming up now. Just here on the left.'

Bob slowed the car as they approached the entrance. He turned off the road and steered the car through iron gates hung on tall stone pillars. The wheels clattered over a cattle grid. Ahead the driveway disappeared around a bend to the right. A large notice board announced that this was Goodmanton Children's Home, administered by the County Council. The drive was short, and almost immediately a large, stone building came into sight.

'This is it,' was Jane's unenthusiastic comment.

Bob stole a quick glance at her. He knew the visit wasn't going to be a pleasant experience for her. He was about to reply with a few words of comfort, but she spoke again first.

'They've made a car park. That's new since I was here.' She waved a hand in the direction of a sign indicating *All Parking*.

Bob turned into the parking area and parked the BMW neatly between two other cars. There were already six or seven vehicles there. Together they walked back towards the main building.

Jane was unusually silent. A kind of sadness had enveloped her as memories of the time she had spent in this establishment came back to her.

Bob took her hand and gave it a squeeze. 'It'll be all right,' he whispered.

'I know. It's just memories,' Jane replied in a quiet voice.

'Thank goodness the weather has improved,' commented Bob. The rain had stopped halfway through their journey and now the sky was lightening, with a hint of blue to come.

'I'm glad you did the driving,' said Jane. She gave a little smile. 'I hate driving in the rain.'

A few minutes' walk brought them to the main building. Once an extremely large house with many windows, it now had a kind of businesslike atmosphere about it.

'That was my dormitory,' Jane commented, pointing to a window on the second floor.

Bob looked up at the window and then turned his attention to the inscription carved in stone above the front door of the building. *Founded 1850 by Sir Edward Ashington as a charitable institution, for orphans of the district.*

'Who was Sir Edward Ashington?' he asked quietly.

'I think he was a wealthy local man,' replied Jane, and then in almost the same breath she remarked, 'I think we have to go round the side.' She pointed to the notice on the wall beside the front door with its clear message. *All enquiries to the office.* A large arrow accompanying the notice made its meaning quite clear.

'The office used to be inside the house when I was here,' she remarked.

They walked in the direction indicated by the arrow, turning the corner of the house, and immediately came to a new brick building tacked onto the side. In front of them was a door marked Reception and Office.

'This is all new since my time,' observed Jane, looking around. She tapped on the door.

From inside, a voice bade them enter. Jane pushed open the door and they both went in.

They found themselves in a bright, roomy office. The sole occupant was a middle-aged woman with glasses, seated at a desk.

'Yes, can I help you?' she asked in a slightly irritated voice.

'I'm Jane Carroll,' replied Jane nervously, 'and this is Bob

Harker, a friend of mine. I have an appointment with the manager at 10 o'clock.'

'Oh, yes,' replied the woman. 'I'm Laura Brompton, the manager of the home.' She indicated two chairs facing the desk. 'Please take a seat.'

Jane and Bob sat down. The manager looked at Jane. 'What can I do for you?' she asked, her tone hardly inviting.

Jane opened her file and started to relate her story. 'I was placed in this orphanage at a very early age. I'm not sure who my parents were. I'd like to know what information you have on me.'

There was almost a sigh from Laura Brompton. 'I'm not sure that we can give you any information on that.'

She began to say something else, but Jane butted in. 'But I can prove who I am,' she protested. 'I have my personal papers here.' She started to open her shoulder bag.

There was a definite pursing of the manager's lips. After a slight pause she said, 'Let me explain the situation to you. We are now run by the county council. I have no early records. All I have are the computer records that were compiled when the home was taken over five years ago.'

This was a blow to Jane, but she was determined to persevere with her quest. 'Can you tell me who arranged for me to come here?' she queried.

The manager shook her head. 'I don't have that information,' she replied curtly.

'What do you have on me?' Jane persisted.

The manager opened a drawer and pulled out a sheet of paper. She looked at it for a second. There was an audible sigh before she replied. 'The computer records show that you were admitted in 1981 and were discharged in 1991 to live with…' She paused a moment to refer to the paper she held, then continued. 'Derek and Mabel Watkins,' she concluded.

'Yes, that's correct,' said Jane somewhat glumly. She had not anticipated this lack of available information.

'What happened to the original records?' It was Bob who asked the question. So far he had merely sat and observed the proceedings.

Laura Brompton turned to him sharply with a cold stare. Bob's input, and his question, were clearly not welcome.

'Some were destroyed in an office fire some years ago and the rest were lost when the home was taken over by the county council,' she replied abruptly, as if the question irritated her.

There was a few seconds' break in the conversation. Jane was desperately trying to think of more questions to ask.

It was a futile exercise, because suddenly Laura Brompton looked at her watch and then at Jane. 'Is there anything else you want to ask me?' she enquired with obvious lack of enthusiasm.

'No… I think that's all,' Jane replied, rising from her seat. It was clear that the interview was over.

'Thank you for seeing us,' said Bob as he stood up.

Farewells were brief as Laura Brompton watched them leave her office. It was abundantly clear that Jane and Bob's visit had been an irritation and an inconvenience to her.

Once outside, Bob let off steam. 'Phew! Talk about being given the cold shoulder,' he remarked.

Jane did not reply. The meeting had been too negative and destructive for her to cope with.

When she eventually turned to Bob, her face was a picture of misery, and tears were close to the surface. 'First last week, and now this. I feel completely gutted. I don't think I can cope with any more.' Her voice was full of emotion.

Bob put his arm round her and pulled her towards him. 'It'll be all right. You'll see. Don't let this meeting get you down,' he said gently, as he started to lead her in the direction of the car park.

'I'm usually quite strong about things, but the last two weeks have really got to me.' Jane stopped and turned to face Bob. She spoke slowly, as if she was thinking about each word. 'It's just this feeling of not knowing who I am. I'm officially a dead person. I don't exist.' She looked appealingly at Bob.

Bob continued to lead her to the car. 'We'll get to the bottom of things. There must be an answer somewhere. We've just got to find it.'

His words were comforting to Jane, but the doubts and anxieties remained. 'But where do we go from here? I really thought we would get somewhere today.' She looked at Bob, desperately seeking inspiration.

'It's certainly a blow, but we can't let it put us off track. There's got to be another way of finding out about the real you.'

He was trying to be as cheerful and optimistic as he could, for Jane's sake, but deep down he wondered where they could go next.

'And that awful woman,' said Jane. 'She wasn't interested in me, you, or anything we asked.'

'I know,' agreed Bob. 'Made it pretty clear as well.'

They reached the car. Bob led Jane to the passenger door. Neither of them paid any attention to the small Ford that was parked a few cars away, or to the petite, blonde-haired young woman who emerged from it. The woman stared at them for a few seconds and then let out almost a shout.

'Jane! It is you, isn't it?'

There was no mistaking who was being addressed. The woman started to walk towards them.

Chapter 12

The sound of the voice shook Jane and Bob out of their discussion.

Jane hesitated for a second and then could not conceal her excitement. She rushed towards the owner of the voice, at the same time almost squealing, 'Lucy!'

The two women hugged each other.

It was Lucy who pulled free first. She looked at Jane, her face beaming. 'Jane! What are you doing here again?' she enquired excitedly.

'It's a long story,' replied Jane, smiling for the first time. She studied Lucy briefly and then asked the first of the many questions that were bubbling inside her. 'But what about you? What are YOU doing here?'

Lucy laughed. 'I work here,' she explained.

Jane suddenly remembered Bob, who had been observing their excitement with amusement. She turned to him. 'Bob, this is Lucy. We were in the orphanage together. Lucy, this is a friend of mine, Bob.'

Bob moved forward and was greeted with a handshake and a kiss on the cheek from Lucy. He and Jane had hardly any time to say anything before Lucy piped up again.

'I'm so excited at seeing you again! It's made my day. But I still want to know what brings you here.'

'Well—' Jane started to explain, but Lucy interrupted.

'Look, I don't know how you are for time, but I've only called in to collect something I left here yesterday. I'll only be about five minutes. How about we have a cup of coffee together? Then we can chat. There's a lovely little tea-shop here now.' She nodded in the direction of the village and looked hopefully at Jane and Bob.

Jane turned to Bob. 'Shall we?' she asked.

'Sounds a great idea,' enthused Bob.

'Super,' said Lucy, clearly pleased.

'Shall we wait for you?' asked Jane.

Lucy was full of smiles. 'I suggest you go on ahead. I'll follow in five minutes. You should find the tea-shop OK. It's called The Pop Inn and you can park right opposite.'

'Right. See you there.' It was Bob who spoke this time. He was already moving towards the driver's door.

'Great!' Lucy gave them a huge grin and hurried away on her flip-flops. At one point she turned and gave them a cheery wave.

Jane waved back and then slipped into the passenger seat. 'Fancy bumping into Lucy!' she exclaimed. 'I'm really quite excited. She's the first person I've met from the orphanage since I left there.'

Bob started to reverse the car out of the parking place. 'How long did you know her?' he asked.

'Almost the whole time I was there. We were quite good friends,' replied Jane. She suddenly thought of something and smiled. 'We were a pair. We used to get into all sorts of scrapes together.'

'Who was the leader?' Bob asked, smiling.

Jane turned to him. 'Usually it was Lucy. She's a year or so younger than me.'

Bob turned the car out of the drive onto the road and towards the village. Goodmanton appeared to be quite large, with a wide main street and quite a number of shops on both sides; there was even a bank. As they entered the village proper they passed the church, which had an amazing tall steeple.

'That's the church we used to go to,' Jane pointed out.

'Every Sunday?' enquired Bob, without taking his eyes off the road.

'Only on special days.' Suddenly she thought of something else. 'They had a Brownie pack there, and Girl Guides. I was in both.'

Bob laughed. 'I'd have liked to see you as a Girl Guide,' he chuckled.

'Hey, I'll have you know I got all my badges,' retorted Jane, feigning indignation.

Bob was pondering a suitable reply when she piped up again. 'Look. There's The Pop Inn, and there's a parking space.'

Bob glanced in the direction Jane indicated, turned the car and parked neatly between two other cars. They crossed the road and went into the tea-shop. It was larger inside than the outside indicated, but already quite crowded. Jane looked around anxiously, and then she spotted two elderly women getting up from a table in an alcove. In two seconds she was at the table, Bob following at a more leisurely pace.

They had hardly sat down before a pretty young waitress appeared before them.

'What would you like?' she asked.

Jane, menu card already in hand, had a quick glance at a nearby table and then looked at Bob with a mischievous glint in her eyes.

'Let's have a coffee – and let's be absolutely wicked and have some scones with jam and cream.'

'A good idea,' replied Bob with an enthusiastic nod.

Jane put the menu card down and addressed the waitress. 'Two filter coffees and a plate of scones with jam and cream, please,' she announced firmly.

The waitress took their order and disappeared with a flourish.

'I'm glad you met Lucy,' Bob remarked suddenly. He meant it. He had noticed immediately the change that had come over Jane when she encountered her old friend. She had been quite sad after the negative interview with the manager, but on meeting Lucy she had brightened up considerably.

'So am I,' replied Jane with a little smile. 'After that awful woman, it was like a breath of fresh air.'

'Funny that Lucy should be working at the orphanage,' Bob remarked thoughtfully.

'I couldn't have done it,' observed Jane. 'Once I'd left, I never wanted to see the place again.'

'Was it so bad?'

Jane did not reply immediately. She seemed to be analysing the question deeply. When she eventually spoke she chose her words carefully.

'Oh, it wasn't bad in one sense. I mean, we were looked after fine. It was just that...' she paused for a second, thinking and then continued. 'It was just that I desperately wanted to be part of a normal family, like some of the girls I met at school. They did things I could never do. Do you understand?' She looked at Bob appealingly.

Bob nodded. 'I think I do,' he replied.

Jane was in a reflective mood as she continued to remember her days in the orphanage.

'All I ever knew was living there with lots of other children,' she explained to an attentive Bob. 'Sometimes it was the little things you noticed most. I never had a bedroom of my own, with all my own things around me, and I could never invite my friends home like other girls could.'

She studied Bob, assessing his reaction.

'You must have felt a bit isolated at times,' he suggested.

'Different, I suppose you could say,' she replied.

At that moment the door of the tea-shop opened and Lucy appeared. She obviously knew the staff, because she had a word with the waitress who was passing and then continued towards the table where Jane and Bob sat.

'Here I am,' she announced breezily, slipping into a chair opposite them. She looked around the room briefly and then concentrated her gaze on Jane and Bob. 'I come here quite often for lunch,' she announced.

Jane was anxious to know more about Lucy's past. 'So what happened to you after you left the orphanage?' she enquired.

Lucy responded immediately. 'Well, soon after you left I was sent to live with a family in Bristol, and then when I left school I did an office course – you know, typing, office management, that sort of thing – and then I got a job with a firm of solicitors.'

She stopped talking for a few moments, as if to ensure that she had Jane and Bob's attention, and then with a grin she announced, 'I ended up marrying one of the younger partners in the practice. We live in the next village and we have a two-year-old daughter. Raymond's mother lives next door to us and she looks after Patty when I'm working.'

Jane was enthralled and wanted to know more. 'But how did you end up working at the orphanage?' she asked.

Lucy chuckled. 'I saw the job advertised and I applied and got it,' she replied.

Jane would have asked more questions, but the pattern of conversation was broken by the arrival of a cup of coffee for Lucy. She immediately gave it a stir and then took a sip. Replacing the cup in its saucer, she looked straight at Jane. 'And now I want to hear what brings you to Goodmanton,' she said firmly. 'The last I saw of you, you disappeared to this couple in Bristol. I want to know everything that has happened to you since.'

Jane started to relate the events of her life since leaving the orphanage. She touched briefly on her life before university, her marriage and Graham's death, her job and her current quest to find her identity.

Lucy listened intently, and when Jane had finished she let out a gasp of astonishment. 'Gosh, that's quite a story,' she commented thoughtfully, but almost in the same breath she announced with a grin, 'Well, as far as I'm concerned you are Jane Carroll.'

Jane gave a little forced smile before she responded. 'But unfortunately not on my official records.'

Lucy appeared to be deep in thought for a few seconds; suddenly she looked directly at Jane. 'Who did you talk to today?' she asked. 'Laura Brompton?'

'Yes,' Jane replied, wondering why she had asked.

'She wasn't very helpful,' butted in Bob, making his first contribution to the conversation.

Lucy received the comment with a confirmatory nod.

'Hmm… I thought so,' she said. She leaned towards Jane and Bob and lowered her voice. 'She's only been in the job six months and she's completely useless as a manager. She's leaving at the end of next month, thank goodness.'

'Perhaps that's why she was so offhand,' suggested Bob, 'and unhelpful.'

Lucy shook her head. 'No. She's always like that. She's upset a lot of people. If she hadn't been leaving, I would have done. I really can't stand working under her,' she added most emphatically.

'I expect lots of things have changed since we were there,' Jane suggested.

Lucy nodded again. 'Absolutely. A lot more changed when it came under the umbrella of the local authority. It's very different now from when we were there. Even the name has changed,' she added with a grin.

Jane was going to ask another question but was stopped by Lucy, who suddenly grinned at her. 'Do you remember when we used to be naughty and got sent to bed without any supper?' she asked, still smiling.

'Yes, I do,' replied Jane.

Lucy continued with her reminiscing. 'And then if we were really naughty we used to have to stand in a corner in the dining room in our nighties as well while the others had supper.'

Jane made a face. 'I remember that. I had to do it once. It was awful.'

'I did it three times,' Lucy remarked gaily.

Before Jane or Bob could answer, Lucy piped up again. 'They aren't allowed to do it now,' she observed thoughtfully.

'Perhaps something to do with human rights,' suggested Bob. He had been amused by the friends' confessions and the different reaction each had to her punishment. He was waiting for more reminiscences, when Lucy posed her next question.

'So where does all this leave you now?' she asked. 'I mean, with finding out who you are.'

'Stuck,' Jane replied glumly. 'I really hoped I might find

something out today, here at Goodmanton.' She sighed. 'But it hasn't happened.'

There was a few seconds' silence between the three of them. Lucy appeared to be thinking. Suddenly she looked at Jane and Bob. 'Look. I can't promise anything, but there are some old documents in the store room. They are in a pretty awful state, because they were damaged by fire and then water, but I'll try and look at them and see if I can find anything relating to you.'

'Oh, would you please? I'm quite desperate now,' Jane answered quickly. Then she had a thought. 'But Laura Brompton may have looked there already,' she suggested, a bit concerned.

Lucy made a face and shook her head. 'I doubt it. She wouldn't get her fingers dirty.'

Her reply prompted a smile from her companions.

The three of them chatted for a while longer; most of the conversation was between the two friends remembering and reliving their past life at the orphanage. Bob listened politely, making a comment or observation here and there.

It was Lucy who broke up the party. Suddenly she drained the last of her coffee from her cup and looked at her watch.

'Heavens! The time! I must get back to Patty. I said I'd only be half an hour.' She was already getting up from the table.

'I hope we haven't made you late,' exclaimed a concerned Jane.

'It was worth it. It's fantastic meeting you again.' Lucy was delving into her bag. She produced a scrap of paper, placed it on the table in front of her, rummaged for a pen and then started to write.

'Look. Here's my address and phone number. Give me yours so that I can get back to you.'

She gave Jane the piece of paper. Jane was already extracting a card from her file. She handed it to Lucy. 'Actually, it's time we were getting back, too. I'll walk over to your car with you.'

The two old friends left the café, leaving Bob to settle the bill. He had already volunteered for that task, thinking that perhaps they might like a few minutes alone together. There was a small queue at the counter, and it was a good three or four minutes before he joined them at Lucy's car.

Their goodbyes were brief. Lucy hugged Jane and Bob and hurried into her car. She wound down the window.

'I'll do my best for you,' she called out as she started the engine and gave a final wave of her hand.

'Thanks a million,' Jane called out, waving as Lucy drove off.

She turned to Bob, smiling. 'And that', she remarked gaily, 'was Lucy.'

Bob grinned. 'Quite. a live wire,' he said.

'She hasn't changed a bit. She comes over as being a bit scatterbrained, but actually she is quite clever.' Jane was moving towards their car as she spoke.

Bob was making for the driver's side of the car, but she stopped him. 'No. I'm going to drive. You drove all the way here.'

'Agreed.' He laughed and handed her the car key.

Jane settled herself into the driving seat and had the usual search for her shoes, helped by Bob, who found one of the sought-after items under his seat.

As she was changing footwear, Jane turned to Bob. 'What do you think? Shall we have lunch somewhere, or do you want to go straight back?'

Clicking his seat belt into place, Bob was quick to reply. 'How about if we go back now? After all, we've had those scones and cream – and we are going out tonight.'

'My sentiments exactly,' said Jane, adding, 'I don't want to put on weight.' She turned to Bob with a coy smile. 'You wouldn't like me fat.'

'No. Stay as you. Slim and trim.' He gave a little laugh.

Jane eased the car out onto the main road again. She giggled. 'Graham threatened to put me in a corset if I put on a lot of weight.'

'Good for him. I must keep that in mind,' Bob quipped, faking a serious note.

'Pig,' retorted Jane, not taking her eyes off the road, but letting a slight grin escape.

It was late in the afternoon when Jane turned the car into the drive of Bob's house. Bob was already out of the car and opening the front door by the time Jane had changed shoes and locked the car. She followed him into the hall. He had just picked up the post and was glancing through it. He stopped and looked up as soon as she appeared.

'How about a cup of tea?' he suggested.

The thought of a cup of tea was inviting. 'Great,' replied Jane. 'Shall I make it?'

Bob shook his head. 'No. You're a guest. You go into the lounge and leave it all to me.'

Jane was pleased to carry out his suggestion. She had driven all the way back and she was feeling just that little bit tired. She wandered into the lounge. It was a pleasant room, now amply lit by the late-afternoon sun. Sparsely furnished, it was functional rather than homely. A three-piece suite dominated the seating area, and in one corner stood a dining table and chairs. Several well-stocked bookcases, and that was it.

Jane was intrigued by the various framed photographs that adorned the walls. These were clearly examples of Bob's handiwork. Some were still life photographs; others were landscapes. There was even a head-and-shoulders study of a young woman. Jane wondered whether she was Bob's ex-wife. She was still looking at the photographs when he appeared with the tea.

'Some of my early work,' he observed, putting his loaded tray down on the coffee table.

'I like that one,' Jane commented, pointing to the photograph of the young woman.

'That's Janice,' Bob responded hurriedly, almost as if he would like to change the subject.

Jane, however, was impressed by the photograph and wanted to know more. 'I like it very much,' she said. 'Particularly the way the lighting is used.'

Bob joined in her study of the photograph for an instant. 'It's a studio shot,' he commented.

There was a few seconds' silence, both of them lost in thought. Eventually Bob broke the silence. He cleared his throat.

'Perhaps I could take a similar photograph of you some time,' he suggested. He hesitated for a moment and then asked, 'Would you do it?'

Jane turned to him with a smile. 'Of course I would. I'd love to.'

'We could do it in the studio one evening,' Bob continued, enthusiasm beginning to bubble up.

'I'll look forward to it,' enthused Jane.

She changed the subject. 'Gosh, I'm dying for a cup of tea. Shall I pour it?'

'Good idea,' replied Bob. He, too, was ready for a drink. They had only made one comfort stop on the way back and it was hours since they had had the coffee and scones in Goodmanton.

Jane sat down on the settee and started the pouring process. Bob sat down beside her.

When she handed him a mug of tea, he looked at her and voiced his thoughts. 'How are you feeling now? About today's trip, I mean.' He studied her face, waiting for a reaction to his question.

Jane nibbled one of the biscuits from the tray. She thought briefly. 'It's funny, but after we had the interview with that horrible manager, I felt really down and miserable.'

'I could see that,' Bob interrupted.

She nodded agreement and then continued. 'Meeting Lucy changed everything. After that I felt much more optimistic and positive.'

She took a sip of her tea and replaced the mug on the table. She turned to Bob; her face was serious and thoughtful. She spoke again slowly, thinking as the words flowed out.

'You know, Bob, I don't know why, but somehow I have a hunch that Lucy is going to come up with something really exciting.'

Chapter 13

They lingered a long time over their tea, chatting about the day's events. Jane suddenly became concerned about the time.

'When do we have to leave?' she asked a bit anxiously, glancing at her watch.

'I've booked a table for half past seven,' replied Bob, looking at his own watch. 'It's about a twenty-minute walk.' He was quite casual about everything.

For Jane alarm bells rang. 'Heavens!' she exclaimed. 'It's turned six already.'

The thought of getting ready in a strange environment for an evening out alarmed her.

Bob smiled at her. 'We've got plenty of time, but I suggest you get ready first,' he suggested.

Jane was already up and making a move. 'I'll be as quick as I can,' she called from the hall as she collected her weekend case from where she had deposited it earlier in the day.

She was climbing the stairs when Bob called out from the bottom. 'By the way, it's a walk over fields, but at one point we may have to paddle over a stream if the water is high.'

'No problem. I won't be wearing tights,' Jane called back before disappearing.

She went straight to the main bedroom and dumped her case on the floor. She looked around. It was a pleasant room, dominated by a king-size bed. Fitted furniture gave a neat atmosphere. The duvet had been turned back, revealing a crisp white sheet and pillows. She was amazed how tidy the room was, with everything obviously put away.

It was a two-minute job for Jane to unpack. Her dress for the evening; her nightdress – the one she had bought for the previous weekend – she placed neatly on one of the pillows. Grabbing her cosmetic bag, she disappeared into the bathroom. Twenty minutes later she was back downstairs. Bob was not in the lounge or the kitchen, but suddenly he appeared from the second ground-floor room.

He looked approvingly at her. 'You look very glamorous!' he exclaimed. He kissed her. 'And you smell delicious, as usual,' he added.

Jane grinned at him and then looked down at her pretty knee-length summer dress. She had complemented it with a necklace, earrings and bracelet. She glanced at her shoes. 'I'm sorry these aren't the best shoes for walking,' she said, 'but if we're going to be walking over grass…' She looked at Bob for his opinion. She had decided to wear the high-heeled shoes instead of the flats she had brought.

'They'll do fine,' said Bob, following her gaze. 'The ground is quite dry and firm now.' He looked at his watch. 'Give me ten minutes,' he announced. He pointed to the doorway he had just emerged from. 'Have a look at my studio while you're waiting,' he suggested.

He departed up the stairs and Jane wandered through the doorway. She found herself in a typical photographic studio with white walls, flood lamps and camera tripods. A quantity of photographic equipment stood on shelves and tables. Two walls were adorned with large photographs. A few landscapes were in colour, but the majority were in black and white. There were also several still lifes. Jane was intrigued by two photographs featuring women. One was of a reclining nude; the other was of a young woman putting on a pair of stockings, clipping a suspender in place.

Jane was still looking at the two pictures when Bob reappeared. He had changed into a pair of cream casual trousers, an open-necked shirt and a jacket. He came over to her.

'The nude is my sister,' he remarked. 'She wanted it as a Christmas present for her boyfriend a couple of years ago.'

'I quite like it,' said Jane. 'It's rather nice – not too explicit,' she added thoughtfully.

'That's what she wanted,' Bob explained with a smile.

'And this one?' Jane pointed to the glamour picture.

'One of my early photographs.'

Jane looked at him and then back at the photograph. 'I've never quite understood the attraction stockings and suspenders have for some men,' she said, adding with a smile, 'but then I'm not a man.'

Bob grinned at her. 'A man hasn't lived until he has removed a woman's shoes and stockings,' he said.

Jane looked at him, wide-eyed.

He smiled again and answered her silent question. 'And a woman has not lived until she has experienced her lover removing her stockings.'

'Oh. Now I understand,' Jane responded politely, at the same time revealing a slight grin.

'It's a prelude to greater things,' laughed Bob.

'Well, I'll have you know I have worn them.' Jane gave him one of her coy looks.

Bob was going to ask her to explain, but she was already preparing to elaborate. She spoke in a more subdued voice. 'I wore them from time to time when I was married. Graham liked me to.'

'Good for him,' laughed Bob.

'I like this one as well.' Jane pointed to another picture. It was a still life of a spider's web with dew sticking to it and the sun shining through.

'I took that in the back garden a few years ago. It was one of those unique opportunities.'

'I wish I knew how to take better photographs,' commented Jane, almost to herself.

'I could give you a few tips,' offered Bob.

'I'd really like that. But I think I'd probably need a different camera.' She was remembering her frequent failures with photography.

'What sort of camera have you got?'

'Oh, just a basic one, but I think it's a bit out of date now. I need an upgrade.' Jane smiled as she spoke.

'I'll have a look at it next time I'm over at your place,' said Bob. The thought of helping Jane with her photography appealed to him.

Bob would have lingered in the studio, but Jane suddenly looked at her watch and exclaimed, 'Hey, it's nearly seven! Perhaps we should start to walk.'

Her suggestion stirred Bob into action. Five minutes later they set out. The earlier rain had long since disappeared and it was now a pleasant warm June evening. Jane wandered outside first and then Bob followed, carefully locking the door. He had a camera slung over his shoulder. He noticed Jane's glance.

'I like to carry a camera when I'm walking. You never know what you'll come across in the photography line,' he explained.

Jane smiled at him. 'Always on duty,' she replied gaily.

Bob was concerned at her remark. 'You don't mind, do you?' he asked anxiously.

Jane gave a little laugh. 'Of course I don't silly,' she replied, smiling.

'Good,' replied Bob, somewhat relieved.

He immediately took Jane's hand as they set off. The first five minutes or so were along a leafy lane, which led into a path through a wood. After they emerged from the trees, their route skirted an open field. At the end of the field, they came upon a fast-flowing stream. It was about ten feet across, but a series of large, flat stones ensured a dry crossing.

'This is the bit you sometime have to paddle across,' remarked Bob. 'If there's been a lot of rain, the water flows over the stones. I thought it might be like that tonight.'

'I'm glad I didn't wear my wellies,' joked Jane. She had already taken off her shoes for safety and was walking barefoot over the stones. She was halfway across when she heard Bob call.

'Hold it there.'

She turned to look at him. He had his camera at the ready.

'OK. Stand there. Lift your arms up.'

Jane obediently obeyed the instructions.

Bob was the professional at work. 'OK. Arms a bit higher, outstretched. Stand on tiptoe. That's it. Smile.'

The camera clicked as Jane posed. Bob took several photographs and then seemed satisfied.

'That's fine,' he announced, moving to catch up with her.

When they were on the other side of the stream, he smiled cheerfully at her. 'Thank you. You're a good model. I'll get those printed out back home.'

'I'll look forward to seeing them,' Jane replied eagerly. She dropped her shoes onto the ground in front of her. She gazed at the grassy route ahead as she put them back on.

'I'm always tempted to walk barefoot on grass,' she admitted with a shy grin.

'It's magical, isn't it?' agreed Bob, as he took her hand again.

The incident stirred memories for Jane. She turned to Bob as they walked. 'You know, in the orphanage we were never allowed to go barefoot outside the dormitory. We had to wear these horrible slippers everywhere inside, all the same kind.' She paused for a few seconds, remembering, and then continued her reminiscing. 'I was already in my teens and I was allowed to go camping with the Girl Guides for a few days. That was the first time I ever experienced going barefoot outside on grass. It was fantastic.'

Bob nodded. 'I know the feeling,' he agreed. 'My childhood was a bit similar in that respect.' He smiled. 'Perhaps that's why I'm always strutting about at home without shoes on.'

Jane turned to him with a little laugh. 'I do the same,' she admitted. She smiled again. 'It can be a bit embarrassing at times,' she remarked, remembering the way Gerald had looked at her a few days previously.

'In our Western culture we have a problem with bare feet. It's not considered polite, or something like that. Eastern countries don't appear to have that problem,' observed Bob thoughtfully.

'Have you been to lots of countries?' asked Jane, always eager to learn more about his past.

'Quite a few. India, China, Japan...' he reeled off. 'Oh, and Australia and New Zealand as well.'

'Gosh, that's quite a lot.' Jane was surprised. 'What about America?' she asked.

Bob chuckled. 'I've travelled across it from East to West,' he answered.

'Phew. That's a long way.' Jane was impressed.

'What about you?' asked Bob.

Jane was thoughtful for a second. 'Quite a bit, I suppose. I did more when I was married, because Graham travelled quite a bit and could sometimes take me, but I couldn't always go, because of my work.'

Their conversation was interrupted by the sight of rooftops ahead. Two minutes later they were walking down an alleyway between some houses. Soon they were in the main street of the tiny village.

'Here we are,' announced Bob, with a wave of his hand.

Jane looked where he was pointing. Almost opposite them was a picturesque village pub, its walls superbly decorated with hanging baskets bright with flowers. A hanging sign advised potential customers that it was The Gamekeeper.

'It looks really nice,' remarked Jane, who was quite eager to see inside.

They crossed the road and entered the pub. After the bright sunshine outside, at first it seemed to be quite dark, but their eyes quickly grew used to the environment. Jane became aware of a low-ceilinged bar, with lots of beams and gleaming brass-work, before 'mine host' swiftly ushered them to the dining room at the rear of the pub. The dining room was quite small, no more than a dozen tables. They found themselves seated in an alcove with a window overlooking a pleasant garden.

'It really is a lovely place,' observed Jane, looking around.

Bob followed her gaze. 'They do quite a lot of bar food here,'

113

he explained, 'but the dining room is quite small, as you can see, and you have to book early. It's quite popular.'

'I'm rather glad you did. It's a bit more intimate,' replied Jane.

Their conversation was interrupted briefly by the arrival of the waitress, who enquired whether they were ready to order. They asked for another few minutes.

When it eventually came to ordering, they both choose the same thing: asparagus soup followed by a salmon steak with new potatoes. Bob ordered a bottle of wine to top everything off.

During their meal they started to chat again about the day's events. In spite of her early optimism that Lucy was going to come up with something, little moments of concern were now starting to creep into Jane's thoughts. The congenial atmosphere of their surroundings and the effect of the wine made her voice her worries to Bob. Taking another sip of wine, she paused and looked anxiously at him.

'You know, Bob, I still have this feeling that Lucy might come up with something about my past, but I'm beginning to get concerned about what will happen if she doesn't find anything. What do I do then? Where do I go from there?'

Bob thought for a moment. This was something that had occurred to him from the start, but he had decided that nothing helpful could come from voicing his concern. For Jane's sake, he felt that he had to remain positive and supportive.

'Well,' he began, 'we don't know yet that she will find nothing, but even if she does there must be other avenues of research to pursue.' He paused for a few seconds. 'I can't help thinking that somewhere along the way some error has crept in, perhaps a wrong name entered on some document. It could be simply that. If we keep plugging away at it, we must eventually come up with the answer.'

Bob's comments were of some comfort to Jane. He was always so calm and logical.

'I suppose you're right,' she replied. 'It's just this feeling of not knowing who or what I am. Technically I don't exist.' She looked at him pleadingly again.

'We'll get to the bottom of it,' he replied. He placed his hand on one of Jane's briefly. 'I'll help you,' he assured her.

'That's another thing,' remarked Jane with a bit of a wry smile. 'I seem to be leaning on both you and Gerald quite a lot.'

Bob shook his head. 'I enjoy doing it, and so does Gerald. Don't worry about that,' he replied firmly.

Jane forced a smile. 'I know,' she said. I'm sorry about that. I'm just being a bit silly and getting myself all worried about things.'

'In the circumstances it's quite natural that you should feel like that. I'm sure anybody would,' Bob replied sympathetically.

'I wonder if it happens very often,' she pondered.

'I expect it does.' Bob gave a little smile as he spoke. He thought of something else to add. 'I do think that in your case it is most likely to be an error somewhere with paperwork. It shouldn't happen, but apparently it has.'

'I expect you're right.' Jane forced herself to smile again. She was glad of Bob's approach to things and it was silly to get all worried at this stage. Bob could be quite correct: it could be a simple mistake somewhere. She just had to find it, and she could not have better helpers than Bob and Gerald. She made a point of changing the subject. 'Do you come here often?' she asked, indicating their surroundings.

Bob shook his head. 'No, not that often, but it has quite a good reputation with the locals.'

He took another drink of his wine as he finished speaking. Then he looked at Jane and grinned. 'Angus Pike lives not so far away,' he remarked casually.

Jane made a face at him. 'Thanks for reminding me,' she laughed.

The rest of their meal was quite leisurely and congenial. Jane began to feel more relaxed and they chatted about a wide range of topics, perhaps both making a point of not talking about Jane's family history. It was close to ten when they finally left The Gamekeeper.

They walked back to Tatting Green the same way they had

come, hand in hand, and then suddenly Bob put his arm around Jane. She followed his lead and placed her arm around his waist. They walked on, happy and contented. Dusk was already beginning to fall, and at one point Jane suddenly exclaimed. 'Look! There's the moon.' She pointed up at the sky to show Bob. An almost full moon was just beginning to show above the trees ahead.

'Full moon tomorrow,' murmured Bob. He suddenly drew Jane towards him and they kissed passionately, the cares of the day forgotten.

Their interlude was quickly interrupted by the sound of voices not far away. They continued their walk hand in hand, and within a few minutes another couple passed them walking in the opposite direction.

When they eventually came to the fast-bubbling stream, Jane released Bob's hand and stooped down, intending to take off her shoes again, but suddenly Bob bent down next to her, and the next minute she was in his arms. She felt him kick off his own shoes and then he was carrying her over the stream. Once he had reached the other side, he deposited her safely on her feet again.

Jane nuzzled him. 'Mmm. That was super. Thank you, Sir Galahad,' she murmured.

Bob gave her a quick peck on the lips and then dashed across the stones again to collect his shoes. When he returned, Jane smiled at him as she took his hand again. She looked at him in the gathering dusk. 'Do you do that with all your women?' she asked breezily.

Bob squeezed her hand. 'Only those I'm falling in love with,' he replied, laughing.

Chapter 14

Jane awoke to a bright sunny morning. She did her usual thing of glancing at the bedside clock and then, satisfied that she had not overslept, lay there for a few minutes, contemplating the day ahead. It was the start of a new week. She had always been inclined to be a bit 'Monday morning-ish', but lately she had felt even more reluctant to get up. So much had happened over the last few weekends that when Monday came she felt she wanted to rest and absorb the events of the previous two days. Today was no different, and it was the weekend that dominated her thoughts.

Before the meeting with the orphanage manager, Laura Brompton, she had had high hopes that she would learn something that would establish who she actually was; when the meeting proved to be so negative, she had been plunged into despair and left feeling completely miserable. The unexpected encounter with Lucy had immediately lifted her out of her misery, and when Lucy had suggested that perhaps she could delve deeper into the orphanage records, Jane had been filled with optimism. Somehow she felt confident that Lucy would produce something.

As usual Bob had been supportive and attentive and she had been glad of his down-to-earth and easygoing attitude to everything. He had been superbly patient when she met Lucy. The two old friends had chatted continuously while he sat quietly waiting for them to finish, and he had shown an interest in their conversation by making the odd comment or asking a question.

Jane had been aware for some weeks that she was steadily falling in love with Bob. His caring, unhurried approach to things suited her. It kept her feet on the ground and in a way reminded her of Graham. She needed somebody like that around. She had been unsure whether Bob shared her feelings about their relationship, but she strongly suspected that he did. Now and then he would let his feelings show, and that always gave her a big boost. She suspected that beneath his calm exterior a fire waited to be ignited. Over the weekend, things had changed. She knew now that Bob felt the same about her as she did about him. Their relationship had taken on a new dimension, and she liked it.

The time she had spent with him over the weekend had been extremely enjoyable. On the Saturday evening it had been late when they eventually retired to his bedroom. Their lovemaking had been slow and passionate and it had been almost the next morning before sleep had at last overtaken them.

The next morning Jane had woken up slowly, at first slightly disorientated at finding herself in a strange bed. Bob was no longer beside her, but she could hear some movement downstairs. Perhaps he was making some tea. That would be nice, she contemplated. She lay there contented, with little inclination to stir further at present.

Suddenly Bob appeared in the doorway, his face full of smiles. He was barefoot and was wearing a tee shirt and jeans. He was holding something close to his chest.

He bent down to kiss her. 'Good morning,' he greeted her. Jane raised herself in bed to meet his lips, remembering to hold the duvet against herself to cover her nakedness. She put one arm around him and drew him towards her.

'Good morning, darling.' It was the first time she had called him that.

Bob suddenly backed off and displayed what he had been holding to his chest. It brought a squeal of delight from Jane.

It was a large photograph – the one Bob had taken of her the previous evening. It showed Jane standing on tiptoe on a stone in the middle of the stream. Her arms were outstretched, and in each hand she was holding a shoe. She was looking straight at the camera and laughing.

Jane could not conceal her delight. Words poured out in a torrent. 'It's beautiful! When did you do it? Can I keep it?'

Bob grinned at her, pleased at her reaction to his handiwork. 'Of course you can. It's a present for you,' he replied. He decided to elaborate a bit more. 'I knew it would turn out to be a good shot. I got up an hour ago to print it out and mount it.'

'It's fantastic. Thank you.' Jane moved to kiss him again.

It was Bob who broke off their embrace. 'I've got some tea here,' he announced cheerfully, retreating to the landing, where he had left a tray with two steaming mugs on it. He handed Jane one and then perched on the side of the bed with the other.

They spent a long time sipping their tea and chatting, and then Bob politely announced that he was going to 'get some breakfast going', leaving Jane to get up and have a shower.

After a relaxing morning pottering about and going for a walk, they prepared lunch in Bob's kitchen. It was late in the afternoon when Jane took her leave and drove back to Kew, remembering that she had a few routine jobs to do at home before the new week started.

The sound of a car starting up brought an end to Jane's reminiscing, reminding her that she had a train to catch. In a flash she was out of bed and heading for the bathroom. As she passed the dressing table, she could not help pausing to look once again at the photograph Bob had given her. Just looking at it gave her a thrill. For her it firmly cemented in place her relationship with Bob.

Less than an hour later, after a quick shower and a hurried breakfast, she was making her way down the stairs to the front entrance. Usually she did not meet any of the other residents, but this morning, just as she opened the front entrance door, Gerald appeared. He had been out for his morning paper. He beamed when he saw her.

'Ah, Jane. Just the person I wanted to see. I wanted to ask you something – and also, how did you get on at the orphanage on Saturday?'

'Hello Gerald,' Jane responded cheerfully, at the same time conscious that she had only just enough time to catch her train. As briefly as she could, she related Saturday's events to Gerald, finishing with her hope that Lucy might come up with something.

Gerald thought for a few seconds, absorbing the news. 'So we'll have to wait and see what comes up,' he remarked thoughtfully.

'Yes. I hope she contacts me soon. I'm sure she will,' Jane replied quickly. She was beginning to panic about her train. It prompted her next comment. 'I'm just dashing for my train now. We could chat about it tonight if you're free,' she suggested, at the same time trying to ease herself away from Gerald.

'Yes, yes, of course. Don't make yourself late.' Gerald was on the verge of being embarrassed.

'No, I'm fine. I'll just about make it.'

Her reassuring smile encouraged Gerald to ask the question he had on his mind. 'I just wanted to ask you if you could confirm the name of the matron at the orphanage. I seem to remember you said it was a Mrs Marshall.'

'Yes, it was a Mrs Marshall,' said Jane hastily, already turning away to leave Gerald.

'Excellent. I'll talk to you later,' he called after her. He had taken her hint and was moving towards the entrance door as he spoke.

'Fine,' Jane called over her shoulder as she hurried on her way.

She almost had to run to the station. She wondered why Gerald had asked her about Mrs Marshall, but her curiosity was overtaken by the fear that she might miss her train. Luck was on her side. The train was a couple of minutes late and she just made it to the platform as it arrived. It was the usual packed environment, but she managed to grab a seat.

It was a few minutes to nine when she pushed open the heavy door of the office and climbed the stone staircase to the first floor and the offices of *Discerning Woman*. Margaret was already seated at her desk. She greeted Jane with a smile and a cheery 'Good morning!'

'Good morning, Margaret,' Jane replied cheerfully as she walked past.

Once in her own tiny office she dumped her bag on the floor beside her desk and gave her customary glance at the items from Friday that needed her urgent attention this morning. A coffee would be a good idea before she started, she decided. She made her way to the tiny kitchen, passing Amy's desk on the way. It was unoccupied: Amy was rarely on time for work. Five minutes later, Jane arrived back at her desk, a mug of coffee in her hand. She had hardly put the mug down before the internal telephone rang. It could only be one person: Annette Burrows.

Jane picked up the handset and gave her usual reply. 'Jane.'

'Ah, Jane, you are there. Can we get together?' It was indeed Annette.

Jane looked at her desk and stifled a sigh. 'I'll be right up,' she replied.

'Can you get Amy up as well?'

Jane glanced through the glass partition wall of her office. She could see that Amy had just arrived at her desk. 'I'll tell her,' she said.

There was a curt 'Fine', and then a click as Annette put the phone down.

Coffee in one hand and notepad in the other, Jane was on her way. As she passed Amy's desk, after her good morning greeting she whispered, 'Annette wants to see us.'

Her announcement brought forth the usual grimace. 'What's she want now?' grumbled Amy.

'Most likely wants to find us some more work to do,' Jane replied breezily. After her weekend with Bob, not even Annette could spoil her morning.

They made their way upstairs to Annette's office. Annette was on the phone, but she put it down as she gestured to them to sit down.

Greetings were brief. Annette picked up some paperwork from the side of her desk and, placing it in front of her, started the proceedings. She clasped her hands together for an instant, looked at Jane and Amy and then announced, 'I've been thinking.'

121

There was a slight pause as Annette looked closely at her audience as if to ensure that she had their full attention. She need not have been concerned on that point: as soon as Jane and Amy heard her statement, they were fully alert. Whenever Annette made such a remark, there was little doubt that it would mean some disruption or alteration to their work. Satisfied that they were listening, Annette continued.

'I think we need a book review section. It's the one thing we lack. What do you think?'

Jane and Amy were taken slightly off balance. Jane for one was completely aware that although Annette was asking their opinion this was a completely cosmetic exercise – she had already made up her mind to do what she was proposing. Jane's normal reaction to such suggestions was to accommodate them as best she could, and with the least disruption. She thought for a second, and then made a calculated reply.

'It might mean we would have to drop some other feature to do it,' she suggested tactfully. Then, as another thought came to her, she added, 'That is, unless we increased the number of pages.'

Annette had already thought of this. 'That's all in hand. I've had a word with the printers and it's arranged. We can take in more advertising to cover the additional cost.'

'Who would do the book reviews?' asked Amy.

Annette immediately snuffed out any problem with her reply. 'I know a few people in that line. And I thought we might be able to do some of the reviews in-house.'

'I don't think I'd have time for that,' remarked Amy bravely.

Jane was more diplomatic. 'It might be best to have an experienced person, at least initially, to do them,' she suggested.

Annette did not respond directly to Jane's remark. Instead she went on to outline how she thought the review pages should look and the type of books they would feature. It was more than evident that Jane, with Amy's help, would have to sort out all the practical details. It wasn't until a good hour later that they were able to return to their own desks.

Amy's first remark summed up her feelings. 'Bloody cheek, expecting us to do the reviews.'

Jane burst out laughing at her colleague's outburst. 'I doubt if it'll come to that. She said she's already got somebody lined up for that job. Most likely one of her friends,' she added.

'Well, I'm not doing it,' grumbled Amy. In the next breath, she asked, 'Do you want a drink?'

Jane grinned. 'A cup of tea would go down well,' she replied.

Amy disappeared into the kitchen, and Jane retreated to her office to tackle the items on her desk.

Despite the early disruption to her plans, Jane's day went quite well. She ploughed through her work and managed to get through to everybody she wanted to talk to on the phone. She even had time to take a proper lunch break and do some shopping. It was bang on half past five when she said her goodnights and left the office.

Several times during the day she pondered over the question Gerald had asked her. Why did he want to know about Mrs Marshall? No doubt he would enlighten her in due course. During her time at the orphanage, Mrs Marshall had seemed a remote figure, someone she had learnt to respect and, in a way, fear. Certainly she had only spoken to the matron when addressed by her, or when she had been summoned to her presence – usually when she had done something wrong or something was about to happen that would affect her personally.

As the working day drew to a close, Jane's thoughts turned to Lucy. Dared she hope for a telephone call from her that evening? She prayed it might happen. For her, so much depended on what Lucy might come up with. Her time with Bob over the weekend had diverted her from her anxiety, but now that she was on her own she realised that her concerns were always just under the surface. Who was she? What was her background? She was desperate to find answers, and Lucy had now become a key part of her search.

It was close to half past six when Jane let herself back into her apartment. She carried out her usual routine, changing out of her business suit and busying herself making an evening meal. All the time she had her ear alert, listening for the telephone and the doorbell. Would Lucy ring tonight? She also knew that most likely Gerald would like to see her. She regretted not giving Lucy her mobile number. She used her mobile more and more now, and there were times when she debated the logic of still having a landline, as she found that she was not using it so often now.

By half past seven she felt she could wait no longer. She would just have to go down to Gerald's apartment and satisfy her curiosity. She hoped Lucy wouldn't phone while she was out. After making sure that the answering machine was switched on and working, she made her way downstairs.

Gerald and Anna were clearly expecting a visit from her. Anna immediately ushered her into the lounge and announced that the coffee was ready. Gerald was sitting on the sofa, some papers close at hand. He greeted Jane with a beaming smile.

'Ah. Hello, Jane. I've got some news for you,' he announced.

'He's been on that computer all day,' laughed Anna. 'I've hardly seen anything of him,' she added, hurrying to the kitchen, assuming that Jane wanted some coffee.

'I think I'm taking up a lot of everybody's time,' said Jane as she sat down opposite Gerald. She was concerned that so far she had only had a fleeting look at the family history program on her computer. She felt that she was relying on everybody else to delve into her past.

Gerald did not reply.

Anna reappeared in the lounge and stood in front of her. 'Now, young lady,' she asked, 'have you had anything to eat?' Her stance was that of the critical mother.

Jane gave a little smile as she replied. 'Yes, I have, thank you, Anna. I made myself a meal as soon as I got home.'

Anna looked at her as if she did not believe her. 'You young girls don't eat enough,' she commented, almost disapprovingly, scrutinising Jane's lean frame.

Jane just smiled again and remarked, almost under her breath, 'Oh, but I'm fine.'

Anna gave up and retreated to the kitchen. As she departed, she remarked over her shoulder, 'It's all to do with fashion. Young women have to be underweight these days.'

Jane looked at Gerald. He was grinning at her and gave her a wink.

'She's only jealous,' he whispered.

Jane just smiled politely. She had grown used to Anna's approach to eating and had long since realised that this was the reason for her overweight appearance.

Gerald looked at Jane over his half-frame spectacles. 'I've found out something about your Mrs Marshall,' he declared, almost triumphantly.

'What is it? Tell me!' Jane was full of expectation.

Gerald had a confident smile on his face. He waited a few seconds and then calmly announced: 'Mrs Marshall is your aunt.'

Chapter 15

Jane stared at Gerald with a mixture of shock and disbelief. It took her several seconds to assimilate what she had just been told. When she did reply her response was loaded with questions and doubt.

'But how can that be? Mrs Marshall treated me exactly the same as all the other children in the orphanage.' She thought back to her time there. Then another thought struck her. 'And if I had an aunt, what was I doing in an establishment for orphans?'

Gerald glanced at her again over his spectacles. 'It certainly is most odd,' he agreed.

Their conversation halted briefly as Anna returned with a tray bearing the coffee and a plate piled with slices of fruit cake. A mug of coffee was placed in front of Jane and the plate of fruit cake offered.

'Now, you must try this cake. I baked it especially for you today,' Anna insisted.

Jane didn't really want anything more to eat, but out of politeness she took the smallest piece of cake she could see.

Anna sat down opposite Jane and Gerald.

It was Jane who took up the conversation about her past again. The constant nagging thought struck her yet again as she nibbled her cake. She took a sip of coffee and then voiced her anxiety.

'I still don't understand why I have a dead person's identity. It doesn't seem to make any sense.'

'It certainly is most peculiar,' remarked Gerald. Perhaps as a bit of reassurance to Jane he added, 'But there's got to be an answer somewhere.'

Pausing in her eating and drinking and lifting her hand as if to silence them, Anna suddenly asked, 'Do you know what I think?'

Jane and Gerald waited, both interested to hear her view of the situation.

Anna continued. 'I think this Mrs Marshall could be your mother. Perhaps you were an illegitimate child.' She waited to learn how her idea grabbed the other two.

It was Gerald who responded first. 'It's not impossible,' he observed.

Jane was now even more puzzled. 'But in that case why reject me and yet at the same time have me close to her?' she asked. Anna's suggestion had added yet another dimension to her concerns.

'Perhaps she just wanted to keep an eye on you,' said Anna.

Gerald put his mug of coffee aside. He took hold of his paperwork again and scrutinised it for a few seconds. When he spoke, he addressed his remarks to Jane. 'It's an odd situation, I have to agree, but I do think there's an answer somewhere. We just have to keep plodding away at the problem. I'm almost convinced that the clue lies somewhere with the Carroll family.' He studied Jane's face for a reaction as he finished speaking.

His comments, while comforting, raised another worry in Jane's mind.

'But I feel that I'm leaning an awful lot on you,' she said. 'I've barely glanced at the computer program you helped me with. You're doing so much for me. It all seems a bit unfair.'

Gerald just laughed. 'Don't worry about that,' he assured her with a chuckle. 'I'm in my element with family history. It gives me something to do in my old age.' He finished up laughing.

'It gets him out of my way,' piped up Anna.

Jane smiled at them both. Gerald's remark had comforted her a good deal and allayed her concerns. It did prompt another question from her, however. 'So what do you think is the next step?' she asked, really addressing Gerald.

Gerald's response was immediate. 'I assume you haven't heard from the friend you bumped into on Saturday – the one from the orphanage,' he said.

Jane shook her head. 'Lucy? No. Not yet. I've been hoping she might ring me this evening, so I don't want to be away from the phone for too long.' She glanced at her watch.

'Let's see if anything comes up there first and then if not, we'll try to delve deeper into the Carroll family,' proposed Gerald, putting his paperwork down.

Jane nodded. There wasn't much more either she or Gerald could do for now. She voiced one concern that was nagging her, though she smiled as she spoke. 'The trouble is that whenever I use anything with my name on now, I get a horrible feeling that I'm doing something illegal.'

'I shouldn't worry too much at this stage,' Gerald responded. 'Who knows? It might be your correct name.'

His calm, methodical approach to things helped to calm Jane's fears once again. The three of them chatted for another ten minutes or so and then Jane, conscious that she might have a phone call from Lucy, extricated herself from her hosts. Thanking each in turn, she made her way back to her own apartment. Once there, she immediately checked the answering machine for any messages. There was nothing.

She shrugged off her disappointment. It was quite possible that Lucy hadn't found the time to do any searching. After all, she had a husband and a daughter to look after, as well as her job at the orphanage. Jane was still confident that Lucy would eventually phone her.

She pottered about for a while and then at ten called it a day and retreated to bed with a book. As soon as she started reading, tiredness caught up with her, and she was abruptly woken up by the noise of the book dropping onto the floor. She had fallen asleep over the pages. She turned out the bedside light and settled down to sleep again.

She awoke to a wet morning. It felt quite unusual to walk to her train under an umbrella. Once at the station she was dismayed to learn that her train had been cancelled. It meant a fifteen-minute wait for the next one. Inevitably this was already packed when it arrived. She managed to squeeze in, but any chance of a seat was completely impossible. By the time she got to the office she was a good twenty minutes late. On top of that, despite the umbrella, rain had seeped into her shoes and her feet were cold and wet. She was glad to change into the spare pair of high-heeled shoes she kept in the bottom drawer of her desk for occasions such as this.

She had hardly completed the task before Amy appeared carrying a mug of tea for her.

'Good morning, Amy,' Jane greeted her. And then, eyeing the mug of tea, she added. 'Oh, marvellous! Just what I need. My train was late.'

'I thought that might have happened,' said Amy. It was unusual for Jane to be late.

'And the next one that came was packed to suffocation,' commented Jane, clasping her hands around the mug of tea.

'I know the feeling,' replied Amy, making a face.

Jane remembered that Amy frequently grumbled about her train always being crowded or cancelled.

Then Amy piped up, 'Queen Bee has phoned. She's not coming in this morning.' There was almost glee in her voice.

Jane laughed. 'Well, that will at least allow us to get on with some work,' she replied.

Amy muttered something and then retreated to her own desk.

Jane smiled to herself. Amy was one of those people who were never at their best first thing in the morning. When she encountered people like that, she felt glad that she was always quite perky when she woke up.

With the thought of no interruptions from the editor-in-chief, Jane took the opportunity to work her way steadily through quite a lot of work during the morning. When Annette did eventually make an appearance, she appeared to be tied up with several meetings with various visitors, and her contact with Jane was brief.

As a result Jane even found the time to do a little groundwork on the forthcoming book review feature. At the end of the day she was pleased with what she had achieved.

When it was time to finish and go home, she was relieved to discover that the rain, which had persisted all day, had now cleared away and it was now a rather pleasant sunny evening. Even her wet shoes, which had been lodged under her desk for the day, were now dry enough to wear.

As she let herself into her apartment, the thought uppermost in her mind was whether during the evening she would receive the expected phone call from Lucy. After a quick shower to freshen up, she busied herself preparing a meal, at the same time listening out for the telephone. By half past seven she had eaten her meal and washed up. She wandered back into the lounge and picked up her laptop, intending to check her emails and then play with the family history program. All the time her attention was half on the telephone, waiting for its shrill notes to pierce the quiet of her apartment. But it remained silent.

The next day – Wednesday – followed a similar pattern, even to the shower of rain Jane had to walk through to get to the station. Fortunately, the train was on time, and she arrived at work before most of the other staff. It was an uneventful day. Annette only wanted her briefly on one occasion, and on the whole the day went well. Only the evening was less positive. There was still no call from Lucy.

Jane was disappointed, but logic told her that she could not expect Lucy to put all her other chores aside just to help her with her family history; after all, she reasoned, only two days had passed when Lucy might have had time to look into her affairs.

When Thursday came and there was still no contact from Lucy, Jane was becoming just a little bit more concerned, particularly when during the evening Gerald contacted her to enquire whether she had received any news. She wondered whether she should telephone Lucy, but thought that might appear too pushy. In the circumstances it would be better to wait a few more days.

Friday was not such a good day at work. Annette was in the office most of the day and seemed intent on causing as much disruption as possible to other people's work. First thing, she announced that she wanted to see Jane and Amy to discuss a feature that was due for the next issue of *Discerning Woman*. Amy had done some work on this and Annette found fault with it, much to Amy's dismay and indignation. It was left to Jane to comfort her after the meeting and pour oil on troubled waters. On top of that, Annette announced that she had contacted someone who could do the book reviews for the magazine and had invited her for a meeting that afternoon. As Jane had only just started to look into various possibilities, she felt she was being put under a bit of pressure unnecessarily. Fortunately, when the arranged meeting took place, Bobby, the prospective reviewer, was quite easy to get on with, and a bonus for Jane was that she announced that she could not do anything for the magazine for at least another couple of months. That took the wind out of Annette's sails, and she was forced to concede that the project could not be rushed. That did not stop her wanting another meeting with Jane after Bobby had left, to consider whether they should try to find somebody else. Jane did her best to try and eliminate that suggestion, but it was hard work. By the time half past five came she was more than ready to call it a day. She left the office with a grumpy and grizzling Amy.

Back home in her apartment she felt quite exhausted. Even preparing some sort of meal seemed for once to be a bit of a trial. Now she was on her own in the apartment, her thoughts turned again to the possibility of a call from Lucy. As each day passed and there was no contact from her, Jane became more despondent. She was trying to relax with a mug of tea after her meal, stretched out on the sofa, when the phone rang.

She jumped up, spilling some of her tea on the table in the process. She dashed to the phone and picked it up. 'Hello.'

A strange foreign voice answered. 'Am I speaking to Mrs Carroll?'

'Miss Carroll,' Jane corrected.

The voice continued. 'I'm Ralph Santos from Billgrave Marketing. We're doing some research in your area and wonder if you would help us by answering a few questions. It won't take up much of your time, and you will be entered into our competition to win a holiday.'

Jane had felt sure that the call was from Lucy. She felt miserable as she answered the caller. 'I'm sorry, but I don't want to,' she responded curtly.

'But it will only take a few minutes, Miss Carroll, and you could win a wonderful trip to Venice.'

'I'm sorry, but I don't want to take part. Thank you for your call. Goodbye.'

She put the phone down before the caller could reply. Bitterly disappointed, she wandered back into the lounge and sat down on the settee again. She didn't feel like doing anything. She noticed the tea she had spilt on the table and jumped up and went into the kitchen to fetch a cloth to mop it up.

As she returned she was alerted to another noise. It was the unmistakeable, distinctive ring of her mobile phone. That could only mean one thing: it was somebody she knew. She only gave the number to selected people. For a split second she wondered where her mobile was, but the sound directed her. She had left it on the settee. Two strides, and she snatched it up, clicked the button and held it to her ear. 'Hello.'

A familiar voice answered. 'Hi, Jane. It's me – Bob.'

Jane was surprised and delighted. Bob didn't usually call her mobile.

'Bob, what a nice surprise! It's lovely to hear you.'

'I just had to give you a ring. I'm still at the studio. How are you? Any news from Lucy?'

Jane snuggled back into the cushioned settee, pressing her bare feet into the opposite end. She was overjoyed to be able to talk to Bob. 'Oh, I'm fine. Just a bit tired. It's been one of those days at work.'

There was a laugh at the other end of the telephone. 'I know the feeling,' contributed Bob. 'But what news from Lucy?'

His question almost returned Jane to her worried state. 'Not a word. I really thought I'd have heard from her by now. I'm a bit gutted.'

There was a slight pause before Bob replied. 'Hmm. She could be busy, or perhaps she's not had the opportunity to have a look for anything.'

Inwardly, Jane had to agree. 'Yes, I know. I guess I'll just have to wait.'

'You could give her a ring,' suggested Bob.

'I did try today, but I don't want to appear too cheeky. I thought I should give it a few more days before contacting her.'

'That might be a good idea. It sounds as if this Laura Brompton is a bit difficult to work with.'

Jane took up his suggestion. 'Yes, of course you're right. Lucy may not have had a chance to look yet.'

Jane felt that Bob's thinking reinforced her own ideas on the subject. She would just have to be patient a little longer.

A sudden thought prompted her to change the subject. 'But you're still at work!' she exclaimed. 'It's turned eight o'clock.'

Bob sounded a bit more serious as he answered her question. 'That's one of the reasons I wanted to talk to you.'

'Tell me more.'

Bob clearly hesitated before replying. 'It's just that this big opportunity at the studio has come up. Jeff and I have taken over an assignment at the last minute from another company that let down the client. It means we'll have to slog all weekend to get it done.'

'But that's wonderful for you.' Jane tried her best to be positive and not let her disappointment show. It was pretty clear that she would not be spending any time with Bob this weekend.

Bob confirmed her worst fears. 'Poppet, it means I won't be able to see you.'

Jane was determined not to let her disappointment filter

through. 'But of course you must do it. And we'll make up for it another time.' She made her reply as cheerful as possible. There was also another angle to the weekend that had been concerning her, but now there seemed to be a get-out. She thought carefully before adding to her comment. She decided to plunge in. After all she knew Bob well enough by now to broach such matters.

'Bob, don't feel too bad about it. It works out quite well, really. It's the wrong time of the month for me.'

Bob answered quickly. 'Point taken.' Then he asked, 'What will you do with yourself?'

Jane gave a little laugh. 'Miss you terribly and perhaps catch up on one or two drudge jobs – you know, cleaning, washing…'

There was another pause from Bob. Clearly, he was thinking about the situation. When he did reply he spoke without conviction. 'I might be able to see you on Sunday, but I'm not sure about it.'

Jane was quick to quash the idea. 'No. Don't worry about it. Concentrate on the weekend's work. We'll make up for it perhaps next week.' She was trying her best to sound upbeat and cheerful for his sake.

'We'll have to plan a more exciting weekend soon.' He sounded quite buoyant again.

'Anything in mind?' Jane was enthusiastic.

'I'll think of something. Something different,' he added quickly. Then his thoughts obviously turned to more mundane matters. His next comment was less enthusiastic.

'Well, I guess I'll have to wander my weary way home.'

'How long have you been there?' asked Jane.

She could hear a bit of a laugh from Bob. 'Since ten this morning,'

'Gosh. That's a long day. You must go home now and get some rest.' Jane's caring side took over.

'I will. I'll say goodnight now and give you a ring over the weekend.' Bob did sound tired.

'Look forward to it. Missing you. Bye for now,' Jane chipped in.

'The same. Bye.'

The phone went dead at the other end and Jane clicked off her own mobile. She settled back into the settee. The phone call from Bob had made her evening. Now, if only she heard from Lucy, things would be even better. She waited until the hands of the clock reached ten, but no call came.

Chapter 16

For some reason Jane woke up early on the Saturday morning. Perhaps the reason for this was that on the previous two Saturday mornings she had had to get up early and drive up to Bob's house. This time it was different, and she awoke to the realisation that there was no rush to get up.

Her first action was to glance at the bedside clock. It was just coming up to six. She waited for a few minutes and then, throwing back the duvet, she thrust her feet out of the bed and stood up. She went over to the window and peeped out through the curtains. A bleak grey sky greeted her. She looked down into the parking area and spied her car standing there. She watched one of her neighbours walk to his car, which was parked next to hers, reverse out of the space and drive away.

She closed the curtains and wandered into the bathroom and then the kitchen and made herself a mug of tea. There seemed to be a slight chill in the air and her bed tempted her once again. Snuggling into its warmth, she sat up and pulled the duvet around her, her hands clasped around the mug of tea.

She went over the events of the last few days. The last week had fully cemented into place her relationship with Bob. Somehow it seemed they got on together and were an admirable support for each other. She guessed that under his calm façade he could perhaps be quite adventurous, yet at the same time remain fully grounded. She liked that in a man; it was what had attracted her to Graham. Last week Bob had shown that he was immensely fond of her. Things were moving in the right direction. She glanced towards her dressing table, where the photograph he had taken of her the previous weekend was propped up. In a way it said everything.

She finished her tea and lay back in bed. This was a rare luxury, and it had been a hard week. On the one hand the extra effort she had had to make at work, and on the other the waiting for a phone call from Lucy. Prior to Bob's advice she had rung the orphanage the previous day – and had immediately received a rebuff. It had been clear from the start that the person answering was the manager she and Bob had met the previous weekend.

'Good morning. Is it possible to speak to Lucy Whitney?' Jane had asked.

Immediately the voice at the other end of the phone had changed. 'She's not here at present. Is this a personal call?'

'Yes, it is.'

Jane had been ready to identify herself and explain the reason for her call, but the opportunity was denied her. 'Staff have been instructed not to make or receive private telephone calls here. Please don't do it again.'

'I'm sorry. I wasn't aware of that. I—'

'That's all right,' the woman had cut in. 'Goodbye.'

With that, the call had ended before Jane could say anything more.

She had been a bit put out by the response she had received and on top of that she had not achieved her objective to contact Lucy. This had all added to the difficult day she had been experiencing.

The sound of a church clock striking somewhere jerked Jane's thoughts to the present. A glance at the clock, and she realised it was time to get up. Yesterday, she had managed to get a last-minute appointment at the hairdresser's, and it was for half past eight. She also had some shopping to do.

Twenty minutes later she had showered and had put on a pair of comfortable trousers and a casual blouse and was in the kitchen having a bowl of muesli and another mug of tea. She turned on the radio for a bit of company, but the programme was uninteresting and she quickly turned it off again. It was past eight when she looked out of the window again to check on the weather. It was raining steadily. This brought forth an 'Oh, no' from her lips. The thought of walking to the shops in the rain was not appealing. She would have to take the car. She knew somewhere to park close to the hairdressing salon.

By the time Jane had finished at the hairdresser's and made a visit to the supermarket, the morning was well advanced. Fortunately, the rain had stopped for a while and she was able to carry her bags of shopping to and from the car in the dry, without having to struggle with an umbrella to protect her hair.

Once back in her apartment, after a much desired coffee she threw herself into washing and cleaning. It was while she was vacuuming the lounge that she heard the sound of the telephone. It must be Bob, she thought. Switching off the vacuum cleaner, she dashed to the hall and picked up the receiver.

'Hello,' she said.

A woman's voice answered. 'Jane, it's Lucy.'

Jane was ecstatic. 'Lucy, how marvellous! How are you?'

A somewhat subdued Lucy answered. 'Oh, I'm fine. It's just that… Well, you must think me awful for not contacting you before this.'

Jane could sense that Lucy was a bit embarrassed. She tried to hide her own stress of the past week. 'Not at all. You must have lots of other things to do besides dabbling in things for me.'

Her strategy appeared to work. The voice at the other end of the line sounded more like the old Lucy she had known. 'I felt terrible about not getting back to you sooner, but it's been a most awful week.'

Jane could immediately empathise; she gave a little chuckle as she responded to Lucy's comment. 'I know the feeling. My week has been pretty hard going, too. Tell me about yours.'

Lucy was quick to take up her offer. 'Well, first of all, we've had the auditors in at work and I don't know whether I've been coming or going. Then Laura Brompton has been in a foul mood all week because of the auditors being around.' Lucy paused for an instant and then continued. 'On top of that, Patty looked as if she was coming down with something or other, and then to crown it all somebody ran into the back of my car.'

Jane could see why Lucy hadn't contacted her. 'Phew,' she replied. 'That's a lot at one time.' Then she asked, 'But how is Patty now?'

'She seems to have got over whatever it was, thank goodness,' replied Lucy.

'And your car?'

'A write-off. I'll have to get something else. I'm driving my mother-in-law's car at present.'

'Gosh. You've had quite a week.' Jane had almost forgotten about her own problems.

It was Lucy who changed the subject and brought the conversation round to Jane. 'Now for you and your dark past.' There was a bit of a laugh at the other end of the telephone. She was already sounding more cheerful.

'Oh, don't worry about me. You've got enough on your plate without my problems.' Jane felt she had to say it, though she was disappointed. But Lucy's next sentence changed things.

'Oh, but I *have* found out something.' Lucy sounded quite excited.

'Tell me,' Jane urged her. She couldn't wait to hear what Lucy had to say.

'Well, Laura was correct. There is no trace of you on the computer system.'

Lucy's confirmation brought Jane a stab of despondency. Once again it looked as if she had struck a dead end. Lucy's words brought forth a spontaneous reaction from her.

'But why on earth should that be? I spent years in that place.'

Lucy took Jane's reaction in her stride. She was quite philosophical about it. 'I don't know, really. Somebody could have made an error when entering the original details on the computer and left you off, or, you know computers: one slip of the finger, and you can delete something. On top of that there was a fire in the office and a lot of documents were burnt.'

Jane was forced to agree, but she felt the news still left her high and dry. Her response to Lucy's comment reflected her gloom. 'I know. It's just that I feel so despondent at the moment with all this. I don't know who I really am and I'm apparently using the name of a dead person.'

'It must be awful for you. But I know you were at the orphanage – and I think I may have discovered something else.'

The last bit of Lucy's statement hit Jane with full force. 'Tell me,' she prompted; there was urgency in her voice. She listened intently as Lucy continued.

'Well, I've been breaking every rule in the book; I knew there were some old hand-written documents somewhere in the storeroom. I managed to find them, but I was so busy with the auditors around that I couldn't get a chance to look at them properly, so in the end I took them home with me.'

'Gosh. That was a bit of a risk.'

Lucy seemed unconcerned. 'Not really. I don't think anybody except me knows they're there. They were supposed to have been destroyed after we had the fire in the office.'

Jane was still anxious to know the extent of Lucy's finds. 'But what else did you find about me?' she asked.

'Well, I managed to find the old hand-written admissions book. It was in a pretty bad state – it was partly burnt and had got wet – but I did manage to find the year you were admitted.'

'So what did it say?' asked Jane anxiously, grabbing the notepad and pen that she kept next to the phone.

'There were six children admitted to the orphanage that year...' Lucy stopped for a second as if she were reading, and then she continued. 'Now, this is the odd bit. That particular page of the book has a second page stuck down over the original. It had got wet and I managed to prise it off the original one. And here is the interesting bit: all the names matched on the two pages except yours.'

'What was the difference?' Jane could hardly contain herself.

There was a slight pause, as Lucy was obviously checking something, and then she continued. 'On the page that's been stuck down over the original it's got your name, but on the original it's Ruth Ashington.'

'But why has the name been changed, and when was it changed?' Jane was almost thinking aloud as she spoke. Suddenly she thought of something else. 'But why Ashington – and where have I heard that name before?'

'It must have been changed a long time ago,' answered Lucy. Then she added excitedly, 'But don't you remember? It was the Ashington family who founded the orphanage.'

Lucy's remark stirred Jane's memory. 'Of course! The name over the front door. Sir Edward Ashington.'

'Do you think my efforts will be of any help?' asked Lucy.

'I don't know,' replied Jane. 'I hope so, but at the moment it's all a mystery.' She thought for a moment, and then added, 'I don't know how I can thank you for all your efforts – particularly with the kind of week you've had. I really appreciate what you've done.'

'Forget it. I enjoyed doing it for old times' sake, and if I can do anything else, just ring me,' retorted Lucy.

That reminded Jane of something. 'Give me your mobile number,' she suggested. 'I forgot to ask you for it.'

'No problem; it's…'

Jane made a careful note of the number. 'Got it. Thank you so much for that.' She felt quite pleased that she now had both numbers.

It was Lucy who ended the call. 'I'll have to go now, Jane. We're all going shopping and the others are all ready and waiting for me.'

'Oh! You must go. Thank you again for all your help. I'll let you know how I get on from here.'

'Please do. And why don't you and Bob pay us a visit sometime?'

'That would be lovely. I'll say goodbye for now, but perhaps we could do that at some point.'

'Great. Look forward to it. Bye. Coming!' Lucy ended with a shout to somebody in the background.

'Bye,' said Jane; but Lucy had gone.

For a few seconds Jane stood looking at the details she had taken down on the notepad. Though she was still a bit excited by Lucy's telephone call, the content had left her puzzled. Why had the names been changed in the book? Could she really be Ruth Ashington? It seemed as if every twist and turn of trying to establish who she actually was left her even more in the dark, with more unanswered questions.

Chapter 17

For a good five minutes Jane pondered over her conversation with Lucy. Still clutching the notes she had taken, she wandered into the lounge and sat down, her cleaning abandoned for the moment. None of it seemed to make any sense to her. Her past was still as big a mystery as before.

The sound of her mobile alerted her from her musing. It could only be one person. She dashed into the kitchen where she had left it, and picked it up.

'Hello.'

'Hello, Jane. It's Bob.'

'Bob, darling, it's great to hear from you. How are things going?' Jane was a bit ecstatic now.

'Not bad at all. But we've a lot more to do. How are you getting on?'

Jane had cheered up a bit now that she was talking to Bob. 'Missing you terribly. I'm in the midst of cleaning at present, but...' She hesitated to give more emphasis to what she had heard that day. 'I've got some news for you. I've been talking to Lucy.'

'Great! I wanted to ask you about that, but I've also got some news for you.'

'That sounds exciting. Who's going first?' Jane was now intrigued as well.

'You are.' There was a chuckle at the other end.

Jane accepted the prompting. 'Well, Lucy told me...' Slowly and methodically she relayed the contents of Lucy's telephone call. Bob listened intently. When she had finished, Jane asked the question that was nagging at her. 'What do you make of all that?'

'Absolutely weird.'

'It looks as if somebody wanted to hide the first name,' she observed.

'But what on earth for? Why put it down to start with?' Bob appeared as perplexed as Jane.

'That's what I'd like to know. Do you think I might actually be Ruth Ashington?'

'That's certainly possible,' agreed Bob.

'So I'm still in limbo about who I really am,' she sighed.

'There must be an explanation somewhere,' Bob reassured her.

'I know – but where? It's got to the point now that whenever I see my name somewhere, I suddenly wonder whether it's my real name or not.' Jane was letting her worries creep to the surface again.

'We've just got to keep at it. Somebody somewhere knows why and how that name was deliberately changed.' Bob did his best to sound positive. Before Jane could answer, he suddenly spoke again. 'The matron at the orphanage when you were there – Mrs…?' He searched for the name.

'Mrs Marshall,' Jane chipped in.

'Yes. Mrs Marshall. I wonder if it would be possible to contact her.'

'Gosh,' said Jane. 'That's an idea. She should know something. She would have been there when it all happened.'

'See if you can get hold of her,' urged Bob.

When Jane replied, she was almost thinking aloud. 'I wonder if Lucy knows where Mrs Marshall lives.'

'Give it a go.'

'I will. I'll give her a ring. I'm going to see Gerald in a minute. He might have some ideas.'

'Good idea,' enthused Bob. 'That man is a mine of information on family history matters.'

Jane chuckled to herself. 'He's been at it for a long time,' she said.

Suddenly she changed the subject. 'Hey, what's your news? All we've talked about is me.'

There was a slight hesitation at the other end of the phone, and then Bob announced, 'I'm planning a night out. How do you feel about a dinner dance?'

'Fantastic. I haven't been dancing for ages. When?'

'A week on Friday. It's a prestige affair. Evening dress for men and women.'

Jane was already thinking ahead. 'I'll buy a new dress. Something nice.'

There was a bit of a laugh from Bob before he replied. 'I'll have to see if the moths have left anything of my evening togs.'

'You can always hire an evening suit,' suggested Jane tactfully.

'I know. Might do that.'

'What time does it start?'

'Eight-thirty,' Bob replied quickly, 'but it goes on till one in the morning. We'll have to stay over in town. I'll book everything. Leave it to me.'

'I'll most likely take a day or an afternoon off work,' Jane chipped in.

'Good idea. Now I'd better get some work done.'

Jane took the hint. 'Yes, you must. Darling, thank you for the call and the invitation. I'm looking forward to it already. I haven't been to anything like that for ages and ages.'

'I haven't, either. Listen, I've got to go. Somebody's after me.'

'OK. Bye for now. Missing you.'

'Me too. Bye.'

Jane clicked her mobile to end the call. Talking to Bob had lifted her spirits. She was excited about his invitation. She was already planning what sort of outfit she would buy: something completely feminine to please Bob, she had decided, and she knew just the shop to purchase it in. Next week she would take an extended lunch break and go there. She wondered what the event was and what the occasion. No doubt Bob would enlighten her nearer the time.

The sight of the vacuum cleaner lying on the floor where she had abandoned it brought her down to reality. She just had to finish the dusting and vacuuming, and then she would go and see Gerald.

It was over an hour later and close to midday by the time she had finished – quite a bit later than she had planned. Slipping her feet into a pair of flip-flops and clutching her keys and the details from Lucy, she made her way downstairs to Gerald and Anna's apartment. She rang the bell and waited.

It was Anna who opened the door. 'Jane, how lovely to see you. Come in.'

'Hello, Anna.' Jane stepped into the hallway.

'Come and sit down. Would you like a drink?' Anna enquired cheerfully, making a move towards the lounge.

Jane hesitated. 'Thank you,' she said, 'but I'd better not. I'm in the middle of cleaning.'

'Oh, what a pity. Never mind. Another time.' Anna received Jane's refusal with her usual homeliness. She was still edging towards the lounge.

'Is Gerald in? I've got some new information I would like to share with him. I've heard from the old friend I met last weekend.' Jane did not want to linger if Gerald was not around.

Anna shook her head. 'He's out most of the day. He's meeting an old friend in town. I'm not expecting him back until late afternoon.' She was looking quite concerned.

Jane responded quickly. 'Don't worry. I'll pop down later on if I may.'

'Is Bob coming to see you this weekend?' Anna suddenly asked.

Jane shook her head. 'No. He has to work this weekend,' she replied, wondering vaguely why Anna had asked.

Anna was immediately full of sympathy. 'Oh, what a shame! He's such a nice young man and you seem to get on so well together.'

'He and his partner have some important work to do at the studio,' explained Jane.

Anna's face suddenly lit up. She looked at Jane and beamed. 'I have an idea. If you're not doing anything, why don't you come and have some dinner with us this evening? Then you can tell us all about your friend.'

The idea quite appealed to Jane. After her previous Saturday nights with Bob, making a meal and being on her own was not inviting. She gave Anna a friendly smile. 'That would be lovely. About what time?'

'Shall we say six o'clock?'

'Super.'

Jane took her leave soon after that. While she quite liked Anna and accepted her mothering and fussiness in good part, she was glad she had managed to avoid wasting a chunk of a precious Saturday sitting around drinking coffee. She knew that Gerald and Anna led quite a quiet, secluded life, which perhaps explained Anna's readiness to socialise at any given moment. Still, she quite liked the idea of meeting them later in the day and talking to Gerald.

Back in her own apartment, she threw herself into various domestic chores. Several times, remembering Bob's advice to try and locate Mrs Marshall, she tried unsuccessfully to phone Lucy. In the end she left a message on the answering machine, remembering to add that she would most likely not be available during the evening.

It was late in the afternoon when she was in the bathroom that she heard the unmistakable sound of her phone. Desperately diving out of the shower and wrapping herself in a towel, she dashed into the hall with wet feet, every second fearful that the phone would stop ringing before she got to it. She grabbed it just in time.

'Hello.'

'Hello, Jane. It's Lucy.'

'Lucy, great! Thanks for coming back to me. I was in the shower.' She giggled. 'I'm dripping everywhere.'

Lucy joined in Jane's mirth. 'It's what's called an inappropriate moment,' she said breezily. Then she went on. 'Sorry I was out when you rang, but we've all been shopping and we got wet. It's pouring with rain here.'

'It's raining here as well.' Jane gave a glance towards the window, where the rain was running down the windowpane.

'You wanted me?' asked Lucy.

'Well, if I could ask for your help again…' began Jane. She explained why she wanted to contact the former matron of the orphanage. She ended up by saying, 'Bob thinks she may have some information about the change of names.'

'She retired before I went to work there. I'm not sure if there's anything about her around…' Lucy seemed to be slowly speaking aloud her thoughts. Then she responded quite positively. 'But I'll have a look and see what there is.'

'It would be marvellous if you could. I'd really appreciate that. Just so that I can contact her.'

'Leave it with me. I'll see what I can do.' Lucy sounded quite upbeat about everything.

Jane was about to thank her, but Lucy interrupted. 'Jane, I must go now. Patty wants me. But leave everything with me and I'll contact you again.'

'Super. You're an angel in disguise,' said Jane.

There was a chuckle at the other end of the phone. 'I wish Laura Brompton thought so. Must go. Bye for now. Talk to you soon.'

'Bye,' Jane called out into the phone. But Lucy was gone.

Jane put the phone down and hurried back into the warmth of the bathroom. Standing only for a few minutes talking to Lucy, but practically naked and sopping wet into the bargain, had made her feel chilly.

It was coming up to six when once again Jane made her way to Gerald and Anna's apartment. She had hardly rung the bell before Anna opened the door.

'Now come right in, Jane. Dinner's nearly ready. Gerald's in the lounge.'

Jane stepped into the hallway with a smile and a brief, 'Hello again.' At the same time Anna called out, 'Gerald, Jane's here.'

As they moved towards the lounge, Anna suddenly turned and looked at Jane admiringly. 'You look very pretty,' she said. 'That dress really suits you. Look what Bob is missing.' She laughed.

Jane almost blushed at Anna's comment. Instead she smiled

cheerfully and said, 'Thank you.' Her dress, a pretty floral one with an open neck and short sleeves, was an old favourite that had been in her clothes collection for a long time. For comfort and to match the dress she had decided to wear her soft white pumps. She also knew that if Bob had been around she would have taken more time and care in choosing what she wore. Still it was nice to receive compliments about her appearance.

It was at that moment that Gerald appeared in the lounge door, newspaper in hand. He grinned at Jane and greeted her. 'Hello, Jane. Welcome.'

'Gerald, get a drink for Jane while I finish off the dinner.' Anna appeared to be in her element organising her husband.

Jane found herself in the lounge sitting opposite Gerald, a sherry in her hand. She began to relate to him the contents of her telephone conversation with Lucy. It was a lengthy process, with much repetition, because Anna kept popping in and out from the kitchen, so that Jane often had to repeat something to include her in the update.

When she had finished, Jane waited for Gerald's opinion. Gerald was quiet for a few seconds, and then he stroked his goatee beard thoughtfully. Jane had noticed before that he often did this when he was pondering a situation.

She suddenly thought of something she hadn't mentioned. 'I spoke to Bob earlier and he seemed to think that the best solution was to try and contact Mrs Marshall, the matron of the orphanage at the time I was placed there.'

Gerald was almost thinking aloud. 'There are several options we could try,' he replied. 'We could check out other families in the area with the name Carroll, but that could take some time. I think the best and immediate thing to do would be to try and contact this Mrs Marshall, as Bob suggested.'

'I phoned Lucy to see if she can find a contact address for her,' added Jane.

'That's good. She should know something,' replied Gerald with a smile.

It was at this moment that Anna returned to the room. 'Now, Jane,' she said. 'Come and sit down at the table. Dinner is all ready.' She turned to Gerald. 'Gerald, wine!' Anna was enjoying herself. Gerald grinned at Jane, disappeared for an instant and returned carrying a bottle of wine.

Jane obediently sat herself down where Anna directed her. This was the first time she had been invited by the couple for dinner. Her previous contact with them had been simply as nearby neighbours. It had been her recent involvement in family history and the role Gerald had taken on in helping her that had placed the relationship on a friendlier basis. She had grown to appreciate Gerald's advice and help with her research, but there were times when she had to admit to herself that she found Anna's fussiness a bit over the top. This was quite evident tonight.

'Jane! You've hardly got any food on your plate. Do help yourself to more potatoes and vegetables.' Anna pointed to the dishes piled with food.

Jane smiled and nodded. Out of politeness she said, 'Perhaps later. Let me get through this first.'

Even that was not enough for Anna. 'Bob won't like you if you're thin,' she joked. 'Most men like their women to have a bit of meat on their bones. It makes them more cuddly in bed.' She ended with a laugh.

Jane was about to say that she didn't consider herself too thin and that all the men in her life so far had liked her just as she was, but she realised that it was best to just let the incident pass. There was no point in having a disagreement with Anna. Instead she changed the subject. Turning to Gerald, she asked a question that had been bothering her ever since her conversation with Lucy.

'Gerald, what do you think about the name Ruth Ashington, which had been erased from the orphanage records?'

When it came to family history, Gerald was immediately alert. 'Ah, now that is extremely interesting. Not only from your point of view, Jane, but also the name itself. I seem to think I've encountered that name before somewhere. I must look into that.'

Suddenly Anna piped up, 'Gerald, what about Eric? He would know.'

Gerald's face lit up. 'Yes, of course. Eric would most likely know something. I'll contact him next week.'

He turned to Jane and explained. 'I have this friend I've known for many years. Eric Alcott. He's a real family history enthusiast and has delved deep into family names.' He laughed. 'You can't ask him the wrong question,' he added.

'Perhaps you're descended from aristocracy,' suggested Anna, addressing Jane.

Jane made a face. 'I'm not sure about that,' she replied, laughing.

'Well, you never know,' insisted Anna.

The evening continued in quite a light-hearted fashion. In the end Jane quite enjoyed Gerald and Anna's company. It was nearly ten o'clock when she finally took her leave, after her offer to help with the clearing and washing up was firmly refused by Anna.

Letting herself into her apartment, the first thing she did was to check the answering machine. There were no messages. The most likely people to have called were Lucy and Bob. She knew Lucy would not be contacting her until the coming week, and Bob was obviously tired out.

She considered getting her laptop out and playing with the family history programme, which so far had received little attention from her. However, she changed her mind almost as soon as the idea cropped up. That was something she could do tomorrow. Ten minutes late she was tucked up in bed.

Chapter 18

It was on the Monday evening that Jane heard from Lucy again. She had returned from work and was busy preparing a meal when the phone rang. She rushed to answer it.

'Hello.'

'Jane, it's Lucy.'

'Lucy, how marvellous!'

'I thought I'd give you a ring before I put Patty to bed. Raymond is amusing her at the moment.'

'No more sign of the problem you had with her last week?' asked Jane.

'No, thank goodness.'

Before Jane could reply, Lucy burst out with, 'Anyway, I've got some news for you!'

'That sounds really interesting!' Jane could hardly contain her excitement.

Even Lucy sounded quite exhilarated as she continued. 'Well, I managed to find some details about Mrs Marshall. I found an old letter file and in it was a letter written after she'd retired, thanking all the staff for her retirement present. The letter has an address on it.'

'Gosh, that's fantastic!' exclaimed Jane. 'What's the address?'

'Hang on. I've got it here somewhere.' Lucy paused for a second. 'Ah, here it is. It's number 10 Tipton Street.'

Jane was busy writing. 'Is that near you?' she asked.

Lucy chipped in immediately. 'No. This is the good bit. It's in your direction. South-east London. Postcode is—'

'Just a minute!' Jane wailed. 'My pen's run out.'

It took a minute for her to find another pen from her work bag and continue taking down the details. When she had finished she was full of praise for Lucy's efforts.

'Lucy, that really is fantastic. I can't thank you enough for finding this for me.'

'All part of Goodmanton Orphanage's service,' laughed Lucy. She became more serious. 'I hope it turns out to be of some help,' she said.

'So do I,' replied Jane. 'Mrs Marshall should know something. After all, she was in charge of the orphanage when I darkened its doors.'

'Well, I should hope so.' Jane heard Lucy give a little sigh. 'Now I'd better get some supper for that husband of mine.'

Jane immediately took the hint. 'Yes, you must. Don't let me keep you.'

'Oh, it's OK,' said Lucy casually.

Jane could feel that Lucy wanted to end the call. She took matters into her own hands. 'Well, once again, thank you for your efforts. I'll say good bye for now.'

Lucy took the offer up. 'No problem. Let me know how you get on.'

'I will. Bye for now.'

'Bye,' Lucy called, and then the line went dead.

Jane returned to the kitchen and her evening meal. She was well pleased with Lucy's efforts. Tomorrow she would try phoning the address to see if she could talk to Mrs Marshall, or better still, meet her again. She wondered if the former matron would remember her. She thought perhaps not. Suddenly a thought occurred to her. She had no phone number for her. Perhaps she could get it from Directory Enquiries. She hadn't used that for years. But didn't you need the name of the telephone account holder? She wasn't sure. An idea came to her. She would ask Gerald. He would be sure to know.

She was still thinking about everything as she finished preparing and eating her meal. As soon as she had washed up her few dishes, she headed downstairs to Gerald and Anna's apartment. It was Gerald who answered the door. It seemed that they had been watching television, because Anna called to Jane from the lounge to come in.

Jane stepped into the hallway, but she was conscious that she had perhaps interrupted Gerald and Anna's entertainment, so she decided to make her visit short. She gave Gerald brief details of Lucy's phone call, and explained her concern about obtaining a phone number.

Gerald was his usual helpful self. He wrote down the address and said with a smile, 'Leave it with me. There are ways and means of doing it.'

At that point Anna appeared in the lounge doorway and scolded him for keeping Jane in the hallway. Then she wanted to make Jane a coffee.

Jane declined politely, explaining that she had just eaten and was rather tired that evening, which was quite true, as it had been a hard day at work. She said goodbye and left. She was growing more and more aware that she was leaning heavily on Gerald for help with sorting out her past, but he always insisted that he enjoyed doing it and it gave him something to amuse himself with, as he termed it.

Back in her own apartment, she fiddled with her laptop for a while. While she was playing with her family history programme Bob phoned. He had called her every day over the weekend. She still had a lot to tell him. First was the telephone call from Lucy, and then all the gossip from her day at work. Then Bob told her he had fixed everything for the dinner dance. That reminded her that she would have to take a few hours off work to sort out a dress for the occasion. Bob was on the phone for over half an hour, and by the time they had finished Jane decided to call it a day. By half past ten she was in bed.

It was a busy week for Jane at work. Not only were there the regular features on the magazine to handle, but there were several new ones planned, including the book review section, which had meant extra work for both Jane and Amy. Fortunately, Annette was out of the office quite a lot, and this enabled them to get on with some work, although they still had to endure Annette's early-morning meetings when she was around.

When Jane returned home on the Tuesday evening, she discovered that a note had been pushed through her letter box. It simply said:

Here is the telephone number you need. Let me know the outcome.
Gerald

Jane was thrilled. Good old Gerald, she thought. He comes up trumps every time. Now she held the key to the next stage of her research. Dumping her bag on the floor, she glanced at her watch. It was only just after six. Why not now? The next instant she was dialling the number. She had not planned what to say, but she would let that take its course. The phone at the other end of the line started to ring. It rang and rang. Jane hung on, hoping against hope that it would be picked up, but clearly nobody was there to answer it. Slightly disappointed, she replaced her phone and went into the kitchen.

She tried again later that evening and then next day at work, but it was always the same – no answer. Each time she tried and failed, she grew more frustrated. Sometimes it seemed as though she were just hitting a brick wall trying to establish exactly who she was. Now every time she saw her name somewhere, a pang of anxiety clouded over her. Was she really that person? And if not, who was she? What was her real identity?

A highlight of the week was when she took an extended lunch break one day and went shopping for a new dress for her evening out with Bob. She was let down with the first shop she went to. She had been sure she would find something there, but she was disappointed. Luck was with her at the next shop she tried. They had exactly what she had in mind. As soon as she tried the dress on, she knew it was the right one. It was long, in a pleasing shade of blue, with a plunging neckline. She hadn't worn anything like that since her marriage, but on this occasion she was determined to surprise and please Bob. On top of that she knew the dress suited her and she had the figure to wear it. The sales assistant packed the dress up into a box and Jane paid the bill. She felt the price was a bit more than she had expected to pay, but she compensated that with the thought that she didn't go to a dance every week. Of course, when she returned to work, before she could hide the box away under her desk the other members of staff spied it and started to ask questions.

The first was Margaret. 'And who's been out shopping for clothes?' she piped up.

Jane laughed. 'It's a new dress for a dinner dance I'm going to next week.'

'Let's see it.' Both Margaret and Amy, who had joined her, uttered the same request.

Jane obediently unfastened the box and revealed the dress.

'Oh, it's lovely!' exclaimed Margaret.

The response from Amy was a bit more subdued. 'I wish I could wear something like that,' she remarked glumly. She was rather overweight.

Jane was surprised at what Margaret said next.

'The problem is that we women spend a fortune on a dress like that and the only thing men can think about is getting it off us in the fastest possible way.'

Jane laughed. 'It's not always like that, surely.'

Margaret sniffed. 'I don't know about that.'

Jane thought that was a bit odd, coming from Margaret. She knew Margaret was married and the remark made her wonder if Margaret's relationship with her husband was all that good. Margaret rarely talked about her private life, unlike Amy, who constantly moaned about her partner. The party was broken up by the appearance of Annette returning from a late lunch. Jane was glad to get the box with its dress safely stowed away under her desk.

She had just reached home that evening when her doorbell rang. Immediately she guessed it was Gerald.

She opened the door and flung it wide open. She was correct. Gerald stood there beaming at her.

'Ah, Jane. I wasn't sure if you were home yet.'

'Just got back. Do come in, Gerald,' she invited.

Gerald stepped into the hall. 'I don't want to delay you. You need to make yourself a meal, but I just thought I'd give you a bit of information I've discovered.'

Jane was immediately intrigued and curious. Gerald usually came up with something interesting. 'Will you come and sit down?' she asked, nodding towards the lounge door.

Gerald shook his head. 'No, Jane. I won't hinder you, but I just wanted to let you know a couple of things.'

He hesitated and looked at her. She smiled encouragingly.

Gerald continued. 'I've been looking into this name you discovered in the orphanage records – Ashington. It appears to be quite an old and prosperous family. They hail from the Bristol area, which all fits in. They were originally ship owners and later owned sugar plantations in the West Indies.'

'Gosh, that's interesting!' exclaimed Jane.

'I've also had a word with Eric – Eric Alcott, my friend I told you about. I told him what you said about the unexplained change to the orphanage admissions book and that you were wondering whether you might be Ruth Ashington, and he is going to delve a bit deeper into the family history.'

Jane felt a bit embarrassed. 'You're all working so hard on my behalf, and so far I feel I've not done very much research on my own.'

'Oh, but you are,' Gerald protested. Then he added with a wink, 'Anyway, it keeps us old codgers' brains active.'

Jane laughed. Then she suddenly thought of something. 'Above the front door of the orphanage there was a plaque that said it had been founded by Sir Edward Ashington. That must be the same family.'

'Most likely. I'll tell Eric about it,' Gerald replied. Then he asked, 'Have you managed to get hold of this Mrs Marshall yet?'

Jane shook her head. 'No. I keep on trying every day, but there's no answer.' She was now getting quite concerned over her lack of contact.

'Keep at it,' Gerald exhorted her, at the same time turning to leave.

'I might try and go down to the address this weekend,' suggested Jane. It was something that had just occurred to her.

'Good idea.' Gerald's hand was already on the door latch. 'I must go now and let you get your meal.' He opened the door.

'Thank you again – and greetings to Anna,' Jane called after him as she stood in the doorway and watched him make his way to the stairs. He put up his hand by way of acknowledging her words.

Immediately after Gerald had disappeared, Jane closed the door and, kicking off her shoes, wandered into the lounge. She picked up the file containing all her family history notes and scribbled the new information Gerald had given her on a bit of paper. Gerald had told her from the start to make a note of everything they found out, and now she tried her best to do this methodically. He had impressed upon her that sometimes the most trivial bit of information can suddenly be of prime importance.

After she had eaten, Jane spent the rest of the evening pottering about in her bedroom, sorting out the accessories she would need for her night out with Bob. Her dress was already hanging up behind the bedroom door. Jewellery? Well, she had the necklace with the deep blue stone in it, and she also had the fancy silver bracelet that incorporated a watch, which she could wear on her wrist. But what about shoes? When she looked at the silver ones she had in mind, she was not impressed. They looked decidedly old and shabby. She could not and would not wear them. This would mean a lunchtime forage for a new pair.

The next few days flew past. Jane had tried several times each day to telephone the number she had for Mrs Marshall, but it was a lost cause: there was no answer. Each time she tried, she became a little bit more despondent; sometimes it seemed as if everything was against her. Only Gerald and Bob kept her going with optimism. They would get to the bottom of everything at some point, Bob assured her.

On the Thursday evening, Bob rang her again. Once the preliminaries of their conversation were over and they had caught up on the last few days' news, Bob turned their talk to the coming weekend. By now it was a generally accepted agreement between them that they would spend the weekends together whenever possible.

'About this Saturday…' Bob began.

Jane's heart sank. Immediately she felt that he was going to tell her that he couldn't see her all weekend. She waited anxiously as he continued.

'Jeff has to go to a wedding in the family, so I've got to cover for him at the studio.'

Jane couldn't help but let her disappointment come through in her reply. 'Oh… Does that mean I won't see you this weekend again?' she asked.

Bob jumped in immediately. 'Heavens, no. It just means I won't be available until mid-afternoon Saturday.'

Jane was instantly upbeat. 'Oh, that's fine. I just thought you were going to leave me all on my own this weekend.'

She heard a chuckle at the other end of the phone.

'No fear of that,' he said.

'I missed you terribly last weekend,' she admitted.

'I missed you too,' replied Bob. 'I kept thinking about you, wondering what you were doing.'

Jane's brain was suddenly working overtime. The idea she had thought of was suddenly blossoming. If Bob was working the first part of Saturday, she would have time to put her vague plan into action.

The next instant she spelt her idea out to Bob. 'Bob, I've been thinking. If you're going to work Saturday morning, I might go and see if I can find out if Mrs Marshall still lives at that address. I

159

mean, the neighbours might know something even if she's away somewhere. What do you think?'

Bob was a bit studious in his reply. 'It seems a good idea,' he replied slowly, but then suddenly he asked, 'But will you have time?'

Jane had already thought out some of the details. 'Oh, yes. Heaps. I'll do some shopping for us Friday evening, hairdresser's first thing Saturday morning, and then I'll go straight there. I'll be back here in the early afternoon. I'll cook us a meal for when you come.'

'I'll look forward to that,' enthused Bob. Then he asked, 'Where does this Mrs Marshall live exactly?'

Jane had already checked out the location. 'It's in south-east London, Charlton way. I'll drive there. Saturday morning the traffic should be fine.'

'I wish I could come with you,' said Bob, perhaps a bit concerned.

'So do I. But I'll be fine. I'm a big girl now.' She laughed.

Bob laughed in turn at her reply. 'I believe you,' he said cheerfully.

It was Jane who changed the subject. She was still planning Saturday in her head.

'What time do you think you'll get here on Saturday?' she asked.

Bob hesitated for a second. He was also planning his day. 'Hmm… Five or six, I should think.'

Jane was quick to reply. 'Make it six-ish – that will give me plenty of time.'

She heard a forced sigh at Bob's end of the telephone. 'OK. If I must be prevented from sharing your company for an extra hour, then so be it.'

Jane took on the faked disappointed tone. 'Darling, I'll make it up to you. I promise.'

'OK. I'll hold you to that,' retorted Bob.

They chatted for another five minutes or so and then Bob said he had better get back to his accounts and Jane responded that she had better do the washing up before she went to bed.

160

They were both looking forward to the weekend – particularly Jane, who was already working out the final details.

Unfortunately, despite all her careful planning, Saturday did not turn out as she had intended.

Chapter 19

Jane had everything planned for Saturday. She would go to the hairdresser's at half past eight and take the car with her. As soon as she had finished there she would pop into the supermarket to do some extra shopping for food to share with Bob over the weekend and then drive to Charlton. She figured out that she would then have heaps of time to make herself and everything else nice for the Bob's arrival at six, including having a meal all ready. Then she and Bob could have a cosy evening together. If the weather was nice perhaps they could go for a walk along the river later.

But on the Friday evening her plans went awry. She had hardly arrived home when the doorbell rang. She opened the door to find a rather flustered Gerald standing there. She greeted him in her usual cheerful manner.

'Hello, Gerald. Come in.'

She held the door wide open and Gerald stepped into the hall as he answered her greeting.

'Good evening, Jane. I'm sorry if I disturbed you as soon as you got home. But I have some important information and I wanted to ask you something.' He looked distinctly concerned.

'Of course. Come into the lounge.'

Jane started to turn to go in that direction, but Gerald shook his head. 'I don't want to hinder you,' he said.

Jane could see that he was worried about something and didn't know the best way to tell her. She immediately offered her encouragement. 'So what's happened?' she asked gently.

It seemed to do the trick. Gerald appeared more relaxed. 'Oh, nothing serious,' he said quickly, before continuing more thoughtfully. 'It's good news, really. For you, I mean.' He smiled at Jane.

Jane was intrigued and anxious to hear more. She almost interrupted Gerald. 'That sounds exciting. What is it?'

Gerald still seemed a bit perturbed. He hesitated. 'Well, you remember I told you about my friend Eric Alcott?'

Jane nodded, anxiously waiting.

'He's been doing some more research into the Ashington family. Apparently he's found out quite a lot and he'd like to see you.'

'I'd love to see him,' responded Jane quickly.

Gerald hesitated again. 'That's just the problem. He wants to come over tomorrow evening.'

It was Jane's turn to be concerned. She had made all her plans to have a nice evening with Bob, and it seemed they were to be thwarted.

Before she could answer, Gerald spoke again.

'Anna's going to make a meal for us all, and we wondered if you could come as well.' He looked at Jane appealingly.

Jane's brain raced. She didn't want to offend Anna or Gerald, but nor did she want to make a habit of having meals with them and being fussed over by Anna. In any case, this time she had Bob to consider. It was this that gave her the answer.

She responded graciously. 'Oh, that is sweet of you. But Bob's coming over for the weekend and he won't be getting here until about six – or perhaps even later.'

Gerald's face took on the concerned look again. 'Well,' he replied, 'I'm sure Anna can manage an extra person.' He seemed to be thinking and speaking at the same time. 'I can go and get some more food tomorrow.'

Jane seized the advantage his statement offered her. She shook her head. 'No. It's not fair on Anna.' She thought for a second. An idea came to her. She immediately outlined her solution to the problem. 'Why don't you all have your meal as arranged and then

Bob and I can pop in later in the evening – say, about half past seven?' she suggested as tactfully as she could.

This seemed to go down well with Gerald. 'Well, if you're quite sure. That seems like a good arrangement.' His face started to beam again.

They left it at that, and a much-relieved Gerald departed to relay the decision to Anna.

Jane closed the door and breathed a sigh of relief. Her diplomacy appeared to have worked. True, her plans for the evening had been altered, but she had avoided another meal with Anna.

Saturday morning began well. She was the first client at the hairdresser's, and as soon as she emerged from there she went straight into the nearby supermarket. She raced quickly around and fifteen minutes later was depositing two shopping bags in her car boot. A quick visit to her apartment to put some perishable items in the fridge, and then she was on her way to Charlton.

Crossing London held no fears for her. She had learnt to drive there, and during her marriage she had used the car a lot. She had studied the London map before leaving her apartment and she was confident of the main route and where she needed to turn off for Tipton Street.

Soon after she left the main road she became lost in a maze of side streets that all looked the same. She pulled up when she spied a postman emerging from a garden. In answer to her query, he promptly replied, 'First left and then second right.' After that it was easy finding her goal.

Tipton Street was a comparatively quiet tree-lined backwater. On both sides of the road stood rows of small Victorian terraced houses, each with a tiny garden and a tiled path leading up to a porch and front door. Most had bay windows.

Jane drove slowly along the street, noting the house numbers where she could. When she got to number 14 she parked alongside the kerb in a convenient free space. It was now well past mid-morning. She quickly got out of the car and looked for number 10. A minute or so later she was pushing open the metal gate. The front door was in the traditional Victorian pattern with glass panels in the upper half. Jane quickly grabbed hold of the stout iron knocker and gave several sound knocks. The noise carried across the road and alerted a middle-aged, grey-haired woman with a sad demeanour who was just coming out of a house opposite. She eyed Jane up but said nothing. Jane waited, trying to rehearse what she would say when the door opened. She waited a few minutes. Nothing happened. There was no movement inside the house.

'I think she's gone away.'

Jane turned round to see where the voice was coming from. The woman from across the road was standing on the pavement looking at her.

Jane immediately fixed her attention on her. 'Oh,' she said. 'Do you know where she is?'

The woman shook her head. 'No. I did hear she went to Australia to visit her sister.' She continued to stare at Jane. Suddenly she volunteered more information. 'Beth at number 14 might know when she's coming back.'

Jane smiled politely. 'Thank you. I'll try there.'

The woman nodded and muttered something like 'OK' and then went on her way.

Jane went back down the path and shut the gate behind her. Number 14 was next door but one. She walked up the path and this time rang a bell. There was the noise of a dog barking, but nobody answered the door. She tried again with the same result. It was abundantly clear that there was nobody at home.

Undaunted, and desperate now to try and obtain some information, Jane tried the houses on either side of number 10. The man who opened the door of number 12 was quite pleasant, but, no, he declared in a soft Irish accent, he didn't know much about the lady next door. She kept herself to herself. Jane asked him if her name was Marshall, but he didn't know. She fared no better at number 8. Here the door was opened by a young woman holding a baby. No. They had only just moved in and they had only spoken briefly to their neighbour. They weren't sure if her name was Marshall.

Disappointed, Jane returned to her car. She sat in the driving seat wondering what she could do next. It seemed as if her bright idea of making a visit to Mrs Marshall's house had come to naught. She had encountered the remote pattern of living that existed in large cities. People didn't know their neighbours any more. Despondency began to cloud over her once again. It seemed as if every avenue she tried in order to establish who she really was just became blocked to her.

She suddenly spied the postman she had spoken to earlier. She waited until he came closer and then hopped out of the car again and walked towards him.

'Excuse me,' she said. 'Could I ask you a question?'

He looked up from the packet of letters he was studying. He grinned at her and gave a brief 'Yes.'

'I was wondering if you knew the name of the lady living at number 10. Is it Marshall?'

He looked at her for a moment. 'I don't think I can help you there. I've not been on this route long and I tend to look at the numbers more than the names.'

'Oh, yes, I see. Thank you, anyway.'

The postman nodded and smiled at her again. He moved on about his work.

Jane retreated to her car once again. She sat there for five minutes or so, vainly hoping that the occupants of number 10 or number 14 might return, but no one appeared. She glanced at the clock on the dashboard. It was already approaching midday. There seemed to be no point in hanging about any longer. Her mission had failed. She started the car and moved off, with one last regretful look at the empty house number 10.

The journey back to Kew was fraught with delays. At one point Jane encountered an accident area and the road was cut back to one lane. The traffic was backed up and it was a case of moving a few yards and then stopping for three or four minutes. Then it started to rain, and she sat there in the queue of traffic listening to the windscreen wipers carrying out their monotonous thumping sound. She switched on the radio for company but quickly became disinterested and turned it off again. Eventually she was clear of the area and was able to drive normally.

It was close to half past two when she arrived back home. It was still raining and she had to run from the car into the building to try to save her hair arrangement, so beautifully done earlier in the day.

Back in the apartment, she made herself a cup of coffee and a cheese sandwich and then set about preparing the evening meal. By four o'clock she had everything ready. The tuna steaks she had bought were ready to pop into the oven later, and the salad was made. She had laid the table carefully and had even added a candle to give a bit of a romantic touch. The bottle of wine she had purchased was chilling in the fridge. She felt quite pleased with everything.

When it came to getting changed, she took her time. She spent ages in the bathroom and then a long time deciding what to wear. After some deliberation and taking various garments out of her wardrobe for consideration she finally selected a pretty green floral short-sleeved summer dress. She hadn't worn it for some time, so it required the extra attention of the iron before she was satisfied with it. She had a necklace with green stones that matched the dress perfectly. When it came to shoes, she spent a good five minutes making up her mind which to wear. In the end she chose a pair of sandals. They could hardly be called that, because they consisted of just two strips of leather to hold them on. Flip-flops with high heels, somebody had once called them. For an extra bit of wickedness she dug out a delicate gold anklet Graham had given her, and clipped it around her left ankle. It always intrigued her how men's eyes were drawn to it. She couldn't wait to see Bob's reaction, although she was already pretty sure what it would be. Satisfied with her appearance, she popped the shoes near the front door to put on later and then went into the lounge for a well-earned rest while she waited for Bob.

It was only just past six when there was the familiar buzz of the outside doorbell. She scurried to the hall and answered it.

'Hello.'

'Hello. It's me.' It was Bob's cheerful voice.

Jane pressed the release button and called into the speaker, 'You're in.'

While she was waiting she slipped her feet into her shoes. After a minute or so, she heard footsteps outside. She opened the door wide. Bob stood there with a rucksack on his back and carrying several plastic bags. He was dressed in a green sports jacket with an open-necked pink shirt. He grinned at Jane and stepped into the apartment.

'Hello again.' Bob's greetings were always low-key.

Jane closed the door and the next moment her arms were around him. 'Darling, it's so good you're here. It's been two whole weeks since we were last together.'

'Two weeks, five hours and six minutes,' he replied.

The next second they were kissing each other passionately.

After a while they broke off. Bob held her close. 'Mmm... You always smell so nice,' he murmured.

'It's different from my usual perfume. Do you like it?' Jane had her face burrowed in Bob's shoulder as he gently caressed her back with his free hand.

'I do,' he replied. He added, 'I like your other one as well.'

Suddenly Jane disentangled herself from their embrace. She stood back, glanced down at herself, and then looked at Bob with a cheeky grin.

'What do you think of my outfit?' she enquired, looking again at her dress. 'It's the alluring me,' she laughed.

Bob scrutinised her garb, and his eyes finally rested on the gold anklet. 'It's quite different, but I like it. Anklet as well.'

Jane followed his gaze. She blushed just a little. But her strategy had worked.

'My little bit of wickedness. I haven't worn it for years,' she replied with a shy grin.

'It's perfect.' He added quietly, 'Janice used to wear one occasionally.'

'It's got a tiny label attached to it with my name on it. See?' Jane bent down and turned the anklet round to show Bob. She was going to say that Graham had bought it for her, but she decided against it. She stood up again, a mischievous grin on her face. 'Anyway, which do you prefer? Plain Jane, or Wicked Jane?'

Bob pretended to be deep in thought for a second. 'Plain Jane by day, Wicked Jane in the evening, and Sexy Jane in bed.' He laughed.

Jane made a face at him and then grinned. 'I'll have to remember that,' she replied gaily.

The next instant reality bounced back. She remembered the dinner. 'Hey! I've got a meal to cook. You put your things away and go into the lounge.'

It was the end of their frolicking. Jane hurried in the direction of the kitchen. Just before she disappeared she called out, 'Would you like something to drink?'

Bob called back from the bathroom where he was depositing his toilet kit. 'I'd love a cup of tea. Shall I make it?'

'No, I'll make one.' Jane was already busy with the tuna steaks.

A minute or so later Bob appeared in the kitchen door. 'Can't I help?' he asked.

'Certainly not. This is my show. You go and relax while I cook.'

'I brought some goodies for us.' He glanced down at the carrier bag he was carrying.

'Mmm, that sounds interesting. What have you got?' Jane turned from closing the oven door.

'There's a bottle of wine, a couple of bottles of beer, some grapes... Oh, and a cake.' Bob started to put the items on the kitchen table.

'Fantastic! We can have the wine with our meal if you prefer it to the one I bought. Have a look – it's in the fridge.'

Together they sorted out the things Bob had brought and then Jane insisted that he go and sit in the lounge. A few minutes later she brought him a mug of tea. Then she produced a photograph album and placed it on the settee beside him.

'There you are. I told you I was in the Girl Guides.' She indicated the open page.

Bob picked up the album.

'Have a look through it,' Jane encouraged him. 'It's all about my dark and distant past – or what I know of it,' she called over her shoulder as she hurried back to the kitchen.

Bob scanned through the album. Most of the photos were of Jane, sometimes as part of a group, and sometimes a shot of her alone. Nearly all of them appeared to be of her life in the orphanage and at university. There were just one or two taken when she was obviously on holiday. One early photo showed her with a friend, wearing a rather old-fashioned badly fitting one-piece bathing suit; another was more modern and showed her clad in a trim bikini. There were several photographs of her with an older couple – clearly, Bob thought, the people who had fostered her when she left the orphanage.

When Bob put the album down to take a drink of his tea, a large brown envelope dropped out. It fell onto the floor, and as he picked it up the flap opened, revealing part of a photograph. He pulled it out to look at it. It was a black and white nude photo of Jane in a pleasing kneeling pose, with her body partly turned away from the camera. Bob was intrigued. At the same time, he was viewing the image through the eyes of a photographer.

'Oh, you horror! You weren't supposed to see that!'

Bob hadn't heard Jane walk into the lounge. She stood behind the settee watching him. He quickly turned to look at her.

'It's quite good,' he said. 'I like it.'

As soon as he spoke, he could see that Jane was just a little bit embarrassed, as he was. 'I'm sorry. It fell out of the album,' he explained hastily.

Jane recovered quickly. 'It was the one Graham took of me. We hadn't been married long,' she said slowly. She paused, looking down at the photograph. 'I'd forgotten I'd put it in that album,' she admitted ruefully.

Bob smiled at her reassuringly. 'It's a good shot,' he admitted. 'It does you credit. Perhaps the lighting could have been improved a little.'

170

'Graham was only an amateur,' said Jane. For a second she seemed in deep thought.

Bob was still holding the photograph. 'I'd like to take one like that of you sometime,' he said.

Jane gave him one of her coy smiles. 'You'll have to marry me first,' she retorted light- heartedly.

Bob grabbed her hand, which was resting on the back of the settee. He pulled her towards him.

'I'll do that any time,' he murmured softly as he kissed her.

Chapter 20

After the brief interlude with the photograph, Jane and Bob enjoyed a leisurely meal, accompanied by the bottle of wine Bob had brought. They took slightly longer over it than Jane had anticipated, and she became increasingly concerned that they would be late for their meeting with Gerald, Anna and Eric. As she and Bob had been apart for two weeks, there were numerous snippets of news and gossip to exchange, which accounted for the slightly rushed situation towards the end of the meal. Nevertheless, it was only a few minutes after the agreed time when they rang the bell of Gerald and Anna's apartment.

It was Anna who opened the door.

'Hello. It's lovely to see you. Now come right in. We're all ready for you. I'm just making the coffee.'

She ushered them into the lounge, where Gerald and his friend were sitting, and immediately started the introductions. 'Eric, this is Jane and this is Bob.'

Gerald and Eric had already jumped up. Eric stretched out his hand. He was a tall, thin man dressed in a formal suit of sombre grey stripe set off by a rather crumpled shirt and tie that had seen better days. He peered at Jane and Bob over a pair of half-frame spectacles.

'Ah, a member of the Ashington family,' was his jovial greeting to Jane.

'We're not really sure about that,' replied Jane, smiling politely as she shook his hand.

'A most interesting family,' was Eric's remark as they all sat down.

Eric cleared his throat. He regarded Jane and Bob across the coffee table. 'I—'

He got no further. He was interrupted by Anna.

'Eric, wait a minute while I get the coffee. I want to hear all about it as well.'

For a second Eric looked a bit embarrassed, but a wink and grin from Gerald smoothed things over as Anna hurried to the kitchen.

The conversation was of a trivial nature until Anna returned with the coffee. Gerald produced a bottle of liqueur and poured some out for everybody. Neither Jane nor Bob really wanted any, but they politely accepted the glasses he handed them.

At last Anna settled in her seat beside her husband. 'Now I'm all ready,' she announced, taking up her cup of coffee.

It was Bob who brought the conversation back to family history matters. 'Can you tell us a bit about the Ashington family background?' he asked Eric.

Eric took a sip of his liqueur. He looked at Bob and Jane over his glasses. Clearly this was a habit of his. He took his time before speaking.

'I looked into the Ashington family some years ago, when I became a professional genealogist. A most interesting family to research.'

'Can you tell us where the family roots are?' asked Jane. Though apprehensive about what she might learn, she still was anxious to know about her possible roots.

Eric resumed, his gaze centred on Jane. 'Until comparatively recently, they were centred very much in Bristol and the surrounding area. In the eighteenth century two members of the family, Henry and John Ashington, were ship owners operating out of Bristol.'

'Gosh, that's interesting. Can you tell us any more?' Jane took the opportunity to comment as Eric took another sip of his liqueur.

Eric resumed his narrative.

173

'The family began to own sugar plantations in the West Indies and sadly started to import slaves from Africa to work on them.'

'You mean they were actually involved in the slave trade?' Jane looked shocked.

Eric nodded. 'Unfortunately, that's true, for a period of time. Yes, they were involved. They had the sugar plantations, which needed workers, and they had the ships to transport them.'

'It's horrible to think that a family like that was involved in such a vile trade,' said Jane.

Bob glanced at her. She appeared to be quite upset at Eric's revelation. He hadn't seen her quite like this before. This prompted him to ask a further question.

'I seem to have got the impression that the Ashingtons were very much a wealthy family based in England. So how did owning sugar plantations fit into that scenario?'

Eric laughed. 'You're quite correct in your assumption. Sugar cane made the family very wealthy, but when the slave trade ended, so did the family interest in sugar-cane growing. The later members of the family turned their attention to the rise of industry in Great Britain.'

'What kind of industry would that have been?' It was Bob who again asked a question.

'Certain members of the family were very far-sighted. They seemed to recognise early on how a new industry was going to develop, and they invested in the new enterprises accordingly.'

'What industries were they?' Gerald repeated Bob's question.

Eric turned his attention from Jane and Bob and focused on Gerald. 'Coal mining, for one,' he replied simply.

Eric took another drink of his coffee. He looked at his audience again and continued. 'It was Samuel Ashington who first took an interest in coal mining.'

'Can you tell me roughly what year that would have been?' asked Jane.

Eric picked up a file from the floor beside his chair. He took out a piece of paper and looked at it. 'Samuel was born in 1796,' he replied. 'It was Samuel and later his son Edward who expanded the business. They owned several coal mines, including one in Yorkshire.'

'Gosh, that's a bit of a spread of interests!' exclaimed Bob, intrigued by Eric's revelation.

Eric nodded. 'It was,' he agreed. 'The family were extremely successful in their business ventures.'

Jane had been listening intently, trying to work out how her possible roots fitted in with the information Eric was providing. Suddenly she asked a question that was perplexing her.

'I'm a bit baffled. If the Ashington family were originally living around Bristol and then became involved in coal mining in Yorkshire, why would Ruth Ashington have been placed in an orphanage in Gloucestershire?'

She paused, a puzzled look on her face, but before Eric could answer, she suddenly thought of something else. 'And there's another thing. How is it that the orphanage was founded by an Ashington?'

Her questions stirred comments from both Gerald and Anna.

'Could it be that there were several members of the family involved, with interests in the two places?' asked Gerald.

'Perhaps they split their time between the two counties,' suggested Anna, looking at everybody in turn.

Eric thought for a few seconds. 'We have to remember that we are dealing with several generations of the same family. Their interests often tended to change with each new generation. By the late eighteen hundreds they had become wealthy estate owners, with land and homes in both Gloucestershire and Yorkshire.'

He paused and looked directly at Jane. 'It would be Edward the son of Samuel who founded the orphanage you were in,' he added. He looked at his audience for a second and then thought of something else he wanted to say. 'Being wealthy landowners didn't stop the Ashington family from having lucrative business interests as well.' He smiled.

'But Gloucestershire and Yorkshire are so far apart,' protested Jane.

Eric nodded. 'Agreed,' he said, 'but you have to remember that by the mid-eighteen hundreds rail travel had become quite normal.'

'I suppose so,' replied Jane thoughtfully.

Eric had more information. He cleared his throat, glanced at his papers again and faced his listeners. 'It was the Great War of 1914 to 1918 that really decimated the family and affected the future generations badly.'

'In what way?' asked Bob.

'A James Ashington had three sons and two daughters. Two of his sons were killed in the war, John in 1916 and Charles in 1917. The remaining son, Edward, carried on the family's business interests.'

Jane already had another question to ask. 'Do you think there's a connection between the name Ruth Ashington in the orphanage admissions book and this family?'

'It's quite possible,' replied Eric. He glanced at his paperwork. He looked up at Jane and Bob and then spoke again. 'Sadly, from the time of Edward Ashington on, the family dwindled in numbers. Not only did he lose his two brothers in the war, but one of his sisters never married and the second sister's marriage produced no children.'

'What about Edward? Did he marry?' asked Jane.

'Yes. He did. In 1946, but unfortunately his wife Jessica died two years later. She was only thirty-three years old.'

'What about children? Are there any from the marriage?' Jane was still thinking about Ruth Ashington.

Eric nodded. 'Yes, there was one daughter, Ann, born in 1948. She was only eighteen when her father died suddenly.'

'What happened to her?' asked Jane.

Eric put his papers down and drank the last of his coffee. He adjusted his spectacles and resumed his narrative to his waiting audience. 'Well, she was of course an incredibly wealthy woman. She seems to have been a bit of a recluse and apparently frequently ill.'

'Do you know where she is now?' Bob had been listening

intently and doing mental calculations. He elaborated. 'She would only be in her fifties.'

Eric shook his head. 'She died in 1980,' he said simply.

'How was it that such a wealthy woman didn't have any suitors and get married?' piped up Anna.

Eric smiled at her. 'She did,' he explained. 'In 1978. She married a Miles Ashington.'

'It seems a bit odd that she married somebody with the same name,' remarked Jane. She too started to do some calculations. Her next query reflected this. 'But she was only married two years before she died.' She looked at Eric with a questioning gaze.

Eric seemed unperturbed by her observation. 'Yes, indeed. That is so,' he replied.

'I'm puzzled about the marriage to a person with the same name,' persisted Jane.

Eric smiled at her. 'In family history one does come across that happening. Perhaps cousins marrying, or it could be a brother marrying a widowed sister-in-law,' he explained.

There was a brief silence as they all digested everything Eric had related.

It was Eric who spoke again first. 'I have to say that most of my research dealt with the earlier members of the family. Given the present situation, some further research could prove interesting.' He looked at Jane as he finished speaking.

Jane was deep in thought. What she had just heard Eric describe seemed to be completely remote from her own situation, yet at the same time there was Ruth Ashington to consider. How did she relate to the events Eric had described?

'Where do you think Ruth Ashington fits into all this?' she asked. 'And why would her record in the admissions register have been obliterated?'

Eric thought for a second. 'She could be a distant cousin of the family,' he explained. He paused again. 'Unfortunately, the answer to your question why records have been amended must lie with the orphanage, or with somebody who worked there.'

Jane was disappointed. She had been hoping that this meeting with Eric would reveal some clues about her past, but things were not turning out that way. Though Eric's information about the Ashington family was interesting, his knowledge ended at just about the period she was most interested in. She felt as if she had come up against yet another closed door, and the cold fact remained that any clues to her ancestry lay with the orphanage or with people connected with it. She was about to ask Eric another question, but was beaten to it by Anna stating almost the same thing she had been thinking.

'Perhaps this Ann Ashington had a daughter,' suggested Anna.

'It looks as if it could be a likely answer to me,' observed Gerald.

'Did you never find anything when you did your research into the family?' asked Jane.

Eric chuckled wryly. 'As I said, I was chiefly concerned with the earlier history of the family. I did trace Ann Ashington's marriage, but it would be worth another look in the records to see if there was a birth, illegitimate or otherwise.'

Eric had hardly finished before Gerald chipped in. 'We could definitely do that,' he said, looking at Jane.

His remark prompted a wave of concern in Jane. 'I feel that I should do that. Up until now I seem to have had everybody else doing my family history for me.'

Gerald gave a little laugh. 'It keeps us old men busy and the brain working,' he remarked.

'It keeps him out of my way as well,' added Anna. She suddenly changed the subject. 'Now, anybody want more coffee?'

After that the conversation strayed away from family history and Jane's problem. Eric had learnt that Bob was a photographer, and it turned out that that was another of Eric's interests. He asked Bob's opinion of a new camera he intended to buy.

At last the conversation wound down. Eric looked at his watch and said he must be going. This was the signal for Jane and Bob to depart. Thanking their hosts, and in particular Eric for his interest in Jane's affairs, they returned to Jane's apartment.

As soon as they were in the hallway and Jane had closed the outer door, Bob placed his hands on her shoulders and drew her towards him. 'Darling, you're disappointed with tonight's results aren't you?' he asked gently.

Jane looked at him, her face sombre. She nodded. 'Just a little bit.'

He put his arm around her and led her slowly into the lounge. As soon as they had sat down on the settee, Jane added to her previous statement.

'It was super that Gerald contacted Eric and really nice of Eric to come and see me, but in spite of what he said I still feel in limbo. I still don't know what my real name is.'

'I know. It must be pretty frustrating and worrying, but I'm convinced there's an answer somewhere.'

Jane gave a little sigh. 'It's just this feeling that every door seems to get slammed in my face. We get one lead that seems as if it might have the answer, and then it just produces another query.'

Bob drew her towards himself. 'Unfortunately, that's family history. But we'll find out who you really are in the end. I'm sure we will.'

Jane forced a grin. 'I'm being a bit of a misery, aren't I?'

'No. Just concerned.' Bob gave her a quick kiss on the lips.

Immediately she relaxed. She suddenly looked at him rather coyly. 'I've got my dress for next Friday,' she announced proudly.

'Let's see it,' demanded Bob.

Jane thought for a second, a frown on her face. Suddenly she jumped up and headed for the bedroom. 'You can have a sneak preview and that's all,' she announced over her shoulder. Two minutes later she reappeared, carrying the dress by the hanger.

Smiling broadly, she held it against herself. 'I'm not going to let you see me wearing it until the actual night,' she replied in answer to Bob's quizzical look.

'Spoilsport,' he said, with a grin.

'What do you think? Do you like it?'

'I think it looks fantastic. I can't wait to see you wearing it.' Bob sounded as if he meant it.

'I'm really looking forward to Friday,' said Jane. 'I haven't been to anything like that for years.'

'The hotel's all booked. I'll give you all the details and I'll meet you there.'

'I'm going to take at least an afternoon off work so that I'm nice and fresh.'

She started to carry the dress back to the bedroom. Something was worrying her.

'There's just one thing,' she announced, concern in her voice. Bob looked at her enquiringly. 'What's that?' he asked.

She looked slightly anxious. 'Shoes. I've not been able to find any anywhere. I thought about silver, but the only ones I've come across have been sandals, and I didn't really want sandals.'

She was already in the bedroom before she finished speaking. A few seconds later she returned with a pair of silver shoes.

'I've got these, but they're a bit old now.' She displayed the shoes for Bob to see. The next instant she was trying them on. 'What do you think?' she asked, looking down at the shoes and then enquiringly at Bob.

'I think they'll be OK if you can't get exactly what you want,' he replied.

'I suppose so.' As an afterthought Jane added, 'Perhaps it's just me who had set my heart on a new pair.'

Bob smiled at her. 'You look nice in anything,' he said.

'Flatterer,' Jane retorted, making a face at him.

The next second he ducked as she hurled a nearby cushion at him.

Chapter 21

The new week started badly for Jane. On the Monday morning she was dismayed when she arrived at the station to discover that her train had been cancelled. It followed that the next one was packed, and she had to stand all the way to her destination. On top of that, she eventually arrived at work to learn from Margaret that Amy had rung in to advise that she was sick and would not be coming in. This was a blow because Amy had been working on a project that had a deadline that day and Jane had to reschedule her own work to incorporate Amy's.

Fortunately the extra workload did not dampen her enjoyment at looking back over the events of the weekend. In spite of the disappointment of not learning any more about her past from the meeting with Eric, after her initial reaction she had become more philosophical about the whole thing and had settled down to enjoy the rest of the weekend with Bob.

They were now completely comfortable with each other's company. When Bob had found the nude photograph, she had at first been a bit embarrassed, but then she suddenly realised that she didn't mind him seeing it at all. In fact, she was rather proud of it. After all, she reasoned, Bob had held her naked in his arms on more than one occasion now and she had been happy about that. She had been quite at ease answering his questions about the photograph. In Bob she felt that she had at last found another soulmate after losing Graham, and although they had not discussed their future in any detail, there now seemed to be an understanding between them that said it all.

Perhaps the only minor obstacle was that she could not be certain if she was who her documents said she was. As far as she was concerned it was a constant worry and a stumbling block in her relationship with Bob. On one occasion she had almost revealed this in a joke when they had been discussing her past in a light-hearted way:

'We can't get married yet, because I don't know who I am. We could both be accused of something or other and end up in prison.'

Bob's reaction had as always been down-to-earth and completely spontaneous. 'I'll ensure that I get a lighter sentence as the more innocent party and then I can visit you in prison,' he had replied gravely, hiding his humour.

It was his upbeat attitude that helped Jane through her despondency when she was failing to make any definite headway in finding out who she really was.

She worked hard that Monday, not taking any lunch break and working right through to well after her normal finishing time. Her only sustenance had been a sandwich brought in to her by Margaret, and endless cups of tea and coffee. When she got home she was worn out and she had a headache. Even preparing a meal for herself was quite an effort. Gone were her plans to spend some time on the computer playing with the hardly used family history program and doing another search for Ruth Ashington. By half past nine she was in bed asleep.

She felt a bit better when she woke up the next morning. Monday's grey sky had been replaced by bright sunshine. It was pleasant walking to the station and also comforting to find her train running as normal and having a more relaxing journey to work. When she arrived at the office, any apprehension about the day was lifted still further. Amy appeared to have made a miraculous recovery and was at her desk drinking a cup of tea.

Jane greeted her. 'Morning, Amy. Are you feeling better?'

Amy went into a long, detailed account of her sickness and finished by asked Jane if she could get her a mug of tea. Jane readily accepted the offer and then turned her attention to the pile of work on her desk.

During the afternoon her spirits were lifted still further. She had taken a slightly extended lunch break and managed to squeeze in some much-needed shopping for cosmetics. When she returned to the office Margaret greeted her with excitement.

'Jane, while you were out a courier left something for you.' She dived under her desk and produced an intriguing rectangular parcel. 'It's not very heavy,' she announced, handing it to Jane.

'It looks like a pair of shoes.' Amy had suddenly appeared.

Jane looked at the handwriting on the label. She recognised it immediately. It was Bob's. But what could he have sent her?

'Are you going to open it?' Olive from advertising was also taking an interest in what was going on.

Jane could see that her audience were not going to be satisfied or disperse until she had opened the parcel. Besides, her own curiosity equalled theirs.

Carefully, she tore off the brown paper wrapping. What looked like a new shoebox appeared. She placed it on a nearby chair and lifted the lid. When she pulled aside the tissue paper covering the contents, a squeal of delight came from her colleagues. Comments and questions were directed thick and fast at her.

'It *is* a pair of shoes.'

'Where did they come from?'

'Try them on.'

Jane took a shoe out of its tissue-paper packing. It was a silver high-heeled court shoe with a dainty filigree bow on the front. She held it up to show her admiring audience.

'They're beautiful.'

'Where did you get them? I've never seen any like that.'

'Are they for the dinner dance you're going to?'

Jane continued to be bombarded with questions. Then Amy spotted something else in the box.

'Look, Jane. There's something in with them.'

Jane looked in the box and sure enough there was an envelope tucked in. She took it out and opened it. Her colleagues waited expectantly.

The envelope contained a pretty card with flowers on it. Jane read the simple message inside in Bob's handwriting: '*And Cinderella shall go to the ball.*'

She felt obliged to show the card to the others. Reading it brought further questions from her audience. Who had sent her the shoes? Was it anybody they knew? Where exactly was she going?

Jane answered as truthfully but as vaguely as she could. Just at present she didn't want to advertise the fact that she was in a serious relationship. She merely explained that her boyfriend was taking her to a dinner dance and that she had had problems obtaining a pair of shoes to go with the dress she had bought.

'Are you going to try them on?' It was Amy again.

Jane obediently slipped off one shoe and tried on the silver one she held in her hand. It fitted perfectly and she was relieved to discover that though the heel was high it was of a practical height to be comfortable, and sensible for dancing.

'How does your man know your size?' asked Olive.

Jane had no idea. As far as she could remember she hadn't mentioned her shoe size to Bob.

'If a man's bought them you'd better try the other one on as well,' said Olive.

'My other half wouldn't have a clue what size shoes I take,' muttered Margaret.

Jane tried the second shoe on. It fitted just as well as the first one. She was then expected to model her new accessory for her admirers. She walked up and down, turning her feet and pointing her toes to display the shoes.

The show was brought to an abrupt halt. A sound alerted the four of them to the entrance door. Annette had just returned from her lunch break. She eyed them all in silence, taking in every detail, and then she quickly continued to her office without comment.

Everybody quickly dispersed. Margaret hurried to the reception desk, Amy to hers, and Olive to the advertising department. Jane took a more leisurely pace. She took off the shoes, replaced them in the box with the envelope and slipped on her other shoes again.

She couldn't wait to get home and phone Bob. She had to be patient until she thought he might be back, which made the time seem to drag. Eventually, relaxing on the settee, she dialled his number on her mobile. She could hear the phone ringing at the other end.

'Bob Harker.'

'Bob, it's Jane. I've got your lovely present. I'm over the moon! Thank you.'

She heard a chuckle at the other end, and then, 'Great. Do they fit OK?'

'Of course they do. How did you know my size?'

'Ah. Secret.'

It was Jane's turn to give a little laugh. 'OK. But I'm intrigued where you got them. I searched and couldn't find anything like them.'

There was another chuckle from Bob. 'That's a secret as well. But it needed a bit of inside knowledge.'

Jane was about to answer in the same vein, but Bob spoke again.

'I've got another surprise for you.'

'Oooh. What is it?' Jane responded eagerly.

'That's a secret as well. I'm going to tell you on Friday.'

'Oh, no. You're horrid to me. I'm already eaten up with excitement.'

He laughed. 'I'm looking forward to it as well. I haven't done anything like it for years.'

'I'll make sure you enjoy it,' quipped Jane. She added wickedly, 'You don't know me when I taste the high life.'

'I can handle you,' laughed Bob.

Their conversation gradually became more serious. Bob wanted to know whether Jane had had any luck contacting Mrs Marshall, and the question immediately brought her back down to earth when she had to admit that she had been so busy the last two days that she hadn't managed to try phoning again. She made a mental note to do so the next day.

At last Jane confessed that she hadn't done the washing up yet, and Bob admitted that he hadn't had his evening meal. It was the signal for them to end their conversation.

The Wednesday morning proved to be even more exhilarating for Jane. She arrived at the station before her usual time and caught an earlier train. It was less crowded, and she wondered whether it might be a good idea to catch this one in future. No one else was at the office when she arrived, and she had to use her keys to get in. She made herself a cup of tea and was already hard at work at her desk when a surprised Margaret arrived. It was Margaret who usually got there first as she lived much closer to the office than everybody else.

'Good morning, Jane. Gosh, you're here early,' she said.

Jane nodded. 'Good morning, Margaret. Yes. I caught a different train.'

Margaret disappeared to make herself a drink, and Jane got back to work. She still had a bit of a backlog from Monday because of Amy's day off sick.

It was mid-morning when she suddenly remembered her intention to try and phone Mrs Marshall again. She was about to do so when the internal phone buzzed. That could only be one person, she thought. She was correct in her assumption. As soon as she put the receiver to her ear, Annette's voice came over.

'Good morning, Jane. Are you free for a few minutes?'

'Good morning, Annette. Yes, of course. Shall I come up now?'

'Yes, that will be fine.'

'I'll be right up.'

Jane replaced the handset, stifling a sigh. Usually a meeting with Annette meant more work or an alteration to work already done. And she had been getting on so well that morning!

Grabbing her notepad, she made her way upstairs and tapped on Annette's office door before opening it.

'Ah, Jane. Come in and sit down.'

Annette was sitting at her desk, the current issue of *Discerning Woman* open in front of her. She looked up as Jane sat down opposite her. 'Would you like a coffee?' she asked.

'That would be nice. Can I get you one?' enquired Jane politely. She didn't really want any coffee herself, but thought it diplomatic to accept the offer. Annette had her own coffee machine in her office for entertaining visitors. Jane was about to get up, but Annette immediately jumped up and waved a hand for her to remain seated.

'No, no. You sit there and relax. I'll get it. Milk and sugar?'

It was unusual for Annette to offer her staff a cup of coffee from her machine, let alone serve them. Jane immediately started to wonder what she had up her sleeve.

Annette returned with two cups of coffee. She handed one to Jane and then, placing the other on the desk in front of her, she settled back in her plush chair. Jane waited.

Eventually, Annette glanced down at the magazine in front of her and then immediately at Jane. 'I think last month's issue was really good. That feature that you did on Gilli Jameson was quite impressive.'

'I'm glad it turned out well,' responded Jane, sipping her coffee. Gilli Jameson was an author whose work Jane and Amy had showcased for the magazine.

Annette picked up her cup and looked at Jane again. Suddenly she volunteered another snippet of information.

'I had a meeting with Olgans on Monday.'

She paused for a second, taking a sip of her coffee and seemingly slowly relishing the taste. Jane waited, wondering what was going to come next. Olgans was the company that owned *Discerning Woman* and a few other magazines.

Annette was taking her time. After what seemed an age to Jane, she added to her original comment. 'Olgans are very pleased with the way things are going. Sales and our circulation have continued to rise.'

'That's nice to hear,' agreed Jane politely. It was rare for staff below Annette to hear comments from Olgans unless some changes were afoot.

Annette had more to say. 'It all started with that article on Angus Pike. Circulation has been increasing steadily every month since.'

'I'm glad it went down well after the struggle we had to get the interview with him,' replied Jane.

'That was really thanks to your perseverance and hard work.' Annette paused and studied Jane for a second. Then, before Jane could answer she continued. 'You seemed to get on well with Angus Pike. He had quite a high regard for you.' She studied Jane again, at the same time drinking her coffee.

Jane's spontaneous reaction was to give a little laugh. 'Perhaps because he wanted me to model for him,' she remarked dryly.

'Did you? Or are you going to?'

Jane shook her head. 'No way,' she replied, smiling.

Annette nodded. 'That's good. Never mix business with pleasure.'

Jane made no reply to Annette's remark. She had actually forgotten all about Angus Pike's interest in her. As to appearing in one of his paintings, that idea was quite repulsive to her. Appearing nude in a photograph for someone you loved was one thing. Being exhibited naked to the public was a totally different kettle of fish.

Annette continued the conversation. 'You work very hard, Jane. You sometimes don't take a lunch break and often work late. Be careful you don't burn yourself out.'

Jane was a bit surprised by this remark. Annette was not known for showing concern about her staff. She vaguely wondered how Annette appeared to know so much about her working hours. She considered her answer carefully.

'I manage OK, but at times a bit of an extra effort is needed.'

'You haven't taken any holiday leave yet this year,' observed Annette.

It was quite true. Except for the odd day here and there, Jane had to agree that a holiday had not been high on her agenda. She and Bob had vaguely discussed a holiday break, but that was as far as it had got. Somehow work had got in the way for both of them.

'I'll have to think of something,' she said, hoping that a vague reply might steer the conversation away from her and back to work.

Annette was not to be fobbed off. She smiled at Jane. 'I saw you trying on a pretty pair of shoes yesterday. Are they for a special occasion?'

Gosh, thought Jane, she sees and remembers everything. 'My boyfriend is taking me to a dinner dance on Friday evening,' she replied.

She thought that was sufficient information on the matter, but Annette immediately wanted to know what and where it was. Jane's vague answer seemed to satisfy her.

Jane was completely thrown by Annette's next question.

'You're taking Friday afternoon off, aren't you?'

Jane nodded. 'Yes. Just to give me time to get myself ready.'

'You must take the whole day off.'

'But...' Jane started to protest.

Annette immediately shook her head. 'No. I insist. You must take some time for yourself, Jane.'

Jane caved in. She knew that just half a day for everything that she wanted to do would have been a rush. Now she had a full day to look forward to, despite the thought at the back of her mind that she would have to reschedule Friday morning's work.

The conversation lasted for ten minutes or so, gradually veering away from Jane to the current work in hand on the magazine. At last Annette put her cup and saucer down and glanced at her watch. This was a clear indication that the interview was over, which pleased Jane. She had been surprised by the sudden appearance of Annette's caring side and it had been quite pleasant to be praised, but she had a deskload of work to do downstairs. Gratefully, she

189

took her leave. This appeared to suit Annette, who picked up her telephone as Jane was closing the door.

Of course, Amy wanted to know what had happened. 'What did Queen Bee want?' she asked as Jane was passing her desk.

Jane grinned. 'Oh, she was quite pleased with how the magazine is going and complimented us on the Gilli Jameson article.'

Amy's response was to make a face and utter a simple 'Oh, is that all?'

Jane left it at that. During the afternoon another event occurred to brighten her day. She had taken a short lunch break, buying a sandwich and having it at her desk with a mug of tea while idly considering some of the work in front of her. It was then that she suddenly remembered her intention to try once again to get in touch with Mrs Marshall. She had dialled the number so many times that she now almost knew it by heart. The telephone had rung so many times without anybody answering it that on this occasion she was hardly anticipating a reply. She concentrated on her work with the handset held to her ear.

Suddenly the telephone stopped ringing and a voice answered. 'Hello.'

Jane's heart missed a beat. Could this be Mrs Marshall at long last? She almost struggled at first to find some words.

'Hello. Is that Mrs Marshall?'

There was a slight pause at the other end.

'No. This is her sister.'

Jane thought quickly. 'Oh, I'm sorry. Would it be possible to speak to Mrs Marshall?'

She waited for the answer but was not prepared for the information it contained.

'I'm sorry. My sister passed away two years ago.'

The reply threw Jane for an instant. She had not expected such news. She did her best to forge a suitable reply. 'I'm dreadfully sorry. I had no idea. I do apologise.'

'That's all right. What did you want to talk to Susan about?'

190

It was clutching at straws, but Jane was determined to exploit any opportunity to solve the mystery of her past. She explained her mission as briefly as she could.

'Well, what it is, really...' She paused for a second. 'My name is Jane Carroll and I was at Goodmanton orphanage during the time your sister was in charge. I've been trying to trace my family and I was hoping your sister might have been able to help.'

'Oh, I don't know...' Elizabeth's answer was disappointingly vague.

Jane was about to try and elaborate, but Elizabeth asked another question.

'What did you say your name was?'

'Carroll. Jane Carroll.'

'Oh, I see.'

Despite Elizabeth's unencouraging response, Jane thought she detected an interest deep down. She decided to take the bull by the horns.

'I was wondering if I might come to see you.'

She waited. She knew she was clutching at straws.

Elizabeth's answer was not encouraging.

'Oh. I don't know.' She added, 'You see, I don't know you.'

To Jane her reaction was completely understandable. But Jane was not going to give up. She racked her brain quickly to try and think of something to say to achieve her objective. The answer suddenly came to her.

'I quite understand your caution. As you say, you don't know me, but I was wondering if you know or read *Discerning Woman* magazine?'

She waited. She knew it was a faint hope, but she felt a twinge of encouragement at Elizabeth's answer.

'Yes, I know it. Sometimes my neighbour gives it to me to read when she has finished with it.'

This was progress. Jane jumped at the opportunity.

'Do you have a copy of the magazine handy?'

'I might have – or my neighbour would have one. But why do

191

you ask?' Elizabeth was clearly being very cautious, but Jane could tell that she was curious.

'Well, if you look in the front of the magazine, you will see my name listed. I'm the features editor.'

Jane waited for a response.

'Oh. I see.'

The reply was hardly encouraging, but Jane was determined. 'If you telephone the magazine, they will confirm that I work there. Ask for Margaret. Can I give you the number?'

'All right.'

It was a minute or two before Elizabeth found a pen and paper and managed to get the number down correctly, but at last it was done. When they had completed the task, Jane reinforced her request.

'Please phone them.'

'Perhaps I will.'

'Please,' Jane pleaded. 'It's very important to me.'

'All right.'

'Thank you. I'll let my colleague know you'll be ringing. Who shall I tell her to expect?'

'My name is Mrs Barton – Elizabeth Barton.'

'I'll look forward to hearing from you, Mrs Barton. Thank you very much for your help. Goodbye for now.'

'Goodbye.'

The telephone went dead.

Jane sighed. Well, she had given it her best shot. She could do no more for now. It was up to Elizabeth to take the next step. She knew it was debatable whether her request would be carried out.

That evening, after Jane had eaten, she decided to load the family history program she had purchased and search for Ruth Ashington's birth. She went through year after year, scouring the indexes without success. She tried again the following evening. The outcome was the same. She found no recorded birth details for anyone by the name of Ruth Ashington.

Chapter 22

When she woke up on the Friday morning, Jane felt quite pleased with herself. Not only did she have a whole day to herself and time to prepare for the evening, but ever since Annette had insisted on her taking the whole day off she had worked extremely hard and was well pleased with her output. Only one thing dampened her exuberance slightly, and that was the fact that she had heard nothing from Mrs Marshall's sister. She had hoped for a call from her all day Thursday, but none had come.

Her immediate reaction on waking was to automatically glance at the clock on the bedside cabinet. It was part of her usual routine, but as she was doing so she remembered that today was a holiday, and she would not have to rush to work. However, that did not stop her thoughts straying to the fact that the previous day she had changed her hairdressing appointment to an earlier time, and that meant she had to be up and about.

By half past eight she was sitting in the hairdresser's, and after her session there she popped into the beauty salon next door to indulge herself with one or two other refinements to her appearance, including having her nails changed to a delicate shade of pink.

After a short visit to the supermarket, she was back in her apartment by lunchtime. Just as she was entering the building she bumped into Gerald coming out. He immediately greeted her with his usual friendly smile.

'Good afternoon, Jane.'

Jane smiled at him. 'Hello, Gerald.'

'Not at work today?' he asked.

'I've taken a day off. Bob and I are going to a dinner dance in town tonight,' replied Jane, but even as she spoke her thoughts had already turned to a more important issue. Before Gerald could respond she was already expressing her worry. 'Gerald, I'm so glad to see you.' She paused for a moment, ensuring that she had his full attention. 'I've been looking at the birth records on the computer program you installed for me.' She hesitated again, her concern showing. 'I can't find a birth recorded for a Ruth Ashington anywhere in the Gloucestershire area.' She looked at Gerald, waiting for his reaction.

Gerald smiled again. 'I've found the same,' he said simply. Then he asked her, 'How many years did you go through?'

'Ten.'

'Hmm... I went through fifteen,' he mused.

'What can we do now?' asked Jane.

Gerald was deep in thought. 'It's very strange,' he admitted.

'But where can we go from here?'

'We have to try a different line of research,' replied Gerald. 'Extend our search area.' He added, 'Or perhaps an error has been made somewhere... Incidentally, have you had any contact with Mrs Marshall?'

Jane suddenly remembered the small amount of progress she had made. 'Not Mrs Marshall, no. Apparently she died two years ago. I spoke to her sister on Wednesday.'

'Any information?' Gerald asked eagerly.

Jane shook her head. 'No. Her sister was a bit hesitant over the telephone, but I'm still hoping I can get to see her.'

Gerald nodded. Suddenly he glanced at his watch. 'Oh dear. I must go. I've got an appointment at the dentist.'

'Oh, you must. Don't let me keep you.'

With that Gerald went on his way, muttering something about seeing Jane over the weekend.

'Bye,' Jane called after him.

Gerald raised his hand as he disappeared from view.

Jane made her way up to her apartment. Meeting Gerald had

brought back the surprise –shock, almost – of finding no record of Ruth Ashington's birth. It seemed almost unbelievable that she had come up against yet another block in her efforts to find out who she really was. It always surprised her that Gerald appeared to take everything in his stride when it came to these obstacles in family history. In her circumstances it was something of a comfort and she was glad of his calm and methodical approach to things. She was quite confident that he would come up with the answer about Ruth Ashington.

She had a snack for her lunch and then began to make preparations for the evening. She dug out her small suitcase from the tiny storeroom each apartment had and started to collect together the things she needed for the evening and the overnight stay.

While she was doing this her mobile phone rang. There was no mistaking the distinctive sound. Must be Bob, she thought. She retrieved it from the bed where it was lying with a host of other things ready for packing and pressed the button.

'Hello,' she said gaily.

But it was a woman's voice at the other end.

'Is that you, Jane?'

Jane thought the voice sounded familiar, but she simply answered, 'Yes.'

'It's Margaret. I'm dreadfully sorry to call you at home on your day off, but I thought you might like to know that Mrs Barton phoned.'

Jane was suddenly quite excited. She responded cheerfully, 'No, that's fine, Margaret. What did she say?'

Margaret sounded relieved. 'Well, she asked an awful lot of questions about you – did you work here? What did you do? What were you like? She even asked how old you were. I told her we'd been expecting her to phone, as you'd asked me to, but of course I didn't tell her anything personal about you. She ended up by asking me to get you to phone her. I wrote down her number—'

'That's fine, Margaret,' broke in Jane. 'I've got her number. I

195

really appreciate you letting me know. I'll give her a ring straight away. She's somebody who I think can help me with my family history.'

After Margaret's helpful gesture, Jane felt obliged to give those brief details of what it was all about. So far nobody at work knew about her search. She would certainly not say anything about not knowing who she really was at this stage to work colleagues.

Margaret appeared to accept the explanation without question. 'I didn't know you were into that,' she said. 'My sister's husband has been researching their families.'

'It's a popular pastime now,' added Jane.

It was Margaret who ended the conversation. 'Jane, I must go. There's another call coming in.'

Jane quickly responded. 'Thanks awfully for phoning me.'

'No problem. Have a lovely evening.'

'Thank you. I'll tell you about it on Monday. Bye for now, and thanks again.'

'Bye.'

And with that Margaret was gone.

Suddenly everything had changed. Elizabeth Barton had rung the office to make enquiries about her. It must mean that she would agree to a meeting. Jane couldn't wait to make that important call. She dashed into the hall to retrieve her notebook from her work bag. Even though the number was now quite familiar, she didn't trust her memory enough to dial without checking – just in case.

With trembling fingers she keyed the number. The telephone seemed to ring for a long time. Suddenly it was answered. Jane recognised Elizabeth Barton's voice.

'Hello.'

'Hello. Is that Mrs Barton? This is Jane Carroll. I've just received your message.'

'Oh, hello dear.'

Plunge straight in, thought Jane. 'I was wondering if you would be agreeable to me coming to see you now.'

There was a slight pause. 'Well... I suppose so.' Elizabeth sounded quite hesitant.

Jane was determined. 'When would it be convenient for me to visit you?'

'Well, not Monday or Wednesday mornings and not Thursday afternoons.'

Jane already had a day in mind. 'What about Tuesday afternoon?' she asked hopefully.

'Yes... That would be all right.' There was again some hesitation in the reply.

'About two o'clock?' suggested Jane. She could take an extended lunch break.

'Yes. That would be all right.'

'I'll look forward to seeing you then.' Jane was keen to get everything fixed.

'Very well, dear.'

'Until Tuesday then. I'll look forward to meeting you.'

'Yes. Goodbye.'

'Goodbye, Mrs Barton.'

There was a click at the other end of the line. Jane felt ecstatic. The day was getting even better. She had an appointment with Mrs Marshall's sister! She had a lot of news to tell Bob now. That thought brought her down to earth with a bump. If she was to stick to the schedule she had worked out, she had to get a move on. She hurried back into the bedroom.

It was close to half past four when she checked into the hotel where Bob had booked accommodation for the night. She was surprised to find that it appeared to be quite an upmarket establishment, and bigger than she had expected. There was an even greater surprise when she took the lift up to the fifth floor and found the room. Turning the key in the lock she threw open the door and almost gave a gasp of astonishment. She was in a small sitting room. Dumping her suitcase on the floor and closing the door, she explored her surroundings. A large en suite bedroom opened up from the sitting area. The bathroom had a giant bath in it as well as a shower. This was a VIP suite, she decided. Bob had certainly pushed the boat out.

She quickly unpacked the few items she had brought. Bob had told her that he would most likely arrive by half past five, but as he was working in London he said he would telephone her when he was on his way. That gave her plenty of time to be ready by the time he arrived. She wandered into the bathroom. She was tempted to try out the gorgeous bath but decided that could be a treat for later and made do with a shower to freshen up. Her mobile rang just as she was finishing. Enveloping herself in one of the large bath towels provided she dashed into the bedroom and picked up her mobile from the bed, where she had dumped it.

'Hello,' she answered quickly.

'Hi. It's Bob. I'm just leaving work. See you in twenty minutes.'

'Super. See you soon.'

They didn't waste time on niceties.

Jane flew back into the bathroom and stood there pondering as she hastily dried herself. Should she change into her dress, or not? She decided against it. No. She would make the grand entrance later. Instead, she slipped into her cosy white dressing gown. She even put on the flimsy travel slippers she had brought but seldom wore. An idea was bubbling in her brain for later.

She had just sat down in one of the easy chairs in the sitting room when there was a tap at the door. She glanced at her watch. Bob's timing was just a minute out.

She threw open the door. Bob stood there smiling, a suit in a plastic cover in his hand and a shoulder bag over his arm. He stepped into the room past her, dropped his bag and draped the suit over the back of a convenient chair. The next instant he had her in his arms.

'Hello again, gorgeous.' He kissed her several times.

'You kept me waiting twenty-one minutes. You told me twenty.' Jane pretended to scold him.

Bob grinned at her. 'Sorry. I had to wait for the lift.'

'OK. I forgive you.'

Jane put her arm around his waist and gently walked him towards the armchairs. Bob gratefully sank into the comfort of one of them.

'How was work, darling?' Jane asked, briefly kneeling in front of him.

Bob sighed. 'The studio is actually quite busy, and there was a last-minute job to finish.'

'You must be tired out. Have you had anything to eat or drink?'

Bob thought for a second. 'Yes and no,' he replied. He elaborated. 'Yes to the first – but seeing you has revived me. No to the second. I've had nothing since a cup of coffee and a roll at lunchtime.'

'Oh, poor you.' Jane suddenly had an idea. She looked at him enquiringly. 'Shall I make you a cup of coffee or tea?' she asked.

Bob glanced across at the side table with the tea-making facilities on it.

'That's the best idea you've had so far,' he replied, grinning.

Jane pretended to pout for an instant, but she was already at work on his shoes. She pulled them off, one after the other.

'You sit here and relax. I'll make us something. Tea or coffee?' She had already jumped up.

'Coffee, please,' replied Bob. 'It might keep me alert.'

'I'll do that without any coffee,' Jane quipped cheerfully over her shoulder as she walked over to the side table.

She made two cups of coffee and brought them to the low table in front of the two armchairs. She sat down facing Bob, pulling the dressing gown tightly around her body. She looked around the room. Then she asked the question that had been on her mind ever since she had arrived. 'Bob, this room must have cost the earth.' She looked enquiringly at him.

Bob took a sip of his coffee. He gave a little smile. 'Not really. There's a story attached to it,' he remarked casually.

'But it's a VIP suite,' Jane protested.

Bob stretched out in his chair and glanced around him. He looked at Jane and smiled. 'Actually, the explanation is that Jeff and I have been taking some photographs of the hotel for a publicity brochure they are going to produce. I've got to know the manager quite well and as I was looking for somewhere to stay tonight I mentioned it to him. This is the result.'

'But it must he horrendously expensive,' Jane butted in.

Bob shook his head and smiled again. 'A VIP suite if it was not already booked, for the price of a standard double room – that was the deal.'

'It's fantastic! You haven't seen the bathroom yet – or the bedroom,' Jane added, raising her eyebrows.

He grinned. 'Pleasures for later.'

Jane was thinking of a suitable reply when Bob changed the subject. As he took another sip of coffee he became more serious.

'Any developments on the family history front? Any contact with Mrs Marshall?' he asked, studying Jane's face for her response.

Jane suddenly remembered that she had a lot of news. She started to tell Bob everything that had happened recently, ending up with the announcement that she had an appointment with Elizabeth Barton the following Tuesday.

Bob listened intently, waiting until she had finished before he responded, 'That's fantastic! Well done!'

'I am worried about there being no birth record for Ruth Ashington, though,' remarked Jane.

Bob thought for an instant. 'I can think of one or two possible explanations,' he replied.

Jane looked at him hopefully.

He continued. 'Her mother might have been married before, or Ruth might have been an illegitimate child.'

They looked at each other for a second, Jane trying to take in Bob's suggestions. Suddenly, the penny dropped.

'Of course!' she exclaimed excitedly. 'That could well be the explanation.' Her brain raced into action. 'I must see what Gerald thinks of that idea.'

'Perhaps Elizabeth Barton will be able to come up with something,' suggested Bob.

'I do hope so,' replied Jane wistfully.

They chatted on for a while, covering a range of subjects while they finished their coffee. At last they had exhausted all their news.

Bob suddenly looked at his watch, then at Jane. 'Time to get ready, Cinderella,' he announced, grinning.

Jane already had another plan in mind. 'No. I'm almost ready except for my ball gown. You go first,' she said firmly.

Bob readily agreed. He could sense that something was in the air. He was up in an instant and collecting his bag from the floor where he had abandoned it earlier.

He fumbled in the bag for a second and then produced a small, gift-wrapped package. The next second he was presenting Jane with it.

'A little something for this evening,' he explained to a puzzled Jane.

His remark produced a squeal of pleasure from her as she caught sight of the package. 'A present for me? Can I open it?'

'Of course. That's the idea.' With that, he disappeared grinning into the bedroom.

Jane carefully unwrapped the small box, revealing a tiny bottle of scent. She could not resist trying out the contents on her wrist.

It was fifteen minutes before Bob appeared, dressed in an evening suit complete with a frilly shirt and cufflinks. Jane thought he looked extremely handsome. As soon as she saw him she leapt up and threw her arms around him.

She planted a kiss on his lips. 'Thank you for my present, darling.'

'Do you like it?' asked Bob, bemused.

'Mmm. It's wonderful. Here.' She held a wrist up to his nose.

Once he had approved, Jane stood back to admire him. 'You look fabulous! And the shirt — is it new?'

Bob laughed. 'Mrs McGinty's handiwork. You should have seen it before she got to work on it. I haven't worn it for years.'

'She's done a marvellous job,' Jane agreed, laughing.

Bob prompted her to get ready.

'Give me five minutes,' she called as she disappeared into the bedroom, adding, 'I'm going to wear your present.'

The five minutes became ten, before Jane reappeared fully dressed apart from her shoes, which she carried. She felt good in the dress, and her earlier fear that it exposed too much of her had disappeared completely. Her necklace with the deep blue stone really set everything off.

She went over to Bob and sat in a chair opposite him, dropping her shoes on the carpet. Stretching out her feet in front of her, she announced with a wicked grin, 'Prince Charming, do your duty.'

Bob immediately fell into the part. He carefully took Jane's foot and guided it into one of the shoes. When the second one was in place, Jane jumped up and looked down at them admiringly.

'Don't they look great?' she asked. 'They really are beautiful. Thank you, darling.'

Once again she kissed him. Bob held her in an embrace. Her perfume was tantalising. Jane looked at him enquiringly.

'Do you like my new perfume?' she asked.

'It suits Cinderella perfectly,' he replied.

Jane enjoyed every bit of the evening. It was close to eight when they took a taxi to the venue for the dinner dance. The distance from their hotel was walkable, but Bob pointed out that it was better to make the grand arrival by taxi, a decision Jane welcomed. For one thing it was not easy walking in a long evening gown, and for another she had no wish to walk in shoes not intended for dirty pavements.

Jane was surprised to see the attention the guests received on arrival. A small crowd was gathered around the entrance and press photographers' cameras flashed.

'I didn't realise it was an event that attracted so much attention,' she whispered to Bob as she took his arm and they entered.

Bob smiled at her. 'It's very popular with the entertainment world and celebrities,' he replied quietly.

When the dancing started, Jane was pleased to discover that her old skill had not diminished from lack of use. She had learnt to dance while still at the orphanage and had become quite proficient. She and Graham had frequently attended events where there was dancing. However, she could now count the years since she had been on a dance floor, and she was afraid her skills might have grown rusty. She was surprised and intrigued to discover that Bob's skill surpassed even her own; he whirled her around the dance floor like a professional.

'Where did you learn to dance so beautifully?' she whispered.

'When we were teenagers my sister wanted to learn to dance and I was dragged along as well,' Bob explained with a chuckle.

'But you're so good!' Jane exclaimed in his ear.

'We used to go in for medals. I got a silver. Cissy got a gold.' He laughed.

'I'd like to meet her.'

'You will,' replied Bob firmly.

Towards the end of dinner, during the serving of coffee, Bob suddenly took hold of Jane's hand across the table. 'How's Cinderella?' he asked, looking admiringly at her.

Jane leaned towards him. 'Darling, I feel fantastic. It's made me forget all about work and about my ancestry – who I am or who I might be. I really feel like Cinderella tonight.'

She stroked Bob's hand. 'How about you?' she asked.

He smiled. 'I was just thinking of another Cinderella.'

Jane waited. She knew there was more to come.

Bob continued, his eyes fixed on her. 'I was thinking of the Cinderella I found stranded late at night. The one who walked barefoot in the snow.'

'And the one who locked her bedroom door,' said Jane with a wicked grin.

Bob was more serious. 'I'm glad you did in a way. It showed me what you were made of.' He still had hold of her hand.

Jane smiled at him. 'I know what you mean,' she replied softly.

'We've come a long way since then, haven't we?' asked Bob, still studying her intently.

Jane nodded. She was beginning to guess where the conversation was heading.

'And I've enjoyed every minute of it. I've felt alive again.' She smiled.

Bob hesitated for a few seconds. He seemed to be uncertain how to proceed.

Jane jumped in. 'And you – have you enjoyed my company?' she asked, her voice very soft.

Bob nodded. 'Absolutely.' He fumbled in his pocket with his free hand. 'That's why I would like to cement our friendship with this.'

In his hand he held a ring. 'May I?' he asked.

'Yes, please,' whispered Jane.

The next instant he had slipped the ring onto her engagement finger. 'Is it a yes?' he asked.

Jane nodded. She felt quite choked up. She strove to recover. 'Of course it is,' she replied. 'Yes, a thousand times over.' Her emotions were getting the better of her. 'But I feel all soppy and tearful, just when I should be the opposite,' she almost sobbed.

She could never remember clearly quite what happened in the next few minutes. There she was, boiling over with pleasure and happiness, yet with tears threatening to engulf her. Bob continued to hold her hand. It was only when their actions were beginning to attract the attention of nearby diners that they released hands.

Later that evening reality crept up on Jane again. She returned from the ladies' room proudly displaying the ring with its blue stone, a good match for the necklace she was wearing. As she sat down opposite Bob again, he could see that there was something on her mind she wanted to say. It was not long in coming.

She looked at the ring on her finger, then at Bob. 'Darling. I've been thinking. I'm going to wear the ring on my finger for the rest of this evening, but after that I'm going to wear it round my neck until I know who I really am. Then you can put it on my finger again for keeps.'

It was the early hours of the next day by the time they returned to their hotel. As they emerged from the lift, Jane put her arm around Bob.

'The end of the ball for Cinderella,' he said in a hushed voice.

Jane halted briefly and obediently slipped off both her shoes, abandoning them on the carpet.

'I was supposed to do that at midnight,' she whispered, giggling.

Bob chuckled as he opened the door and let a barefoot Jane walk past him into the room. He disappeared for a second and then reappeared a moment later with the shoes. Jane was sitting in an armchair, admiring the ring on her finger. She looked up as Bob walked towards her.

He placed the shoes at her feet. 'No point in trying them on. We know they fit.' He laughed.

Jane continued examining the ring and then looked up at Bob. She spoke softly. 'Darling, you have made me very happy tonight.' She was quite serious. And then, as if speaking her thoughts, she added, 'Happiness I once thought I'd never experience again.'

Bob knelt beside her. He took hold of her left hand. 'Then we are matched in our happiness,' he whispered, as he leaned across to kiss her.

Chapter 23

It was the knocking at the door that jerked Jane out of sleep. For a moment she wondered where she was. Then, realising that she was in the hotel, she grabbed Bob's arm to rouse him.

'There's somebody at the door!' she almost shouted in his ear.

Bob was alert immediately. 'It's breakfast arriving,' he announced as he swung out of bed and hurried into the sitting room, struggling to get into a dressing gown as he went. Jane heard him call out, 'Coming!'

She lingered for a couple of seconds and then it occurred to her that she needed the bathroom urgently. She leapt out of bed and dashed to the desired comfort zone in a flash, in the process almost falling over her nightdress, which had been cast off a few hours previously. Five minutes later she reappeared, refreshed and wearing one of the fluffy white dressing gowns provided by the hotel. Bob had wheeled the breakfast trolley into the bedroom.

'Mmm, breakfast in bed!' she exclaimed excitedly, as she crept under the duvet once more.

Bob disappeared into the bathroom for a couple of minutes. When he came back he busied himself with the trolley.

'Tea or coffee, madam?' he asked, turning to Jane.

Jane stifled a yawn. 'It had better be coffee. It might wake me up. I'm still half asleep.'

Bob handed her a cup of coffee and a plate with croissants, butter and jam. As soon as he had served himself, he returned to bed. Jane was admiring the ring that now graced her finger. She turned to Bob, her lips ready for a kiss.

'Darling, it's a beautiful ring and it was a marvellous night. It couldn't have been better.'

'Let there be many more like it,' replied Bob as he moved towards her to meet her lips.

They kissed briefly and Jane looked at the ring again before turning her attention to breakfast. 'You don't mind if I do as I said I would, do you? About the ring, I mean,' she asked anxiously.

Bob smiled at her. 'Of course not,' he said simply.

Jane tried to explain how she felt. 'It's just this not knowing who I am. I want to be sure of my name before I make any commitment. I know it's a bit silly, but that's how I feel.' She looked at Bob for reassurance.

He smiled at her again. 'I know how you must feel. As soon as we find out your real name, we'll do it all over again.'

Jane snuggled up to him. 'Thank you,' she whispered.

It was late in the morning when they returned to Jane's apartment. Apart from a walk along the river and a refreshing drink at a local pub, they did little for the rest of the day except chat about their new status. They agreed that for the present they wanted to continue as they were without any definite plans for the future. As far as they both were concerned, getting engaged was merely a sign of their approval of an event in the distant future.

Jane kept to her vow. A little later, when she was in her bedroom unpacking her suitcase, she took the opportunity provided by being on her own. She gave one wistful look at the deep blue stone in its diamond setting as she slipped it slowly off her finger. As she did so she wondered vaguely how Bob had known which size to buy, for it fitted perfectly. It had been the same with the shoes. He seemed to have an uncanny knack of finding out these intimate details without actually asking her. Even Graham had not been too ingenious on such matters. She rediscovered the fine gold chain she knew lurked in her jewellery box and threaded the ring onto it. Next she hung the chain round her neck. When she was with Bob in the future, she vowed, that's where the ring would be, close to her heart, until she really knew who she was.

When she went back into the lounge, she perched on the settee beside Bob, unfastened the top button on her blouse, and then slowly and silently drew out the chain with the captured ring to show a bemused and wondering Bob.

'You see, darling, I kept my promise. The next time your beautiful ring is on my finger I'll know who I really am.'

'I'll make sure it's the first thing I do – return the ring to its rightful place.' Bob placed his hand behind her neck and slowly drew her towards him.

'I can't wait for it to happen,' murmured Jane.

They kissed briefly, and then Jane drew away from Bob. She looked at him, her expression serious and enquiring. 'You do think we'll find out, don't you?' She now had a concerned look. 'I mean, find out what my proper name is.' She searched his face for some reassurance.

'We have to,' he replied with conviction. 'If we keep pegging away we're bound to come up with the truth at some point.'

'I do hope so,' Jane replied, with a little sigh.

'You don't know what sort of information you may be able to obtain from Mrs Marshall's sister on Tuesday,' Bob pointed out.

'No, I suppose not.' Jane gave another sigh, almost to herself, and then suddenly looked at her watch. 'Hey, look at the time!' she exclaimed. 'Time we had some lunch.'

Bob wanted to take her out to a pub for a meal, but she shook her head.

'I've got some salad for us,' she explained. 'Too many meals out will make me fat,' she added, making a face at Bob as she got up to go into the kitchen. 'You like me nice and slim, don't you?' she called over her shoulder, smiling.

'Sure do. Keep it that way,' Bob called after her, laughing, as he stood up from the settee to help her.

They prepared the meal together, Bob busy at the sink washing a lettuce, and Jane slicing up tomatoes and dealing with the ham she had bought.

While they were relaxing in the lounge with a mug of coffee

after their meal, Bob outlined his plans for starting up a new business with Jeff. 'We've taken the photographs for several advertising projects, such as the one for the hotel we stayed at last night. Jeff and I believe there is very good potential to develop this kind of work. We think we can offer a package for the whole job and produce the entire brochure.'

He looked at Jane for her thoughts on the subject.

'That's a fantastic idea!' she exclaimed. 'But won't it be expensive to set up a business like that?'

Bob shook his head. 'Comparatively low, in fact, as we already have the premises. We can set up an office on the floor above.' He was eager to explain a bit more. 'We feel that we do a greater part of the job already. The rest is really just words, tweaking the design and sourcing a good firm of printers to work with.' He added with a grin, 'We have a company in mind.'

'That sounds brilliant,' Jane replied enthusiastically. 'Perhaps I could even help out,' she enquired tentatively, with a smile.

Bob chuckled. 'I'm sure we could use your talent at times. That is…' He hesitated, smiling again. 'If you aren't too expensive.'

Jane gave one of her little laughs. 'Oh, I'm horrendously expensive. And there would have to be strings attached,' she joked with a wicked little grin.

'I would have to consider any offer you made very carefully and in great detail,' Bob replied, joining in the humour.

They talked for quite a long time. Gradually their conversation became more infrequent and after a while they both dozed off, Jane's head resting on Bob's shoulder. It was the sound of the telephone ringing that shocked Jane awake. Half asleep, she stumbled into the hall. She grabbed the telephone as she stifled a yawn.

'Hello.'

A familiar voice answered. 'Ah, Jane. You are in. Gerald here.'

'Hello, Gerald.'

'I hope I'm not disturbing you.'

Jane smiled to herself. Gerald was always so polite. 'No, not at all. It's always nice to hear from you and Anna.'

'Anna's gone shopping, but I was wondering…' There was a slight hesitation before Gerald. 'I was wondering if I might see you for a few minutes.'

'Of course you can. Now, if you like. Shall we come down to you? Bob is here with me.'

'I'll come to see you in a few minutes, if I may.'

'That's fine. See you soon.'

'OK. Goodbye for now.'

Jane replaced the handset. She guessed that Gerald did not want to invite anybody in while Anna was out. She hurried back to the lounge. Bob was still sitting on the settee. He turned to look at her enquiringly.

'That was Gerald. He wants to come up.'

'Perhaps he's found out something more about your past,' suggested Bob cheerfully.

'Oh, I do hope so.'

It was at this point that Jane remembered her tousled appearance and Gerald's old-fashioned view of women. She dashed to the bedroom to freshen up. The front door bell rang while she was still absent. It was Bob who answered Gerald's ring.

'Hello, Gerald. Come in.'

He stepped aside to allow Gerald to pass.

'Hello, Bob. I don't want to intrude on your afternoon…' began Gerald, looking a little anxious.

'No, it's fine. Come into the lounge, Gerald.' Jane had just reappeared from the bedroom.

'No, no. I won't stay. But I just thought you should know about a new development in your family history.'

Jane was of course immediately eager to know what Gerald had found out. 'Oh, please tell me. What is it?' she asked.

Gerald fumbled to extract a piece of paper from his pocket. He looked at it and then cleared his throat. Jane and Bob waited.

Gerald started to speak. 'I just had to let you know about this.' He looked at the piece of paper again. 'I heard from Eric this morning. He's been doing some more research into the Ashington family.'

He stopped and looked first at Jane and then at Bob before continuing. 'I knew Eric would. He doesn't like unanswered questions.'

'But what's he found out?' Jane was becoming anxious.

Gerald looked at them both again, almost as if to ensure that he had their full attention, and then he announced, 'Ann Ashington was married twice.'

'What!' Jane was quite taken aback.

'Do you have the details?' asked Bob.

Gerald nodded. 'Yes. Ann Ashington was briefly married to a John Henderson. Ann's daughter Ruth was born after they divorced.'

Gerald looked at his audience for a reaction.

Jane collapsed onto a nearby chair. She struggled to fully comprehend this new information.

'But... but...' she stammered, fighting to get the words out, 'that means I could be that child – Ann Ashington's daughter.'

She looked up at Gerald, seeking confirmation.

'It's quite possible,' he replied calmly.

'Is Eric sure about this new information?' asked Bob.

Gerald nodded. 'Absolutely. Knowing Eric, I'm confident he wouldn't make any statement unless he was one hundred per cent sure of his facts. I'll guarantee he will supply us with documents to prove what he has found out.'

Jane was still sitting on the chair. She was now trying to work out how everything fitted together. Her face had a puzzled expression. 'But if I had a mother and apparently was part of a wealthy family, why was I put into an orphanage and why was my name changed on documents?' She looked at Gerald, hopeful of some sort of explanation.

'That's what is intriguing Eric,' he replied. 'At this stage it doesn't all make sense. But I'm confident he will come up with some answers.'

'But it feels as if everybody else is doing my family history for me, and I feel quite embarrassed by that.' Jane was looking quite worried.

'Don't worry about that,' Gerald replied with a little laugh. 'When it comes to family history, both Eric and I are fanatics and we both like a mystery to unravel.'

Jane was about to comment, but Gerald spoke again. 'It will be interesting to see whether you can glean any new information on the subject of the name change at the orphanage when you meet Mrs Marshall's sister.'

Jane suddenly remembered that she had not been able to update Gerald on her efforts in this direction. She felt even more embarrassed by her delay. 'Oh, Gerald, I'm dreadfully sorry, but I've not given you the latest on this. Being busy with other things most of yesterday drove it right out of my head.'

Gerald smiled at her sympathetically.

'We had a night out last night, and didn't get back until this morning,' explained Bob.

Jane hastened to fill Gerald in on her progress. 'I managed to speak to Mrs Marshall's sister on the phone yesterday. I've got an appointment to see her on Tuesday.'

'Excellent. Let's hope that she can throw more light on things,' replied Gerald.

'Sisters often confide little secrets to each other,' remarked Bob thoughtfully.

Gerald nodded enthusiastically. 'That's absolutely correct.' He turned to Jane. 'You know, Jane, in family history research, the biggest clues can come from the most unexpected sources. Don't dismiss any opportunity.'

Jane smiled at him. 'Thank you for all your encouragement and your involvement in my quest. I do really appreciate it. And thank Eric for me as well.'

'I will.' Gerald glanced at his watch. 'Oh dear. I must go now. Anna will have returned from the shops.'

There was a bit of a flurry as he departed hurriedly in the midst of expressions of thanks from Jane and Bob. 'Our greetings to Anna,' Jane called after him. As soon as he had disappeared from view, she and Bob returned to the lounge.

Jane sat down on the settee again. In spite of her enthusiastic response to Gerald, now that she was alone with Bob a state of gloom swept over her. She put her head in her hands.

Bob sat down beside her. He took hold of one of her hands.

'Cheer up,' he said, rubbing her back.

Jane looked at him, anxiety written on her face. When she spoke it was slowly, searching for the words as she went. 'It's this feeling of not knowing. Now it looks as if I could be one of three people – Jane Carroll, Ruth Ashington, or now, it seems, even a Ruth Henderson.' She took a pause, still deep in thought. Then she continued. 'It's all the questions that keep coming up. Why was I in an orphanage? Why was there a name change?'

'There's got to be an answer somewhere. It's just finding it. If we keep chipping away at it, we must find something at some point,' replied Bob.

'That's fine, but in the meantime I feel as if I'm a fraud. I don't know my real name.'

Jane looked miserable and Bob could sense that tears were close to the surface. He did his best to be logical. 'This guy Eric seems to know what he's doing. I was very impressed with what he's come up with regarding Ann Ashington.'

'That's another thing. He and Gerald seem to be doing all my family history research while I sit about and do nothing,' replied Jane glumly.

'Except sit and moan,' Bob suggested, starting to laugh.

It was the tipping point. Jane suddenly snapped out of her gloom. Her face broke into a smile. 'You're right. I'm a misery, aren't I? I'm getting all this free help from good old Gerald and his friend, and all I do is grizzle.'

Bob was about to butt in, but Jane suddenly thought of something else. She looked at him with a serious expression on her face. 'You know, I'm actually looking forward to meeting Mrs

Marshall's sister on Tuesday. I've just got this feeling that she may have some information.'

'Good for you. That's the spirit,' said Bob with a laugh. He became more serious again as he followed up with a question. 'What makes you think so?' he asked.

Jane thought for an instant and then with a little smile replied, 'Oh, just a woman's intuition.'

Chapter 24

Jane found the journey to Elizabeth Barton's house more difficult by public transport than she had anticipated. By the time she had left the bus in the High Street and navigated her way through several roads with the aid of her A–Z map, it was already a minute or two past two when she reached the house. This time she marched up the path and sounded the knocker on the door. She heard somebody moving somewhere in the distance. She waited for what seemed quite a few minutes before the door was opened.

A grey-haired elderly woman stood in front of her.

'Mrs Barton?' asked Jane holding out her hand. 'I'm Jane Carroll.'

'Yes, that's right.' Elizabeth Barton's voice sounded much more powerful to Jane than it had over the phone.

'I'm very pleased to meet you, Mrs Barton.'

The handshake that greeted Jane was limp, but her host was smiling. 'Do come in, dear,' she said, standing aside to let Jane enter the narrow hallway.

Jane followed her into the sitting room. She was surprised to see how agile she appeared to be – quite the opposite of what her telephone voice had conveyed.

As they entered the room, Jane was surprised to see another woman of a similar age to Mrs Barton sitting in one of the chairs. 'This is my neighbour, Mrs Beth Browne. I invited her to keep me company,' explained Mrs Barton. 'And this is Jane Carroll,' she added, addressing her neighbour.

Jane could see that the neighbour's presence made sense. It

offered just that little bit of security for an older person living alone.

Jane received a fragile handshake from Mrs Browne, and a brief 'Hello' in reply to her greeting of 'Good afternoon.'

'Do sit down, dear,' said Mrs Barton. Jane selected a chair and immediately her host grabbed up some clothing that was lying on the seat. 'I'm so sorry this room is in such a mess, but I've only just returned from visiting my sister in Australia,' she explained.

'Did you have a nice time?' asked Jane politely, as she sat down.

'Yes, thank you, dear. But such a journey. I had no idea it was such a long flight.' Mrs Barton was beginning to look stressed.

Jane took the opportunity to change the subject by opening her bag and taking out the latest issue of *Discerning Woman*. She had popped it into her bag as a little act of courtesy and also because she thought it might help to reassure Mrs Barton that she was who she said she was. She handed it to her host. 'I brought this for you. It's only just gone on sale.'

The magazine was accepted with a cautious smile. 'That's very nice of you, dear. Thank you,' said Mrs Barton. 'Now,' she asked, 'can I get you a drink of tea?'

Jane smiled politely. 'That would be lovely,' she replied.

Mrs Barton hurried away and almost immediately her neighbour followed her, muttering something about giving her a hand.

Their absence gave Jane an opportunity to glance round the room. It was small, as the house itself appeared to be, and had a very old-fashioned air to it. The furniture and carpet were long past their prime. A cabinet full of china ornaments stood against one wall and there were large flowerpots dotted around filled with leafy plants. The mantelpiece above the old-fashioned fireplace with its wood and tile surround was crammed with more china ornaments and photographs. Prints of Victorian paintings decorated the free wall space. It was a rather depressing room with a musty smell and the feel of not being used a lot.

After only a short time the two women returned, Mrs Barton

216

bearing a tray with cups and saucers and a teapot with a tea cosy, and Mrs Browne carrying a tray with cake and plates. Once the refreshments had been placed on a side table, Mrs Barton turned her attention to Jane and asked her whether she took milk and sugar. Jane accepted the delicate china cup and saucer and selected the smallest piece of cake from the plate offered. When everybody had been served, her host sat down opposite her.

'You said that you would like to see me about something, dear,' was her opening remark.

'Yes, that's correct. I was wondering if you could help me solve a question about my past,' explained Jane.

'Well I don't know if I can, dear, but I'll do my best,' replied Mrs Barton with a smile.

Under the watchful eyes of the two women, Jane put down her tea, opened up her briefcase and took out a copy of her birth certificate. She began to explain her mission. 'Well, you see, Mrs Barton—'

'Oh, do call me Elizabeth, dear.'

Jane gave a smile of acknowledgement. 'Thank you, Elizabeth...' She hesitated for a second, picking up the strands of what she wanted to say. She continued quickly. 'Most of my early life I spent in the orphanage where your sister was matron. When I left there I was given this birth certificate, which says my name is Jane Carroll.'

She handed the certificate to Elizabeth and waited a few minutes while she put spectacles on and looked at the document. When Elizabeth eventually looked up, Jane continued, 'I started looking into my past recently and I discovered that the Jane Carroll named on the certificate had died as a baby.'

She took a few seconds to let Elizabeth absorb what she had just related. As there was no response from her, Jane carried on. 'I went back to the orphanage and discovered that I had been admitted there under the name of Ruth Ashington. I had been hoping that your sister could tell me what happened.'

Once Jane had finished speaking she again looked at Elizabeth for a reaction. It was not long in coming. Elizabeth handed the certificate back to her. 'The details you have are correct. I'm afraid Jane Carroll, my niece, did die as a baby. James Carroll was my brother.' She waited a few seconds and then added. 'I'm very sorry, dear.' There was clearly a tenseness about her now.

Jane's brain plunged into overdrive. Here she was, just receiving information she already had. If she was to find out any more about her past, she knew she had to proceed slowly with Elizabeth. After taking a sip of her tea, her next remark sounded almost casual and inconsequential.

'Obviously a mistake has been made somewhere, but what is puzzling is how the name Ruth Ashington is involved.'

As if to emphasise the unimportance of the comment, she turned her attention to her piece of cake.

Her downbeat approach seemed to work. After listening intently, Elizabeth appeared to relax a bit. She gave Jane a little smile. 'Well, Jane… Can I call you Jane?'

'Yes, of course,' Jane responded quickly.

'Jane, I have no idea how you became to be called Carroll. Perhaps a mistake was made.' There was a slight pause. Elizabeth was clearly pondering what to say as she took a sip of her tea. She replaced the cup on its saucer. 'But I can tell you a little bit about Ruth Ashington.'

'Please do.' Jane tried not to sound too eager.

Elizabeth smiled again. 'You see, I looked after Ruth Ashington from the time she was very young until she went into the orphanage.'

The significance of Elizabeth's words suddenly struck Jane. Her response came out in a rush.

'But… But that means you were the person who took me to the orphanage – and that would then mean that my real name is Ruth Ashington.' She looked at Elizabeth for confirmation.

Elizabeth's reaction was almost casual. 'Well, I certainly took a Ruth Ashington to the orphanage,' she replied with a slight smile.

Jane was not going to give up. 'I remember being taken there. I remember crying a lot and I also remember I had a doll with a red dress.' Once again she waited for Elizabeth to confirm what she had just said.

Elizabeth seemed somewhat taken aback by Jane's statement. She reacted almost excitedly. 'That's right. I bought you that doll.'

The facts were seeping into Jane. Here was virtual proof that her real name was Ruth Ashington. But why, and how? The questions still raged through her thoughts. It seemed to her that it was ages before she was able to respond to Elizabeth. When she eventually spoke, it was slowly and calmly.

'That does really make it appear as if I am Ruth Ashington, but can you tell me a little bit more about my early life? Can you tell me about my parents? What were they like?'

Elizabeth seemed to be quite happy to talk about this subject. She took a moment, clearly recalling a time past, and then started to chat quite freely. 'I never knew your father. You were a baby when I was employed by Miles and Ann Ashington to look after you.' She interrupted herself to explain. 'You see, dear, I obtained the job through an employment agency in Bristol.'

Jane thought for a few seconds. She remembered something else she wanted to say to Elizabeth. 'A friend of mine, who is helping me with my family history, has discovered that Ann Ashington was married to somebody called Henderson. I could be from that marriage.'

Elizabeth's reply was brief and vague. 'I never heard anything about that, dear.'

Jane decided to change the subject. 'Can you tell me something about Ann Ashington – my mother?' she asked.

Elizabeth thought for a moment. 'She was a very reclusive person, so strange in a young woman. She was incredibly wealthy, yet she lived alone in a huge house with just a few servants around her. She didn't seem to have any social life.'

'What about me? How did she come to have me?'

Elizabeth gave a little laugh. 'That puzzled everybody. Apparently she disappeared for a few months and then reappeared with a baby. Certainly no explanation was given to anybody I knew.'

'Did she like me? Was I a wanted child?' Jane asked.

Elizabeth shook her head. 'It never appeared so. She hardly came near you. She left everything to me. It was quite odd, really.'

There was a few moments' silence between them, Jane trying to absorb what she had just been told, and Elizabeth waiting for a response from her.

It was Elizabeth who spoke first. 'I'm sorry if what I'm telling you is upsetting, dear,' she said kindly.

Jane forced herself to give a reassuring smile. 'I'm sorry. It's just that I'm trying to take everything on board. There still seem to be so many unanswered questions... That is...' she paused for a second. 'That is, if I *am* Ruth Ashington.'

Elizabeth was very sympathetic. 'I'm dreadfully sorry I have to relate all this to you. It must be very stressful for you, but if I can help in any way, I will.'

Jane smiled at her again. 'Thank you. That's really very sweet of you.' She thought for a few seconds and then asked the question that was uppermost in her mind. 'Can you tell me how I came to be in the orphanage?'

Elizabeth responded quickly. 'That was Miles Ashington.'

'How does he fit in?'

Elizabeth fiddled with her teaspoon in the saucer. She appeared to be thinking deeply. There was a brief silence before she answered. As she spoke, she gazed at the cup and saucer she was holding.

'I understand that he appeared when you were still a baby. Apparently quite suddenly Ann introduced him as her husband and he became the master of the house.'

'Just like that? There was no previous knowledge of him?' Jane was puzzled.

Elizabeth shook her head. 'Certainly none that I and the other staff knew about,' she replied, looking at Jane again.

Jane remembered another question she wanted to ask. 'How come he was called Ashington as well?'

Elizabeth shook her head. Her reply was vague. 'I don't know. I did hear once that he was a distant cousin of the family.' She added,

'I know some people thought he had married her for her money.'

'Perhaps he did,' suggested Jane.

Again Elizabeth shook her head. 'I don't think so. They appeared to be very much in love.'

'But what about my mother?' Jane was determined to glean as much information as possible from Elizabeth.

Elizabeth readily continued. 'A few months after her marriage to Miles she became pregnant. Sadly, she lost the child and after that she always seemed to be ill. She became quite depressive and at times suicidal, I believe.'

'And Miles – how did he cope with that?'

Elizabeth smiled at the recollection. 'He was always so supportive and caring. He was a charming man. He was quite distraught when Ann died.'

'When was that?'

'You were only two at the time,' answered Elizabeth.

Jane returned to her original question. 'But the orphanage,' she asked. 'How did I get there?'

Elizabeth answered her immediately. 'I looked after you for a while and then Miles Ashington felt that it would be better if you spent some time with other children, so it was arranged that I would take you there.'

She looked at Jane with a mixture of affection and sadness. 'I was very sad. I had grown so fond of you.'

'I remember that day. I know I cried for a long time and everything was very strange.' A feeling of sadness came over Jane. It had not been a pleasant time in her life. Her memories of the event prompted another question. 'But I was there for years and years. Nobody came near me. I thought I really was an orphan with no family.'

'I left the employment of Miles Ashington immediately after that,' replied Elizabeth. 'I had no idea what happened to you. I didn't see my sister very often, and she never talked about the orphanage when we did meet.'

Elizabeth finished looking at Jane, almost as if she required

Jane's forgiveness, in spite of sounding almost defensive during her explanation.

The sadness continued to cloud over Jane. 'Did you never think about me?' she asked softly.

Elizabeth was eager to answer. 'Well, you see, dear, just after that I met my future husband. We got married and moved to London and I've been here ever since.' Elizabeth smiled at Jane. 'Are you married, dear?'

Jane shook her head. 'I was married for a short time, but my husband died.'

'Oh, I'm sorry to hear that, dear.' Elizabeth looked quite concerned.

'Can you tell us what happened?' It was Mrs Browne who asked the question.

Jane was surprised to hear her speak. So far she had not joined in any of the conversation. She turned to her. 'Graham was killed in a plane crash,' she replied.

Exclamations of sympathy came from the two women, but Jane felt no desire to elaborate and was glad that Elizabeth then changed the subject.

'I hope what I've told you has been of some help, dear.'

Jane did her best to shrug off the melancholy she now felt. She forced a smile. 'It's been quite helpful. Thank you very much for seeing me.'

'Oh, I'm so glad, dear. If there is anything else you want to know, I'll try and help.' Elizabeth sounded as if she meant it.

Jane suddenly thought of something else. 'There is just one thing – Miles Ashington. What happened to him?'

Elizabeth seemed quite surprised. She looked at Jane almost with amusement. 'My dear! Didn't you know? He's quite well known.'

Jane struggled to comprehend. Then the penny dropped. 'You mean…' she stuttered. 'You mean he's the businessman and celebrity who's often in the news?'

Elizabeth smiled. 'Yes, of course.'

Jane was struggling to remember something. Suddenly it came

to her. She voiced her recollection, though it was almost as if she were talking to herself.

'Now I remember! Just after I joined *Discerning Woman*, we did a two-page feature on him. I wasn't involved myself, but apparently he was very charming.'

Elizabeth and her neighbour nodded as if in agreement. The conversation stayed on Miles Ashington for a while, particularly in respect of his public life, which the two women seemed to have gleaned from the media.

After refusing a second cup of tea, Jane took her leave, explaining that she had only taken a few hours off work to be there. Mrs Browne shook her hand and expressed her pleasure at meeting her, and Elizabeth showed her to the door. Jane thanked Elizabeth again and gave her one of her business cards, with the request that she contact her if she recalled anything else she thought might be useful to her. After a handshake and a rather formal kiss on the cheek from Elizabeth, she went on her way.

Elizabeth Barton was worried about Jane's visit. It was something she had not expected to happen, but on the whole she felt that she had handled things very well. Nevertheless, she felt perturbed. After Jane left, Beth wanted to chat, and Elizabeth indulged her, even to the point of making another pot of tea. When Beth eventually departed, Elizabeth became more and more agitated. She tried to take her mind off things by doing the washing up, and then she glanced through the copy of *Discerning Woman* Jane had given her, but it was no good – trying to read it only increased her concerns even more. She knew what she had to do, but she found it difficult to accomplish the task. She picked up the old exercise book she kept all her telephone numbers in and searched its pages for the number she knew was there somewhere. She found it in the end, almost obliterated by the dog-ears at the bottom of the pages. She picked up the telephone several times and replaced it. At last she found the courage to initiate the call she had never anticipated she would have to make.

Chapter 25

Back in the office, Jane found it hard to concentrate on her work. The information that she had received from Elizabeth made her both sad and preoccupied with her past. She had desperately wanted to find out about her ancestry, but now that she was a step nearer to finding out her true name, she found it difficult to relate to the circumstances of her early life. From what Elizabeth had told her it certainly looked as if she was born into the Ashington family, but rather than simplifying things, that discovery seemed to bring up more unanswered questions. Why the secrecy over her birth? Why did Ann Ashington, who was apparently her mother, not want to acknowledge her? Why had her name been changed in the orphanage records? The questions whirled around in her head. On top of that was the problem of her new identity. How was she to prove that? And what would happen then? Would she have to go to some record office and say 'I'm not Jane Carroll any more – I'm now Ruth Ashington'? And where did the Henderson bit fit in? It was all too complicated to work out.

At last it was half past five, and Jane was relieved to leave the office and make her way home. Usually it was Amy who left first, but tonight Jane felt that she needed time and space to be on her own. Even the journey home she did automatically, scarcely noting what was happening around her. She picked up an evening paper, but it failed to hold her interest until she found a page relating to a gala night that had been held the previous evening. One photograph immediately grabbed her attention. It was of a white-haired elderly man with a much younger woman on his arm. Both were in evening dress, the woman in an extremely revealing gown and rather high heels. The caption identified the couple as Miles Ashington and his wife Gail. Jane stared at the photograph. Am I really related to that family? she asked herself. It seemed hard to believe.

It was almost half past six when she reached her apartment. She followed her usual routine of kicking off her shoes and changing out of her business suit into a more casual shirt and jeans. Somehow this evening she could not even stir herself into making a meal. She made do with a tin of soup she had bought ages before as a standby. After washing up the dirty utensils, she made herself a mug of tea and wandered into the lounge. She stretched full length on the settee, clasping the mug and relaxing back into the cushions. Her mobile was close at hand on the coffee table. She knew there were several phone calls she should make. She had to ring Bob to let him know what had happened on her visit to Elizabeth. Then there was Gerald. She had also promised to keep Lucy up to date on what was happening. She felt she had to contact all three that evening, but just for the moment it was nice to sit quietly and go over the events of the day.

It was a good half-hour later that she phoned Gerald. It was Anna who answered. Gerald was out for the evening and wouldn't be back until late, but would Jane like to come and wait for him? Jane declined the offer, explaining that she was rather tired that evening. Of course Anna wanted to know all about her visit to Elizabeth, and Jane did her best to explain without going into too much detail.

Anna's reaction to learning that Jane was most likely a member of the Ashington family was rather amusing. 'Goodness!' she exclaimed. 'Coming from a wealthy family like that you could be worth a fortune.'

The comment made Jane laugh. She had never thought of that. She conversed politely for a few minutes with a chatty Anna and then managed to extricate herself.

She also phoned Lucy, but Lucy's husband answered. Lucy was also out for the evening, but he agreed to let her know that Jane had called.

Jane clicked off her mobile and lay back on the cushions. It was too early to phone Bob. He would most likely not be home yet. She knew he was working in London that day.

The sound of her mobile ringing awoke her with a start. She grabbed it, at the same time stealing a quick glance at her watch. She had been asleep for over an hour.

'Hello.'

'Hi. It's Bob.'

Jane was embarrassed and apologetic. 'Darling, I'm dreadfully sorry. I intended to ring you, but I fell asleep.'

'Ah, that's the high life at the weekend catching up with you.'

Jane could sense Bob laughing as he said it. 'When can we do it again?' she joked breezily.

'Any time,' he quipped. Then he became more serious. 'How did the meeting with Mrs Marshall's sister go?' he asked.

'She was quite sweet really, but from what she said...' Jane paused. 'Well, it looks as if I am Ruth Ashington, though we still don't know how the Henderson bit fits in. I might even be a Henderson.'

'Tell me more.'

Jane related in as much detail as she could remember her conversation that afternoon with Elizabeth. Bob interrupted from time to time to ask a question.

'The problem as I see it,' concluded Jane, 'is to get some proof.'

'That will be the next step,' replied Bob.

'But how?' she asked.

As usual Bob was logical in his review of the subject. 'There's got to be someone somewhere who can vouch for your birth. A midwife or hospital, or even somebody who knew Ann Ashington well,' he explained.

'Hmm. I suppose so.' Jane was still unsure.

Bob was quick to recognise her concern. 'Don't worry. We are making progress. It's only a matter of time before we crack everything.'

His encouragement made Jane feel better. 'I'm a bit of a misery, aren't I? I'm sure you're right.'

'Absolutely.'

While she was speaking to Bob, something occurred to Jane. She was immediately prompted to voice her thoughts with a mixture of concern and humour.

'Bob, I just had a thought.'

She waited a second for him to respond.

'I'm all ears,' he chipped in.

Jane smiled as she formulated a reply. 'Well, I was just thinking. That beautiful ring you gave me at the weekend. You gave it to Jane Carroll. Now it seems you may have given it to Ruth Ashington. How does getting tied up to a Ruth Ashington grab you?'

Bob chuckled. 'I think that's the best idea I've heard in years,' he said. 'Coming from a family like that you must be a very wealthy woman. I can't go wrong.'

Jane took up the humorous tone. 'Of course if I'm so wealthy I'll have to review my options. There could be more eligible men out there, more suitable for my status.'

She heard Bob sigh.

'I know. It's a hard life for a mere male these days.'

It was Bob who brought their conversation back to a more serious level. 'I've just had a thought.' There was a slight pause. 'I think you – or we – should contact Miles Ashington. After all, he was married to Ann Ashington. He must know something about you.'

The suggestion immediately excited Jane. 'Of course! Why didn't I think of that? You're quite right. He must know something.'

'Have a go. Try and contact him,' Bob encouraged.

'I will.'

Jane was taken up with the idea, but already uncertainty was creeping in. 'But do you think he will talk to me? I mean, he's such a well-known person, and so busy. I don't know if he'll want to be bothered with such a trivial matter.'

'Have a try. It's not so trivial. Nothing ventured, nothing gained.'

227

Jane was thinking again. 'I've just thought of something else. Just about the time I joined *Discerning Woman* they were doing a feature on Miles Ashington. We must have the files somewhere, and there must be some contact details.'

Another doubt surfaced. 'Of course, it was over three years ago, so everything may have changed.' She spoke almost to herself.

'It's a starting point,' urged Bob.

'OK. I'll make it tomorrow's job to dig out the old files and see if there is a phone number or address for him,' replied Jane with conviction.

They chatted on for another ten minutes or so. Talking to Bob had snapped Jane out of her immediate concerns, and after she had finished speaking with him she felt much better. Tomorrow she would look for the old files on the Miles Ashington article and see what they revealed.

Jane's plans did not go exactly the way she had intended. The next day was very busy at work, with several new projects landing on her desk. During her lunch break she managed to go into the filing room and hunt for the file on the Miles Ashington feature. The person who had handled the interview had left the magazine soon after Jane started her job, so there was nobody she could ask for more information. All that would be available was the original file – with, hopefully, all the details.

She found it without too much difficulty and carried it back to her desk. The information it contained was going to be helpful. There were several letters from Miles Ashington with a London address and telephone number, and the magazine article itself was interesting reading for Jane. Up until then Miles Ashington had merely been a name that had popped up in the news from time to time. Jane was aware that Miles Ashington was a very successful businessman who owned several companies, and she knew that his business interests frequently brought him into the company of politicians. The magazine article was more revealing. She learned that he had been married three times, and that he owned a yacht and had houses in several parts of the country. The most valuable thing of all to Jane was the telephone number. She carefully made a note of it before returning the file to its home.

She had no opportunity to make a phone call to Miles Ashington that afternoon. She returned home in the evening without her plans being completed.

It was that evening that she received the anticipated visit from Gerald. He was most interested in the details of her visit to Elizabeth and kept asking for more details than Jane had. In the end he agreed that the next stage should be to try and contact Miles Ashington, and left Jane with the statement that he was going to tell Eric what had happened.

After supper Jane decided to open her laptop and play with the family history program. She had hardly started when the phone rang. This time it was not her mobile, which was on the table beside her, but her landline. She dashed to the telephone. It was Lucy returning her call from the previous evening.

The two friends spent a long time talking. Lucy wanted to be completely updated on what had happened with Jane's research, and then they started to chat about old times. It was a good half an hour later that their conversation ended.

Back at her computer, Jane started to type names such as Ann Ashington and Ruth Ashington into the search area to see what came up. She found Ann Ashington's marriage without too much difficulty. She made a careful note of the reference numbers just in case she wanted to obtain a copy of the marriage certificate. Next she turned her attention to the name Henderson in the births section. She found several that looked as if they might be likely candidates. As she soon found out, this was confusing, because the records listed gave no details of parents. All she had access to were the name and the reference number that would enable her to obtain a certificate.

Her research was suddenly brought to a halt again by her mobile ringing.

'Hi. It's me again.' It was Bob.

His voice brought almost a squeal of delight from Jane. 'Gosh! How lovely to talk again so soon!' She sensed that something was in the air.

Bob was quick to elaborate. 'I've just been talking to Mum and Dad.' He paused. 'How about we drive down there and look them up this weekend? They are mad keen to meet you.'

'I'd love to! What have you got in mind?'

'I thought we might drive down Saturday morning and spend the day there. It's not all that far.'

'It sounds a super idea. Shall I pick you up early again?'

'No. I'll come over to you on the first available train. They start quite early. You can have a lie-in.' She heard Bob chuckle as he finished speaking. His next comment was more serious. 'I really must get a decent car soon instead of just talking about it.'

Jane was quick to chip in. 'Bob, don't. There's not really any need unless you want it for local trips. I've got mine and it needs to be used.'

Bob was philosophical. 'I suppose you're right. I only use it for going to the local shops anyway.'

'There you are, then. Listen to a woman's logic.' Jane laughed.

Bob suddenly thought of something else. 'Oh, by the way, Cissy will be there this weekend as well.'

'That's marvellous! I want to meet her.' Jane followed up by asking the question that had been on her mind ever since the first time Bob had mentioned his sister by name. 'By the way, why is she called Cissy?'

Bob laughed. 'It was me who started that off when I was a kid and she was small. I think it was meant to be for sister, but somehow the name stuck. Her real name is Jocelyn.'

Jane was pensive. 'Well, at least she knows her proper name,' she commented quietly, her thoughts turning to her own situation.

Bob picked up her concerned thinking at once. 'Don't worry. We'll sort you out in the end. It's only a matter of time.' He added for good measure, 'And who knows what we might glean from Miles Ashington?'

They continued to discuss family history, and in particular Jane's problem. It was only after a good ten minutes that during a lull in their conversation Jane brought the topic around to the weekend again.

'Bob, what do you think I should wear this weekend?' she asked.

Bob thought for a second. 'Hmm. Something nice and simple, and perhaps not too showy.'

Jane knew the kind of thing Bob had in mind. Perhaps his parents were a little old-fashioned when it came to appearances. Graham's parents had been much the same. 'I think I know what you mean. I've got just the thing,' she replied.

Their chatter continued for a while longer, until eventually Jane had to stifle a yawn. She commented she had had a hard day, Bob replied that he had to get up early in the morning, and they ended the phone call.

The following day Jane had the opportunity to phone Miles Ashington. During a relatively quiet period in the afternoon, she took out the details and dialled the number.

The telephone was answered almost immediately. It was a woman's voice. 'Miles Ashington's office.'

'Good afternoon. Would it be possible to speak to Miles Ashington, please?'

Jane held her breath. Was she speaking to a secretary who vetted her employer's telephone calls, or would she manage to speak with Miles Ashington?

'I'm sorry. He is not in the office at present.' The reply was not unfriendly.

Jane was not going to give up easily. 'I see. Would it be possible for me to phone later?'

'He won't be in the office until Monday. Can I ask who is calling?' The tone of the voice was more formal now.

Jane knew she had to tread cautiously if she was to succeed in speaking to Miles Ashington. She chose her words carefully. 'My name is Jane Carroll and I work for *Discerning Woman* magazine. We ran an article on him several years ago.'

'I would suggest that you call again on Monday, or I can take your number and ask him to call you.'

The last thing Jane wanted was for Miles Ashington to ring her at work. She thought quickly. 'It might be more convenient if I phone him,' she suggested.

'As you wish. I'll tell him you asked for him and that he can expect another call from you on Monday.'

'Thank you very much.'

'Goodbye.'

'Goodbye.'

Jane put the telephone down. So far, so good. There was nothing more she could do until Monday. She suddenly had a horrible thought. Suppose Miles Ashington phoned *Discerning Woman* before she had a chance to call him? Her logic soon dispersed that fear. That was highly unlikely to happen. People like Miles Ashington were too busy.

Now she would concentrate on the weekend ahead and her introduction to Bob's parents.

Chapter 26

Jane was up early on the Saturday morning. So far, she was well pleased with her plans for the weekend. The previous day she had had a brief lunch with Bob at The Green Man and he had outlined his intentions. He would arrive at her apartment at around nine and then they would have a leisurely drive down to Kent to get to his parents' house in time for lunch. Jane had been fortunate in securing a late appointment with her hairdresser after work on the Friday. She planned to be ready and waiting when Bob arrived.

Breakfast was a quick affair, and then she took her time getting ready. She had decided on an old favourite, her navy blue skirt and jacket. She had an open-necked white blouse to go with it. Shoes were another old favourite, a pair of matching navy blue court shoes with a medium heel, her 'old comfortables', she called them. She had had one last-minute idea. For the first time for months she put on a pair of tights. She rummaged in her dressing-table drawer and found a new pair. The label claimed that the contents were 'almost invisible and the next best thing to bare legs'. She decided to give them a go and see what Bob thought. The wickedness in her had originally intended to buy a pair of stockings the day before to tantalise him, but because she had met him for lunch she did not have enough time. It was an escapade that would have to wait.

By half past eight she was almost ready. She was in the middle of going through the contents of her bag to ensure that she had such essentials as her keys, mobile, driving licence and lipstick when the outside buzzer went. She dropped the bag on the settee and hurried to press the entryphone button.

'Hello.'

Bob's voice answered loud and clear, 'Hello you. It's me.'

'Come in. I'm all ready.'

Jane pressed the button and waited at her door until she heard Bob's footsteps outside, and then she threw the door open wide. She stood behind the door to let Bob enter. As soon as she had closed the door, she threw her arms around him.

'Darling, it's lovely to have you here.'

Bob kissed her. 'The minutes dragged until I got here,' he replied with a grin.

As Jane separated from him, she giggled. 'Now you've got lipstick on your face.'

Bob glanced in a convenient mirror and grinned.

'Would you like a drink, darling?' she asked.

'Coffee, please,' Bob replied, wiping off the lipstick.

'You go into the lounge. I'll make us one.'

Jane disappeared into the kitchen. A few minutes later she appeared in the lounge with two mugs of coffee. She put them down on the table in front of the settee and then stood back, holding each side of her skirt; she glanced briefly down at her outfit and then concentrated on Bob.

'How do you like my outfit? Do you think your parents will approve?' She had been slightly worried about her first meeting with Bob's parents, and she had noticed that Bob was wearing a jacket with an open-necked shirt.

Bob smiled at her. 'I think it's just right,' he said.

'What do you think of my tights?' Jane asked, looking down at her legs. 'The packet claims they're supposed to be almost invisible.'

Bob scrutinised Jane's legs. 'They very nearly are,' he laughed.

'Well, I want to make a good impression on your parents.' Jane picked up her mug of coffee and sat down beside him.

Bob smiled again. 'You will,' he announced simply, turning his attention to his drink.

'What time did you get up?' asked Jane.

Bob made a face. 'The middle of the night.'

'Right. I'll drive, then, and you can have a snooze,' Jane announced firmly.

They left her apartment soon after they finished their coffee. Jane drove while Bob dozed. Jane was quite good at navigating and quickly found her way to the South Circular Road. Fortunately, on a Saturday morning the traffic was light, and they made good progress. As a bonus, the earlier grey morning had now changed to a bright sunny one. It was only when they left the M25 and headed deeper into Kent that Jane began to turn to Bob, who by now was wide awake, for directions.

While she was driving she updated herself on Bob's family. 'What did your father actually do for a living?' she asked. She remembered Bob once telling her that his father had worked in the City before retirement.

'He was a banker,' Bob replied. 'I think he was quite good at it. We had a very comfortable lifestyle.'

'What about Cissy? What does she do?'

Bob grinned. 'She's in PR,' he replied. 'She works in Manchester.'

'And she's much younger than you?'

'Only two years. We used to fight quite a bit when we were younger, but we get on fine now.'

'It must be nice to have a brother or sister,' commented Jane, almost as if she were speaking to herself.

Bob looked at her. He knew what she was thinking. It must be lonely at times being an orphan. 'I understand,' he assured her.

It was just coming up to eleven when they arrived at the village near Canterbury where Bob's parents lived.

'Take the next turning on the right,' said Bob.

'How long have your parents lived here?' asked Jane, signalling to make the turn.

'We moved here when I was five or six. There's a railway station just down the road, and that was convenient for Dad to commute to London,' replied Bob, adding quickly, 'Here we are, through those iron gates.'

Jane turned off the road and through the gateway. A large, substantial house stood in front of them. There were already two cars parked on the gravel in front of it, one of them a sports model.

'That's Cissy's.' Bob nodded towards the sports car.

Jane was glad to get out of the car and stretch her legs. They were busy getting the few items they had brought out of the car boot when Bob's mother, a sprightly grey-haired woman, appeared from the house.

'Bob! Lovely to see you.' She embraced her son and kissed him.

She immediately turned to Jane. 'And you must be Jane. It's so nice to meet you. Bob's told me a lot about you.'

She gave Jane a hug. 'It's nice to be here,' replied Jane. She took to Mrs Harker immediately. She handed her the bouquet of pink roses she had bought for the occasion.

'Thank you. They're really beautiful – and they're my favourite. How did you know?'

Jane smiled at her. 'I had inside information,' she laughed. They had stopped on the way to buy the flowers and Bob had advised her which ones his mother liked.

'Come along in.' Bob's mother ushered them towards the house. 'Now Bob, you must show Jane where everything is. Your dad's in the garden. I told him half an hour ago to get ready.' She turned to Jane and shook her head. 'Men,' she said, with a little laugh.

Jane smiled again. They had now entered the large hallway of the house. A graceful staircase swept up to the next floor. Jane liked the house straight away. It had a nice homely feel about it.

'Where's Cissy?' asked Bob.

'She's around somewhere,' said his mother. She went to the foot of the stairs and called out. 'Cissy! CISSY! They're here.'

From somewhere upstairs there was a muffled answer, and a minute later a young woman with blonde hair bounded down the stairs, carrying a pair of stilettos.

'Hi!' she greeted Bob and Jane breathlessly as she slipped into her shoes.

It was clear that Cissy was not one inclined towards formal introductions in family matters.

Bob's father, a white-haired man with spectacles, came into the house at that moment in his gardening clothes, embarrassed and apologetic about his appearance. He was immediately dispatched to change by his wife, while she ushered her guests into the lounge. Coffee was produced at about the same time as he reappeared, and the process of absorbing Jane into the family progressed, mostly by bringing the conversation round to her and asking a lot of questions.

A good half-hour later, during a break in the conversation, Bob's mother announced, 'We thought we'd all dine out today, so we've booked a table at The Golden Lion.'

Jane hardly had time to respond before she addressed her daughter. 'Cissy, why don't you take Jane upstairs and show her where the bathroom is?'

Cissy immediately obliged. She gave Jane a cheeky grin as she stood up. 'This way, Jane.'

Jane obediently followed her.

When they reached the foot of the stairs, Cissy removed first one shoe, and then the other. She leaned towards Jane and whispered, 'I caught my heel a few years ago and fell down the stairs.' She pointed to her forehead. 'I had a cut here and had to go to A & E. Mum makes me take off my shoes now.'

Jane muttered a few words of sympathy, and as they started to climb the stairs she took off her own shoes. Her heels were not as alarming as Cissy's, but she took the hint.

Cissy led the way to a bedroom first. 'You can use my room if you want to. Sorry it's a bit of a mess.'

Jane immediately saw why the comment had been made. Clothes and other items were strewn everywhere. The state of the room rather amused her, particularly as she had learnt from the conversation in the lounge that Cissy had only arrived the evening before.

Cissy gave her a smile. 'How long have you known Bob?' she

asked Jane. There was a friendly inquisitiveness in the tone of her voice.

'I met him earlier this year,' Jane explained.

'I'm glad he's picked up with someone nice like you.' Cissy grinned.

Jane had no time to answer before Cissy pointed to two framed photographs hanging on the wall.

'They're Bob's,' she remarked casually, studying Jane's face for a reaction.

Jane smiled. 'I thought they might be,' she replied politely. She had noticed them as soon as she entered the room. One was a summer scene in woodland, and the other was the same scene in winter.

Jane was quite unprepared for Cissy's next question.

Cissy lowered her voice. 'Has Bob taken a picture of you yet – in the nude?'

Jane struggled for a few seconds to find a suitable answer. In the end she just replied with a smile, 'No. Not yet.'

'He's taken one of me,' announced Cissy.

Jane almost laughed. There was a hint of one-upmanship in Cissy's statement. She did not let on that she had seen the photograph of Cissy. She was beginning to like her a lot. Bob had already warned her about Cissy's forthright approach to everything, but she started to wonder what Cissy's next question might be. It was clear that she wanted to extract as much information as possible from her. She continued to ask Jane questions about her relationship with Bob, to most of which Jane thought up suitably vague answers.

A shortage of time saved Jane from more interrogation. Bob's voice called up the stairs, 'Are you two ready? We're about to leave.'

They took the hint. Jane flew into the bathroom, leaving Cissy to struggle out of the jeans and man's shirt she was wearing into something more appropriate.

Jane enjoyed the rest of the day. She felt that she was getting to

238

know Bob's family. All of them were friendly and welcomed her into their midst. She had been just a tiny bit worried about meeting them all, but any fears were quickly dispelled. Bob's mother was clearly very loving towards her and appeared to be more than willing to take her on as an extra daughter. Even Bob's father, after a slow start, had warmed towards her. Later in the afternoon he had insisted on showing her round his garden and then spent some time introducing her to his collections of various things, including old banknotes from around the world, which he kept in a small room in the house. Cissy had been spontaneous and friendly and seemed quite happy to have Jane be an additional member of the family.

It was late in the evening when Bob and Jane finally took their leave and drove back to Kew. It had been a good day and it had taken Jane's attention away from her concerns over her past. She had not heard from Gerald for a few days and her own efforts on her laptop had not produced any further evidence. Now it seemed that the only glimmer of hope lay with Miles Ashington, but the big question there was whether she could get to see him − or, to be more correct, whether he would condescend to see her.

Chapter 27

During a quiet spell at work the following Monday morning, Jane tried again to contact Miles Ashington. She was disappointed. He was out of the office for the rest of the day, the receptionist told her. Yes, he would be in the office on Tuesday. Jane felt disappointed, but there was nothing she could do about it. She would just have to try again the next day.

She felt pleased about the weekend she had just spent. The time with Bob's family had been particularly enjoyable, and she felt that now they were more to her than just names referred to in casual conversation. She and Bob had taken things leisurely on the Sunday. They had gone for a walk and then Jane had cooked a simple lunch for them while Bob played on her laptop, trying to glean more information from the family history program. Bob had needed to be home early to prepare for some work he and Jeff had undertaken to do in the coming week, and despite his protests Jane had decided to run him back to Tatting Green. It was after six when she had finally taken her leave. On her way home she had been held up by an accident ahead of her that had resulted in a blocked road and a delay of over an hour. It was nearly nine when she had finally arrived at her apartment. After pottering about for a while, she had decided to have an early night.

For once Monday was an uneventful day at the office. Nevertheless Jane was glad when the office clock showed it was time to finish for the day. The sky had clouded over, and by the time she left her train at Kew station it was raining quite heavily. She had an umbrella with her but decided to wait in the station foyer and see whether it eased off. This proved to be futile. The rain continued to fall steadily and it looked as if it would remain that way. After five minutes she decided to make a move. By the time she reached her apartment, though the umbrella had kept her head and shoulders dry, the lower part of her was decidedly wet. She could feel the water running down her legs into her shoes.

She was glad to be back in the comfort of her apartment. She had felt cold walking home from the station and she had been aware of the thinness of her business suit. She lost no time in discarding it and having a hot shower to warm up. While she was eating a hastily prepared evening meal, the telephone rang. She rushed out to the hall and picked the handset up. It was a familiar voice.

'Jane, it's Gerald. I hope I haven't interrupted your meal. I was wondering if I might pop up for a few minutes. I have some interesting information for you.'

Jane was immediately curious and slightly excited. What had he found?

'That's fine, Gerald. Do come up. I'm quite intrigued to know what you have for me.'

There was a little nervous laugh at the other end of the telephone before Gerald replied. 'Oh, I don't want to raise your expectations too high, but I think it's information you should have.'

Jane smiled to herself. Gerald was always so precise. 'I'm still curious,' she replied cheerfully.

'Would it be convenient to come now, or later?'

Jane thought quickly. She was in her dressing gown. Memories of appearing in that garb in front of Gerald on a previous occasion rushed into her mind. 'Could you give me ten minutes?'

'Yes, of course. Let me see... I'll see you...' there was a brief pause as Gerald must have looked at his watch. 'I see you at half past seven, if that would be all right.'

'That's fine. See you soon. Bye for now.'

Jane hardly heard Gerald's goodbye. She was already replacing the handset.

She dashed back into the kitchen. She hurriedly finished her meal, gulped down the cup of tea she had made and then flew into her bedroom. Her dressing gown was flung onto the bed and she quickly put on a pair of jeans and a blouse and slipped her feet into the white pumps she sometimes wore at home. A touch of lipstick and a dab of perfume, and she was just about ready as the front doorbell rang.

Gerald stood there, a folder in hand.

Jane flung open the door wide. 'Hello, Gerald. Come in,' she greeted him breezily.

Gerald followed her into the lounge.

'Now what have you got for me?' she asked cheerfully.

Gerald took the seat she indicated and placed his folder on the coffee table. Jane sat down opposite him.

He started to open the folder. 'I've been purchasing some certificates.' He took out a piece of paper and handed it to Jane. 'Ann Ashington's birth certificate,' he announced calmly.

Jane started to read the writing aloud. 'Father Edward Ashington, mother Jessica, mother's maiden name Bantree.'

She looked up at Gerald, who immediately handed her another certificate. 'Have a look at this one,' he said.

Jane studied the contents of the certificate for a second and then read out the name. 'Name Ruth, mother Ann Ashington.' She paused and looked at Gerald questioningly. 'The birth was registered in Yorkshire.'

Gerald gave a hint of a smile. 'That's why we never found a birth for Ruth in Gloucestershire. She was born in Yorkshire.'

Jane looked at the certificate again and then, mystified, at Gerald. 'But there is no father on it,' she remarked.

Gerald smiled at her. 'Exactly,' he said.

Jane was still puzzled. 'But does that mean that Ruth was illegitimate?' she asked.

'It certainly looks that way.'

'But what about this John Henderson Ann Ashington is supposed to have married?'

Gerald took another piece of paper from his folder. 'I've got a copy of the marriage certificate,' he declared casually, handing it to Jane.

Jane studied the certificate. 'John James Henderson, bachelor, and Ann Ashington, spinster.'

She looked at Ruth's birth certificate again and then held the two documents side by side. She looked up at Gerald in bewilderment.

Gerald smiled at her. 'The interesting bit is that according to Eric, Ann Ashington and John Henderson were divorced eighteen months before Ruth was born.'

'So that really confirms that Ruth was illegitimate,' Jane suggested, looking at Gerald for confirmation.

Gerald was cautious. 'It's never a good thing in family history to assume things, but I would agree that in this case it does look as if she was.' He did not give Jane time to respond, but spoke again almost at once. 'What we really need is to talk to somebody who knew Ann Ashington at this period of her life.'

Jane was deep in thought for a few seconds. 'Elizabeth, Mrs Marshall's sister, was around when I was small. She took me to the orphanage, but she can't tell me anything about my birth.'

Gerald stroked his beard as if for inspiration. 'What about Miles Ashington?' he asked. 'Any luck there?'

Jane made a bit of a face. 'I've not managed to make contact with him yet,' she replied.

They continued to chat for a further five minutes or so and then Gerald declared that he had to get back to Anna. Jane could see that there was little else that could be done at present. She remembered that Gerald had purchased the certificates and she insisted on paying him for them. After that, with his usual courtesy, Gerald took his leave.

Afterwards Jane felt a bit downhearted. It seemed as if, despite Gerald's efforts, she was getting nowhere in establishing her true identity. So much now seemed to depend on finding somebody who could confirm that she was Ann Ashington's daughter. She realised that a lot now depended on a meeting with Miles

Ashington – if he would see her. She thought about phoning Bob, but she realised that there was really nothing new she could tell him. She would just have to wait and see if she could make contact with Miles Ashington.

The following afternoon at work, feeling almost as despondent, Jane found a few minutes to try and telephone Miles Ashington's office once more. The same receptionist answered the telephone and Jane repeated her request. This time the response was, 'I'll see if he is available. Will you hold, please?'

Jane waited for what seemed a long time, her expectations dropping further with each second.

Suddenly a man's voice answered. 'Miles Ashington. How can I help you?'

Jane's heart missed a beat. She was actually able to talk to Miles Ashington! She knew she had to choose her words carefully if she was to achieve success. She took a deep breath and began.

'Good afternoon, Mr Ashington. My name is Jane Carroll and I think you may be able to help me sort out a problem with my ancestry. There is some evidence that I may be related to the Ashington family.'

There was silence for a short time on the other end of the telephone. Jane held her breath.

'That sounds very interesting. How do you think I might be able to assist you?' The answer was cautious but not unfriendly.

'Well, you see...' Jane gave a brief account of her problem. When she had finished, again there was a pause before Miles Ashington responded.

'I see.'

Jane felt that the reply was not unsympathetic, but she needed to make further progress. 'Would it be possible to come and see you and ask you a few questions?'

That's it, she thought. I've done it. There's not much more I can do if it's a refusal. She waited anxiously for a reply. It was not long in coming.

'I'm afraid I'm tied up for the next two days, but would Friday suit you?'

Jane was on cloud nine. An interview with Miles Ashington was in the offing! 'Yes, it would,' she replied quickly.

'Do you live in London, Miss Carroll?'

'I live at Kew, but I work in central London,' she replied.

There was another short wait. Jane held her breath. He was clearly consulting his schedule.

'I shall be at my house in Maida Vale on Friday afternoon. Would half past two be any good for you?'

Jane's thinking raced. She had nothing major on this Friday. She could come into work early, work her lunch hour, see Miles Ashington and still perhaps be back in the office before the end of the day.

She tried to sound not too eager as she replied. 'Yes, that would be fine.'

'I'll put that in my diary. Can I get my secretary to email the address to you?'

Jane was puzzled for an instant, but then she suddenly realised that well-known people had to be especially careful about security.

'Yes, of course.' She gave him the email address.

She was unprepared for his response.

'Ah yes, of course. *Discerning Woman*. I've met Annette Burrows socially on several occasions.'

Jane's heart sank slightly. The last thing she wanted was for Annette to know what she was doing, but logic told her there was no reason why Miles Ashington and Annette Burrows should not be acquainted. Her reply was deliberately vague. 'That's interesting.'

It seemed to work. Miles Ashington's next sentence returned to the business in hand. 'I'll get that confirmed, then, and I'll see you on Friday.'

'Yes, of course,' answered Jane. 'Thank you very much. I look forward to meeting you.'

'Exactly. Goodbye.'

Jane just had time to say 'Goodbye' before the line went dead.

She put the phone down. She suddenly felt good. She had got a meeting with Miles Ashington! Surely he must have some information about her roots. Dared she hope that their meeting would reveal who she really was?

It was Amy appearing in her office and asking a question that brought Jane down to earth again.

That evening Jane just had to phone Bob and tell him the good news. He was almost as enthusiastic as she was and they chatted for quite a long time. Towards the end of their conversation Bob made a suggestion.

'I've been thinking,' he began, and then slowly continued. 'I promised I'd take a portrait of you sometime. The studio is free on Saturday afternoon. How would you feel about it?'

For a couple of seconds Jane was completely thrown. Bob's suggestion had come completely out of the blue, but she remembered when he had first expressed a desire to photograph her. She had been agreeable then, so why not, she thought.

'I'd love to,' she replied.

Bob was immediately enthusiastic. 'Great. I'm working Saturday morning, but what I suggest is that we meet up somewhere for lunch, then go to the studio and perhaps do something in the evening.'

'That sounds super, and I can get my hair done on Saturday morning then.' Jane was already planning the day.

'That would work out fine,' replied Bob. 'I'll think of somewhere nice for us to go in the evening.'

'That would be great.'

Jane suddenly decided to be a bit humorous and tantalising. 'I hope you're not suggesting that I pose nude.'

Bob took up the challenge. 'Ah. I'm disappointed. I suppose I'll just have to wait.' Jane heard a faked big sigh.

'I might – I say might – agree to it once I am a married woman and respectable. A single girl has to protect her modesty.' Jane started to giggle.

'I shall have to make it a condition of marrying you,' remarked Bob, almost casually.

'In that case I may have to review our current agreement,' said Jane haughtily.

'I think you're being extremely difficult over such a minor issue,' retorted Bob, echoing her manner.

Jane started to laugh. She decided to change the tone of the conversation. 'Seriously, I'd like a photograph similar to the one you've got hanging up in the studio – the black and white head and shoulders one. It looks really nice.'

'That's what I have in mind for you,' replied Bob.

Before Jane had a chance to reply, he broke in again. 'Jane, I've got somebody at the door. I think it's Mrs McGinty. She'll have some bits and pieces for me. Can I ring you later in the week?'

'Yes, of course. Bye for now, darling.'

There was a hurried 'Bye' from Bob, and she heard him call 'Coming' as the telephone clicked off.

Jane was also determined to tell Gerald her news that evening. It was Anna who answered the telephone. She immediately insisted that Jane come down to their apartment. As soon as Jane arrived, Anna offered her a cup of coffee. She accepted, as she had not had a drink since the afternoon, although she declined any cake, explaining that she had just eaten.

Gerald was quite enthusiastic about her forthcoming meeting with Miles Ashington and kept thinking of questions he thought she should ask him. It was a good hour later when Jane at last managed to take her leave.

Back in her own apartment, she decided to call Lucy. Patty had been put to bed, Raymond was out, and Lucy had time to linger on the phone. They chatted for a long time, first about Jane's meeting with Miles Ashington, and then about old times at the orphanage. It was Raymond's return home that ended their conversation.

Jane went over the day's events. Despite a rather depressing start she felt that she should be pleased with how things had gone. She had at last got an interview with Miles Ashington. The big question was, how much information would he be able to give her? And if her real name was Ashington, what then? How should she deal with that situation? She would just have to wait until Friday to find out.

Chapter 28

Jane made a point of being in the office well before her usual time on the Friday morning. She caught a much earlier train, opened up the office, and was already hard at work when Margaret arrived. Margaret popped her head round the door of Jane's tiny room on the way to make herself a drink.

'Good morning, Jane. You're an early bird today!'

Jane looked up. 'Good morning, Margaret. Yes – I have to go out later on and I wanted to finish a couple of things first.'

Margaret gave a quick glance at Jane's desk and then asked, 'Can I get you a drink?'

Jane grinned as she handed Margaret her mug. 'Marvellous. Yes, please. I'd better have a coffee. I was up at the crack of dawn.'

Margaret took the mug, at the same time scrutinising Jane's outfit. 'You're dressed up this morning. Something on?' she asked, smiling.

'I've got an important appointment,' replied Jane, and left it at that.

To Jane's relief Margaret accepted her explanation without any further questions. She did not want to elaborate or to explain why she had taken special care with her appearance today. Instead of her normal work outfit of a jacket and matching trousers, she had opted to wear a skirt suit. She had even put on a pair of tights, albeit the sheer ones. The black shoes she had chosen sported rather higher heels than usual, so she had opted to travel to work in flats for comfort.

The morning went quite smoothly. There were few interruptions. Annette was not in the office that day so there was

249

no urgent summons to her office. Jane was surprised how much work she managed to get through. By lunchtime she was well pleased with her efforts.

It was early afternoon when she left the office and set off for the address Miles Ashington's secretary had emailed to her. She had looked up the address in her A–Z and found the road without difficulty. It was one of those tree-lined roads with large Victorian four-storey terraced houses on each side. It was an upmarket area and even had an inner road separated from the main one, which provided parking for the residents. Many of the houses appeared to be expensive rental apartments, but when she came to the house she was looking for, it had all the appearance of being owner-occupied. It was just coming up to half past two when she mounted the short flight of steps to the front door. She pressed the doorbell and waited.

The door was opened by a young woman in a maid's uniform of black dress and white apron. She stared at Jane for an instant. 'Can I help you?' Her voice had a slight foreign accent.

'Yes. I have an appointment with Mr Ashington at half past two.'

'What name, please?'

'Jane Carroll.'

'Come in, please, and wait here.'

Jane stepped inside and the door was closed quietly behind them. The maid walked silently up the majestic staircase and disappeared from view. This gave Jane the opportunity to quickly glance at her surroundings. The house had an air of elegance about it. The tiled hallway, the thickly carpeted stairs, the paintings on the walls, the chandelier... All reflected the affluence of the owner.

The maid reappeared at the head of the stairs.

'Will you come up please?'

Jane made her way up the stairs. The maid led her a short distance down a corridor, pushed a door that was already ajar, and held it wide open for Jane to enter the room.

Jane found herself in a small office-cum-sitting room. A leather three-piece suite occupied one end, and there was also a large desk with an ornate table lamp burning. But it was the figure standing ready to greet her that most interested Jane. Miles Ashington.

He held out his hand. 'Miss Carroll, I am pleased to meet you.'

Jane held out her hand, and it was grasped firmly. 'Thank you for seeing me, Mr Ashington.'

'A pleasure. Do come and sit down.' He waved his hand towards the seating area.

'Thank you.'

Jane's first impression was that Miles Ashington was quite friendly. He was a tall, white-haired man dressed in a beautifully cut suit and an expensive shirt and tie. There was a faint smell of aftershave about him.

Jane took a seat as indicated. Miles Ashington smiled at her briefly.

'Can I offer you some refreshment? Tea or coffee, perhaps?'

'Tea would be lovely,' answered Jane with a courteous smile.

There was a minute's silence between them as he went over to the desk and picked up a telephone to arrange for some tea to be brought. He returned to Jane and sat down opposite her. He smiled at her again.

'So I'm talking to a long-lost member of the illustrious Ashington family.' Miles Ashington chuckled as he finished speaking.

'That's what I'm not really sure about. You see...' Jane had rehearsed the next bit many times. As briefly as she could, she outlined her search for her true identity. Her host listened intently.

When she had finished he asked quite kindly, 'So how do you think I can help you?'

Jane was anxious to make the most of the occasion. She thought carefully for a few seconds before answering. 'What I would really like to know is whether I am Jane Carroll, or Ruth Ashington. I don't seem to be able to get any proof of either.'

Miles Ashington appeared to be deep in thought. He smiled at her. 'Well, I can't help you with the Jane Carroll bit, but I think I can be of assistance with Ruth Ashington.'

A flurry of excitement flushed through Jane. Here at last was somebody who seemed to know about her past. She was determined to exploit the opportunity that lay in front of her. She formed her next question carefully.

'I'd really like to know something about my early life – if indeed I am Ruth Ashington. For example, I don't know who my father was.'

Miles Ashington paused; he sat looking at her, his hands in front of him, almost as if he was in prayer, but with the fingers separated. He spoke slowly, choosing every word carefully.

'My wife Ann was a very beautiful woman. We met and fell in love very quickly. At the time she was embarrassed that she had a baby, born apparently out of wedlock. But it didn't matter to me. I was in love with her.'

He looked at Jane, studying her reaction.

Any possible reply from Jane was interrupted by the arrival of the maid with the tea. She placed a tray on the low table between them. After she had departed, Miles Ashington took up the teapot.

'Shall I pour for us?' he asked cheerfully.

Jane smiled her agreement, adding 'Please do,' and waited while her host poured the tea into a fine bone china cup. He handed her the cup and saucer with the offer of milk and sugar. The tea service had every appearance of being extremely expensive china. Miles Ashington offered a plate of fancy biscuits, but Jane refused. She carefully stirred the milk into her tea as she formed her next question.

'So I'm not the daughter of John Henderson?' she asked.

Miles Ashington took a careful sip of his tea. He shook his head as he looked up at Jane again. 'No, I'm afraid not. My understanding is that you were the result of a slight indiscretion on Ann's part.'

Jane reacted quickly. 'You mean it was a sort of brief affair?' she asked.

Miles Ashington gave a quick smile. 'I suppose it would be called today a one-night stand,' he explained with a sigh.

'Did Ann never say who my father was?'

Again Miles Ashington shook his head. 'No. Only that you were the result of going to a party and having too much to drink.'

Jane was doing her best to absorb what she was being told. There was one question that was uppermost in her mind. She took a sip of tea before asking it.

'I was speaking recently to the woman who looked after me when I was small – Elizabeth Barton – and—'

'Elizabeth Barton?'

'Yes. I think you would probably know her as Elizabeth Carroll.'

'Ah, yes. The nanny Ann and I employed to look after you.'

Jane continued. 'She told me that my mother didn't show very much interest in me.'

Miles Ashington placed his cup and saucer on the table. He spoke softly. 'I'm afraid that's quite true. It was a situation that worried me, but Ann could be quite stubborn at times. The cold fact is that she did not want to know you in any way. You were a reminder of a past that she preferred to forget, and she didn't even want to acknowledge that you existed.'

His statement shocked and saddened Jane. It prompted a sudden reaction from her. 'But why?' she asked. 'I was her daughter. She gave birth to me.'

She looked at Miles Ashington in puzzlement, looking for an answer.

'My dear, I am extremely sorry if what I have said is upsetting.' Miles Ashington regarded her almost as if he were talking to a fond daughter.

Jane choked down her emotion. 'Can you tell me a bit more about my mother? What was she like?' she asked.

Miles Ashington pondered the question carefully. 'As I have said, she was a very beautiful woman. She lost her mother and father quite early in life, and that left her incredibly wealthy. Sadly, it never brought her happiness. She became withdrawn, sometimes depressive. There was a brief and disastrous marriage to John Henderson. She always remarked that I was the first person she had met whom she could trust.'

Jane was silent for a few seconds, taking in what she had just heard. 'I'm glad she felt that way about you,' she said softly.

Miles Ashington offered more tea, but Jane refused. One question still needed an answer.

'Can you tell me why I was placed in the orphanage?' she asked, doing her best to control the emotion that kept threatening to overwhelm her.

'I am sorry to say this, but your mother did not want to recognise you in any way as her daughter or as part of the Ashington family. I tried many times to talk her round, but she was adamant. It was almost her dying request that you be placed in an orphanage. Eventually, I complied with her wish and sent you to Goodmanton. The Ashington family had supported that institution for many years.'

Jane looked at him in astonishment. 'But I was shut away there. Nobody ever came near me,' she protested. She was close to tears now.

'It was your mother's wish.'

Jane was silent for a few seconds. She had the answer now that she had sought, but she wished it could have been a happier one.

Miles Ashington looked at her. He could see that she was upset by what she had just learnt. He spoke again. 'After a period of time the Goodmanton orphanage was taken over by the County Council and the Ashington family ceased to have any involvement. I did try to make contact with you at one stage, but you had already left the establishment and apparently disappeared.'

Jane looked at him enquiringly. 'But I was sent to live with somebody when I was a teenager. The orphanage must have had a record of that.'

Miles Ashington shook his head. 'When I enquired, they had no record of you whatsoever.'

'That would be because you were looking for Ruth Ashington and by that time I was known as Jane Carroll.'

He pondered her suggestion for a moment. 'Given the circumstances, one has to assume that some sort of administrative error was made during your time at the orphanage.'

'But why the name Carroll?' asked Jane.

'I'm afraid the only person who could answer that question is the one who made the error – or Mrs Marshall, who was in charge of the orphanage then.' He studied her for a second. 'But as you have learnt, she passed away.' He added quickly, 'I think it is most unfortunate for you.'

Jane did her best to respond positively. 'It's a bit of a startling situation to have to deal with,' she remarked, with a little smile.

She suddenly thought of something else. 'Can you tell me how my mother died?'

For a moment Miles Ashington looked quite sad, and Jane wished she had not asked the question. However, he recovered quite quickly and seemed pleased to answer.

'Ann had always been subject to mood swings and fits of depression. She was treated by various doctors for this problem. I discovered this soon after we were married, and sadly I did not seem to be able to help her recover from this distressing condition.' He paused, apparently recalling events, and then he continued. 'She was taking a lot of drugs, and one morning her maid found her dead in bed. It was assumed at the time that she had taken an overdose.'

Jane waited until he had finished, and then offered her sympathy. 'But that must have been awful for you. I was obviously too young to know anything was happening.'

He nodded. 'It was. I was devastated.'

Jane felt sad about what she had just learnt. She did her best to throw off her gloom and ask a less distressing question. 'Can you tell me anything more about Elizabeth Carroll?' she asked quickly.

Her strategy appeared to work. Miles Ashington responded with a smile. 'Ah, yes. Elizabeth was a charming person. She looked after you like her own daughter. She was quite upset when you went to the orphanage.'

'That's nice to hear,' Jane replied softly.

It was Miles Ashington who wound the meeting down. 'Do you have any other questions you would like me to answer?' he asked.

Jane took the hint. It was clear that though her host was being very polite it was possible that he had other commitments and wanted to draw the interview to a close. She took one last opportunity to add to her information. She smiled at him. 'Just one. I'm intrigued how you have the name Ashington. Can you explain that?'

Miles Ashington chuckled. 'I have a connection with the family going back a long time. I think Ann and I were cousins, perhaps twenty-nine times removed.' He laughed.

Jane joined his mirth. 'Oh, I see,' she said with a little laugh.

She stood up, her hand out to shake his. 'Thank you for seeing me, Mr Ashington, and thank you for answering all my questions.'

Miles Ashington gripped her hand firmly. 'It's been my pleasure, Jane… I can call you Jane, can't I?'

Jane smiled. 'Yes, of course you can.'

She prepared to take her leave. Her host hesitated for a second. He looked at her. 'May I ask if you are married, Jane?' he asked suddenly.

'I was married, but sadly my husband was killed in a plane crash just over three years ago. I have a fiancé again – Bob.'

Miles Ashington hesitated. 'Would you and Bob join Gail – my wife – and me for dinner one evening?' he asked.

Jane was caught off balance for an instant. She had not expected such an invitation, but it might be an opportunity to learn more about her new acquaintance in a more relaxed setting. She recovered quickly from her surprise. 'That would be very nice,' she replied readily.

'We will try and arrange something. May I have your telephone number?'

Jane dived into her bag and produced one of her personal cards, which had her home and business telephone numbers on it as well as her mobile.

'Thank you.' He glanced at the card for a second and then hurried to the desk. He put her card down and took one of his own from a silver box on the desk. He handed it to her.

'My card, Jane. It has my personal number on it, so you will come straight through to me. If you think I can be of any further help to you in any way, please do give me a ring.'

Jane thanked him and he led her down the stairs in silence to the front door, Jane taking careful steps in her high heels.

Courteous goodbyes were expressed between them on the doorstep and then Jane was alone again. As she walked away, she felt a mixture of emotions. She had wanted so much to find out who she really was, but her meeting with Miles Ashington had saddened her at times. If she was Ruth Ashington – and there was now every indication that she was – then her own mother had rejected her. The thought of that made her feel emotional again. She had been shut away in an orphanage, believing that she was alone in the world, when in reality she belonged to a very rich family. It didn't make sense. Then there was Miles Ashington. Where did he fit into all this? He had been very charming to her this afternoon, but apparently he had been part of the plot. He had knowingly allowed her to be placed in an orphanage. It was all so complicated. And if she was now Ruth Ashington, what did the future hold for her?

Chapter 29

It was later than she had anticipated when Jane returned to her office. As she walked through the main office to her tiny den, the hands of the office clock showed well after four. Soon after leaving Miles Ashington's house, she had been so deep in her thoughts that she had taken a wrong turning on the way back to the tube station and temporarily lost her way. It had delayed her return to work. Back in the office everybody seemed to be preoccupied with their own affairs and nobody asked her where she had been or why. She was glad of that: she was still so full of the events of the last few hours that she did not feel inclined to become involved in conversation.

She did one or two small jobs, made several notes for Monday morning, and left it at that. For once she was among the first to leave the office. Even on her way home the events of the afternoon still occupied her thoughts. She picked up an evening paper but hardly glanced at it.

Walking back home from the railway station, she encountered her neighbour Margot with her pug dog Sam out for an evening stroll. She exchanged pleasantries with Margot, but could hardly remember afterwards what she had said. She was glad to reach the seclusion of her home.

She had hardly entered her apartment and closed the front door when the telephone rang. Thinking it would be Bob, she was disappointed to discover that it was a nuisance sales call. She politely explained to the caller that she already had double glazing and was not interested, before quickly putting down the handset.

Kicking off her shoes, she removed a few important items from her bag and then went into the bedroom. Two minutes later she was in the shower. Refreshed, she changed into the comfort of her dressing gown and wandered into the kitchen to make herself something to eat. The thought of preparing a meal was irksome, but hunger was already reminding her that she had not taken a midday break and had scarcely had any lunch to speak of. In the end she made herself an omelette and ate it with some tomatoes that were in the fridge and going soft. She finished by making herself a mug of tea and taking it into the lounge. She knew she should contact Bob and Gerald to tell them what the afternoon's meeting with Miles Ashington had revealed. But for the moment it was nice to just rest and think. Relaxing on the settee, she once again went over the events of the afternoon.

Now it seemed that she had to accept that she was Ruth Ashington instead of Jane Carroll. She preferred to be Jane Carroll, but that person did not really exist. Only Ruth Ashington existed on paper. Even being that person was hard to accept. Why had her mother rejected her? Thinking about that again easily brought emotion to the surface. And why had she been placed in an orphanage and ignored by those who should have loved and cared for her? It was all almost too complicated and stressful to think about.

The sound of her mobile alerted Jane. She woke up with a start, stretched full length on the settee. She must have fallen asleep, lying there and thinking about things. For a few seconds she struggled to recall where the ringing was coming from. Then she realised she had left her mobile on the dressing table. She dashed into the bedroom to retrieve it. Grabbing it, pressing the answer button and putting it to her ear came automatically.

'Hello.'

'Jane, it's Bob. I've been trying to get you on your landline for ages. It's always unobtainable.'

Jane glanced at her watch. She had been asleep for over an hour.

She gave a hurried 'Give me a second' and hastened into the hall. She picked up the telephone handset and clicked it into place. It had not been replaced correctly.

She spoke to Bob as she returned to the lounge. 'Darling, I'm dreadfully sorry. I had one of those wretched sales calls earlier in the evening and I can't have put the phone down properly. I really am sorry.'

She heard a chuckle at the other end of the line. 'Oh, that's OK. I just wondered where you were. You know, you can register with a number to eliminate those calls.'

'Yes, I know. I did do it once, but it's possible it's run out or something.'

'Anyway, how are you? You sound a bit down this evening,' said Bob..

Jane knew it was true. She struggled to be a bit more cheerful. 'Darling, I am sorry. I'm missing your company. It's just that the meeting with Miles Ashington has made me a bit emotional. I'm feeling better just talking to you.'

'That's what I was ringing about. How did things go?'

Jane thought for a second, recalling the afternoon's meeting, before answering. 'He was quite helpful really, but from what he told me it looks as if I am Ruth Ashington.'

She hesitated for a second before asking the question that had suddenly occurred to her. 'How do you fancy tying up with Ruth Ashington instead of Jane Carroll?'

'Poppet, I don't care if you're called Dracula. I will still love you.'

Bob's reply almost brought tears to Jane's eyes. His reply had sounded so loving. Her voice was soft and quiet when she replied. 'Darling, thank you for saying that.'

Bob wanted to know more. 'So, what did you find out?' he asked eagerly.

Jane thought for a moment, formulating a brief résumé of the afternoon's events, and then related as much as she could remember.

When she had finished, Bob's reaction was immediate. 'Phew. That's a bit of a load to accept all at once,' he replied thoughtfully. 'I mean, being rejected by your mother and then put in an orphanage is a bit weird.'

A slight wave of emotion swept over Jane as Bob reiterated the circumstances of her upbringing, but she managed to control it.

'So what will the next step be?' he asked.

Jane forced a little laugh. 'I'm not sure. Accept that I'm now called Ruth Ashington, I suppose.' She thought for a second. 'I'm not really sure I want to be Ruth Ashington. I think I prefer to be Jane Carroll – but that person doesn't exist,' she said quietly.

Bob was quick to make a suggestion. 'It's not all that difficult to change your name,' he pointed out.

Jane had to agree. 'Yes, I know. I did have some experience of that when I lost Graham. I changed my surname back to Carroll. My married name was Hawkins.'

Bob did not respond to Jane's reply. Instead he started to ask her more questions about her visit to Miles Ashington: where did the well-known businessman live? What did he look like? Did they talk about anything other than Jane's early life? He had a host of questions to ask.

Answering Bob's questions lifted Jane briefly out of her gloom. It was good to change the subject and talk about other aspects of the afternoon, including Miles Ashington's dinner invitation. When she had finished she was not quite prepared for Bob's next suggestion.

Bob hesitated a second before speaking. 'I've just been thinking. Since you're feeling a bit sad about this afternoon, would you like to cancel the session at the studio tomorrow?'

Jane reaction was immediate. 'No, no! I want to do it. I'll be there as we arranged.'

It was a turning point. Jane did her best to throw off her gloom and they chatted over their plans for the following day. They talked for a long time. By the time they had wished each other goodnight, it was already turned half past nine.

The following day did not start well. Jane had had a disturbed night. Though she had gone to bed at her normal time, sleep had not come immediately. She had started to go over the events of the afternoon again, and her thoughts had kept her awake. It had been early morning when she had finally dropped off. The result was that she overslept.

She woke from a muddled dream and for a second or two had a job to remember where she was. As recollection jolted her back into reality, a quick glance at the bedroom clock told her that she was late. The hands indicated that it was a quarter to eight. Remembering that she had a hairdressing appointment at half past eight made her jump out of bed in a flash. A quick shower and a hurried cup of coffee was all that time would allow. Desperation prompted her to use the car to get to her appointment on time.

Emerging from the hairdressing salon, she made a quick call into the supermarket close by to stock up on provisions. She purchased more than she had intended and in the end was glad she had the car with her.

While she was struggling up the stairs leading to her apartment, she met Gerald and was reminded that despite her good intentions she had not contacted him the previous evening to tell him what she had learnt during her meeting with Miles Ashington.

On seeing her, Gerald's face immediately broke into a smile. 'Ah, Jane, good morning. I was just thinking about you.'

'Good morning, Gerald. I've been meaning to contact you and update you on what's been happening. I'm sorry I didn't make it yesterday evening.'

Gerald brushed aside her apology. 'You're a busy person,' he commiserated.

'Would you like to come up now, and I can tell you all about it?' she suggested politely.

Gerald hesitated. 'Well, if you're sure it isn't inconvenient, I could come up for a few minutes,' he replied, looking a bit anxious.

Jane's response was to smile at him and start climbing the stairs again. Gerald offered to carry one of her bags, for which she was grateful. Just in the short trip from the car the plastic handle had been biting into her hand.

They arrived at her apartment. Jane fumbled for her keys and let Gerald into the hall. They were both relieved to put down the bags of shopping.

'Will you come into the lounge and sit down for a minute?' asked Jane.

Gerald shook his head. 'No. I can't stay very long. I'm meeting Anna at the shops.'

Jane felt relieved. She knew that time was already running out for her meeting with Bob.

'Anna and I are most interested to hear what happened when you went to see Miles Ashington,' said Gerald.

Once again, Jane related briefly the information she had gleaned from Miles Ashington. She finished up by stating her new identity. 'So it now looks as if I have a new name – Ruth Ashington.' She forced a smile and then added quickly, 'But I think I'll remain Jane Carroll for the present.'

When Jane had finished, Gerald's reaction was spontaneous. 'Well, of course we expected that. What we need to do now is to fill in the details.'

Jane was a bit surprised by Gerald's matter-of-a-fact answer. It seemed to her that he was quite happy to acknowledge that she was now Ruth Ashington. She was formulating a suitable reply, but Gerald seemed keen to tell her something.

'But I've got a bit of new information for you,' he said.

The tone of his voice stirred Jane's curiosity. 'Tell me,' she prompted.

Gerald needed no urging. 'I told you Eric had the bit between his teeth,' he announced with a smile. He continued before Jane could say anything. 'He's been delving into the Ashington family. He's discovered that Miles Ashington changed his name to Ashington just before he married Ann Ashington.'

The news brought an exclamation of surprise from Jane. 'Gosh!

He never mentioned that to me. He said he was a distant cousin of Ann's.'

'It's quite possible,' Gerald pointed out quickly.

'I suppose so,' said Jane thoughtfully, her initial surprise dispersing.

'But here's more from Eric,' Gerald remarked.

'Please tell me,' urged Jane.

'Miles Ashington was married previously. He was divorced shortly before marrying Ann Ashington.'

'That's odd. I thought it was his first marriage.'

Gerald shook his head. 'At the time of his marriage to Jane he had a seven-year-old son.'

'Phew. That's interesting,' said Jane. 'He never mentioned any of that yesterday.' She added thoughtfully, 'But I suppose he didn't have any need to. We were talking about me.'

Gerald nodded in agreement. 'Absolutely,' he said.

Suddenly he glanced at his watch. 'Goodness!' he exclaimed anxiously. 'Anna will wonder what's happened to me. I must be on my way.'

Jane ushered him out. 'Thank Eric for me, and I hope I haven't made you late.'

Gerald was already hurrying away, talking as he went. 'Oh, he'll most likely find out more. He doesn't give up.'

He had disappeared before Jane could say anything else.

Jane closed her door, realising that she, too, was late. Gone were her plans to do a few jobs before going to meet Bob. Now she only just had time to get ready.

Gerald's revelation about Miles Ashington had been most interesting. It made Jane wonder what other dark secrets about the Ashingtons would come to light. Somehow she had an inkling that there was more to learn about the family she was apparently part of.

Chapter 30

Jane arrived for work early on the Monday morning. For several days now she had made a point of getting up just those few minutes early and catching an earlier train. Her strategy was twofold. One, the train was less crowded, and two, arriving first in the office gave her the opportunity to do one or two jobs and plan her day without any interruptions.

She felt quite buoyant. In spite of her initial reaction on the Friday to her meeting with Miles Ashington, by Saturday evening after talking things through with Bob she had begun to see things in a different light. Bob had been extremely supportive, and his logical reasoning had filtered through to her. She had become much more philosophical over the whole thing. As Bob had pointed out, she was still the same person as before Friday, and it would not be too difficult to change her name.

She had enjoyed Saturday, in spite of the late start and the time spent talking to Gerald. In the end she had had to call Bob on his mobile to tell him that she was running late. She had eventually met him in a pub close to his studio. Being Saturday, it was not at all busy, and they had had a quiet drink and a spot of lunch, taking their time and chatting about the events of the previous few days. Talking things over with Bob had allayed many of Jane's fears and worries, and when they eventually emerged from the pub she was feeling much better about things.

In the studio, Bob made them both a mug of coffee and Jane sat and enjoyed watching him set up the lighting to take the photograph of her. When he announced that he was ready, she obediently slipped out of her jacket and blouse and sat as she was directed. Bob took a number of head and shoulder shots of her and at one point asked her to take off her necklace. She enjoyed seeing Bob at work and admired his skill and dedication. When he at last announced, 'That's it. Finished,' she wanted to see the photographs, but Bob insisted on not showing her anything until they had been printed.

For the first two days of the week Annette was out of the office a good deal and the staff only saw her briefly at intervals. Jane and Amy were pleased about this, because it enabled them to concentrate on their work without the interruptions that usually took place when Annette was in the office for any length of time.

It was on the Wednesday morning that things started to happen. Jane was again in the office early and was surprised to see Annette also arrive extremely early, long before the official starting time for the office. She continued working, expecting to hear the buzz of the internal phone. It did not happen for several hours. There was no mistaking the voice on the other end when she answered it.

'Have you got a minute to come up, Jane?'

'Yes, of course. I'll come right away.'

Grabbing her notepad in case she needed to take any notes, Jane made her way up to Annette's office. Amy made the usual face as she passed her desk. She had heard the phone ring and knew where Jane was heading.

Annette looked up from her desk as Jane entered the office. An almost full cup of coffee was beside her.

'Come and sit down, Jane. Would you like a coffee?'

Out of politeness, Jane helped herself to half a cup. She did not really want it, as she had just had a mug of tea made for her by Amy.

She sat down opposite Annette and waited for the usual flow of questions about work, or the sudden ideas about future projects. This time it did not happen immediately.

Annette looked at Jane for a second and then with a slight smile she announced, 'I was talking to a mutual acquaintance of ours the other evening.'

Jane was thrown off balance initially. Who on earth could

Annette know who knew her? All she could answer was, 'Oh. That's interesting.'

Annette studied Jane for a reaction. Perhaps she had expected her to ask who it was they both knew, but as no enquiry was made she was forced to reveal the name anyway. She said just two words.

'Miles Ashington.'

Jane did her best to hide her surprise. The last thing that she wanted was to talk to Annette about Miles Ashington, least of all about her own involvement with him. She struggled for an instant to find a suitable reply. In the end all she could find to say was, 'I wondered who it was.'

Annette did not seem inclined to leave the matter at that. Instead she volunteered more information. 'You appear to have made quite an impression. He asked a lot of questions about you.'

Jane gave a forced little laugh, more to hide her anxiety than anything else. Her reply was deliberately vague. 'Nice ones, I hope.'

Annette nodded. Taking a sip of her coffee, she glanced over her cup at Jane. 'Miles was most interested in you. He wanted to know a lot about you.'

Jane was stumped for a suitable reply for an instant. She need not have worried. Annette was in full control of the conversation. After taking another sip of coffee, she replaced her cup and saucer on the desk and looked at Jane again with a rather curious smile.

'I am extremely intrigued why you wanted to see Miles. Was it something to do with work?' She stopped suddenly in mid-track, remembering something, and then added quickly, 'You know we already did an article on him some years ago?'

Jane's heart sank. It was no good. Annette was clearly too curious to let the matter drop. She seemed determined to find out some information from Jane, but the last thing Jane wanted to do was discuss her meeting with Miles Ashington. She thought desperately for a solution to her predicament.

She answered Annette's question first. 'Yes, I know. It was just about the time I joined the magazine.'

She sipped her coffee to stall for a bit more time. As she did so she formulated a brief reply that she hoped might satisfy Annette. She made eye contact as she spoke again. 'I wanted to have a short discussion with him, because I've been looking into my family history and there's a possibility I am related to the Ashington family on my mother's side.'

Having delivered her explanation, Jane waited. Would it be enough to stop Annette asking further difficult questions?

Her idea appeared to work. Annette beamed admiringly at her. 'Well, you couldn't be connected with a more influential and respected family,' she remarked.

Jane decided that perhaps her best strategy now would be to ask questions instead of answering them. 'What's Miles Ashington like?' she asked quickly, before Annette could say anything else.

Annette took up the prompting. Looking at Jane all the time, she delivered her appraisal. 'He is a most charming man. I have met him on a few occasions socially. His wife, Gail, is very nice as well. They are quite well known in town for their entertaining, and their dinner parties are legendary. I've been invited to a few of them.'

It was a surprise to Jane that Annette was so well acquainted with Miles Ashington. She decided to try to find out a bit more about him while she had the opportunity. 'He appears to be a very wealthy man,' she observed casually.

Annette nodded. 'He is,' she said. 'Extremely wealthy. He is head of I don't know how many companies and has several houses dotted about the country, as well as a yacht somewhere. He is also a generous donor to charity and political campaigns.'

She ended by looking at Jane, as if to determine how she was reacting to the information.

Jane responded with another comment. 'I believe he has a son from a previous marriage.'

Annette thought for a moment before answering. 'Yes, I met him once, briefly.' She hesitated again, and then added quietly, 'I cannot say that I was as impressed with him as I am with his father.'

'What does he do?' asked Jane. 'The son, I mean.'

Annette laughed. 'Much the same as his father – heavily

involved in business interests – though I think he is taking a bigger load off his father's shoulders these days.'

'Are there no other children?'

Annette shook her head. 'None that I am aware of,' she replied. 'Miles has been married at least four times,' she added casually. 'He has only been married to Gail for about three years.'

Jane's reply was equally casual. 'Perhaps something to do with his wealth,' she remarked dryly.

Annette steered the conversation back to business. Quite out of the blue she asked, 'How's the Rompton feature coming along?'

She was referring to an article about the author J.C. Rompton, which Jane and Amy were preparing and was similar to the Angus Pike feature. It was due to appear in the next but one issue. As Annette knew the author personally, she had been keeping her eye on what Jane and Amy were going to produce and had been checking on their progress at regular intervals.

Jane had an answer ready. She was glad the conversation had turned away from Miles Ashington. 'Very well. We've got the photographs now, and the text is all ready. No changes since you last saw it.'

Annette seemed satisfied with the update. She went straight on to her current favourite topic: the forthcoming book review pages.

Jane took up the challenge and explained how things were going. It was a good half-hour before she was able to take her leave.

As she passed Amy's desk, Amy looked at her enquiringly as usual, concerned that Jane's meeting with Queen Bee might involve her in some way.

Jane grinned, remarked that Annette had wanted an update on work in progress, and left it at that. She had no intention of discussing her family history with any other member of the staff. Amy was satisfied. With a shrug of her shoulders she returned to her work.

At the end of the week Jane received an unexpected telephone call. She was working away quietly in her office one morning, when the shrill noise of her telephone disturbed her. She made a grab for it, at the same time continuing her work.

'Jane Carroll.'

A man's voice was at the other end. 'Jane, good morning! Miles Ashington here.'

It took a full two seconds for Jane to overcome her surprise, but she regained her composure quickly. 'Hello, Mr Ashington. Good morning.'

She waited. What could Miles Ashington want with her? Perhaps he had been serious about inviting her and Bob to dinner. She had thought at the time that he was simply being courteous.

He quickly explained. 'Jane, I've been thinking about you. I was at my house in the West Country over the weekend and I came across some old photographs I think you might be interested in. For example, there is one of your mother.'

Jane's heart gave a leap. Of course she was interested! Her reply echoed her excitement. 'I would love to see them.'

'I will have some copies made and let you have them.'

'That would be lovely,' replied Jane. 'Thank you.'

There was a slight pause, and then Miles Ashington spoke again. 'Jane… I was wondering whether you and your fiancé would like to join Gail and me for dinner one evening soon. I could have the photographs ready for you.'

'I'd really like that,' said Jane. 'When were you thinking of?'

There was another silence. Jane could tell that Miles Ashington was consulting his diary.

'Let's see… This Saturday evening is out… What about Saturday week? Would that suit you?' he asked.

'I think that will be OK, but I'll have to check with Bob, just in case he has something else on,' replied Jane.

'Yes, of course. Let's make that a date. Shall we say 7pm at my house? You have my telephone number. Give me a ring if it isn't convenient, or if you can't get hold of me, leave a message with my secretary.'

'That will be lovely.' The idea was beginning to appeal to Jane.

'Excellent. We will look forward to seeing you both.'

He was preparing to ring off, but Jane suddenly thought of something. 'That will be the house where I met you last week?' she asked hurriedly. She had a horror of going to the wrong place, after Annette's disclosure earlier that week.

She was quickly reassured.

'It will be indeed. Goodbye for now.'

'Goodbye... and thank you.'

Jane just had time to get the words out before the line went dead.

She was quite excited about the phone call. She had been reasonably impressed when she met Miles Ashington, but she hadn't really expected him to phone her. Now it seemed that he really wanted to help her. She just hoped Bob would want to come with her.

She need not have worried. That evening when she called Bob on her mobile and told him about Miles Ashington's invitation, he said straight away, 'I'd like to meet him.'

During their conversation Bob mentioned something Jane had had on her mind ever since Miles Ashington's phone call. 'I imagine it will be a collar and tie affair,' he said.

'I've been wondering about that too,' replied Jane. She went on, almost speaking her thoughts, 'I should think it would be.' She thought of something else. 'I suppose I could ask Annette. She goes to his dinner parties.' Even as she said it she was not keen on the idea. She really had no desire to discuss Miles Ashington further with her boss.

'We'll play it safe,' Bob chipped in. 'I'll dig out my best suit and tie and get Mrs McGinty to wash my shirt.' He laughed.

Jane knew he was joking about Mrs McGinty washing his shirt. Bob was always well turned out, even when he was dressed casually. His suggestion had given her an idea.

'I've got a cocktail dress I can wear. You've never seen it, but it's quite pretty.'

'I'll look forward to seeing you dressed up, then,' said Bob.

Jane knew he was joking, but she took the bait and pretended to be shocked. 'Darling, how can you say such a thing? You know I'm always dressed up for you. I've a good mind to wear something awful you won't like.'

Bob was quick to reply. 'Poppet, you will look beautiful in anything.'

'Hmm. Just you wait and see. You don't know me yet,' Jane replied breezily.

'Nothing you do will shock me,' Bob chipped in quickly.

With that their conversation returned to more mundane matters. Bob wanted to know where they were going for dinner with the Ashingtons, and at what time. Jane wanted to know how the photographs had turned out, and Bob told her she would have to wait and see. In the end they chatted for over half an hour.

When she returned home the following evening Jane had another surprise. In her post was a slim package. The address was written in neat handwriting that she did not recognise. Before she did anything else she tore open the package to reveal a paperback book. She glanced at the title: *A Short History of the Ashington Family and Ashington House*. There was a note tucked inside it. Jane quickly read it, puzzled as to who had sent the book:

Hi Jane,
I saw this lying on a stall at our local boot sale. I thought of you and immediately snapped it up for the grand sum of 50p. I hope you enjoy reading about the history of 'your' family.
Talk to you soon.
Love,
Lucy

Jane smiled to herself. Good old Lucy, she thought. Just like her to do this sort of thing.

She had already made up her mind that she would spend the rest of the evening reading more about the family that everything now appeared to point to her being part of.

Chapter 31

Jane was pleased with her day so far. Saturday had loomed bright and sunny and she had walked to her early-morning hairdresser's appointment. Then it had been a quick dive into the supermarket to top up on one or two things. Walking back to her apartment she had encountered Margot and her faithful Sam out for their walk. They had chatted for a few minutes until Sam decided that he wanted to continue his exercise.

Back home, Jane had quickly changed and flung herself into cleaning the apartment and doing some washing. It was close to one in the afternoon by the time she finished. She made herself a bite to eat, and topped everything with a cup of coffee, which she took into the lounge. She was just relaxing on the settee when her mobile rang. She knew it must be Bob; he was working, but he would be coming over towards evening.

She pressed the answer button. 'Hello.'

Bob's voice came through. 'Hi. It's me.'

'Hello, darling. Are you still slogging away at work?'

'We're nearly finished. I'll be able to join you earlier than I thought.'

'Super! About what time?'

'Three-ish.'

'Marvellous. We can have a cup of tea when you get here.'

She was about to say something else, but Bob beat her to it. 'I've got a surprise for you.'

'Ooh, what is it? I can't wait.'

She heard a chuckle at the other end.

'Not going to tell you.'

273

Jane almost wailed, 'Oh, no! Now I'll be all eaten up with excitement.'

Bob was enjoying himself. 'Good. I'll let you into the secret later.'

'Oh, you're horrid to me,' Jane complained, laughing. Then she suddenly thought of something else to add to the conversation. 'Anyway, I've got a surprise for you, too – and I'm not going to tell you, either.'

There was a faked sigh at the other end of the telephone. 'OK. I'll wait, but I'll want to know what your surprise is first.'

'You will,' replied Jane breezily.

'I'd better finish up now. I'll see you soon.' Bob was serious again.

'Bye, darling,' Jane replied, with a secret smile to herself.

'Bye, poppet.'

'See you—'

But he was gone.

Jane put down her mobile and relaxed back onto the settee. She sipped her coffee. She was pleased that Bob was coming early and extremely glad that she had got through all her jobs. She wondered what his surprise was, but she could guess: she hadn't seen the photographs he had taken of her yet. As for her own surprise for him, she had been planning it all week, driven by a chance remark he had made during a recent telephone conversation, with just that little bit of wickedness added to her intention. Putting the final touches to her plan was the next item on her agenda. On her way home the previous day, she had popped into Mario's and reserved a table for the evening. At first Mario had protested that the restaurant was fully booked, but after gentle coaxing from Jane he had found room for them, provided they arrived early. In the end she had secured a table for seven o'clock and felt well pleased with her efforts to generate an extra surprise for Bob.

Draining the last of her coffee, she dived into her bedroom. She knew it was there somewhere: the dress she had scheduled ages ago as part of a clear-out she had never got round to. She found it in a bag at the back of her second wardrobe. She pulled it out and held it up, scrutinising it. It was a long-sleeved, drab brown affair, knee length and buttoned up to the neck. She had acquired it during her marriage and had worn it only once. Graham had joked and threatened to divorce her if she ever wore it again. It had been hidden away, regarded as a bad buy on her part. Today she had a use for it.

She spent a while having a relaxing bath and then, worried that the time was slipping by, she started to panic. It was essential to her plan that she be completely ready when Bob arrived. Hurriedly finishing off, she went back into the bedroom.

It did not take her long to put on underwear and slip into the dress. A glance in the mirror confirmed to her how awful it actually was. Next came the cheap tights she had purchased from a market stall a few days earlier: dark brown, with an ugly pattern. When it came to footwear she was stuck for a few minutes. Then she remembered that the only thing she had in her wardrobe that would serve her escapade was the pair of lace-up ankle boots she kept tucked away for walking in the snow. It seemed to take ages to put them on and do up the laces, and all the time she was worried that Bob might suddenly arrive early. She quickly found the never-used dark lipstick she had acquired as a sample somewhere, and applied a generous coating to her lips. Next, dark eyeshadow added to the effect. To complete the makeover, she found a long, hideous string of beads, which she dangled round her neck. A final glance in the mirror made her realise that she found it hard to even recognise her own image. She grinned to herself. She was ready.

It was fast approaching three o'clock when the doorbell rang. It couldn't be Bob, unless somebody had let him into the block. She hurried to the door and looked through the spyhole. Gerald stood on the other side. She flung open the door.

'Hello, Gerald.'

'Hello, Jane. I just—' Gerald stopped abruptly as his eyes regarded her.

Jane realised she must have blushed visibly. 'Oh, I'm sorry, Gerald. I was waiting for Bob, and… I was dressing up for something.'

The words just came out. She had momentarily forgotten how

she was dressed in her haste to answer the door. Fortunately Gerald seemed to accept her explanation.

'Please come in,' she urged.

Gerald stepped into the hall. 'I don't want to hinder you, but I wanted to tell you that Eric contacted me yesterday evening.'

'That sounds interesting. Come into the lounge.'

Gerald shook his head. 'I just wanted to tell you that he is continuing the Ashington family research. He's been very busy on another project recently, but that is now finished and he is taking up the Ashington business again.'

'Oh, that's really sweet of him.' Suddenly Jane remembered something that had been worrying her. She voiced her concern. 'But if he does it all professionally, surely I have to agree a fee with him for his services?' She looked at Gerald for an answer.

Gerald shook his head again and raised his hand in protest. 'No,' he replied. 'Gerald is an old friend. We shared much together and he is doing it as a favour for me – and you, of course.'

Jane was slightly embarrassed. So far, she felt, she had contributed very little to her family history. 'It really is very nice of him, but it does seem a little unfair,' she said.

Gerald smiled at her. 'Eric was very impressed with you when he met you. He wants to help you and he also likes the challenge of a mystery to unravel.'

'What did he do for a living before he started doing genealogy?'

'He was a solicitor,' Gerald replied, with another little smile.

Jane suddenly thought of something she wanted to show Gerald. 'Just a second,' she said.

She dashed into the lounge and returned with the book about the Ashington family. She handed it to him. 'My friend Lucy picked this up at a boot sale and sent it to me,' she explained.

Gerald read out the title. 'This looks very interesting,' he remarked. He studied the contents of the book, turning the pages slowly. 'I wonder if Eric knows about this. I must tell him.'

Jane interrupted his musing. 'I just want to show it to Bob, and then you can borrow it,' she suggested.

'Yes, of course,' replied Gerald, readjusting his spectacles and handing the book back to her. 'Thank you,' he added. 'I would really like to have some time with it.'

They chatted for a few more minutes and then Gerald looked at his watch and said he did not want to take up any more of Jane's time. With a promise from her that she would drop the book in over the weekend, he departed.

Closing the front door, Jane stole another glance in the hall mirror. What must Gerald have thought about her appearance? No doubt he would tell Anna, and Jane would have some more explaining to do, but that was for later. She was rather glad that Bob had not arrived while she was talking to him.

Almost twenty minutes later the outer door buzzer rang loud and clear.

Jane pressed the button to speak. 'Hello.'

'It's me,' answered Bob's voice.

'Come in, me,' she responded cheerfully. She could not help adding, 'I'm all ready for you.'

She stood in the hall, one hand on the door latch. Her heart was thumping. She waited until the doorbell rang, and then she threw open the door.

'Darling, it's marvellous to see you.'

She threw her arms round Bob and nuzzled him for a kiss.

When she broke free from the embrace, she realised that he was looking at her with a mixture of surprise and shock. He closed the door silently and then turned to her without a word as he took in her appearance.

Jane stepped back, beaming at him. She glanced down at her attire, her hands holding her skirt wide.

'What do you think of my new image?' she asked.

Bob was lost for words. 'Well... I...'

Jane was pleased with her escapade. 'You said you wanted to see me dressed up, so this is what I thought.'

Bob was looking glum. 'I'm not sure if I like it,' he replied, scrutinising her outfit.

'Oh, I expect it's just a matter of getting used to it. I'm sure you'll like it in the end,' responded Jane, smiling at him as she turned to walk into the lounge.

Bob followed her in silence. He sat down on the settee. He looked both shocked and gloomy.

Jane sat down opposite him. She was enjoying her prank.

'I thought I might wear this when we go for dinner with Miles Ashington and his wife,' she announced casually, still concealing her humour.

Bob still had an air of disbelief about him. 'Why have you got to change your image?' he asked.

'Well, darling, you said I'd look nice in anything.'

'I'm not sure if I had in mind the sort of thing you're wearing now,' he replied, still staring at her.

'I thought I might change my hairstyle as well – perhaps have it dyed,' Jane remarked, continuing the ruse.

Bob looked at her but said nothing.

Maybe I'll buy some different shoes as well – more like these.' She glanced down at her footwear as she spoke.

'Why not wellington boots?' remarked Bob in a decidedly sarcastic tone.

Jane took up the challenge. 'Darling, you don't seem to like my new image at all.' She gave him a bemused look.

'I preferred you as you were,' he replied quietly.

Jane looked at him. She could see that she had continued her joke long enough. Bob was looking sad and bewildered. The last thing she had wanted was to upset him. Prompted by his remark the previous week, she had planned everything meticulously, but now she realised the folly of her prank. She had initiated something that had gone horribly wrong.

A wave of anxiety swept over her. Had her silly joke damaged her relationship with Bob?

Chapter 32

Suddenly Jane jumped up and went to sit beside Bob. She had to try and do something to rectify the situation. She placed her hand on his arm.

'Darling, I'm sorry if I've upset you with my silly prank.' She looked at him anxiously.

Bob looked at her. There was a glimmer of a smile beginning to appear as he took in her words.

Jane was feeling sad now. She put her arms round him, resting her head on his shoulder. She spoke softly. 'I really am sorry. I didn't mean to shock you or make you angry. It was just something silly I thought up after what you said – and now I've made a mess of things.' As she finished speaking, she looked anxiously at him again. There were almost tears in her eyes now.

For the first time since he had arrived Bob appeared to be more relaxed. 'If you're not careful, I won't give you your present,' he announced, smiling at her.

'Oh, no… Please,' she pleaded.

Bob just grinned at her.

Relieved, Jane took control. She gave him a peck on his cheek and whispered, 'Give me five minutes. I'm going to change.'

She was already jumping up and heading towards the bedroom. She spoke over her shoulder. 'How about a cup of tea? Everything is ready. Just click the kettle on.'

The five minutes became nearer ten. Once in her bedroom, Jane frantically tore off the dress, the ghastly shoes and the tights, but it took her longer than she had anticipated to remove the dark eyeshadow and lipstick. She knew what she was going to wear. She took it out of her wardrobe. It was a pink summer dress with a halter neck. It left her shoulders and a good deal of her back bare, but it was just right, she thought, for the occasion, and when they went out this evening she could drape her white cardigan over her shoulders. She had a pendant necklace to enhance the plunging neckline. It meant that she had to remove the engagement ring on its chain from around her neck. For a second she was tempted to place it on her finger, but somehow she hesitated to do so and instead placed it safely in the jewellery box at the back of her dressing-table drawer, where she kept it hidden whenever she was not with Bob. Replacement lipstick and a dab of perfume were quickly applied. Carrying a pair of soft-topped high-heeled white court shoes she had purchased during the week, she reappeared in the lounge. She lifted first one foot and then the other to slip on her shoes as she entered.

'How's this, darling?' She twirled round, swirling the skirt as she spoke.

Bob looked up from the Ashington book, which he had picked up from the table.

'I like what I see,' he replied, with a smile.

Jane sat down beside him and snuggled up to him. 'Am I forgiven?' she asked softly.

Bob grinned at her. 'I'll think about it.'

'Please,' Jane whispered in his ear.

Bob kissed her gently. 'Don't give me a shock like that again.' He smiled again.

Jane leaned her head on his shoulder. 'I promise I won't do it again,' she murmured.

Suddenly she sat upright and gave him a mischievous grin. 'You can spank me if you want to.' Just to spice up her statement, she added a bit more. 'Graham spanked me once.' She made a face. 'On my bare bottom.'

Bob pretended to be serious. 'Good for him,' he remarked.

He was amused and intrigued by Jane's revelation. He wanted to know more. 'And what had you done to justify such drastic punishment?' he asked.

Jane gave him a coy look. 'I burnt one of his favourite shirts when I was ironing; and then when he was angry about it, I threw a cup of water over him.'

Bob burst out laughing. 'Then you clearly deserved it,' he announced firmly, as if that was the final word on the subject.

'You're not supposed to say that,' complained Jane.

Bob gave her a quick kiss. 'Just behave in future,' he replied.

Jane snuggled up to him again. She clasped her arms around him. 'You wouldn't do that to me would you?' she whispered.

Bob was slow in responding.

Jane shot upright again. 'Would you?' She looked anxiously at him.

'I'll certainly think about it,' he announced, pretending to be serious.

'Oh, no.' Jane wailed. She was not sure if Bob was joking, but she was determined to play the role of the helpless female for a bit longer.

She wrapped her arms around him again. 'If you do, I'll squeal the place down and then all my neighbours will come knocking at my door. Then they'll send for the police and you'll be arrested for beating me,' she said softly.

Bob gave a big sigh. 'Ah, the problems of modern living,' he replied.

Suddenly he gave her a quick kiss.

'Have you noticed anything about me?' she asked.

'I noticed the dress,' Bob chipped in quickly, his eyes on the cleft between her breasts and the pendant hanging there.

Jane held up her hand and displayed her ring finger. 'I should be wearing your ring on my finger, but I've still not got used to my new name. I just want to be Jane Carroll for a bit longer,' she almost whispered as she again burrowed her face in his shoulder.

Before Bob could make any response, she added, almost to herself, 'I suppose I do know who I am now.'

'Ruth Ashington,' said Bob.

Jane was rather pensive. Her thoughts translated into speech.

She sat up again and regarded Bob as she spoke. 'You know, Bob, I don't really want to be Ruth Ashington. I much prefer to be Jane Carroll. I think I really want to remain Jane Carroll.'

'What? Not even Jane Harker?' Bob faked shock.

Jane jumped in quickly. 'No! I don't mean that, silly. I meant until you marry me.'

Bob changed the subject. 'How about that cup of tea?' he asked.

'I'll get it,' said Jane, making a move to get up.

'I made it ages ago. I bet it's gone cold now,' he laughed.

'I'll warm it up.'

Jane was already fumbling for one of her shoes, which had come off during their discourse and disappeared under the settee. As she replaced it and started to walk towards the kitchen, taking careful steps on the new, slippery soles, Bob picked up the book again. 'I'll talk to you about that over tea,' Jane called out just before she disappeared from view.

The tea had gone cold. Jane had to start again. Several minutes later she arrived back in the lounge carrying the tea and a plate of chocolate biscuits – Bob's favourite. Bob was still engrossed in the book. He looked up as she set the tray down on the table.

'This is really interesting,' he commented.

Jane busied herself with the tea and did not reply immediately.

'I've read through it several times,' she replied, handing Bob a cup.

He looked at her. She seemed subdued suddenly, a direct contrast to the teasing and joking of earlier. 'What do you think about it?' he asked, adding a biscuit to his saucer.

Jane thought for a second. 'It's interesting, but the bit about the family being involved in the slave trade really bothers me. Whoever wrote the book seems to glorify in that part of the family history.' She took up her cup of tea as she spoke.

Bob thought for a second about what she had just said. 'Hmm. Perhaps written by an academic who specialises in that bit of history.'

Jane turned to him, concerned. She spoke quietly. 'But, Bob, if I really am Ruth Ashington, and it now certainly looks that way, these are my ancestors who did all those terrible things to poor, innocent people.' She looked imploringly at him.

'Poppet, you can't be held responsible for the actions of your ancestors,' Bob replied. He could see that Jane was upset by the revelations in the book.

Jane was silent for a few seconds. 'Yes, I know, but it's just the thought of what happened to all those people – whole families dragged from their environment and transported all those miles across the sea. They must have been petrified. And then sold and forced to work to make money for my ancestors.'

'It's a pretty bad part of history,' agreed Bob. He was scanning through the book as he spoke. He stopped to look at a page and showed it to Jane. 'Have you seen this picture of Ashington House?' he asked.

Jane nodded. 'Yes, I have.' She thought for a second. 'That's where I must have lived when I was tiny, before I was put in the orphanage.' She looked up at Bob. 'I'd like to see it again,' she remarked quietly.

'We could drive down there sometime,' suggested Bob. A thought struck him. 'Even tomorrow.'

There was a glimmer of excitement about Jane as she poured out her tea. 'Could we? I'd really like that.'

'Why not?' answered Bob. 'We'll get up early,' he added.

Jane made a face, and then looked a bit concerned. 'Darling, I haven't told you yet. I booked us in at Mario's this evening. My treat.'

'We'll have to be careful how much wine we drink, then.' He laughed.

They settled down to have their tea, Bob munching the chocolate biscuits and Jane making one biscuit last to keep him company. It wasn't until they had finished that she suddenly remembered something.

'Darling, do I get my surprise now?' she asked excitedly, adding with a wry smile, 'After all, you've had yours.'

Bob pretended to be serious and offended. 'After that nasty joke, I'm not sure if you deserve it,' he replied.

Jane grabbed his arm. 'Oh, please,' she implored him.

'OK. I'll forgive you. Just this once,' he replied, hiding his amusement at her anxiety.

He got up and went into the hall, where he had left his weekend bag and a rather interesting package that had caught Jane's attention when he arrived. He came back into the lounge, sat down beside her again and handed her the package. 'Here you are, poppet – though I'm not sure you deserve it after your surprise for me,' he said with a grin.

Jane took up the challenge. She planted a kiss on his lips. 'Darling, I'll make it up to you, I promise.'

He laughed. 'I'll make sure you do.' Then he urged her, 'Open it.'

Jane placed the package on her knee and gently prised open the covering paper. Two large photographs mounted in stiff edging frames were revealed. They were the photographs Bob had taken of her the previous week. One was in full colour, the other black and white. In the first she was wearing her necklace, but the second had been taken after Bob had asked her to remove it.

Jane stared at the photographs for what seemed a long time. She was speechless with joy. She suddenly became aware of Bob watching her intently. She lifted her gaze from the photographs. 'Darling, they are beautiful. Thank you.'

She gave him a quick kiss and then turned her attention to the photographs again. 'I never expected anything like this,' she murmured. 'They've come out so marvellous.'

'I'm rather pleased with them myself,' Bob exclaimed with a chuckle.

'I'm going to frame one of them,' Jane announced suddenly. She hesitated. 'The trouble is that they're both so nice that I can't make my mind up which one.' She held them both up, viewing them critically.

'Black and white has a certain quality that is not obtainable with colour,' observed Bob, eyeing up the photographs.

'I'll probably frame both and alternate them,' laughed Jane.

'I've got something else.' Bob returned to his overnight bag and reappeared holding a small paper wallet. He handed it to Jane.

She looked at him, surprised, for a second, before curiosity made her investigate the wallet. There were six photographs inside, taken at the dinner dance several weeks before. Two were of them arriving at the event, and the others were random shots taken at various times during the evening. One even showed Bob placing the engagement ring on Jane's finger.

Jane gazed at Bob questioningly, her pleasure curtailing her speech.

Bob grinned at her. 'I know the photographers,' he explained.

She smiled back. 'Our engagement recorded on film,' she murmured softly.

'No getting out of it now,' chuckled Bob.

Jane gave him a peck on the cheek. 'I don't want to get out of it,' she retorted reproachfully.

She turned to Bob with a look of mock concern. 'That is, unless after my naughty prank you don't want to know me any more.'

Chapter 33

'It can't be far now.' Jane gave a quick glance at Bob before returning her attention to the road.

Bob looked at the map on his knees. 'It's not,' he reassured her. 'I calculate that it's only about another two miles.'

'Great.' Jane had been driving for about an hour and a half and was now looking forward to a break.

She had enjoyed the previous evening. They had made their way early to Mario's and were surprised and delighted to be given one of the best tables in the restaurant. Mario had fussed over them, flirting with Jane and feasting his eyes on her dress. Knowing that they would be driving early the next morning, they had drunk sparingly from the bottle of wine they had ordered. In the end Mario had recorked it and they had departed from the restaurant carrying the half-full bottle in a paper bag.

Once back at Jane's apartment they had made themselves a drink, chatted for a while and then retreated to bed, with the intention of getting up early. Their lovemaking had been brief, which had left Jane slightly disappointed as she was still feeling bad about her prank earlier in the day and desperately wanted to make it up to Bob. She fell asleep vowing to rectify the situation at the earliest possible moment.

That morning Bob had woken up with a headache and Jane had wanted to cancel their excursion. However, Bob had assured her that the problem would soon disappear and that he was happy to go as long as she drove the first half of the way. In the end she had insisted on driving the whole distance so that he could relax. They had made a comfort stop at a motorway service station and

286

in the end had taken time for a cup of coffee. Now the end of the journey was in sight.

'Do you think we'll be able to talk to anybody living in the house?' asked Jane, braking quickly for a sharp bend in the road.

'It really depends on who's there now,' replied Bob. 'We know it can't be Miles Ashington.' He glanced at the map again. 'We must be getting close.' Almost immediately he exclaimed, 'There it is!'

Jane instinctively slowed the car and caught a brief glimpse of two iron gates out of the corner of her eye as they passed.

'There's a layby. We can park there,' said Bob.

Jane had already spied it, just a few yards ahead. She carefully steered the BMW into it. There was just about room for two cars to park off the road.

Bob was the first to jump out. Jane was a bit slower, as she changed her driving shoes for something more elegant.

Jane clicked the car locked and together they walked back to the gates of Ashington House. It was a glorious morning, with the sun shining brightly. Somewhere close by church bells were ringing.

'There must be a village somewhere near here,' observed Jane, with a quick glance in the direction of the sound.

'There it is. You can just see the church, over there.' Bob pointed towards some trees across the fields.

Jane looked where he was indicating and could just see the spire of a church.

They reached the entrance to the drive, and stopped. They both stared in disbelief at the gates and then at each other.

'It looks almost abandoned,' remarked Jane.

The tall iron gates that guarded the entrance were rusty and neglected. A large padlock and a rusty chain secured them. It was obvious they had not been opened for years. Beyond them a drive overgrown with weeds disappeared round a bend not far away. Clearly it had been a long time since any motor vehicle had driven along it.

'Somebody comes in here regularly, though.' Bob pointed to

the half-open side gate. A narrow path had been worn, leading away from it.

'Shall we enquire at the lodge?' asked Jane.

A stone-built lodge stood beside the gates. It had some appearance of being lived in. Curtains hung at the windows and the front garden was tidy, with flowers growing in the beds. Jane opened the little gate and they went up the short path to the front door. Bob pressed the doorbell. Somewhere in the distance they could hear the bell ring.

There was no answer.

'Try again,' urged Jane.

Again they received no answer.

'Nobody at home,' concluded Bob with a sigh.

'Let's walk up to the house,' suggested Jane, with a final glance at the lodge windows.

Hand in hand they followed the worn path along the drive.

'People must walk their dogs here,' Bob observed, pointing to the evidence at the side of the track.

At that instant they reached the bend in the drive and the house stood in front of them. Its appearance prompted an exclamation of surprise and shock from Jane.

'It's a ruin!'

All that was left of a once-elegant house were gaunt, roofless walls reaching up to the sky. The windows were all gaping holes devoid of glass. The whole building had an air of desolation and decay about it.

For several minutes they peered at the scene in front of them, and then they walked towards the building. The front door had long been boarded up, but they peered through one of the lower windows. What once must have been quite big and grand rooms were now a mass of debris and fallen roof timbers. In some places vegetation was well established, growing in areas where it could obtain nutriment.

Jane turned to Bob. She spoke quietly. 'I wonder what happened,' she said casually.

Bob gazed around at the remains of the house. 'It looks as if it was destroyed by fire,' he replied.

'It's rather sad. It must have been such a nice house.'

'Do you remember anything?' asked Bob. 'About living here, I mean.'

Crestfallen, Jane shook her head. 'I was too small. I just remember the orphanage.'

In silence they wandered around what remained of the house. It was the same story everywhere. Everything had been burnt out.

'It must have been a colossal fire to do this much damage,' observed Bob at one point.

Jane did not reply. She was feeling sad and disappointed. She had expected this visit to be more positive and perhaps contribute some more snippets of information about her past. Now it all seemed pretty dismal.

While they were at the back of the house, Jane suddenly clutched Bob's arm. 'Look!' she whispered. 'Someone's watching us.'

Bob followed the direction of her gaze. In the distance, near what might have been the kitchen garden of the house, stood an elderly man. He looked as if he had been pushing a wheelbarrow, but he appeared to have set this down to take his time to observe them.

'I think we'd better go and say something,' whispered Jane.

'Agreed,' muttered Bob. He could not help adding, 'Probably get told off for trespassing.'

They walked towards the man. He stood motionless, regarding them. As they approached, Bob gave out a cheerful 'Good morning.'

'Morning.' The reply was courteous but cautious.

'Good morning.' Jane greeted him with a sweet smile. She felt she had to add something. 'I suppose we're trespassing really, but I just wanted to see the house again. You see, I used to live here.'

The man absorbed the information for a few seconds. When he replied it was with carefully chosen words. 'Nay, it's no problem. Plenty of folk from the village come this way.'

'What happened to the house?' asked Bob. 'When did it burn down?'

Their informant thought for a bit. He pushed his cap back and scratched his head as if seeking inspiration.

'Over twenty years ago,' he eventually replied.

'But how did it catch fire?' insisted Jane.

The man looked at her. 'Well, it was standing empty and then vandals got in and started a fire. By the time the fire brigade got here, there wasn't much left.'

'Why was it empty?' Jane was determined to get as much information as possible.

The man gave a sort of grunt. 'I suppose the Ashingtons didn't want to live here any more.'

'Was that Miles Ashington?' It was Bob who asked the question.

'Aye.'

Jane had more questions she wanted to ask. 'Did you know Ann Ashington?' she began.

The man looked at her. A kind of grin lit up his face. 'I worked for her for ten years. I was the gardener here.'

Jane was about to ask something else when the man interrupted her. 'Did you say you once lived in the house? Were you a servant?' he asked.

Jane shook her head. 'I'm Ruth Ashington,' she explained. It was the first time that she had referred to herself by that name.

The man stared at her with a mixture of surprise and disbelief.

'I'm Ann Ashington's daughter,' she emphasised.

The man continued to regard her with incredulity. 'Were you the baby she had?' he asked.

'Yes, I think so,' replied Jane, with a smile.

'We thought you'd died,' he remarked. The statement was rather matter-of-fact.

Jane could not help giving a little laugh. 'Well, I'm here in front of you,' she replied cheerfully.

The man's face suddenly broke into a smile. 'My Bett would

like to talk to you,' he announced. 'She looked after you when you were a baby.'

A wave of excitement swept over Jane. There was somebody around who knew her in her younger days. 'Is it possible to see her now?' she asked excitedly.

'Aye. Come with me.' As if to give substance to his offer, the man stooped down to pick up his wheelbarrow and started to move towards what looked like a walled garden.

'What's your name?' Jane asked him kindly as they started to walk.

'Albert Simmons.'

'And is Bett your wife?'

'Aye. We live in the lodge,' replied Albert. 'Bett's sight is not so good these days. Doctors reckon they can do something, but we don't know when.'

'Oh, I'm sorry to hear that,' exclaimed Jane, giving him a sympathetic glance.

'Nay. We manage all right.'

They reached the entrance door to what turned out to be the garden of the house. Bob and Jane allowed Albert to enter first with his wheelbarrow, and took in their new surroundings. The garden was large and was surrounded by a high wall. Everything was neatly laid out

'I like your garden!' exclaimed Bob.

Albert gave a chuckle. 'Been at it nearly forty years,' he grinned.

Albert was moving towards an elderly, grey-haired woman who was seated in a chair.

'When it's a nice day, Bett likes to come and keep me company when I'm working here,' explained Albert.

'Can she see anything at all?' Jane asked in a low voice.

'Not a lot.'

They were now close to the woman in the chair. Albert cleared his throat and addressed her. 'Bett, I've got a lady and a gentleman here. Lady says she's Ruth Ashington.'

Bett stirred immediately. 'Come and talk to me, dear.' Her voice was clear and vibrant.

Jane stooped down beside her and took her hand. 'I'm Ruth Ashington. This is my fiancé, Bob.'

Bob shook Bett's hand. 'Hello, Bett. I'm Bob Harker.'

'It's nice to meet you both,' said Bett. 'You say you are Ruth Ashington, dear?'

Jane summed up her background as briefly as she could. She was keen to know more from Bett if possible. 'Yes. I always thought I was Jane Carroll, but I've being researching my family and now it seems that I'm Ruth Ashington. I met Miles Ashington recently and he seemed to confirm this.'

Bett repeated her husband's previous statement. 'We always understood that you died quite young,' she said.

For the second time in ten minutes Jane was puzzled by the comment, but she responded as she had done previously. 'Well it seems that I didn't, and here I am talking to you today.'

It occurred to her that she could furnish some detail. 'I was in an orphanage until I was in my teens,' she added.

'We always wondered where you disappeared to. Nobody said anything about where you were,' remarked Bett thoughtfully.

'Can you tell me more about my early life?' asked Jane, keen to learn more.

'Why not invite them in for a cup of tea?' It was Albert who interrupted the conversation. While Jane and Bett had been conversing, he and Bob had just been standing watching.

'Yes,' replied Bett enthusiastically. 'Do come and have a cup of tea with us, and we can chat more.'

Jane turned to Bob. 'Shall we?'

'I'd love to,' he replied.

'Albert, give me a hand.' Bett was getting up from her chair. Albert sprang into action to help her.

The four of them walked back to the lodge, Bett on Albert's arm. Jane was on her other side, and Bett told her that she had lost her sight gradually over the years, but on her latest visit to the specialist it had been indicated that they might be able to partially restore it. Bob walked beside Albert, chatting with him about gardening.

When they reached the lodge, Jane and Bob were ushered into the tiny sitting room, which looked out onto the entrance gates. Albert hurried away to make the tea, refusing their offers of help.

Once Bett was sitting comfortably in her armchair, she brought the conversation back to Jane's past. 'You said that you were in an orphanage, dear.'

'Yes, that's right. I've been told that I was taken there by Elizabeth Barton when I was quite young. I only remember it vaguely.'

'Elizabeth Barton?' queried Bett.

'Elizabeth Carroll.'

'Ah, yes. Elizabeth, the professional,' recalled Bett. There was a hint of contempt in her voice.

'Can you tell me more about my mother – Ann Ashington?' Jane asked eagerly.

Bett smiled. 'She was a lovely lady. So kind to everybody. But she had a hard life.'

'Why was that?' asked Jane.

'Her mother died giving birth to her, and her father was very strict.'

'In what way?' asked Bob.

Bett turned towards him. 'He sent her to a religious boarding school. She used to tell me about all the things they did to her there, and how the pupils were treated.' Bett hesitated for a second. 'And then her father died when she was only eighteen.'

'Gosh, that's a pretty tough start to life,' empathised Bob.

Bett nodded. 'It was.'

'Who looked after her and sorted out the estate and everything that needed attending to after her father died?' asked Bob, as always interested in practical matters.

Bett pondered the question for a minute. 'Her father had appointed an estate manager, and I think his accountants and solicitors looked after everything else at first. They took everything off your mother's shoulders, but when she reached twenty-one she took on a great deal herself. That's how I understood things, anyway,' she concluded.

'Phew. That sounds an awful life!' exclaimed Jane. 'Even worse than mine,' she added.

The conversation was halted briefly by the reappearance of Albert carrying a tray. For the next ten minutes the conversation was more general as the four of them drank tea and munched slices of fruit cake that Jane and Bob agreed afterwards had been a bit stale.

It was Jane who returned the conversation to her past. She addressed Bett again. 'Your husband said that you looked after me when I was a baby. Can you tell me a bit more about that?'

'I was your mother's maid. I was with you from the beginning,' replied Bett. She started to reminisce. 'You were such a lovely baby, with your big brown eyes and your smile.'

'And then Elizabeth Carroll took over from you,' prompted Jane.

'That was when Miles Ashington came on the scene. I wasn't good enough, according to him.' Once again there was a trace of contempt in Bett's voice.

Jane was determined to exploit Bett's knowledge as much as possible. 'I've been told that my mother was a very reclusive person. Is that correct?'

Bett gave what appeared to be a sniff of contradiction. 'That's what people say who didn't really know her. It was only after she had you that she changed. After that she became very retiring and depressive at times. I know. I was with her all the time.' As she finished speaking, Bett appeared to lapse into a reflective state, playing with the spoon in her cup.

'Can you tell me how she came to have me?' Jane asked softly. She desperately wanted an answer.

The question stirred Bett into talking again. 'The Ashington family had an estate in Yorkshire. It was your mother's habit to spend quite a lot of time there in the summer. One year there was a big ball in the area. All the gentry for miles around were there. That's when your mother got herself pregnant.'

'Do you know who my father was?'

Bett shook her head. 'Nay. Your mother didn't, either,' she replied.

Jane was aghast. 'But how? Why?'

'She had too much to drink. Next morning she had a hangover and couldn't remember a thing about it.'

Jane was still struggling to comprehend what she had just heard.

Bob looked on, absorbed. 'What happened next?' he asked.

Bett seemed quite happy to recount events. She addressed Jane again. 'I remember quite vividly the morning your mother came to me and announced that she was pregnant.'

'What did you say to her?'

'I asked her if she was sure and she said she was. Anyway, I took her to the doctor and it was confirmed.'

'How did she react?'

'She was a bit bewildered – and angry with herself for letting it happen. She didn't know what to do. I think she even thought of getting rid of it.'

Bett was quite matter-of-fact in her explanations, and what she was hearing made Jane feel sad. It was clear that she had been an unwanted child and that no love had been available for her, not even from her own mother. She wanted to ask more questions, but she was beginning to feel that she was hogging the conversation and that it was all about her.

Courtesy made her broaden the topic. 'How long did you work for my mother?' she asked Bett.

'Over ten years. Your mother was only twenty when I went to work for her.'

Jane was going to ask her something else, but Bett wanted to continue. 'We got on well together, your mother and I. She used to tell me everything.'

'What about her marriage to John Henderson?'

Bett gave what sounded like a grunt of disgust. 'I told her from the start it wouldn't work. But your mother could be headstrong at times. I was surprised the marriage lasted twelve months.'

'What happened after I was born?' Jane knew she had to ask just a few more questions.

Bett finished eating her cake before replying. 'After a few weeks in Yorkshire we came back here. I had to travel separately with you. Your mother didn't want to know you.'

Albert entered the conversation. 'That caused a stir among the folk in the village, when they discovered the baby was Ann's.'

'At first they thought you were mine,' laughed Bett.

'When did Ann meet Miles Ashington?' enquired Bob.

'Very soon after we came back here after you were born. He ruled the roost from then on. She was besotted by him. In her eyes he could do no wrong. He employed Elizabeth Carroll to look after you, and I wasn't allowed near you after that. Your mother never even raised a protest on my behalf.'

'That was a pretty rotten deal, after all you'd done for her,' observed Bob.

'I was very upset at the time,' replied Bett. She smiled at Albert. 'But then Albert asked me to marry him and after that I had a family of my own.'

'How many children do you have?' asked Jane.

'We've got a son − John. He's a schoolteacher and lives in Bristol, and our daughter, May, lives in the village. We've got two grandchildren,' Bett announced proudly.

After that the conversation stayed on Bett and Albert. Bett explained how they had always lived nearby, and Albert outlined how they eventually came to live in the lodge at the suggestion of Miles Ashington to become sort of caretakers for the ruined house.

'"E don't charge us any rent,' added Albert thoughtfully, 'and I've got the garden still.'

Jane would have liked to ask many more questions, but Bett dropped a hint that she and Albert were expecting a visit from their son that afternoon, so she and Bob politely took their leave.

'Nice to meet you,' remarked Albert, holding out his hand.

'Come and see us again, dear,' Bett stressed.

As they walked back to the car, Bob asked, 'What do you think about all that? Do you feel happier about your past now?'

Jane was silent for a minute. Something was on her mind. As they reached the car, she stopped and looked at Bob.

'Bob, did you take in what Bett said about me as a baby?' She hesitated. 'She said I had brown eyes – but MY EYES ARE BLUE-GREY…'

Chapter 34

'A welcome return to the long-lost member of the Ashington family.' Miles Ashington raised his glass aloft and regarded Jane with a courteous smile. There were echoes of agreement from around the table.

The sumptuous dinner at the Ashingtons' was in full swing. Jane and Bob had been impressed by the friendly reception they received from their hosts. They had been greeted on their arrival and ushered into a grand sitting room by the same maid Jane had seen on her first visit to the house. Miles and Gail had joined them almost immediately and the conversation over pre-dinner drinks had been relaxed and friendly.

Bob had come to Jane's apartment earlier in the day and they had debated what form of transport they should use to go into London for their dinner date. Unsure of the parking arrangements available at the Ashingtons' residence, they had decided to travel by train and take a taxi at the other end. Jane had produced her pretty, knee-length cocktail dress. Its delicate shade of green suited her well, and she had a pair of green court shoes to match. She decided that in spite of the warm evening she would drape a light jacket over her shoulders while travelling on public transport, for comfort and to eliminate enquiring looks from other passengers. Bob had selected a velvet jacket and a floppy bow tie. They realised with relief that their decision to wear something more formal was the right one as soon as their hosts entered the sitting room. Miles was wearing a smart suit, and Gail a full-length, off-the-shoulder red gown.

Jane had previously only seen a newspaper picture of Gail

Ashington, but meeting her confirmed her impression that Gail was a good deal younger than her husband. At first she thought Gail couldn't be much older than she was, but later she learned that she was nearly forty. Her dark, almost black hair and her slight accent gave her an intriguing air. Much later Jane and Bob found out in conversation that she was from Spain.

Over the pre-dinner drinks Miles produced a brown envelope and handed it to Jane.

'Have a look at these, Jane. They are for you. I think you will find them of interest.'

Eagerly Jane opened the envelope. It contained several photographs. She held one out in front of her so that the others could see it. It was a pretty head-and-shoulders portrait of a young woman with dark hair.

'That's your mother,' announced Miles.

'And this one must be me.' Grinning, Jane held up a picture of a young baby.

'It is. You were only a few months old then.'

For the first time Gail took an interest in the photograph. 'You were a pretty baby,' she observed, smiling at Jane.

Jane wondered whether Gail had had any children or whether she had a secret longing to do so. She felt that it was not an appropriate question to ask at the present time and merely smiled in agreement before turning her attention to the third and last photograph. It was a picture of Ashington House in its former glory.

'Gosh!' exclaimed Bob. 'We were there last week.'

Miles gave him a surprised look. 'Ah. It's terrible to see the old place in such a state,' he remarked wistfully.

'Couldn't it be restored?' asked Jane. 'After all, the walls are still standing.'

Miles smiled at her. 'I did investigate that a few years after the fire, but apparently the walls are unstable and would have to be pulled down. The cost of rebuilding it would be enormous.'

'It's so sad to see it as it is now,' Jane observed, looking at the photograph again.

It suddenly occurred to her that she had not thanked Miles for the photographs. She looked up at him. 'I really do appreciate having the photographs. Thank you very much.'

'It's been my pleasure,' responded Miles, smiling kindly at her. 'Sadly, many items such as photographs were lost in the fire. My caretakers were a bit lax in looking after the place, I think.'

'We met them there last week – Albert and Bett Simmons,' remarked Jane.

Miles Ashington chuckled. 'They've been around for years.'

'Bett said she looked after me when I was a baby,' said Jane.

Miles nodded. 'That's quite true. Betty Simmons is a very charming lady, but unfortunately your mother and I felt that she didn't look after you as well as she could have done, and sadly we had to find someone to replace her.'

'Was that Elizabeth Carroll?'

'Yes, it was,' replied Miles. 'A very capable lady. She was an excellent nanny.'

The conversation was interrupted briefly when Gail excused herself from the group, explaining that she had to supervise the dinner. Miles then asked Bob what kind of work he did. At Bob's reply that he was a professional photographer, he was immediately interested and a brief discussion took place between them.

This gave Jane a few minutes to contemplate things. She would have liked to ask Miles more about Bett's dismissal, but there was no opportunity at present. What did seem odd to both her and Bob was Bett's reference to Jane's brown eyes as a baby. Back in Jane's apartment they had discussed the subject in great detail. Bob thought eyes could change colour; Jane was convinced it wasn't possible. In the end, to try and settle the issue they had searched for information on the internet. Some people apparently claimed that it did happen, but Jane and Bob found no conclusive evidence. In the end they agreed that Bett must have been mistaken in her recollection. As Bob pointed out, she had most likely seen a lot of babies since Jane, including her own. Nevertheless, Jane still felt that something didn't quite ring true.

Gail's return to the room to announce that dinner was served brought Jane's musing to an end and halted the discussion between Miles and Bob. She led the way into an elegant dining room, with an impressive chandelier hanging from the ceiling above the table. All the furnishings in the house had an air of opulence about them.

The discussion over dinner was as congenial as the excellence of the food. The pace of the meal was leisurely, with both Miles and Gail taking an interest in their guests and encouraging them to talk. It was at one stage during a lull in the conversation that Jane plucked up courage to ask a question that had been on her mind since they had arrived.

'Mr Ashington—' she began.

She was halted abruptly by her host, who smiled at her warmly as he spoke. 'Please, Jane. We are family and friends. Call me Miles.'

Jane flushed slightly and continued her question. 'Miles, I was wondering if you could tell me a bit more about my mother. How did she actually die?'

As soon as she finished speaking, Jane wondered if she should have asked the question, particularly with Gail present. However, neither of their hosts appeared to be perturbed by the question.

Miles appeared to be deep in thought. His reply was delivered slowly and thoughtfully. 'When I first met your mother, I was a solicitor in Bristol. She came to me for some advice, which I was able to give her. She turned to me a number of times after that and we gradually got to know each other quite well. Our marriage was quick and simple.'

He paused to take another sip of his wine. Then he continued. 'Soon into our marriage I discovered that she suffered from fits of depression. She would often remain in bed for one or two days while an episode lasted. She had treatment from her doctor for this complaint. Unfortunately, your mother also suffered from severe insomnia. She regularly took sleeping tablets. I was extremely worried about her condition and tried desperately to help her become well again, but one evening she must have taken an overdose – and we discovered her dead in bed the next morning.'

'Oh, I'm dreadfully sorry.' exclaimed Jane, saddened by what she had just heard.

'It must have been a terrible shock for you,' said Bob suddenly.

Miles nodded. 'It was.' Then he added, looking at Gail with a smile of admiration, 'But it was a long time ago.'

Jane hastily tried to think of something to change the subject. To her it seemed a bit unkind to talk about Mile's deceased wife when his present wife was in the room.

However, it was Miles himself who changed the subject. He addressed Bob quite jovially. 'Bob, I am most interested in this idea of yours to start a new promotional company. What have you done so far with it?'

Bob went into brief details of how he and Jeff were intending to branch out into this field, but that the project was still in its infancy due to pressure of work in other directions. Miles listened intently. Jane and Gail merely feigned interest. Conscious of the fact, Bob tried to bring the discussion to a close as early as possible, but Miles continued to ask questions.

Eventually, a glance from Miles at Gail prompted him to end the conversation. 'That's extremely interesting, Bob,' he said. 'Give me your card later and I may be able to put some business your way. I've just started a small company and your services could be valuable to us.'

Bob made the required comments, but was almost interrupted by Gail. She looked at him with a sweet smile as she asked, 'Do you take portrait photographs in your studio?'

'Yes, we do.'

'Will you take a portrait of me?' she asked, with a bit of a bemused look.

Bob was about to offer a courteous reply when he was interrupted by Miles, who threw up his hands and exclaimed, laughing, 'Don't send the bill to me.'

'Miles!' admonished Gail, pretending to be shocked.

The arrival of the maids with the next course saved any conflict and the conversation turned to food, much to the relief of Bob, who had not been quite sure how to handle Gail's request.

Towards the end of the meal, when coffee and liqueurs were being served in the lounge, the topic of holidays came up. Miles said how much he liked the West Country – so much so, that a few years previously he had purchased a small estate in Cornwall, which he used for restful breaks away from the hustle and bustle of business life. It was, he said, his retreat when he required peace and quiet.

'It really is a heavenly spot,' added Gail.

It was she who brought the conversation round to Jane and Bob by asking them whether they had been on holiday anywhere recently. When they both replied that they hadn't been anywhere and didn't have a holiday planned, Gail was aghast. 'But you must!' she exclaimed. 'Everybody needs a holiday. I've been away six times this year. I only came back from a fortnight in Spain a week ago.'

It was Miles who injected humour into the conversation. 'She goes. I just pay,' he laughed.

'But you should go with your wife,' Jane reproached him jokingly.

Miles was serious. 'Oh, I do. We get on very well together on our vacations. Occasionally Gail goes off without me if I'm tied up with a client, but I try not to let my business affairs intrude too much on our private life.' His next remark was addressed to Bob. 'You need to remember that.'

'I'll certainly do so,' replied Bob.

Gail seemed about to say something, but suddenly Miles looked at Jane and Bob intently. 'I've just had a thought,' he announced.

His audience waited in anticipation.

He continued. 'Why don't the pair of you come down and spend a few days at our retreat in the West Country? I have a lovely old barn I converted last year just for this sort of occasion. You would be very welcome to stay there.'

'It really is idyllic,' remarked Gail. She added for more emphasis, 'The sea isn't far away, and you can go swimming – or we have a marvellous swimming pool you can use.'

Jane turned to Bob. 'It does sound lovely.'

Bob was thinking aloud. 'I like the sound of the peace and quiet, and we did say we'd try and have a holiday when my workload permitted.'

'Why don't we, then?' asked Jane.

'It sounds great. I'll just have to check with my business partner first,' he explained to Miles and Gail.

Miles was equally enthusiastic. 'Then it's agreed.'

'We will of course pay for the accommodation,' offered Jane.

Miles turned to her, smiling. 'Jane, you are part of the family. Please let me do this for you. I assure you it will be my pleasure.'

'Of course you're not going to pay,' insisted Gail, almost indignantly.

'That's really very nice of you,' Jane responded politely.

Miles put up his hand as if to stop any protest. 'Just let me know when you'd like to come, and I'll make all the arrangements for you.'

The rest of the evening passed quickly. At half past ten Jane and Bob felt that it was time to go. Bob started to say something about a taxi, but Miles stopped him. 'I will arrange a car for you,' he said.

Jane and Bob were glad to accept his offer. They had both consumed more alcohol than they would have done normally and now they were beginning to feel the effects, making them eager to reach home.

On the way back Jane rested her head on Bob's shoulder. Bob had his arm round her. 'Do you think we'll be able to take up Miles' offer of a break?' she asked, snuggling up to him.

'I don't see why not. I'll just have to agree it with Jeff first,' Bob replied.

"Mmm. And I'll have to check what's happening at work as well.' The practicalities were reaching Jane now.

'We'll make it,' he assured her.

'I'm going to buy a new bikini,' she murmured sleepily.

Chapter 35

To her surprise it was Jane who had difficulty finding a suitable time to take leave from work. When she went into the office on the Monday following the dinner with Miles and Gail Ashington, the first thing she did was to look at the holiday list. It was an unwritten rule that staff tried not to be away at the same time where jobs overlapped. It was slightly more difficult for Jane, because as well as Amy she had Annette to consider. A glance at the schedule informed her that any time during the next month was going to present problems for her. Both Amy and Annette had holidays posted up during this period. The most likely looking time was almost three weeks off. Fortunately it was also convenient for Bob. They decided that the best option for them would be a Thursday-to-Tuesday long weekend break. Jane hoped upon hope that this time would also be convenient for the Ashingtons.

Despite having Miles's personal telephone number, Jane had to try on several occasions before she managed to get an answer. When she did it was almost a surprise to hear his voice.

'Miles Ashington.'

'Miles, it's Jane. I wondered if you had a minute to talk about our proposed break at your cottage.'

The tone of his voice changed immediately from that of a brusque businessman to that of a friend greeting a friend.

'Jane, how nice to hear from you! Did you arrive home safely on Saturday night?'

'Yes, we did. It was a lovely evening. We both enjoyed it very much, but we did feel a bit bad about you paying for our cab home.'

It was true. When they had reached their destination, Bob had jumped out expecting to have to pay a fare. Instead the driver looked at him in surprise and just touched his cap and replied, 'It's been sorted out, guv. It's on account.'

Jane heard a little laugh at the other end of the phone. 'It's my pleasure, Jane. I feel it's the least I can do considering the treatment you have received so far from your family.'

Jane felt a bit embarrassed about Miles's statement, but for the present she decided to let it pass. Before she could reply, Miles spoke again.

'Gail and I enjoyed your company on Saturday evening very much. I intend to contact Bob in the near future. I think I can put some business his way. Gail also wants to see you again some time, Jane.'

Jane took the suggestions in her stride. She just replied with, 'That would be nice,' and left it at that. She and Bob had been slightly embarrassed by the Ashingtons' generosity and had decided not to exploit the various propositions made. However, they were both keen to take up the offer of a few days' break. This was the thought that was uppermost on Jane's agenda. Before Miles could reply to her last comment, she plunged into suggesting suitable dates.

'Bob and I have found it a bit tricky to find a suitable time to take up your offer. Would this be convenient?' She read out the proposed dates.

Miles greeted her suggestion with enthusiasm. 'Excellent. Let's see. I hope so.'

There was a pause as he checked his diary. When he spoke again he sounded quite excited. 'Jane, those dates are very suitable. The cottage is free and Gail and I are planning to be down there ourselves at about that time. That would all work out splendidly. Can we say that's fixed?'

Jane too was excited. 'Oh, yes, please.'

'Excellent. Gail will be pleased as well. I must ring her right away and tell her.'

Jane was already dealing with practicalities. 'We will most likely arrive on the Thursday afternoon,' she advised.

'That's no problem at all. Gail will telephone Mrs Potter and she will have everything ready for you. Mrs Potter looks after the cottage for us,' he explained as an afterthought.

'That sounds super!' exclaimed Jane.

'You'll enjoy being down there,' Miles enthused. He added, 'And, Jane, don't forget to bring your swimsuit. As Gail said, we have a swimming pool, and the sea is close by.'

'Great!' Jane was thinking about the bikini she was planning to buy.

It was Miles who ended the call. 'Jane, I have to go. I have a business meeting starting in a few minutes' time.'

'Me too,' echoed Jane. Amy had just appeared in her office doorway looking worried.

'Goodbye for now, then,' said Miles. 'Excellent that everything is arranged now.'

'Goodbye – and thank you,' Jane called into the telephone.

She turned to attend to Amy.

When she returned home that evening Jane found a note pushed through her letter box. It read simply, *Jane, can I see you sometime? Gerald.*

She took her time changing into a blouse and jeans and preparing a light meal for herself. By the time she had consumed this and washed up the few dirty dishes, a good hour had passed by. She intended to phone Bob this evening and tell him that everything was now fixed for their weekend break, but decided to wait until a bit later to ensure that he would be at home. In the meantime she would pop down to see Gerald and Anna.

Anna opened the door at Jane's ring of the bell. 'Jane, how nice to see you! Come in!' was her greeting.

Jane found herself ushered into the lounge, where Gerald was sitting with a newspaper on his knee. He greeted her as she entered.

'Ah, Jane. You got my note,' he chuckled.

Jane sat down, just as Anna asked her if she would like a cup of tea or coffee. On this occasion, as she had not made herself a drink earlier, Jane was happy to accept a cup of tea.

Anna hurried away on her mission.

Jane turned to Gerald with a smile. 'You've got some more news for me,' she suggested, almost eagerly.

Gerald put his newspaper down and reached for a notepad from a nearby table. He smiled at Jane. 'I had a telephone call from Eric,' he explained.

'Don't start telling Jane about it until I'm there. I want to hear about it too.' It was Anna, calling from the kitchen.

Gerald and Jane indulged in small talk until Anna came back bearing a tray with the tea and a large fruit cake. Several minutes passed before she had served everybody. Jane insisted on having just a very small portion of cake and received the usual admonishment from Anna that she was starving herself to keep thin.

Once everybody was settled, Gerald reiterated his opening statement. 'I had a telephone call from Eric.'

'What did he say?' Anna was as interested as Jane.

Gerald cleared his throat, glanced at his notepad and then addressed Jane. 'Eric has been doing some more research. He's found out a little bit more about Miles Ashington before he changed his name.'

Gerald's remark prompted a comment from Jane. 'When I spoke to him he seemed to indicate that he was a distant cousin or something like that,' she pointed out, recalling her first meeting with Miles.

'That's not impossible, but clearly he wanted to retain the Ashington family name, and that was the easiest way of doing it.' Gerald looked at Jane over his half-rimmed glasses.

Jane thought for a few seconds, assimilating what Gerald had just related. 'What was his previous name?' she asked.

Gerald grinned at her. 'Ah, now that is the interesting bit. You recall that I told you Eric was a solicitor? Well, he knows the practice where Miles Ashington was a junior partner. Apparently at that time his name was Carlton.'

Jane was impressed with Eric's research. 'Phew!' she exclaimed. 'Eric can certainly ferret out information.'

Gerald gave a little laugh. 'There's a bit more he has found out,' he remarked, again consulting his notepad.

'Tell me,' Jane responded, eager to hear more.

Gerald smiled at her as he continued. 'He has discovered that Miles Ashington's son also changed his surname to Ashington a few years ago.'

Jane was surprised. 'Gosh! They certainly mean to keep the Ashington name going,' she laughed. Then she was serious. 'But I'm amazed how Eric manages to find all these things out.'

'You haven't seen him when he really gets going.' Gerald chuckled, almost to himself.

'You know what I think.' It was Anna who suddenly piped up.

Jane and Gerald regarded her, waiting for more.

Anna put her cup down on the table. As she did so she remarked casually, 'I think this Miles Ashington married your mother for her money.'

Anna's remark brought forth a smile from Jane. At one stage before she met Miles she had thought the same.

Gerald was silent. He stroked his goatee beard, as he was in the habit of doing when thinking something through. He was the first to speak. 'One thing that has always puzzled me a bit is why your mother never made any provision to extend some of her fortune to you – her only daughter!'

'She didn't want me. She never came near me. I've been told so.'

'Umm. It's strange, though,' Gerald remarked, still stroking his beard.

'What was this Miles Ashington like to talk to?' asked Anna, moving to offer Jane more tea.

Jane thought for a second before replying. 'Well, before I met

309

him I felt a bit nervous. But I needn't have been. He's really rather sweet and quite easy to talk to.' She hesitated for a second, and then continued. 'He and his wife Gail invited Bob and me to dinner last Saturday. They were both really nice.' She paused again. 'Actually, they've invited us to stay at their cottage in the West Country. We're going there later this month.'

Gerald and Anna were surprised at Jane's news.

'You seem to have made a hit there,' observed Gerald with a chuckle.

'Perhaps he looks upon you as his daughter,' piped up Anna.

Jane smiled. Since Saturday she had begun to consider that possibility herself.

Gerald just smiled back.

The conversation continued for a short while. Anna wanted to know the exact place they were going to for their weekend break and told Jane that she had read in the newspaper that the weather was going to be exceptionally good at that particular time.

Eventually Jane took her leave, anxious now to phone Bob and give him the news.

It was almost half past eight when she eventually called him on her mobile from the comfort of the settee. She could hear the phone ringing at the other end for quite a while before he answered it.

'Hello. Bob Harker.'

'Bob, it's me.'

'Hello, me.'

Jane jumped in with her news. 'Bob, I've got everything fixed. A weekend starting the Thursday we talked about is fine. I'm covered at work and I've booked that slot.'

'Great! That's first class!' Bob sounded as excited as she was.

Jane was anxious to relate the rest. 'I phoned Miles, and Gail is going to arrange everything with the person who looks after the cottage.'

'You've done a good job. I might just keep you on,' Bob was joking with her again.

Jane was more serious. 'Darling, I'm really looking forward to it. A few days away, just with you. And the sea isn't far away – we'll be able to go swimming. I told you I'm going to get a new bikini,' she ended up breezily.

'I'll buy you one,' Bob chipped in suddenly.

'You don't know my size,' Jane teased him.

Bob was confident. 'Yes I do. Dress 12, and size 5 in shoes.'

Jane was surprised. 'How do you know my dress size?' she asked, almost laughing.

'Aha. Ways and means. What I want to know I find out.' She could tell Bob was grinning all over as he spoke.

She feigned a sigh. 'A girl just can't have any secrets these days.'

'I'm afraid not, poppet. Not with me around.'

'Hmm. I shall just have to be more secretive. That's all.' Jane gave another pronounced sigh.

Bob changed the subject. 'Anyway, how's work? Anything to report?'

Jane went into a résumé of snippets of news about things that had occurred at work since she had last spoken to him. In turn she wanted to know what had been happening with him. In the end they were on the phone for over half an hour. Jane spent the rest of the evening playing on her laptop with the family history program.

It was the buzz of her internal telephone that distracted Jane from her work the next morning. It could only mean one thing: Annette wanted to speak to her. She picked up the phone and answered with her usual, 'Hello. Jane.'

Annette's voice came over loud and clear. 'Jane, can we get together sometime this morning?'

Jane smothered a sigh. 'Of course. Now, if you're free.'

'That would be excellent.'

'I'll be right up.'

Jane replaced the telephone. That was the end of her work for half an hour or so. She made her way up to the editor-in-chief's office.

Annette was helping herself to coffee from her machine when Jane entered. She looked up. 'Ah, come in, Jane. Would you like a coffee?'

It was about the time of the morning when Jane or Amy usually made some coffee. Jane readily accepted Annette's offer.

'You don't take sugar, do you?' Annette was already moving towards Jane with a cup of coffee. She retrieved her own and settled herself in her comfortable chair. She regarded Jane for an instant as she sipped from her cup. 'How's the Patterson article going?'

The Patterson article was a feature that Jane and Amy had been working on.

'We're all ready now for publication next month,' Jane assured her.

'Excellent.' Annette took another sip of her coffee. She studied Jane again. 'How long have you been with us now, Jane?'

Jane had not been anticipating a personal question. She wondered what Annette was up to. Her answer was simple. 'Just over three years.'

'How do you like working here?'

Jane could not quite comprehend why Annette was asking such questions. Once again her answer was brief and to the point. 'Fine.'

'And what about the future? What plans do you have?'

Jane was on the point of asking Annette why she was asking all these questions, but she decided to bide her time and simply reply with short answers. 'I have no immediate plans for the future,' she replied, concentrating on drinking her coffee.

'But you have a fiancé. Are you planning to get married?'

This was the limit, thought Jane. 'We have no immediate plans for marriage,' she replied rather curtly. She did elaborate a little. 'We are both quite busy at present,' she added. Then, before Annette could reply, she said, 'Why do you ask?'

Perhaps Annette noticed Jane's concern, or perhaps she had gleaned enough information. Either way, her approach changed. She thought for a few seconds, then looked closely at Jane as she replied. 'I had a big meeting with Olgins last week. We are going

312

to start another magazine and I have been asked to get it under way.'

She paused for an instant and then continued. 'It will mean that I will be away from this office for longer periods.'

Jane wondered what was coming next, but as it looked as if she was expected to respond to Annette's last statement, she gave another vague answer. 'Oh, I see.'

'It has been proposed that we rename your position here Assistant Editor and employ another person in the office to help you and Amy out. What do you think of the idea?'

Annette took another drink of coffee and studied Jane for her reaction.

Jane thought for a minute. What was being proposed was very little different from what was happening now. The main difference would be that Annette might not be around quite as much.

Perhaps Annette read her thoughts, because before Jane could reply she spoke again. 'Of course, it's not such a major change, Jane. After all, you do quite a lot of what's being proposed already.'

'I can't see any major problems,' replied Jane rather cautiously. At the same time she reflected that with Annette out of the office more she and Amy might be able to get on with their work without the frequent interruptions when she was around.

'Of course, you will be reimbursed for the extra workload,' Annette insisted.

Jane smiled slightly. 'That will be nice,' she replied politely.

'Of course, nothing is going to happen for a few months yet,' stressed Annette.

'That's fine,' replied Jane. She then spoke her thoughts. 'That might be a good time to make changes – when the holiday season is over.'

Annette nodded in agreement. Then, concluding that the conversation about Jane's future was finished, she launched into other matters. How was this going? What was happening about that?

It was a good hour later when Jane returned to her desk.

As she had come into the office early, Jane took a slightly extended lunch break and used the opportunity to do some shopping and buy a few items for her forthcoming break with Bob. She spent some time shopping for a new summer dress for the holiday and eventually found just what she wanted: a knee-length white dress with a pleasing neckline and bare shoulders, just right for a warm summer evening. She hadn't intended to buy shoes, but on her way past the shoe department she spied a pair of white high-heeled shoes, a perfect match for the dress she had just bought, and ended up purchasing them. Next, she spent quite a bit of time selecting what she considered were sexy items of lingerie to surprise Bob. She hesitated in the swimwear department, wondering whether Bob would remember his promise to buy her a new bikini. In the end she bought one, remembering that her current swimwear was well past its sell-by date. If Bob did get her a bikini, she would keep this one for a later appearance.

She returned to the office slightly later than she had intended, quite laden with bags but well pleased with her purchases.

Walking home from the station that evening, she reflected on recent events. She felt that life was good. She had a positive and loving relationship with Bob, and at long last she had discovered her true identity, albeit not quite what she had expected. Now she had a pleasant holiday break on the horizon and she was looking forward to a restful few days in the country alone with Bob.

Unfortunately, she was not to know at this stage about the traumatic events that were about to unfold.

Chapter 36

'This must be it.'

It was Jane who uttered the words, as she fixed her attention on the turning off the road that was looming up ahead of them. Bob instinctively slowed the car down.

'Yes, It is. Look.' She pointed to a sign indicating Barn Cottage.

Bob made a careful right turn, bumping over a cattle grid between two stone pillars. The wooden gate was already wide open. Beyond stretched a rough road that eventually disappeared round a corner out of sight.

They drove along the track in silence, each consumed by suspense and curiosity. It had been an early start for both of them. Jane, excited by the prospect of her holiday, had packed everything the evening before. She had arrived on Bob's doorstep just after eight o'clock in the morning. After a quick cup of coffee they had started out for the West Country. Now, almost at their goal, she and Bob both felt that their holiday break had already begun.

All the arrangements had gone to plan and a few days earlier Gail Ashington had telephoned Jane and given her all the instructions. The last days at work had been frantic for Jane as she cleared up items prior to her few days off. She had hardly had any time to think about her proposed new role in running *Discerning Woman* magazine, though she had discussed it with Bob and both of them had agreed that in some ways it was going to be hardly any different from what she was doing now unofficially. The difference, as Bob pointed out, would be that now she would have the official title and receive more money for her efforts.

'Oh! Isn't it charming?' Jane almost squealed with delight as their destination suddenly appeared in front of them. Barn Cottage could not conceal its origin as an imposing stone barn standing on the edge of a large field, but it appeared to have been beautifully converted. Ornate leaded windows had been cut into the stone walls, and the entrance was a solid, varnished wooden door. A wrought-iron handle had been crafted to operate the door bell, and this was matched by the words 'Barn Cottage' scrolled in the same black metal on the wall alongside. Hanging baskets filled to the brim with bright flowers adorned the walls at intervals. Further decoration was provided by several water butts finished to match the door, and an old cartwheel leaning against the wall.

Bob drew the car to a halt on the gravel that surrounded the building. A rather battered 4x4 was already parked there.

'That must be Mrs Potter's,' he remarked as he switched off the engine and prepared to get out of the car. They had telephoned Mrs Potter as arranged from their last stop at a motorway service station, to announce their impending arrival. Jane was already half out of the car and regarding the 4x4. It was certainly an aged and dilapidated model.

At that instant the front door of Barn Cottage opened and a rather plump, cheerful-looking middle-aged woman approached them. She was full of smiles. 'Ah, here you are. Did you have a good journey?'

They did not have a chance to respond to the question before their host held out her hand and announced, 'I'm Maggie Potter. It's nice to meet you both.'

Jane shook Maggie's hand. 'I'm Jane Carroll and this is my fiancé, Bob Harker,' she replied.

Maggie grabbed Bob's hand. 'Pleased to meet you.' She beamed at him.

Bob had no time to reply before Maggie spoke again. 'Now, come inside and I'll show you everything.' She was already preparing to move back towards the entrance door.

Obediently they followed her into the building.

Their first impressions drew exclamations of surprise and admiration from both Jane and Bob.

'Gosh, it's really nice and inviting,' observed Bob, quickly glancing round.

'It's super,' enthused Jane.

From a tiny entrance hall they had entered a large sitting room. Two roomy leather settees faced a stone fireplace with a wood-burning stove. A dining table and chairs occupied one of the walls. An open wooden staircase wound its way up to a balcony, which looked down on the room. Solid wooden doors opened up from there. Freshly cut flowers adorned the room, and a large bowl of fruit stood on the table. For a second or two Jane and Bob stood speechless as they took in the scene.

Maggie watched them, smiling confidently. 'This place was a ruin before Mr Ashington bought it and renovated it last year.'

'Good for him. It's a fantastic conversion,' replied Bob, looking at the exposed beams overhead.

'Gail Ashington chose all the furnishings herself,' Maggie continued. 'She's very talented that way. More so than Mr Ashington's previous wife, Gillie.'

'Have you known the family very long?' Jane asked her, curious to know more.

Maggie seemed to want to give them information. 'I've worked for Mr Ashington for over ten years, ever since he bought the big house near here. Wait until you see that.' She smiled at them.

'Is it far from here?' asked Bob.

Maggie grinned at them. 'Across the fields, it's only about a quarter of a mile, but if you go by road it's a mile or so. Mr Ashington has done wonders with that place as well,' she added. 'It was almost derelict when he bought it twelve years ago.'

Jane was about to ask Maggie another question, but Maggie wanted to talk about something else.

'Gail tells me you're a long-lost member of the Ashington family.'

Jane laughed. 'That seems to be the idea at the moment,' she replied breezily.

'Well, you couldn't be part of a better family,' asserted Maggie. Then she announced, 'Let me show you everything else.'

Three solid doors opened off the room. Maggie proudly threw open each one in turn, extolling the contents of each room beyond. One door led into a bright and cheerful kitchen that looked out onto the entrance road. Another led to a tiny cloakroom. When Maggie opened the third door, both Jane and Bob gasped with surprise. They were looking into a large bedroom complete with its own en suite bathroom. It was the size of the bed that impressed Jane.

'The bed – it's huge!' she exclaimed.

Bob chuckled. 'King-size,' he remarked.

'There's more upstairs,' Maggie announced, leading the way to the ornate staircase.

The three of them climbed the wooden steps slowly and carefully.

'Careful you don't slip,' warned Maggie.

Jane and Bob paused for a second to look down on the lounge below, but Maggie was already opening other doors. One led into a second bedroom, not quite as big as the first, but equally impressive. A second bathroom was adjoining.

Maggie had something else up her sleeve. Smiling at Bob and Jane, she marched to the end of the balcony, drew a curtain and quickly unlocked a glass door, which led out onto an extension of the balcony. She held the door open for Jane and Bob to walk through. Folding chairs and a table were stacked against the wall outside.

'Phew. It's fantastic!' exclaimed Jane, looking around her. The balcony had been built out from the main building of the barn and was almost suspended over the cornfield, which stretched away into the distance, ending at some trees on the horizon.

'An ideal place to have breakfast,' observed Bob, looking over the safety rail at the field below.

'Nice place for a cup of tea,' remarked Maggie, winking at Jane.

'It's wonderful. I am going to enjoy staying here,' replied Jane enthusiastically.

They stood on the balcony for several minutes, enjoying the view and the feel of the warm summer breeze on their faces and the smells of the countryside it brought with it. Eventually Maggie made a move as if she wanted to finish the tour. Jane and Bob took the hint and followed her downstairs.

Once back in the lounge, Maggie supplied them with some last-minute information – how to turn on the hot water heater, and so on. She added, 'Now, there's tea and coffee and a tin of biscuits in the cupboard, and fresh milk in the fridge, and there's a useful little supermarket in the village if you want anything – and the pub does very nice meals in the evening.'

'Super,' replied Jane. Then she asked Maggie, 'How far is the sea?'

'No more than seven or eight minutes' drive. You go through the village and you'll see a turning on the right. It's quite easy to find. And there's a nice beach for bathing.'

'We'll try that out, won't we?' Jane grinned at Bob.

'How far is it to the village?' asked Bob.

Maggie smiled at him. 'It's just a quarter of a mile down the road. You'll pass my cottage on the way, on the right – Rose Cottage.'

Jane could see that Maggie was now anxious to leave them. She smiled and held out her hand. 'You've been very kind and helpful. I know we'll enjoy our stay here.'

'Give me a ring if you need any more help. My number's pinned up in the kitchen,' Maggie stressed, making her way to the door.

'Thank you very much for all your help and advice,' Bob called after her.

They stood at the door and watched Maggie drive away in her battered conveyance. A wave of her hand, and she was gone.

'And that was Maggie Potter,' grinned Bob, as they turned to go back into the house.

'Do you know what I want to do?' asked Jane. 'I want to have a cup of tea on the balcony. I'll make it. You bring in the cases.'

'That sounds like an excellent idea. I was wondering when you were going to get round to it,' replied Bob, making a face at her.

'Pig,' Jane hurled at him as he made for the car.

Ten minutes later they were sitting on the balcony, enjoying a mug of tea and sampling the biscuits Maggie had provided. Bob had set up the metal table and two chairs and discovered that there was an awning to shield them from the hot August sun.

'With the cornfield below us, it almost feels as if we are sitting in the middle of the country,' murmured Jane, leaning back in her chair and momentarily closing her eyes.

'Even down to the flies,' laughed Bob, flicking away one that had suddenly perched on his mug.

'I forgot to bring my sunglasses,' remembered Jane suddenly.

'Perhaps we can buy some somewhere,' remarked Bob casually.

There was silence between them for a few minutes, as they both sat back and enjoyed the break. Jane in particular was feeling rather tired after her efforts of the last few days and being up early. It was just nice to just relax and do nothing.

The silence was broken by Bob, who suddenly got up from his seat and with 'Back in a minute' disappeared down the stairs. Jane was still sitting with her eyes closed when he returned.

'I've got a present for you.'

Jane was immediately alert. Bob had put a small package on the table in front of her.

'Ooh. What is it?' Jane squealed with delight, as her eyes feasted on the package, although she had already guessed what it probably contained.

'Open it.'

Jane needed no encouragement. She had already picked up her present and was carefully undoing the wrapping paper. As soon as she spied its contents, another squeal of delight burst forth from her. She held up a green bikini with white spots.

'It's fantastic! Thank you, darling.' The next instant she was up and planting a kiss on Bob's lips.

The kiss became several before Jane resumed her seat. She held up her new item of clothing. 'I thought you'd forgotten. I thought I was going to have to swim in my birthday suit.' She gave Bob one of her coy looks.

'You can if you want to,' he replied with a grin.

'I did once.'

'When was that'? he asked, immediately curious.

'When I was married.' Bob could see from Jane's suddenly serious face that perhaps it was a happy memory that stimulated unhappy ones. He decided to quickly change the subject.

'We'll go swimming first thing tomorrow morning,' he announced. First one awake wakes up the other one. You can try it out then.'

'That's a super idea.' Jane was full of smiles again.

After their tea break they decided to go and explore the village. It turned out to be closer than they had anticipated. They seemed to have hardly started driving before the first houses appeared. It was a pretty village, with a pub and half a dozen shops, several of them selling antiques. It was the small supermarket next to the post office that was the focus of their attention. Here they stocked up on breakfast muesli, bread and some extras. Bob insisted on buying a couple of bottles of wine as a standby, and the tiny establishment even managed to supply Jane with a pair of sunglasses.

Once outside the supermarket again they decided to investigate the pub and its facilities. They both came to the conclusion that it would be an excellent choice for an evening meal.

The next morning Jane was up first. It was the sound of the birds outside that alerted her to the new day. The sparrows that occupied the ivy covering parts of the outside wall kept up a noisy chatter. She looked at her watch and discovered it was only five. Bob was still sleeping soundly. Her mind made up, she slipped out of bed and tiptoed into the bathroom. Ten minutes later she was putting on the bikini Bob had bought her. She smiled to herself as she did so. It was perhaps more skimpy than she might have bought herself and was probably more suitable for sunbathing than for serious swimming, but as Bob had given it to her she was determined to wear it. She had been unsure whether he would remember his promise to buy her one and had popped the one she had bought herself into the bottom of her suitcase.

She shook Bob's shoulder. 'Wake up, sleepyhead. We're going for a swim.'

Bob opened his eyes and ran his hand through his hair. He looked up. Jane was standing over him wearing a pretty shorty beach robe.

She planted a kiss on his cheek. 'Hurry up, darling. I'm all ready,' she urged.

'Give me a minute.'

Bob was out of bed in a flash and heading for the bathroom.

Jane took the opportunity to put a few items in her beach bag. By the time Bob appeared again, carrying a towel and wearing a tee shirt, casual trousers and flip-flops, she was relaxing in one of the lounge chairs.

'Who's driving?' asked Bob.

Jane held out the car keys. 'You are. I'm going like this.' She glanced down at her bare feet.

Bob took the keys and they headed for the car. A cool breeze met them.

'Hmm. It's a bit colder than I thought,' remarked Jane, picking her way carefully over the gravel and wishing she had worn her flip-flops.

'It'll warm up when the sun gets up a bit,' Bob assured her. He was already in the car. Glancing at the car clock he observed, 'It's not six yet.'

Jane slipped into the passenger seat and dusted off a stray bit of gravel from the sole of her foot. 'I did drive a car barefoot once, when my heel broke,' she related, closing the car door and reaching for the seat belt.

Bob grinned, partly to himself, as he started the engine. 'I think most women have done it at one time or another. Janice used to do it occasionally.'

'It's quite a different sensation,' Jane admitted. 'But I'm not sure if it's illegal.'

'I think it's most likely legal until you have an accident doing it,' chuckled Bob.

The drive to the beach was short, just as Maggie had told them it would be. The road was deserted at this time in the morning. The only other vehicle they passed was a post van. Just after the village they spotted the side road and a sign 'To the beach'.

The road ended on a wide parking strip close to a short, sandy beach hemmed in by rocky cliffs at each end. There was not a person in sight. Bob stopped the car on the strip of stony grass. Jane was out of the car in an instant. Her robe abandoned, she sped across the firm sand towards the sea. Bob followed at a more leisurely pace. Jane waited for him at the edge of the water, the waves lapping her toes. Hand in hand they ran into the sea.

The experience brought forth a gasp of surprise from Bob and a squeal of shock from Jane. 'It's cold!' she shouted, laughing.

Just under an hour later they were back at the cottage, invigorated by their early morning swim, and two swimsuits and two towels were hanging on the line to dry in the gathering sunshine. Bob got dressed in a flash, and while Jane groomed herself he busied himself in the kitchen. By the time he heard Jane reappear, he had two bowls of muesli and a pot of tea with all the trimmings ready on the balcony table.

'Breakfast is served,' he called down to Jane.

Slowly she came up the staircase to join him. She was wearing a pretty summer dress. She paused and gave him a quick kiss. 'Thank you, darling.'

They ventured out onto the balcony. Jane sank into a chair. She looked around at the scenery and then at Bob, who was busy pouring out the tea.

'Gosh, this is heavenly. Even in my wildest dreams I didn't think it would be as good as this.'

Bob nodded at her. 'I know. It's really fantastic. A dream come true.'

Unfortunately, neither of them remembered that sometimes even the most wonderful dream can turn into a nightmare.

Chapter 37

The days flew past as Jane and Bob enjoyed every minute of their mini-holiday. The weather was warm and sunny, and each day began with a trip to the beach and an early-morning swim. The rest of the time was relaxing and restful. Sometimes they went for a walk in the countryside or took a sightseeing trip somewhere. Evenings were usually a meal in the village pub.

On their second morning at Barn Cottage, just after they had finished breakfast, a large and expensive-looking car drew up outside, and Gail Ashington emerged from its interior. Jane rushed outside to welcome their unexpected guest, who was already walking towards the door.

'Hello, Gail. This is a pleasant surprise,' Jane greeted her.

'Darling, how are you? Have you settled in? I was just passing and thought I'd check that everything is all right.' Gail planted a kiss on Jane's cheek.

'Everything is super. Come on in.'

Gail needed no urging. She quickly followed Jane into the lounge. A kiss was planted on Bob's cheek in response to his greeting and then Gail flopped into one of the armchairs. Jane and Bob followed suit.

Gail looked around. 'How is everything?' she asked. 'Is Maggie looking after you all right?'

'Yes, thank you,' replied Jane. 'She really is quite sweet.'

'She's worked for us years,' Gail remarked thoughtfully.

As Jane was about to make another comment about Maggie, Gail said, 'Jane, you are most welcome to come and use our swimming pool.'

'We've been going to the beach first thing in the morning,' explained Bob.

Gail made a face. 'Urgh. I don't like beaches. All that sand that gets everywhere.'

Jane laughed at the description. 'It's not such a problem, is it?' she asked, still smiling.

'It is for me,' retorted Gail. 'That's why Miles had a swimming pool built.'

Before either Jane or Bob could reply, Gail looked at them excitedly and spoke again. 'Look, why don't you both come over this afternoon for tea? I know Miles wants to show Bob his collection of antique cameras, and while the boys are doing that, we girls can enjoy a swim.'

She looked at them expectantly.

Jane turned to Bob. 'Shall we?'

Bob nodded. 'I'd like to see the cameras,' he replied.

Gail seemed pleased. 'It's settled, then. We'll see you about three. How's that?'

'That will be fine with us, won't it, Bob?' Jane looked at him for confirmation.

'Sounds great,' he replied.

'Good. We'll see you then.' Gail continued to chat for several more minutes, and then she suddenly jumped up and announced that she had to go. 'We only came down last night and I've got to go into Truro this morning,' she explained, making for the door.

Jane and Bob watched her go.

'Don't forget to bring your swimming gear, Jane,' she called back as she got into her car. And with that she was gone.

As they went back into the house, Jane turned to Bob and made a face. 'I don't really want to go swimming there, but I'd like to see their house,' she remarked.

Bob grinned. 'Me too – and I'd certainly like to see the cameras.'

A thought struck Jane. 'Did you notice what Gail was wearing?

She could have been going for an evening out instead of just shopping or something.'

Bob smiled. He had noticed Gail's extravagant dress. It would not have looked out of place at a royal garden party. 'How the other half lives,' he laughed.

It was close to three in the afternoon when Jane and Bob arrived at the Ashingtons. They had decided to explore the route over the fields that Maggie had told them about. It took them slightly longer than they had anticipated, because they got lost at one point, but they quickly found the way again and soon they were relieved to see the chimney pots of the house looming above the trees ahead of them.

The track finished close to the house, but it was necessary to go onto the road for a few yards before crossing a cattle grid between two stone lodges that marked the entrance to their destination. The drive stretched ahead to a majestic Elizabethan-style manor house. It seemed to be quite large, with numerous windows.

'Phew. That's some holiday residence!' exclaimed Bob.

'I expected something like this,' remarked Jane, scrutinising the building in front of them.

'Your family,' laughed Bob.

Jane was pensive. Turning to him, she suddenly said, 'You know, Bob, I'm still not sure if I really want to be part of the Ashington family. Except for not knowing my past, I was quite happy as Jane Carroll.'

Bob squeezed her hand. 'Whatever you want to be, I'll still love you.'

Jane would have kissed him, but they were almost at the house. The front door opened, and Gail appeared at the top of the steps. Jane was pleased to see that she had dressed down a bit, a blouse and a pair of casual trousers replacing her elaborate garb of earlier in the day. Jane was relieved that her own choice of a white blouse and pink trousers was a suitable match.

327

'Ah, hand in hand. That's nice to see,' was Gail's greeting.

Jane was thinking up a suitable reply, but Gail was already ushering them into the house.

'Now come on in, both of you. This is our country house, where we like to relax.'

Jane and Bob looked around at their opulent surroundings in silence. From the tiled floor of the huge entrance hall rose a magnificent staircase leading to a balcony on three sides of the upper floor. It was reminiscent of the one in Barn Cottage, but on a much grander scale. The hall was dominated by a large open fireplace stacked with logs, and oil paintings decorated the walls. There was even a suit of armour standing silently observing everything.

'This place was almost derelict when Miles purchased it. The roof had to be replaced and some of the walls were in a pretty bad state,' commented Gail, watching her guests' reaction to their surroundings.

'It's very impressive,' Bob remarked, still gazing around.

'It seems quite large, but at the same time it has a homely feel to it,' observed Jane. She liked the house already.

'I must show you the rest of it,' replied Gail.

The conversation was interrupted by the arrival of Miles Ashington.

'Delightful to see you both again.' He embraced Jane, planting a kiss on her cheek, and shook hands with Bob. 'Welcome to our country house,' he chuckled.

Gail took control. She addressed her husband. 'Now, Miles. You take Bob and go and play with your toys, and I'm going to show Jane around and then we girls are going to have a swim. You can both join us for tea. We'll have it on the terrace.'

Miles gave Bob a wink and a jerk of his head as if to say, 'Come with me.'

And with that the two men disappeared.

Jane was treated to a guided tour. It exceeded all her expectations. The house was extensive and lavishly furnished. The

328

large lounge with its comfortable seating was matched by the dining room with its giant table and panelled walls. A rather sombre library crammed with books from floor to ceiling featured alongside a spacious study. On the upper floor the bedrooms were impressive. They were all sizeable and had en suite bathrooms. She was surprised to note that Miles and Gail had separate bedrooms.

While they were passing a closed door Jane was surprised to hear the unmistakable sound of voices.

Gail turned up her nose. 'That's where the boys are,' she announced, rather disdainfully.

Jane just smiled politely in reply.

At that point it seemed the house tour was over. 'You've seen enough,' said Gail suddenly. Let me take you to the pool,' she urged, already making a move towards the staircase. 'I hope you've brought your swimming gear,' she added over her shoulder.

'Yes, I have,' replied Jane, indicating the bag she was carrying, as she followed Gail down to the ground floor. Then she asked, 'Do you spend a lot of time here?'

Gail shook her head. 'We come here for a few days six or seven times a year. Miles's business concerns keep him in town quite a lot of the time. I keep trying to persuade him to slow down and cut back a bit, but he's quite stubborn about it. He's really a workaholic. '

Jane found it hard to see the point of keeping such a large and expensive house standing unlived-in most of the time. 'Isn't it difficult to keep two houses going?' she asked.

Gail shook her head. 'Not really. We have three staff here – a housekeeper, a maid and a gardener.'

'Oh, I see,' replied Jane. Gail's remark seemed to reflect the wealth she and her husband must possess.

That topic of conversation ended there, as they had arrived at the swimming pool, which was joined to the house by a paved terrace. Jane had not been expecting anything quite so grand. It was much bigger than a normal domestic swimming pool. There were changing booths at one end, and the terrace was furnished with chairs and tables. The umbrellas looked inviting in the heat of the afternoon.

Gail took command. 'You go and change, Jane. I'll see you in the pool. Then we can chat while we wait for the boys.'

Jane obediently made her way to one of the booths. She was really only obliging out of courtesy. She preferred to swim in the sea with Bob, and 'girlie' talk had always tended to bore her.

She quickly changed into her bikini and joined Gail, who was already in the water. She had to admit that it was cool and pleasant in the pool. She wished she and Bob could share it on their own.

After swimming a couple of lengths, she came to a stop beside Gail, who had paused in the middle of the pool. 'It's a super pool,' she said enthusiastically.

Gail nodded. 'I made Miles build a nice big one. I can't stand those tiny little pools you get.'

They swam for another five minutes or so and then Gail appeared to tire of the activity. She made her way to the end of the pool, climbed the ladder and disappeared into one of the changing booths. Jane swam to the other end, left the pool, and walked back along its edge to retrieve her clothes. Once out of the water, she realised how hot the day was. The sun beat down on the tiles, and the heat was almost uncomfortable.

By the time Jane had changed and hung her bikini in the sun to dry, Gail was already relaxing in one of the chairs under an umbrella, her eyes closed. Jane joined her and sat down. As soon as she arrived, Gail opened her eyes and commenced to chat.

Jane was bombarded with quite a lot of questions. First Gail wanted to know about her life at the orphanage, and then about her marriage, and finally she turned her attention to *Discerning Woman*. How long had Jane worked there? What was it like working on a magazine? In the end, Jane felt quite exhausted by the interrogation, particularly as she had had very little opportunity during the conversation to ask Gail any questions about her background. All she had managed to glean was that Gail had once

330

been an actress as well as at one point a personal secretary. She was glad when the conversation changed tack.

Suddenly Gail asked, 'Jane – Monday is your last evening here, isn't it?'

'Unfortunately it is.' Jane wondered why she had asked.

Gail was quick to elaborate. 'Miles's son Ray is down here for the weekend. He owns a pub and restaurant about twenty miles away. He's invited us all over on Monday evening. You'll both come, won't you?'

Jane was thrown a bit off balance for a second, but she quickly recovered. 'I'm sure we'd love to,' she replied.

'Good. There's just one thing…' Gail hesitated.

'What's that?' asked Jane.

Gail screwed up her nose. 'The boys have decided it's to be a men's night.'

'What's that?' queried Jane, smiling slightly.

Gail made another face. 'The men are free to drink, and we girls have to do the driving and look pretty for them.'

Jane wanted to laugh, but she retained her composure. 'Oh, I see,' she responded with a grin.

Gail would have continued on the subject, but at that moment Miles and Bob appeared.

'Did you have a nice time playing with your toys?' asked Gail rather sarcastically.

'Of course we did,' Miles replied jauntily.

Gail appeared to give a sniff of disgust and then announced that she was going to the house to arrange for some tea. Miles and Bob sat down with Jane.

'Has Gail informed you of our little plan for Monday evening?' asked Miles. 'I've told Bob.'

'Yes, she has. We'll look forward to it, won't we, Bob?' Jane looked at Bob for approval.

'Of course we will. It will be a pleasant way to spend our last evening,' he replied.

'Did you enjoy looking at Miles's cameras?' Jane asked Bob.

331

'It's a very interesting collection,' he replied. 'Miles has some very valuable old cameras.'

'I've been collecting for many years,' Miles chuckled.

'Looking at your collection has made me want to start one of my own,' remarked Bob thoughtfully.

'Why not?' exclaimed Miles. 'I can put you in touch with one or two people who might be able to help you.'

Nothing more was said on the subject, because at that moment Gail reappeared carrying a tea tray. She was followed by a middle-aged maid laden with another tray.

For the next hour or so they sat enjoying tea and conversation. Gail kept offering Jane and Bob more sandwiches and cake, and in the end they had to politely refuse. The conversation was congenial and strayed from antique cameras to the rebuilding of the house and the construction of the swimming pool.

It was well after five when at last Miles remarked that he had to make some telephone calls. Jane and Bob welcomed the opportunity to take their leave. Gail insisted on showing them round the garden before they departed. Miles rejoined them briefly and goodbyes were said.

'See you on Monday evening,' Miles called after them as they departed. He added with a wink at Bob, 'Don't forget it's men's night.'

The remark brought a look of disdain from Gail. Clearly she was not in favour of the arrangement, but she waved a friendly hand in their direction as they walked away.

Monday evening seemed to arrive very quickly. As they prepared for their last evening, Bob and Jane became reflective. They were both appreciative of the few days' relaxation they had enjoyed. Over an afternoon cup of tea, Jane expressed her pleasure.

'I've really enjoyed these four days. It seems to have been a bit of heaven.'

Bob laughed. 'It's not completely over yet.' He became more sombre. 'But I know what you mean. It makes you realise that you do need to get away from things at times and just relax.'

Jane was pensive. 'You know, in a way I'm sorry we agreed to go tonight. On reflection I would have preferred to have a quiet meal together somewhere – just the two of us.'

Bob smiled. 'There'll be other times,' he replied. Then he grinned at her. 'Besides, it's boys' night.'

Jane made a face at him that changed to one of her coy looks. 'OK. I'll spoil and indulge you this evening, but you'll owe me one in return.'

'Agreed,' replied Bob, adopting a serious demeanour.

As soon as she had heard about the evening, Jane had been making plans. She did not share Gail's view of things. If Bob was to be spoiled for one evening, that was fine with her. She knew well enough that her turn would come. All she had to do now was put her plan in place.

When it came to getting ready, she had everything under control. She had the pretty new white summer dress Bob had not seen yet. It was going to be just right for the evening and for what she had in mind. She took out the new bra and briefs she had bought to go with it. They were skimpy in the extreme, but tonight she was dressing to please Bob. Before leaving the store she had dived into the hosiery department and purchased a pair of stockings to top everything off. The packet, which lay on the bed as she got ready, promised that the contents were 'sheer and invisible'.

Unfortunately, even the best-organised plans don't always work out as expected. When Jane came to put on her suspender belt, she discovered that it had come apart. She kicked herself for not checking it before throwing it into her case when she was packing. After all, she reasoned, she hadn't worn it for years. A few minutes' work with a needle and cotton might have saved the day, but she had neither. Perhaps if she had found out earlier, Maggie might have helped out. A drastic change of plan was necessary. She hurriedly grabbed the belt and the stockings and hid them in the bottom of her suitcase. The last thing she wanted was for Bob to see what had happened. Her original plans on that front would have to wait until another day. In the meantime she wondered what she could do to spice up her appearance. As she removed the engagement ring from around her neck, she pondered the idea of wearing it on her finger, but again she decided against it. Instead she tucked it safely into the inner pocket of her suitcase. An idea suddenly came to her. In the same pocket of her suitcase was the little gold anklet, which she had put in as an afterthought while she was packing. Now it would come in useful. She had slipped on her dress and was fastening the anklet when Bob appeared. His admiring look told her everything.

Jane looked up at him with a grin. She jumped up and slipped her feet into her new white shoes, which Bob had seen her wearing only once before. They matched the dress perfectly.

'I'm all ready,' she announced breezily.

But Jane was not to know what would be the dramatic outcome of her sudden change of plan.

Chapter 38

In spite of her earlier reservations, Jane was determined to enjoy spending the evening with the Ashingtons, and by the time she had finished getting ready she was really looking forward to it, even down to doing all the driving.

Just before they left, Bob appeared dressed in his cream summer trousers and lightweight jacket. The pink shirt he wore was perfectly matched by the tie he had chosen. Jane was quite thrilled when she saw him. She knew that he regarded the evening in the same light as she did. She was intrigued to see that he was holding a small box. Her eyes were wide in expectation as he handed it to her.

'A present for you,' he announced with a wide grin.

'What is it?' she asked excitedly.

'Open it.'

She was already lifting the lid of the box. As she peeped inside she gave a gasp of delight. A gold locket nestled in the soft padding. She removed it from its fancy packaging and held it up by the chain. Suddenly her arms were around Bob.

'Darling! It's beautiful. Just what I need to go with this dress. Please help me to put it on.'

She stepped back and waited obediently while Bob removed the necklace she was wearing and fumbled with the tiny clasp of the new gold chain. He fastened it around her neck and stood back. Jane ran to the mirror to view her new gift. Three seconds, and she was back and embracing Bob again.

'Thank you, darling.' She kissed him on the lips several times.

They embraced for several minutes. Bob had one arm around her, the other gently caressing her back.

'Save it for later,' Jane whispered, breaking free. She gave a little giggle as she looked at Bob. 'Now you've got lipstick on your face.'

Bob grinned and disappeared to the bathroom to rectify the situation. Jane scurried into the bedroom to check herself out. A glance in the mirror made her stop to admire the locket. It nestled comfortably between her breasts and was a perfect match for the dress. She had been a bit worried after purchasing the dress that the neckline was too deep, but now it seemed to be just right with the new adornment. A bit sexy, but not showing too much of her. Besides, this was Bob's treat night and she was determined to make sure he enjoyed it.

Bob was already waiting for her in the lounge when she reappeared.

She paused in front of him for a second. 'How do I look?' She regarded him, a look of mystique about her.

Bob smiled at her. 'You look great.'

Jane picked up her handbag and car keys. 'Right. Let's go. I'm the chauffeur both ways.'

'I could drive there...' Bob pointed out.

Jane shook her head. 'Nope. My treat this evening. You just relax and enjoy,' she laughed gaily. 'Besides, you need to find the route and guide me.'

She closed and locked the door of Barn Cottage, and together they walked towards the BMW, Jane taking careful steps in the high heels. She had already discovered that the shoes were a bit tight and needed a good deal more wear to be comfortable, but she dismissed the problem quickly. This was Bob's night and she would just have to put up with the discomfort.

It was about twenty-five minutes' drive to their rendezvous. Miles had given Bob details of how to get there and they found it quite easily. It turned out to be a village pub that had been extended with a large restaurant. It was clearly a popular venue, because when they arrived the car park was already quite full. Miles and Gail were already there and greeted them as they entered the foyer.

The formalities of meeting again were hardly over before Miles's son Ray and his wife, Kylie, arrived. Both were immaculately turned-out, Ray in what looked almost like a dinner jacket without a tie, and Kylie in a dress that was quite revealing and left little to the imagination. She wobbled on high heels, completely losing the effect they should have had.

Introductions were polite, though perhaps a little over the top.

'So you're the long-lost member of the Ashington clan,' was Ray's greeting to Jane, accompanied by a limp handshake.

'Something like that,' Jane responded, almost shyly.

'And you're the great photographer my stepmother keeps talking about,' went on Ray, turning his attention to Bob.

'A slight exaggeration, I think,' Bob replied, smiling politely and grasping Ray's hand.

It was Miles's jovial manner that eased the slight tension.

'Now come on, boys and girls. This is a jolly reunion of the Ashington family – and a special welcome to a long-abandoned member!' he exclaimed suddenly, smiling at Jane.

His strategy appeared to work, and a more relaxed mood came over the party.

It was quite clear from the over-attentive behaviour of the staff that Ray was the owner of the establishment. Introductions were hardly over before the head waiter arrived to show them to a table. There was no doubt that it was the best spot in the room. A large, round table in a corner had been selected and marked with a 'Reserved' notice. Once everybody was settled, the conversation began to flow a little more easily. Ray replied to Bob's questions about the restaurant, telling them how he had taken a fancy to the place five years previously, finding it in a rundown state, and had developed it into a sought-after establishment.

Polite conversation was directed at Jane and Bob, with questions about their stay locally and whether they had done this or that. Jane and Bob could not help noticing that both Gail and Kylie seemed to take a disinterested approach to the evening. Gail only put in a remark here and there and Kylie said very little. Ray appeared to have a gluttonous approach to eating, which no doubt accounted for his overweight appearance. He consumed

337

large amounts at each course, and the wine waiter was continually topping up the men's glasses. True to her intention, Jane consumed very little alcohol, making one glass of wine last the evening. She noted that Gail was doing the same, although Kylie drank freely.

On her way back from a visit to the ladies' room Jane almost bumped into Kylie. 'Oh, I am sorry!' she exclaimed.

'It's all right,' Kylie replied somewhat offhandedly. She noticed Jane glancing at her bare feet. 'My shoes hurt,' she explained.

'Ah, I see.' Jane was in a similar situation herself, but she felt uncomfortable at the thought of walking round shoeless in an up-market restaurant. She was about to mention her own problem out of sympathy, but at that point Kylie volunteered other information.

'I don't like it here,' she announced, screwing up her face.

'Oh. Why not?' Jane enquired, intrigued.

Kylie needed no urging. She screwed up her face again. 'We were supposed to go to my best friend's party this weekend, but Ray insisted we come down here. I don't know why. We were only here two weeks ago,' she grumbled.

'Oh, what a shame. I am sorry,' replied Jane.

Kylie nodded. 'Ray likes his own way,' she grumbled, looking to Jane for support.

Jane smiled at her. 'You'll have to try and get your own way more,' she suggested kindly.

Kylie sniffed. 'Chance would be a fine thing,' she replied miserably. 'Anyway, I'm a city girl by heart. I don't like the country.'

'What do you do?' Jane asked, tactfully changing the subject.

'I'm a model.'

'That sounds interesting,' Jane responded.

'I know what you do,' Kyle burst out. 'You're with *Discerning Woman* magazine. I was in a shoot for that once.'

'Small world,' laughed Jane.

They chatted for a few minutes more and then Jane remarked that she had better get back to the rest of the party, and they parted their ways.

As she returned to the table Jane couldn't help wondering what sort of relationship Ray and Kylie had. It didn't look as if they were married, and there appeared to be major differences between them. She wondered why Ray had insisted that they come down to this part of the country, on this particular weekend. Was it just to meet her and Bob? Had Miles told them to come? She had no answers to her questions.

When she returned to the table, she found herself the centre of conversation.

Ray turned to her. 'Dad tells me you're Ann Ashington's daughter. A direct descendant,' he remarked, continuing to look at her.

'It seems to be that way,' replied Jane politely.

'How did you find out you were a member of the family?'

Once again Jane went into brief details of how she was brought up in an orphanage and had always wanted to know a bit more about her past. Several times Ray interrupted her and asked questions. At times Jane felt she was being interrogated and she was glad when Miles politely changed the subject.

The time passed quickly and it was already well past eleven when Ray suddenly looked at his watch, mumbled something about having something to attend to and abruptly left the table. It was a sign for the party to break up. Miles glanced at his watch and announced that he and Gail would soon have to leave. Jane was relieved. Though she had looked forward to the evening it had failed to come up to her expectations. From the start there had been a slightly strained atmosphere. Ray had been quite offhand and overbearing at times, Gail had appeared subdued, and Kylie clearly did not want to be there. Only Miles had been a charming host, involving Jane and Bob in the conversation and stimulating it when it flagged.

Ray and Kylie disappeared quickly, but Miles and Gail walked with Jane and Bob to their car.

'Thank you for a lovely evening – and thank you again for letting us stay at Barn Cottage,' said Jane, as she shook Miles's hand.

'It's been a marvellous little holiday – just what we needed,' said Bob.

'You must come down here again,' cooed Gail.

'What did you think of the evening?' asked Jane, as she drove back to the cottage.

After a few seconds, Bob replied, 'A bit strained, I thought.'

'That's how I felt, and I didn't really like Ray very much.'

There was no reply from Bob.

Jane drove on in silence. After a while she noticed that Bob was strangely quiet. After several miles she could stand it no more.

She tapped Bob on the shoulder. 'Hey, you're quiet. Talk to me!'

Bob stirred. 'Sorry,' he mumbled. 'It's just that I feel so damn sleepy.'

'You need a strong coffee. I'll make you one when we get back,' announced Jane firmly. She grinned to herself. Surely the highlight of her evening was not going to be denied her by a sleepy partner.

'I had two cups of coffee in the restaurant,' Bob replied, yawning.

'OK. You sit back and have a snooze. But I want you awake and active when we get back.' She murmured under her breath, 'I just hope I can find my way in the dark.'

There was no answer from Bob. His head had dropped back onto the headrest.

Jane drove slowly and carefully. She hadn't taken particular notice on the way to the restaurant, because Bob had been giving her directions all the time. Gail, who had driven out of the car park just in front of her, seemed to have disappeared.

In spite of the slight worry, Jane managed quite well and eventually drew up outside Barn Cottage.

She gave Bob another tap on the arm. 'Hey. We're here.'

Bob barely stirred.

Jane was a bit dismayed. She had been looking forward to the

340

last bit of the evening, and now she had a sleepy partner on her hands. It was so unusual for Bob to be like this that she could not be angry. She took her time changing her shoes, in the process making several comments that were apparently ignored by Bob, who only seemed to murmur something at one point.

Wondering what to do, Jane collected her handbag and keys and slammed the car door, hoping that would wake him. Nothing happened. She gave a little sigh. What should she do now?

Suddenly an idea came to her. A wet sponge! That was it. That would be sure to do the trick, and there was a large sponge in the bathroom that would be perfect. She walked to the front door of Barn Cottage, making as much noise on the gravel as she could, still hoping that Bob would wake up.

She unlocked the front door and plunged the room into brightness. Depositing her bag and keys on a convenient chair, she kicked off her offending shoes, went into the bathroom and filled the basin with water. The sponge was dry and it took a couple of minutes to absorb the right amount of water. She grinned to herself. Now for the sleepy Bob, she thought.

As she emerged from the bathroom carrying the wet sponge, something between a gasp and a scream burst from her lips, and she dropped the sponge in shock. A figure stood in the entrance doorway holding a gun levelled directly at her.

Chapter 39

For a few seconds Jane's voice seemed to be frozen. She stared at the figure in the doorway holding the gun. Time seemed to be standing still.

After what felt like an eternity she managed to speak. 'Who are you? What do you want?'

'Don't try anything silly. Just do as you're told.' It was a woman's voice.

Jane's sudden shock was replaced with fear. The gun pointing at her appeared real and menacing. Her brain seemed to be paralysed. Her mouth was dry. 'Who are you?' she managed to croak again.

Her intruder spoke from behind a scarf that covered the lower part of her face. 'Just do as you're told and you won't get hurt. This gun is loaded and I know how to use it. We don't want any violence, but that's up to you. It would be best if you didn't try anything heroic.'

'I have no money.' Jane was beginning to think she was immersed in an armed robbery.

'We don't want money.' The woman moved forward into the room. 'Go and sit there.' The order was accompanied by a slight movement of the gun in the direction of a chair.

For the first time Jane directed movement into her body. She bent down to pick up the sponge, but her attempt was immediately countermanded by her aggressor.

'Leave it. Go and sit down.'

Jane obeyed. There did not seem to be anything else she could do. She walked over to the chair and sat down on the edge of it.

The woman came and sat opposite her, the gun trained on her the whole time.

Jane found herself almost petrified with fear. What was happening? Everything seemed unreal, as if she were in a dream. But the gun levelled at her was real enough. She suddenly thought of Bob. How long ago had she left him? Five minutes? Ten minutes? Oh, if only he would wake up and come to her aid... Please. Please wake up, she prayed. But nothing happened.

How long they sat facing each other Jane could not tell. It might have been only a few minutes, but it seemed to be hours. All the time she was conscious of the gun pointing at her.

At last she found her voice. 'Why do you have to keep pointing that thing at me?'

The intruder chuckled. 'We don't want anything silly to happen, now, do we?' was her reply, but the gun moved position to rest on the arm of a chair.

Jane felt relieved by the action. At least it was no longer pointing directly at her. 'If you don't want money, what do you want?' she asked.

Again there was a chuckle behind the scarf. 'We want you.'

'Who is we?'

'You'll find out.'

Jane suddenly thought of something, 'If this is a kidnap, you've either got the wrong person or got things wrong. Nobody is going to pay a ransom for me.'

'It's not a kidnap.'

'Why are we sitting here like this?' Jane was beginning to feel more forceful in her questions.

'You'll see.'

The reply puzzled Jane. What did the woman want with her? She tried to make her out, but her face was almost obscured by the scarf. From her voice she appeared to be a young woman.

Jane sat consumed with fear. This was something you read about or saw in a film. It didn't happen to ordinary people; but it was happening to her here and now.

There was a sudden noise outside. It caused Jane to shift her position. Could it be Bob? Would he grasp the situation quickly enough to help her? The questions raced through her head.

Her movement caused the woman to react.

'Stay where you are.'

The harsh instruction was accompanied by the movement of the gun towards Jane.

Jane sat still. There was no further sound from outside, and the hope of rescue from Bob began to diminish. Fear still gripped her. She tried desperately to think of some way to overcome her assailant. Could she divert her attention long enough to escape? Could she say she needed the bathroom and escape that way? Each time her strategy was blocked by the thought of the gun.

'How long are you going to keep me sitting like this?' she asked hoarsely.

'You'll see.'

'But why? What do you want with me?'

'You ask too many questions. Be quiet.'

Again the tremors of fear swept through Jane's body. Not only was she being held prisoner, but she also had to be a silent one.

They sat in silence, for how long Jane never knew. Suddenly there was another sound outside and the next instant a figure appeared at the still-open front door. It was another woman, perhaps a year or two older than Jane. She was dressed casually in a tee-shirt and jeans and unlike her accomplice's, her face was visible.

She greeted the first woman. 'Everything all right, Babs?'

'You took long enough. Everything go OK?'

'Sleeping like a babe. He won't wake up for hours.'

The remark puzzled Jane. Who were they talking about? She knew it was pointless asking. Then the attention turned to her.

'How's this one behaving?' asked the second woman.

'Asking too many questions. Let's get on with it.'

The second woman turned to Jane. 'Right, you. Get up. We're going somewhere.'

Jane tried a new ploy. 'I'm not going anywhere until you tell me what's happening.'

Her remark produced an immediately reaction from the second woman. Showing signs of annoyance, she addressed Jane.

'Now look, we can either do this the easy way or the hard way. It's up to you.'

She opened the lid of a small box she was carrying and showed the contents to Jane. The box contained a hypodermic needle and several phials. She continued. 'You can either go willingly or I can inject you with this. It'll put you to sleep in seconds.'

There was a moment's silence. Jane could not bear the thought of being made unconscious.

'What's it to be?' The tone of the voice was impatient.

Jane almost panicked. 'Please don't inject me. I'll go with you.' To demonstrate her compliance she got up from the chair.

'OK. Just do as you're told and everything'll be fine.'

Still consumed with fear, Jane waited. Where were they going to take her?

The second woman spoke again. 'Pick up your bag and keys and put on your shoes. Hurry.' It seemed that she was now taking charge of events.

Jane obediently carried out the command. With the gun still pointed at her, she appeared to have no option. She walked to the spot where she had abandoned her shoes, and stuffed her feet into them. Almost mechanically she picked up her handbag and keys from the chair where she had deposited them what seemed like hours ago now, although perhaps it was only a matter of minutes.

'Turn out the lights and lock the front door. Then walk towards your car. And don't try anything silly.'

Jane followed the instructions. Outside she was again ordered to walk to the car. As she approached it, she noticed that there was no one in the passenger seat. The shock of seeing the empty seat produced an anxious response from her.

'Where's Bob? Where's my fiancé? What have you done to him?' There was panic in her voice.

'Don't worry about him. He'll just sleep for a few hours.'

'But where is he?'

'He's safe.'

Jane had no time to even consider the answer, as they had arrived at the car.

'Get into the driving seat. Babs, you sit behind her.'

Jane found herself sitting behind the steering wheel. The woman called Babs got in behind her. The second woman slipped into the passenger seat.

'Now start the engine and start driving. Don't try anything and remember there's a gun pointing at your back.'

'Where are you taking me?' Jane asked, hesitating and shaking now. It was a futile question.

'Never you mind. Just do as you're told.'

'I told you she asked a lot of questions, Mel,' said the woman in the back seat.

'She'll be quiet soon enough.' The woman called Mel turned to Jane. 'Get cracking,' she ordered.

With a thumping heart Jane started the engine. The BMW sprang into life. Almost in a dream she put the car into gear and they moved off.

Jane drove slowly through the darkness. The clock on the dashboard indicated that it was approaching one in the morning. It seemed ages since she and Bob had left the restaurant. She had been happy as she drove back to Barn Cottage, humming a tune to keep herself company, a sleeping Bob beside her. Now she was driving again, this time to an unknown destination, with a gun at her back. Somehow she had to try and escape from her captors. But how? They seemed so well organised and in control. Perhaps the car would break down, but she knew that was clutching at straws. Could she fake needing petrol? She knew it was no good. The petrol gauge was showing well over half full. Could she force a collision with another vehicle? It seemed a risky idea, and in any case there was no traffic on the road.

They drove on in silence except for the occasional direction from Mel. Jane was driving on unfamiliar roads and needed to concentrate. On top of that she had not had the opportunity or the inclination to change her shoes, and she found driving in high heels difficult. How long the journey took she had no idea. She was too concerned with the predicament she was in.

At last she was directed down a minor road. It was narrow and not very well maintained. The car bounced over several potholes. The road ended abruptly in a flat, stony area overlooking the sea. The water was sparkling in the moonlight.

Mel pointed. 'Park over there.'

Jane brought the car to stop just feet from a dilapidated wooded fence, which appeared to be on the edge of the cliff. She took the scene in with a glance. There seemed to be a gap in the fence, and a path leading down towards the sea. Under normal circumstances the view would have been quite romantic, with the moon shining on a calm sea, but she was acutely aware that this was not a normal situation.

'Stop the engine.' Babs spoke again from behind her. 'Now get out of the car.'

As she issued the instructions, Babs was already opening her own door.

Slowly Jane complied. She was still shaking, and she had not come up with a way of outwitting her captors.

Again she asked the question that dominated her thinking: 'What are you going to do with me?'

'Just shut up.' The command came from Babs, who was looking anxiously around. 'Where are they? They should be here by now.' There was almost panic in her voice.

'They'll be here,' remarked Mel quite calmly.

'I want to get this job finished and get out of here,' Babs snapped angrily.

So there were more people involved in her abduction. What on earth was it all about? Why would anybody want to kidnap her? Surely they must have got the wrong person. That thought generated another fear. What would happen to her when they found out they had made a mistake? And what had happened to Bob? Was he all right? Was he looking for her? The questions raced through Jane's brain in a matter of seconds, and all the while fear was seeping into every part of her body. Fear of what was going to happen to her.

Jane stood motionless by the car. Mel seemed quite calm, but Babs was still looking anxiously around. Suddenly she turned her attention to Jane.

'You. Walk round to the other side of the car.'

With the gun levelled at her again, Jane had little option other than to comply. Slowly, watched by an impatient Babs, she walked round the front of the car to the front passenger door, which Mel had left wide open.

'Now take your clothes off and be quick about it,' barked Babs.

Jane's reaction was swift. 'Go to hell.' For good measure she added, 'I've no intention of doing such a thing.'

Babs shrugged her shoulders. She seemed quite unconcerned.

'Please yourself. There'll be a couple of men here shortly and they can do it for you. They'll enjoy that.'

As if to give substance to her remark, a large black car drew up a short distance away, and two men emerged. Babs immediately beckoned them silently with her hand.

Panic overtook Jane. The thought of strangers stripping her clothing off was unthinkable.

'Please. I'll do it myself.' The words came out automatically.

'Get on with it, then,' Babs snapped at her.

Jane kicked off her shoes and started to take off her dress.

'Put everything on the car seat,' ordered Mel.

With shaking fingers, Jane complied. 'Why are you doing this to me?' she pleaded, close to tears now.

'You'll find out. Just get on with it,' said Babs, brandishing the gun.

'You can keep your bra and pants on,' said Mel. Her voice was almost sympathetic.

Shaking and fighting back the tears, Jane completed the

required task. She placed her dress, neatly folded, on the car seat and put her shoes next to it.

'Take off your watch as well,' instructed Mel. 'You can leave the rest on,' she added, with a glance at Jane's locket and anklet.

Jane looked at her. 'Why?' she pleaded.

'Just do it. We've wasted enough time on you,' snapped Babs.

Jane removed her watch and placed it on top of her dress. She stood there, conscious of her skimpy underwear. Under normal circumstances embarrassment would have overtaken her, but now fear overruled her modesty. What did these people want with her, and what were they going to do to her? Why had she been made to remove her clothes? 'Please tell me what you're going to do with me,' she begged.

'You'll find out soon enough,' smirked Babs.

The two men were now standing with them. They seemed to be a similar age to the two women – perhaps just a bit older than Jane. Their eyes were fixed on Jane, who was standing pathetically by the car. One of them gave a whistle and grinned at her.

'Where have you been all my life, darling?'

Babs immediately took control of the situation. 'You can cut that out. Remember we're doing a job. I don't want you messing things up.'

The man looked a bit sheepish. 'No harm in a joke,' he muttered under his breath.

Babs turned to Jane. With the number of accomplices increased, she was no longer waving the gun around.

'Walk over to the other car,' she ordered.

Jane obediently started to walk in the direction indicated. She felt sick with fear, but for the present there did not seem to be any alternative other than to do as she was told. The situation she was in was the type of thing you read about. Something that happened to other people. But now it was real and it was happening to her.

She walked slowly, surrounded by her captors. It was like a nightmare. She kept thinking that at any moment she would wake up and forget everything. But the rough ground under her bare

349

feet and the cool breeze blowing in from the sea reminded her of the reality of her ordeal.

They reached the other car.

'Kneel down,' growled one of the men.

Jane sank down onto the sharp stones that a few seconds earlier had been tormenting her feet.

She was completely unprepared for the next thing that happened. Her arms were suddenly pulled behind her, almost causing her to lose balance. She noticed the cord in the man's hand and realised his intention.

'No, no! Please don't!' she cried out.

It was to no avail. Within seconds her hands were tightly bound. Her ankles received the same treatment.

Even worse was to follow. Her head was yanked back and a cloth was forced into her mouth. No, it couldn't be happening. They were gagging her! She shook her head violently and protested with muffled sounds. She received no sympathy from her captors. She found herself lying on the ground, her hands and her voice out of action.

'At least that's shut her up for a while,' remarked Babs. 'I'm sick of listening to her questions.' The next instant, Jane heard the boot of the car being opened. Surely they were not going to put her in there? Abruptly she was lifted up by the two men and deposited on the hard metal floor of the boot. She protested as best she could through the gag.

Mel peered into the boot. 'If you don't keep quiet, I'll have to put you out.' She held up the hypodermic box again.

Her threat had the desired effect. Jane ceased her protest. The last thing she wanted was to be injected with heaven knows what. It was best to be quiet for now. The nightmare had to end at some point. Her new strategy was tested when the lid of the boot slammed shut. Panic overtook her. It was dark and cold in her cramped prison. Her heart was thumping. What would happen to her in there? Would there be enough air to breathe?

She was vaguely conscious of people getting into the car and it moving off. She felt every bump as the car jogged over the stones. She tried to ease herself into a more comfortable position, but it was difficult. There was the smell of petrol, and her feet were pressed against metal that was unusually cold. It must be the fuel tank, she thought. By raising her knees slightly, she managed to lift her feet off it. That at least solved that problem.

The jolts from the rough ground ceased as the car began to run over the smoother surface of the road. Jane tried to force her thinking into action. Who were these people who seemed to have planned everything down to the last detail? Where were they taking her? What had happened to Bob? She had been so concerned with her own predicament that she had had hardly any time to think of him. Where was he? Was he looking for her? There were many questions racing through her brain, but no answers came.

She did her best to cope with her strange environment. At least her earlier fear that she might run out of air appeared to be unfounded. If anything, the boot was draughty.

Suddenly a new fear struck her. She started to feel slightly sick. Panic almost overtook her. What if she was actually physically sick? She had heard somewhere of people experiencing being gagged and actually choking on their own vomit. There was no chance of removing the gag with her hands tied securely behind her back. She tried to thump the sides of the boot with her body to attract attention. Any sound she could make was minimal and only hurt her. That was no good. She had to try and relax. That was the thing to do. The sick feeling would pass. It could be the smell of the petrol. Breathe deeply. That was the thing to do. She tried to lie back and concentrate on her breathing, slowly and methodically. The strategy seemed to work. The sick feeling started to abate.

She lay there in her cramped position. The car she was travelling in as a prisoner was taking her to a destination and future that were unknown to her.

Chapter 40

It was the cool wind fanning his body that woke Bob. For a few seconds he lay there disorientated. The bed was hard and unyielding, and he had a pounding headache. He tried to force his brain into action, but it did not seem to work. He started to raise himself up to a sitting position, and he realised that he was naked apart from his underpants, and that his watch was gone. Where on earth were his clothes? Had he removed them? If so, where?

He looked around and tried to work out where he was. He was on a bench on the edge of what appeared to be a playing field. It felt like early morning, and it was starting to rain. He shivered. Where the hell where his clothes? He looked around desperately, but there was no sign of them. The field was small and was mostly surrounded by trees and the backs of houses. Perhaps it was a cricket ground. There was a small pavilion not far away. Maybe his clothes were there. He got to his feet and then realised that he felt pretty groggy. On top of the headache he was beginning to feel sick. Sheer desperation forced him to start walking across the grass to the pavilion. As he did so he heard a clock striking somewhere. He counted the chimes – six. He had been correct. It was early morning.

It was a futile exercise. The pavilion was locked and there was no sign of his clothes. Somewhere at the other end of the playing field there must be a village. The church clock had sounded from there and he could actually see the steeple. He had to get help somehow. Perhaps he could find a sympathetic man who would take pity on him and assist. It was all he could think of.

He staggered back across the grass in the direction of the

church. He felt as if he was going to be sick at any moment and he just wanted to lie down somewhere, but the chill in the air and his predicament drove him on. He tried to nudge his brain into thinking and that produced an alarming question: where was Jane? His last memory was of being in the car with her and feeling sleepy.

He reached the edge of the playing field and discovered a hard track that clearly must lead to the village. It was at this point that his inside finally erupted. He knelt on the grass verge and was violently sick again and again.

'Goodness.' The comment was close by and was one of surprise and disgust.

He looked up.

A middle-aged woman out walking her dog was viewing him suspiciously. He had not heard her approach.

He wanted to say something to her, but with one more brief look of revulsion she turned and hurried away.

'I say, can I talk to you?' he called after her, but she did not reply or look back.

Humiliated, and with temporary relief from his inner turmoil, he continued walking in the same direction. The woman had already disappeared.

It was only a short distance to what was apparently the main street of the village. He crossed the road to a bus shelter and sank thankfully onto one of the benches. He still felt pretty awful and his stomach felt as if it wanted to erupt again. He sat there, almost bent double, waiting for his inside to settle down and at the same time trying to force his thinking into gear. The two main questions were how he got where he was in his present condition, and where Jane was.

How long he sat there he had no idea. He heard the clock strike again, but he wasn't sure if it was striking half past or a quarter to the hour. The sound of footsteps alerted him from his stupor. He looked up. A young woman was approaching the bus shelter. He prepared to speak to her, but the instant she saw him she screamed and fled in the direction she had come from. He sank back onto the bench. Was every inhabitant of the village female?

Ten minutes later the sound of a car drawing up and footsteps approaching made him look up. A burly police officer was entering the bus shelter. A police car was parked outside.

The police officer smiled at Bob. 'A good night out was it, sir?'

At first Bob struggled to reply. When he did it was a brief 'No'.

'Been drinking have we, sir?' asked the police officer as he sat down on the bench beside Bob.

'Only over dinner last night,' replied Bob, wishing that his stomach would stop complaining.

'And where was that, sir?'

Bob couldn't remember. 'We were guests of Miles Ashington and his family,' he tried to explain.

A second police officer now appeared in the shelter.

'We?' asked the first.

'My fiancée and I.'

The second police officer joined the conversation. 'And where is your fiancée?' he asked.

'I don't know,' Bob replied miserably. 'I haven't seen her since last night.'

'What's your name, sir?' the first police officer was pulling out a notebook.

'Bob Harker.'

'And the name of your fiancée?'

'Miss Jane Carroll.' As he replied, Bob wondered if he should explain that Jane was now an Ashington, but the police officer was already onto the next question.

'And you say you were staying with the Ashington family?'

'No. We're staying in a cottage that belongs to them. My fiancée is related to the Ashington family.' At least I explained that, he thought.

The police officer looked up from writing in his notebook. 'I see, sir. We'll get that checked out. Now, can you tell us what happened last night?'

Bob went into a few details, but when it came to his last

memory of the previous night, all he could remember was falling asleep in the car.

The two police officers looked at each other. The second one nodded to the first. He addressed Bob. 'I think you'd better come along with us, sir, and we'll get things sorted out.'

Sheer willpower made Bob get up from the bench. He was still feeling groggy, but at least someone was helping him.

'Where are your clothes?' asked the first police officer.

'I don't know. I woke up like this,' Bob replied miserably.

'Just a minute,' grunted the second police officer.

He disappeared for a minute and reappeared with a blanket, which Bob accepted gratefully.

The two officers led him to their car and deposited him on the back seat. Bob remembered to click home his seat belt.

The second police officer handed Bob a bag as he slipped into the driving seat. 'If you're going to be sick, use this.'

Bob hoped he would not have to use it, though he felt that his stomach was still unpredictable.

He did not remember much about the car journey other than that it did not appear to take very long. They entered a small town, the road sign indicating Stonechurch. They turned off the main road and then into an alleyway, which appeared to lead to the back entrance of a police station.

Bob was ushered into the building. He was feeling self-conscious in the blanket. He avoided the stares of several members of the staff, some of them women. One of the police officers who had brought him to the station led him down some steps and threw open a door.

'We'll put you in here for a while and talk to you shortly,' he explained. He ushered Bob into the room, closed and locked the door, and was gone.

Bob took in his surroundings at a glance. He was in a police cell. It was empty except for a bed against one wall and a toilet without a seat. The sight of the toilet reminded him that he had a desperate need to avail himself of its convenience. Relieved, he sat down on the bed. He tried to think things out. How had he come

355

to wake up almost naked in a strange village? Where had Jane disappeared to? He struggled to remember the details of the previous evening. He could remember saying goodbye to the Ashingtons, getting into the car with Jane, and the first bits of conversation, but that was all.

He suddenly had an overwhelming desire to lie down, just for a few minutes.

It was the sound of the door being unlocked that woke him. Gosh. He must have dozed off. The door opened and the first police officer he had encountered entered the cell, a mug in his hand.

'Here we are, sir. A cup of tea.'

Bob took the mug. 'Thank you,' he responded.

'Feeling a bit better, are we?'

'A bit better, thank you.' It was true. After the short doze, his stomach did seem to have settled down a bit.

'Good. We're going to get the police doctor to check you over, just to make sure it's only a hangover.'

The words alarmed Bob. 'Is that really necessary?' he asked. 'I didn't really have all that much to drink.'

'I'm afraid so,' the police officer replied, ignoring Bob's last statement. He left before Bob could say any more.

Left alone again, Bob became even more alarmed about his predicament. Now it appeared that he was being treated as a drunk after a hard night. At least he now felt a bit better, though he still had a headache. He drank some of the tea, but it had been sweetened and as he did not take sugar in tea or coffee, its sickly taste did not appeal to him.

Not long afterwards he was collected from the cell by the same police officer and taken to another room that was sparsely furnished with just a table and some chairs. A bespectacled man greeted him and announced that he was the police doctor and that he just wanted to check him over.

For the next twenty minutes or so Bob submitted to the routine examination. He answered a lot of questions about his health, and careful notes were taken. He was asked to perform several tasks and then, satisfied that he had not suffered a heart attack or something equally serious, the doctor left the room.

A few minutes later, the police officer returned and Bob was subjected to a barrage of questions. After the doctor's verdict, it became clear to him that he was being treated as a person suffering from the effects of the night before.

At the conclusion of the interview the police officer looked at Bob and made a comment that really worried him. 'You realise, sir, that you could be charged with being drunk and disorderly?'

The news struck Bob like a thunderbolt. Things were going from bad to worse. He struggled to find something suitable to reply. 'I am aware of that. However, I have to say that I did not drink excessively last evening. I only had two glasses of wine.' He thought of something else to add. 'There were six of us dining out. You can check with any of the others.'

His interviewer nodded. 'We shall be doing that.'

It was the mention of the previous evening that once again made Bob concerned. Where was Jane? The clock on the wall showed that it was nearly half past ten. He had been in the police station for four hours.

'That's it for now.' The police officer gathered his papers together and rose from his chair. Clearly the interview was over.

'Can I go now?' asked Bob.

The policeman grinned at him. 'Like that?' He indicated the blanket. He smiled sympathetically. 'Better let us sort something out for you,' he suggested.

Bob did not reply. He was now too concerned to worry about his appearance, but he obediently allowed himself to be conducted back to the cell.

He sat there alone, trying to make sense of everything. Nothing like this had ever happened to him before, not even in his wilder days at university. The pieces of the jigsaw didn't fit together. Jane was uppermost in his mind. Where was she? How did she become parted from him the previous evening?

It was almost an hour later that the cell door was opened again.

A woman police officer stood there. 'Will you come this way, please, sir?' she asked.

Bob followed her back to the interview room. Another police officer he had not seen before was sitting at the table.

'Please take a seat, Mr Harker,' he said.

'Would you like a cup of tea?' asked the woman police officer.

'Thank you. That would be welcome.' Bob's mouth was now dry, though thankfully the nausea had disappeared.

The officer left the room after asking Bob if he took sugar and milk in his tea.

The seated police officer glanced at the papers in front of him and then looked at Bob. He cleared his throat. 'Mr Harker, we have found Miss Carroll's car.'

'Where?' Bob was immediately alert.

The policeman looked at him again. 'It was discovered by a resident of the village of Eldingham out walking his dog. The car was parked in Dolby Cove. That's not far from where you were picked up this morning.'

'But what about Jane?' asked Bob.

The police officer studied him for a second. When he replied, his voice was slightly softer. 'I'm sorry to have to say this, Mr Harker, but the incident has all the appearances of late-night bathing. Two sets of clothing, a man's and a woman's, were found in the car. The man's jacket has your documents in the pocket.'

Bob tried to make sense of what he had just been told. Why on earth should the car have been found miles from where they were going?

'But what about Jane?' he repeated.

The officer glanced at his paperwork again. 'A white dress, size 12, a pair of white shoes, size 5, and a lady's gold watch were the items of clothing found. Officers are still carrying out a search of the car and the surrounding area.'

He looked up at Bob. 'Mr Harker, did you and Miss Carroll go swimming last evening at Dolby Cove?'

Bob protested. He could see the direction the office's thinking

358

was going in. 'That's impossible. Why should we? We had just been out for the evening.'

The officer gave a slight smile. 'Oh, people sometimes get these ideas. A romantic meal out, a moonlit night...'

The interview was interrupted by the woman police officer bearing a tray with two mugs of tea, which she placed on the table.

Bob protested again at the previous suggestion.

'I'm confident we did not go swimming yesterday evening,' he stressed.

'Can you account for the clothing in the car?'

'No.'

By now Bob was both confused and worried. What had happened after he had fallen asleep in the car? How had he come to wake up wearing just his underpants? Where had Jane gone in her underwear? Had they really gone swimming? The questions bombarded him.

There were a few more questions from the police officer, which Bob answered almost automatically. It was concern for Jane that now occupied his thoughts.

The officer had been writing throughout the interview, occasionally sipping his tea. Bob sat with his hands clasped round the other mug.

At last the officer stopped writing and passed a sheet of paper and a pen to Bob. 'I'll have to ask you to provide us with a statement of your side of the events. Please read this and sign it if you consider it a true account of what happened last evening.'

Bob did not reply. He read the document. There was not a lot to it, because he had not been able to tell the police very much other than that he had fallen asleep in the car the previous night and had woken up in a playing field early that morning.

He signed the statement.

'Thank you, sir.' The police officer took the sheet of paper. He looked at Bob for a few seconds and then spoke again. 'Just to let you know, sir, that we have alerted the coastguards in the area and the lifeboat has been called out to do a search.'

359

'I see,' replied Bob. He felt stunned. So that was the way it was. The police were convinced that he and Jane had gone swimming the previous evening and that there had been some kind of mishap.

The police officer spoke again. 'We've also contacted Mr Miles Ashington and he verified that you and Miss Carroll were his guests yesterday evening.'

'Thank you.' Bob uttered the words almost automatically.

'I'm afraid we shall have to ask you to stay here for a while, until the investigation team returns.'

Bob nodded in reply.

He was led back to the cell, with an apology from his hosts for having to ask him to wait in there.

Bob sat alone with his thoughts. He was now extremely worried about Jane. What had happened to her? Another concern was the question of what had happened during the period he could remember nothing about. Had they in fact gone swimming, as the police appeared to think? It seemed too unbelievable to even consider.

Around midday a police officer brought him a plate of sausages and chips, together with another mug of tea. In spite of everything, Bob suddenly became hungry when he saw the food.

A little while later he was led back to the interview room. The officer who had taken his statement was sitting at the table, on which now lay two plastic bags. One clearly contained Bob's clothing, and in the other were Jane's bag, dress and shoes.

The police officer addressed Bob. 'We've recovered these personal items from Miss Carroll's car. We'd like you to check your own items and also verify that the second bag contains the clothing that Miss Carroll was wearing the last time you saw her.'

Suddenly Bob was overwhelmed with misery. Seeing Jane's items in a plastic bag brought reality into focus. He sat down quickly on one of the chairs.

'Are you all right, sir?' asked the police officer.

Bob nodded. 'It's just the shock of seeing my fiancée's possessions like this.'

'I understand sir,' replied the police officer.

Bob said nothing.

The police officer continued. 'We've also recovered Miss Carroll's handbag. It was left on a rock close to the sea.'

He looked at Bob to determine how he received this information. Bob felt too besieged by the questions in his head to even attempt a reply.

His informant spoke again. Closely studying Bob, he made his summing-up. 'I'm sorry to have to say this, sir, but from all the evidence we have seen so far, it would appear that at least Miss Carroll went swimming in Dolby Cove last night.'

'But that's impossible. We would never have done that. Jane must be somewhere.'

'We will continue to make enquiries,' the officer advised sympathetically. 'Now, if you wouldn't mind just looking through these bags, sir…'

Bob carried out the instruction as if in a dream. He checked the contents of the bags as requested and signed various documents. The police officer gave him back his own items but kept Jane's clothing and bag. Then Bob was told that he could leave and that he would be contacted if there were any developments or if he was needed again

With a heavy heart, and carrying his bag of clothing, Bob retreated to the nearby cloakroom. Just to be wearing his own clothes again made him feel a bit more normal.

When he emerged from the cloakroom and was trying to find his way out of the building a woman police officer told him there was somebody waiting to collect him. She led him out into the entrance hall of the police station. A worried-looking Miles Ashington stood there. As soon as Bob appeared, he rushed over and grasped his hand.

'My dear boy, this is a terrible thing to have happened.'

Bob was almost too full of emotion to reply. All he got out was a croaky 'Yes'.

'But what happened?' Miles asked, looking at him anxiously.

'I wish I knew,' Bob replied miserably.

'I'll take you home. I've got my car here,' Miles replied soothingly, taking Bob's arm to guide him to the exit.

'Thank you,' was all Bob managed to say.

He followed Miles out of the building. He was surprised to find himself in bright sunshine. Everywhere he had been in the police station had been away from natural light. Even more of a surprise was to see that the luxurious car that Miles had arrived in was chauffeur-driven. He found himself installed in the back seat with Miles beside him.

They drove in silence. Bob's concern about his own predicament had now been replaced by another serious worry. Where was Jane? What had happened to her?

Chapter 41

Clarity came to Jane slowly. With it also came the reality that she was still travelling in the boot of the car. She could feel every bump from her cramped position. Had she fainted, or had she just fallen asleep? She was not sure what had happened.

She tried to shift her position to ease the ache in her limbs, but it was impossible in the confined space. On top of that her wrists now hurt from being tightly tied. Her only consolation was that the feeling of nausea seemed to have gone away. Two questions were uppermost in her brain: who were these people who had abducted her so violently? Where were they taking her?

How long the rest of the journey took she had no idea, but eventually she was aware of the car slowing down and driving over a bumpy surface. Then it stopped. There was the sound of people getting out of the car, and the next instant the lid of the boot was opened. Babs and Mel peered down at her. Jane looked up at them, pleading with her eyes. It was still dark and they were illuminated by the light in the car boot. Jane was conscious of the two men joining them.

'Get her out.' It was Babs who issued the order.

The two men lifted Jane out of the boot and set her on her feet.

'Let's get her inside quick,' urged Babs.

Mel bent down and released the cord around Jane's ankles. She took Jane's arm and made her walk. Jane could just make out the outline of a large building in the darkness. She staggered the few steps to it. A door was opened and a light turned on, which dazzled her. She was led along a corridor and up some stairs, stumbling as she went, and then into a room.

Mel almost pushed her onto a bed. 'Welcome to the Grand Hotel,' she mocked.

Jane made muffled noises, pleading for the gag to be removed. 'I'll take it off, but if you scream or shout, it goes back on. OK?' Jane nodded. It was all she could do.

Mel removed the gag.

'Thank you,' responded Jane hoarsely, greatly relieved. Another thing was troubling her. Pinioned behind her back, her arms hurt, and she could feel the cords biting into her wrists. 'Please untie my hands,' she pleaded. 'My wrists are hurting.'

Mel nodded. 'OK. But you'll still have to be secured until that lazy partner of mine fixes the window so that you can't escape.'

'Who are you? Why are you doing this to me? I've never done you any harm.'

Jane looked at her captor, begging for an answer, but Mel only looked at her for an instant before turning and leaving the room. Jane heard her run down the stairs, and a few minutes later she returned with a pair of handcuffs.

Jane's hands were untied and the next instant she found her left hand tethered to the iron bedstead on which she was lying. At least the pain from the cords on her wrists was beginning to disperse.

'I'll be back soon.' And with that Mel left the room, closing the door behind her.

Jane tried to take in her surroundings. She was lying on a single bed in a small bedroom. A chest of drawers stood against one wall, and a low table against another. A tatty and rather dirty carpet covered part of the floor. The only window had the glass painted over. Morning was now beginning to lighten it.

Jane lay back on the bed. This was obviously going to be some sort of prison for her. But why? What did her captors want with her? Tethered as she was, she had to remain on the bed. How long were they going to keep her like this? If only she knew what they were planning. It looked as if Mel was now in charge of her. Perhaps eventually she might get some information from her. It was worth a try. The light coming through the window was becoming brighter. It was clearly still early morning, but without her watch it was impossible to know the exact time. It almost sounded as if she was in some sort of farmhouse, because she could hear the clucking of hens and several times a cockerel. There was the distant sound of a meal being consumed. It sounded as if her four captors were all downstairs having breakfast. It must have been at least an hour before things began to go quiet, and then there was the unmistakable sound of a vehicle being driven away somewhere nearby.

Five minutes later the door was opened and Mel appeared again. She carried a plate of toast and a mug of tea.

'I've brought you some breakfast,' she announced. Then with a grin she added, 'We won't starve you.'

Jane had a greater need. 'Please, I need a toilet,' she begged.

Mel hesitated a second, and then sprang into action. 'OK. But no tricks. And you'll have to leave the door open.' She reached into the pocket of her jeans for the key to Jane's handcuffs and quickly unlocked them.

Jane stood up.

Mel opened the door and Jane was relieved to see that the toilet was almost opposite. She had to use it while Mel stood on the landing close by. Normally she might have been embarrassed, but she was already learning that in captivity modesty is of a lesser importance.

However, she was not quite prepared for the next encounter. Emerging from the toilet, she found herself being eyed up by one of her male captors, who must have crept up the stairs behind the waiting Mel.

The intruder gave a low whistle. 'Hello again, darling,' he smirked, feasting his eyes on Jane's scantily clad body.

The sound made Mel turn round quickly to face him. 'You, get back downstairs. And get this window fixed,' she snapped.

With a sulky look the man disappeared down the stairs.

Mel led Jane back into her prison. Jane obediently lay back on the bed and held out her hand to be secured again. She felt that there was little else she could do at this stage.

'Don't worry about Carl. He's all mouth and nothing else. I can handle him,' remarked Mel as she fastened the handcuffs again.

Something else was troubling Jane after the encounter with Carl. Her skimpy underwear had not been intended for public display, but for something completely different. She was now painfully aware of her state of undress.

'Please can I have some clothes to put on?' she asked hopefully.

Mel looked at her, almost smiling. 'Why?' she asked. 'You're not going anywhere.'

The remark made Jane snap. 'Look. You abducted me last night, stripped me of my clothes, trussed me like a chicken and brought me here. You won't tell me why. I'm nearly naked and I'm cold. I want some clothing.'

Her outburst had the desired effect. Mel looked at her for a second, surprised and shocked. She responded quickly.

'OK. Keep your hair on. I'll see what I can find.'

She went across to the chest of drawers and opened one of the drawers. She rummaged for an instant and then pulled out a blanket, which she placed on Jane's legs.

'I'll find you something else later.'

And with that she left the room.

Jane lay back, surprised at the success of her outburst. She pulled the blanket around herself with her free hand and munched the toast Mel had brought her. It was now cold, like the mug of tea, which was sickly sweet, but she was surprised how much she wanted food.

It was some time before the door was unlocked and Carl appeared, carrying some tools. He grinned at Jane and she was glad that she had the blanket pulled tightly round her.

'Hello, darling,' was his greeting.

Jane made no reply.

He set to work. It didn't take long. Two holes were drilled in the window frame, and screws inserted. With a final twist of the

366

screwdriver, he turned to Jane with a smirk. 'That'll stop any little birds from flying away.'

Again, Jane made no reply. It was pretty clear now that Carl was Mel's partner. Jane guessed that he was probably around the same age as Mel, but his unshaven face and greying hair made him look older.

Jane watched as Carl collected his tools together. As he turned to leave the room he hesitated at the side of the bed. He glanced at Jane's tethered hand and then looked at her.

'I could make things better for you, you know.' He grinned.

'Go to hell.' Jane's reaction was automatic.

Carl shrugged his shoulders. 'Please yourself,' he remarked.

As he was leaving, Mel appeared again. She was carrying a bundle of clothes and a bucket.

She looked after the departing Carl and then addressed Jane.

'Don't take any notice of him. He thinks he's Casanova.' She sniffed. 'It takes him all his time to manage it once a week.'

In normal circumstances Jane might have been amused by the comment, but this situation was too serious.

Mel put the bucket down on the floor. 'You can use that when you want a pee,' she announced. The next instant she threw the bundle of clothes onto the bed, over Jane's legs. Next she produced the key to the handcuffs and released Jane's hand. With that she went out of the room, locking the door behind her.

Jane quickly examined the bundle. It contained a blouse, a thin skirt and a pair of shoes. In a second she was off the bed and trying them on. They were quite clearly second-hand. The once-white blouse was greyish in colour and the skirt had a tear in it. Both were at least one size too big but they were garments and she was glad of their covering. The shoes were too loose. They were well worn and one had a hole in the sole, but at least they were shoes.

She lay back on the bed again and tried to think things through calmly and logically. What reason would anyone have for abducting her? At first she had considered it to be a kidnap, but she ruled that out. Why were four peopled involved, and why had she been forced to remove her clothing at the seashore? None of it made sense. Her thoughts turned to Bob. Where was he? Had he been abducted too? For what reason? The whole thing was weird and absurd. She wondered whether she had been reported missing. Perhaps the police were already looking for her. In the meantime, what intentions did her captors have towards her? Again and again she asked herself the question. The more she thought about it, the more concerned she became.

She was now convinced that she was being held on some sort of farm, because again and again she heard animals and the sound of activity outside somewhere below her window. Funny, she thought: Carl didn't look much like a farmer. If only she could see out of the window, but it had been painted over on the outside. There wasn't even a crack to look through.

Sometime later – she guessed around midday – Mel brought her some sausage and mash. As she put the plate down on the table, Jane tackled her again.

'Please tell me what's going to happen to me. Why are you doing this?' she pleaded.

Mel paused and looked at her. Jane thought that yet again she wasn't going to get an answer.

She was wrong. Mel suddenly spoke to her almost angrily. 'Look. Get this. We are just the middle guys, hired to look after you until the next stage. That's our job and as much as I know.'

'But why does anybody want to do this to me?'

Mel shrugged. 'I expect you've upset someone.'

'But I haven't,' protested Jane.

Mel shrugged her shoulders again. 'Somebody must want you out of the way,' she remarked almost casually. Jane's future did not appear to concern her.

'But who? You must know who engaged you to kidnap me,' said Jane anxiously, desperate for an answer.

Mel smiled slightly. 'I value my life too much to tell you that,' she replied.

'What will happen to me?' Jane asked, in almost a whisper now.

Mel shrugged her shoulders again. 'Who knows? Get rid of you somewhere, I suppose.'

Mel's reply struck fear into Jane. What was she hearing? The gravity of her situation was even more apparent. She desperately needed to find out more from Mel while the opportunity was there.

Her next question voiced the fear that was uppermost in her mind. 'You mean they're going to kill me?' Her voice was hoarse.

Mel hesitated slightly before replying. 'I doubt it,' she observed casually. 'More likely ship you off somewhere out of the way.'

'But where?' wailed Jane.

Before she could receive an answer, Carl called from downstairs.

'Mel! MEL!'

'What's he want now?' muttered Mel, preparing to leave Jane. 'Coming!' she called back. She spoke over her shoulder to Jane. 'You ask too many questions.' And with that she was gone, the key turning in the lock once again.

Jane was left with her thoughts. Her brief conversation with Mel had produced a greater fear in her. Her ordeal was no kidnap for ransom as she had first feared. It was something more sinister. Clearly her captors were only part of the plan somebody had for her.

Somehow she had to try and escape. But how could she do that? It was clear that the door was going to be kept locked. Could she overcome Mel in some way? That was difficult. Carl seemed to be around most of the time. Anyway, how would she do it? Hit Mel over the head with something? That was a bit dodgy. She might kill her and then be had up for murder. The window was the only alternative, but Carl had fixed that. Perhaps an opportunity to escape might present itself. She had to be ready to seize any chance that came along.

The afternoon passed slowly. All was quiet downstairs, though she could still hear the sound of the animals close by and occasionally a dog barked almost below her window. It must have been around five o'clock that Mel appeared again, this time with a plate of cheese sandwiches and a mug of tea. Jane had planned to ask her some more questions, but Mel perhaps guessed this, because after depositing the tea and sandwiches, she collected Jane's plate and cutlery from lunchtime and disappeared quickly.

Jane did not want anything to eat. The lack of activity was making her lose her appetite. She only managed to eat half of the sandwiches and, conscious of the primitive toilet arrangements, she only drank half the tea.

The evening passed even more slowly than the afternoon. Jane could hear the sound of a television. Despite her predicament she dozed several times. The light was already fading when Mel appeared again bearing a mug of cocoa. She looked at the half-eaten plate of sandwiches.

'Off our food, are we?' she asked.

'I'm not used to being a prisoner,' remarked Jane sarcastically.

Mel made no reply.

Jane was determined to ask her some more questions.

'What is going to happen to me?' she asked.

Mel looked at her. Her face was quite serious. 'It's better that you don't know,' she replied.

'But why?' Jane pleaded.

'It's just better, that's all.'

Even more worried by Mel's reply, Jane could see that she was not going to make any headway on that subject. She tried a different tack.

'How long are you going to keep me here?'

Mel was non-committal. 'A few days, I guess. Perhaps a week.'

Jane suddenly thought of another question that had been coming into her worried thinking.

'What did you do with Bob – my fiancé?'

Mel grinned at her. 'He's quite safe and sound.'

Jane hardly dared ask her next question. 'Are you holding him prisoner as well?'

Mel shook her head. 'You were the one we wanted.'

370

Jane wanted to continue questioning Mel, but Mel suddenly ended the conversation.

'You're asking too many questions. It's not good for you,' she snapped.

With that Mel left the room again. As she closed the door she spoke to Jane in an almost friendly way. 'Sleep well,' she cooed.

Jane could have wept. Mel's final words had almost been like a doting mother saying goodnight to a beloved daughter.

Jane sipped the cocoa slowly. Whatever these people had planned for her future, it did not seem to be very good. Somehow she had to escape from their clutches. She racked her brain to devise a way of getting her freedom, but each time it came back to one thing. She was locked in a room with only two outlets – the door and the window. The door was kept locked, and the window was screwed shut.

She was to learn that desperate situations often produce desperate solutions.

Chapter 42

Jane slept fitfully. She woke up a few times and immediately remembered where she was: held prisoner for an unknown reason and confined to a tiny room. Eventually she dropped off into a sounder sleep towards early morning and was woken up by the cockerel crowing. It seemed to be only yards from her window.

She lay awake, listening to the sounds from outside. It seemed to be almost another world, remote from her. The realisation came to her that she should have been back at work that day. What would they think when she didn't turn up at the office? She also remembered that she and several other members of staff were due to have a meeting with Annette that morning to discuss future plans. As she was a key player, she wondered whether Annette would cancel the meeting.

It seemed ages before she heard the key being turned in the door and Mel appeared. Mel put a plate and a mug of tea on the bedside table. She looked at Jane.

'Slept well?' she enquired, with a bit of a grin.

'No,' replied Jane curtly.

Mel said nothing. She was turning to leave when Jane broached the subject that was on her mind.

'Can I have a shower or a bath?' she asked. To give more emphasis to her request she added, 'I feel dirty and horrible.'

Mel pondered the request for a few seconds before answering. Then she replied abruptly, 'OK. But it'll have to be later.'

With that, she left the room.

So far, so good, thought Jane. Her request was sincere, but her thoughts were on escape. The room she was in did not seem to offer any options. Her best possible chance would be outside of it. Could she give her captors the slip? It was worth a try.

Satisfied with her strategy, she sat back on the bed to tackle the breakfast Mel had brought. A fried egg swam in a mass of fat, together with two slices of bacon. It was not the sort of breakfast she would normally have partaken of, but hunger forced her to eat what had been provided.

It must have been at least an hour and a half later that Mel returned. She glanced at Jane, who was lying on the bed. 'OK. You can have a bath now. But no tricks, and you'll have to leave all your clothes here.'

This was something Jane had not bargained for. 'Everything?' she queried.

'Yes.'

Jane said nothing. She hadn't quite bargained for stripping off in front of Mel, but if that was the way it was, so be it.

Quickly she divested herself of all her clothes, tossing them casually onto the bed. She removed the two items of jewellery she was wearing and placed them with the clothes, watched all the time by Mel.

Stark naked, she casually picked up the bucket she had had to use and, almost to hide her embarrassment, she announced, 'I'm ready.'

She followed Mel out of the room into the corridor. First she had to empty the bucket in the toilet, and then Mel led her down the corridor to a bathroom. It was old and tatty and none too clean, but Jane was looking forward to immersing her body in water.

'Leave the door open and make plenty of noise,' Mel instructed.

Jane was already running the water.

For ten minutes she enjoyed the feeling of water on her body. All the time she was looking for possible means of escape. She knew Mel was close by somewhere, but that didn't stop her scheming. The window seemed an option. She tried to open it, but although she managed to loosen the catch it refused to budge.

373

'You're wasting your time. It never has opened.'

Mel was standing in the doorway again.

Jane was subdued. She had inadvertently indicated her objective to Mel. It was all or nothing now. Could she dash past Mel and escape down the stairs? It was a possibility. She guessed that in a sprint for freedom she would be faster than Mel, who was a bit on the plump side. So determined was her need, that she would escape stark naked if she had to. The idea brought a whiff of humour into the idea. She might even get arrested for indecent exposure!

She took her time over her bath. She was concerned to note the red marks on her ankles and wrists from being tied up the previous day, but she supposed they would disappear in time. Slowly she dried herself on the rather grey towel Mel had provided, as she quietly planned her next move. She knew Mel was not far away, but could she make the dash for freedom now?

Her optimism was short-lived. She emerged from the bathroom and tiptoed quickly down the corridor, past the room where she had been confined. As she hastened towards where she knew the stairs were, she came face to face with Carl.

Her reaction was to give a piercing shriek. Her two hands flew into action to cover herself.

Carl grinned at her. 'What's the hurry, darling?' he asked.

For a second she stood petrified.

Carl's eyes were all over her. 'Nice body,' he drawled.

The next instant Mel appeared from behind Jane and grabbed her by the arm. 'Get back in your room,' she snapped.

Jane needed no urging. As she retreated into the room she heard Mel berating Carl.

'And you, leave her alone.'

Jane heard Carl's reply as he retreated down the stairs.

'She'll get worse where she's going.'

Back in the room, Jane lost no time in getting dressed. She was in the process of fastening the skirt when Mel appeared in the room carrying the toilet bucket, clearly displeased with what had happened.

'That's the last time you're allowed out of this room,' she said angrily.

Jane made no reply. Mel slammed down the bucket with a clatter and swept out of the room, locking the door behind her.

Jane lay back on the bed once again. She felt defeated and depressed. Her gallant attempt to escape had failed and it now looked as if there would be no further opportunities. And what did Carl mean by his remark, 'She'll get worse where she's going'? It worried her.

The time passed slowly. There was nothing to do except lie back and listen to the sounds that filtered through the window. Around what she guessed was lunchtime Mel brought her a bowl of soup and a roll. She made no comment during her visit and was grim-faced. It was quite clear Jane was not a popular prisoner at present.

It was not until the third day of Jane's ordeal that Mel appeared to mellow slightly. In the afternoon she appeared with a mug of tea.

'I've brought you something to read,' she announced, putting the mug on the bedside table and dumping a bundle of magazines on the bed.

'Oh. Thank you!' exclaimed Jane, appreciative of the gesture. Boredom was beginning to stress her.

Mel seemed to be in a better mood. Jane decided to try and engage her in conversation. 'How much longer am I going to be here?' she asked.

'Hopefully, not much longer,' replied Mel curtly.

Jane was determined to continue the conversation. 'And what will happen to me then?' she asked.

Mel looked at her for a moment, almost as if she was thinking of a suitable answer. 'Someone else takes over,' she replied, almost irritably.

Jane could tell that she wasn't going to glean any further information from Mel by questioning her. She tried another tack. 'I'm sorry if I made you mad yesterday morning, but you can't blame me for trying to escape,' she said softly.

Mel regarded her. There was almost a sadness about her, but she answered immediately. 'I don't blame you. I'd have done the same myself. Actually, I feel a bit sorry for you. It's not your fault you're in this position.'

Jane felt that she was gaining ground. She thought for a few seconds. 'You could let me go,' she said quietly. 'You could blindfold me and drive me off somewhere miles away. I wouldn't know where I'd been,' she suggested hopefully.

Mel laughed. 'Nice one. But I don't fancy a bullet in my back, thank you,' she retorted with a bit of a smile.

'How did you get into all this?' Jane asked as kindly as she could.

The same look of sadness came over Mel, but she quickly recovered. 'You don't know what it's like, the world I live in.' She paused for a second and then continued. 'I was brought up in a rotten family. My mother was on drugs and my father was in and out of prison. I used to tell the other kids at school he'd gone on holiday. I got into trouble before I left school and was on probation by the time I was sixteen.'

She stopped for a few moments and looked miserably at Jane. She seemed to want to continue talking. 'I got into nursing, but I was sacked for trying to steal drugs,' she announced. 'I was in prison by the time I was twenty,' she added casually.

'I'm sorry,' responded Jane.

'Once you've been in prison, it's hard. You go for a job and, yes, they're very polite, but it's always the same: "I'm sorry, we can't take the risk" – or you get a rejection letter.'

'It must be very hard,' sympathised Jane.

Mel went on talking. 'Then I took up with Carl. He's been in and out of prison. We took on this farm, trying to make a go of it, but he's no farmer and now we're in debt and the land is rented out. With the money we get for this job we'll go to Spain and do something there.'

Jane was trying to think of a suitable reply, but Mel spoke again first. 'You're our meal ticket.' She laughed briefly.

'Thanks,' retorted Jane.

Mel looked at her for a moment and then almost as if she had said too much, she muttered, 'I've got to go. I've got things to do,' and left the room.

Alone again, Jane started to glance through some of the magazines. One of them was the issue of *Discerning Woman* with the Angus Pike article. It brought back memories. She remembered her first meeting with Bob and the development of her relationship with him. Now she was held prisoner for an unknown reason and with an unknown future. She wondered whether Bob was looking for her. How would he know where she was? That thought quickly reminded her of the predicament she was in. Carl's words had struck fear into her. She was all the more determined to escape, but the big question was, how? It was now clear that for the rest of her stay in the farmhouse she was not going to be allowed out of the room. That morning Mel had brought a bowl of water for her to wash in. That cut out any hope of escape outside the room. The bedroom window seemed to be her only option, but Carl had secured that on her first morning in the room. If only she had a screwdriver...

Her thoughts were interrupted by the sudden return of Mel. She was carrying a newspaper, and there was the trace of a confident smile on her face.

'Fancy that! You've made the headlines,' she remarked, casually tossing the newspaper onto the bed next to Jane. Then she left the room.

Jane picked up the paper. It seemed to be a local publication, and at first she was puzzled at what she was supposed to look at. Then she found it: a short report in a column.

Tragedy at Dolby Cove. *A tragedy occurred at Dolby Cove on Monday evening. It is understood that a young couple went for a midnight swim there. One of them, Jane Carroll, from London, apparently got into difficulties while swimming and is believed to have drowned. A land and sea search was undertaken by the police and coastguard, but Miss Carroll's body has so far not been recovered. Miss Carroll's partner, Robert Harker, was too upset to be interviewed by our reporter. There are strong currents in the area of Dolby Cove, and swimming is discouraged.*

Jane stared at the article in disbelief. She was reading a report of her own death. Nobody was looking for her alive – only her dead body...

Chapter 43

Jane stared at the newspaper article for a long time. A cold fear now gripped her. She was on her own; nobody was going to come and rescue her. Everybody thought she was dead. Drowned. Even Bob must now think the same. She knew now why she had been taken to the seashore and forced to strip off her clothes. It was all part of the plan, whatever that was.

Somehow she had to escape, but how? Could she break the glass in the window? The idea made her leap off the bed and look for something to use. The room appeared to contain nothing that might serve her. In desperation she picked up one of the shoes Mel had given her. The heel had a metal tip. That might do the trick. Clutching the shoe in one hand, she started to tap the window. The sound it made seemed to be quite loud. She knew she would have to strike the glass much harder to break it and it would take quite a time for her to make a large enough hole to crawl through. By that time Mel and Carl would be alerted. She abandoned the idea.

She examined the two screws Carl had used to lock the window. If only she had a screwdriver. She fingered the slot in one of the screws. If she could find something to fit into it, could she turn the screw? Again she looked desperately round the room for something to help her. The room had been well prepared for her use. It was bare and lacking any object that might be remotely suitable. She looked into the chest of drawers. The first drawer was empty. The second contained some musty blankets. The third yielded nothing. The last drawer offered hope. It contained a few items of clothing and several old handbags. Jane opened each one.

She found a penny in one, but that was going to be too thick. But the second bag she examined contained a metal nail file.

Her heart thumping, Jane examined the file. The end of it was rather similar to a screwdriver. Would it turn the screws?

She went over to the window and tried the file in the slot in the head of one of the screws. It fitted perfectly, but how on earth was she going to hold it in position so that she could turn the screw? At that instant she heard a noise outside the door, and then the familiar sound of the key in the lock. She flew back to the bed. She just had time to hide the file beneath her and pick up one of the magazines and pretend to be reading it.

Mel entered the room. She was carrying Jane's evening meal, which appeared to be a pasty on a plate accompanied by a large portion of mashed potatoes. There was also the usual mug of tea. She placed them on the bedside table and looked at Jane with a grin.

'You're going on your travels tomorrow night.'

'What do you mean?' asked Jane anxiously.

'We're saying goodbye to you.'

'Where am I going?'

'Somewhere safe,' replied Mel casually.

'But where? What's going to happen to me?' Jane almost pleaded.

'It's best you don't know.' Mel was serious now.

Jane wanted to ask more questions, but Mel must have sensed that, and with a brief 'Enjoy your meal' she was gone.

Jane picked at the food, deep in thought and fearful for her future. Where were they going to take her? The hints of something sinister dropped by both Carl and Mel were tinged with menace, and she was now all the more determined to escape. She had only a day and a night to achieve that. She was also conscious that she was beginning to feel unwell. She had a bit of a sore throat, and several times during the day she had felt shivery. She had tried to dismiss the feeling, but now she was aware that something was happening to her body. I can't be ill now, she thought. She just had to fight it.

She did not finish the food. Her appetite had diminished, and she was now more determined than ever to get to work on those screws. Getting them out offered the only hope of escape. It was vital now. Perhaps even her life depended on it.

At first she was unable to hold the nail file tightly enough against the screw to even attempt to turn it. It also hurt her fingers. She thought desperately for a solution. Tearing a page out of one of the magazines, she made a small pad of paper. It worked, but it needed an excessive amount of effort and strength on her part to hold everything in place. She tried with all her might to turn the screw, but it would not budge. All that happened was that on several occasions everything slipped and her hand hit the woodwork.

She tried again and again on both screws without success. Desperation and fear drove her on. How long she wrestled with the screws she had no idea. Almost in tears she pleaded for them to loosen. 'Please, please turn,' she whispered.

Suddenly her prayer was answered. At first she thought the file had slipped out of the slot yet again, but no: there was slight movement. She tried again with all her strength and managed a good half turn. Her hopes rose. She was confident that having moved the screw so far, she could eventually get it out. All evening she persevered. The shadows were already lengthening when she heard Mel's footsteps in the corridor. She was lying on the bed again pretending to read when Mel entered the room.

Mel immediately pressed the light switch and plunged the room into brightness before putting down the mug of cocoa she had brought for Jane. 'You must need a light to read,' she remarked. She glanced at the unfinished food from her earlier visit. 'You didn't eat your tea,' she said, studying Jane.

'I don't feel hungry,' replied Jane. 'I think I've got a cold or something coming on.'

'I'll get you a couple of aspirins,' said Mel, looking at her critically.

'Thank you,' answered Jane, wondering when Mel would bring the tablets. She was desperate to get back to work on those screws.

Normally she was left alone for the night after Mel brought her the mug of cocoa. Now she would have to wait to start work again.

It seemed a long time before Mel appeared again carrying a bottle of aspirins and a glass of water. She deposited the glass and a handful of tablets on the bedside table. 'I don't want you to die on me,' she remarked with a chuckle.

Jane thanked her and with that Mel left her again.

She waited until she heard Mel go back down the stairs, and then leapt into action. Hastily gulping down two aspirins with some water, she returned to the window. The second screw proved to be even more stubborn than the first. Again and again she tried to turn it, but each time she failed. Exhausted, she sank down onto the floor under the window, her back to the wall. She was almost in tears, all hope of escape slowly drifting away from her. On top of that her hands and fingers hurt with her efforts and she was beginning to feel rotten. Perhaps the aspirins would help. She hoped so.

She could hear a television somewhere below the window, and once she heard the dog bark from somewhere in the same direction. It was now completely dark outside. Eventually she got up from the floor. She had to have just one more attempt.

Once again she fitted the nail file into the slot in the head of the screw and pushed with all her might. Nothing happened. She tried again and the file slipped, causing her knuckles to hit the woodwork. In desperation she continued the task, and after a while the screw began to move. Encouraged, she laboured on.

It took her a long time to loosen the screw completely. On each turn it appeared to hit a tight spot and it required extra effort on her part to continue. All the time there was the danger of the nail file slipping or the slot in the screw becoming worn. Slowly she worked away. She guessed it must have taken her almost an hour to completely extract the screw, but eventually she was able to turn it with her fingers. Excitement was welling up inside her when she at long last held it in her hand. She returned to the first screw, which came out comparatively easy.

Her heart was thumping. Now to open the window, she

thought. At first it would not budge, but then slowly she managed to ease it upwards about a foot. She peered out. The first thing that struck her was the cool breeze. For three days she had been cooped up in that small, stuffy room. Now it was a pleasure to breathe the fresh, clean air. She tried to take in her surroundings. The window was right above the peaked roof of some sort of outhouse or extension to the main building. Below and to her left there appeared to be a yard illuminated by the light from a window. She could still hear the sound of the television. She guessed the dog must be somewhere in or close to the yard. That could be a problem: one sound, and it would bark. First she had to get the window open a bit more so that she could get out onto the roof and somehow reach the ground. It stuck, and it required great effort on her part to force it open far enough for her to crawl through. As she pushed the window up it gave a pronounced squeak. She froze. Would the dog bark? To her relief no sound came.

She knew she had to be quick. Desperately looking round the room, she grabbed the pair of shoes Mel had given her and with them in one hand she squeezed through the window onto the slate roof. She had already selected an escape route. She would climb down the roof on the opposite side to the yard, and when she reached the edge she would hopefully manage to get to the ground. There was a pipe that might help her descent.

As she turned to make her way down the roof, disaster struck. One of the shoes slipped from her grasp. She watched in horror as it catapulted down the roof towards the yard. It reached the edge of the roof and then hurtled over the edge. She heard a splash as it landed in some water. Immediately the dog started to bark. Panic overtook her. In desperation she slid down the roof, still clutching the other shoe. She reached the edge and dangled over, clutching the pipe for support as she eased herself downwards, pressing against it to slow her descent.

It seemed a long way down, and as she edged her way she felt the pipe start to come loose. Frantically she fought to reach safety, and just as her foot touched the ground the pipe gave way completely and crashed down, just missing her. She was not so lucky with the gutter, which caught her shoulder with a glancing blow as it fell, knocking her to the ground. The noise stirred the dog into furious action, and it started to bark frantically. There were sounds of movement in the house. Jane heard a door open and a shout. She knew instantly that her absence was about to be discovered. Picking herself up, she was overtaken by panic. She found herself running over soft ground, perhaps a garden; she spied a gate and ran towards it. There was more shouting in the house. Somebody was in the room she had occupied. Any minute now they would be after her.

The gate led directly onto a road. Jane gave no thought to which way to go, but just turned and ran as hard as she could, propelled by one simple thought: escape. The sharp gravel of the road surface was painful to her bare feet, but she hardly noticed, such was her panic. There were sounds of more activity from the house. To her horror she heard a car door slam and a motor starting. She guessed it would be Carl. She knew now she was being pursued. She looked frantically for somewhere to hide, but there was a hedge on either side of the road. On top of that everything was partly illuminated by moonlight. She heard the car pull out onto the road, and to her relief it turned to move off in the opposite direction. Still running, she heard it recede in the distance.

Her relief was short-lived. It was only a short time before she heard the car again. She was sure it must be Carl, who, not finding her on the other section of road, had now turned round and was coming in her direction. The car engine was getting louder by the second. She looked frantically for somewhere to leave the road. Luck was on her side: a field entrance came into view. Panic-stricken at the sound of the approaching vehicle, she climbed over the gate, conscious that the top of it was armed with barbed wire, which pierced her hands. She hardly felt it. In her haste she almost fell off the gate onto the ground on the other side. She searched desperately for somewhere to hide. It was a large field with no cover. Her heart thumping, she crouched in a ditch close to the gate. In order to be less conspicuous, she stretched out full length.

The ditch was wet and muddy. To her dismay she heard the car stop alongside the gate. Somebody got out. The next instant the field was flooded with a powerful light, moving from side to side, searching. She waited, her heart in her mouth, expecting her hiding place to be revealed at any moment.

It did not happen. Carl spent a good two minutes shining his light over every inch of the field, but he missed Jane lying in the ditch. Then the light went out and Jane heard the car door slam. The next second, the car moved off slowly down the road.

Jane climbed out of the ditch and started to run across the field away from the gate and the road. The surface was rough and uneven and at one point she felt a stab of pain in the sole of her foot as she trod on something sharp, but she dared not stop, exposed as she was in the middle of the field. As she ran, a cloud started to move in front of the moon. She was thankful. Darkness might assist her concealment; the only downside was trying to see in the gloom.

By the time she reached the edge of the field, Jane was completely out of breath. She tried to recover as she walked slowly along the hedge trying to find a way out. She reasoned that she must eventually reach a house or a farm where she could get help. She eventually found a wide gap in the hedge and went through it. Now she seemed to be walking over marshy ground. Several times she splashed into water and mud. On one occasion her feet sank into soft mud well above her ankles. This produced a new fear in her. Didn't swamps swallow people up rather like quicksand? She was sure she had heard that somewhere. Fortunately the marshy terrain ended and she found herself walking on firmer ground again.

How long she walked was uncertain. She guessed perhaps an hour or more. Somewhere close by she could hear the sound of sheep calling each other, and from time to time a fluffy shape would scurry out of her way. The terrain was scattered with huge boulders, which she had to avoid occasionally. It was darker still now, and the sky was completely covered with clouds. Suddenly she saw a building start to take shape out of the gloom. Her hopes rose. It could be a farmhouse. Just as she spied it the first drops of rain started to fall, slowly at first and then settling into a steady downpour. She hurried towards the building.

It turned out to be a small cottage with several outbuildings. Jane hurried through a broken gate and spied a door. She lost no time in hammering at it with both hands. Everything was in darkness and she guessed the occupants had long since gone to bed. She had no idea of the time but she supposed it must be long past midnight. No answer came. She knocked again and waited. Still nothing. Then she saw something she had not noticed in her earlier relief at finding habitation. The windows were boarded up.

Despair seeped into her. She wandered round the cottage and onto a single-track road. It was raining heavily now and she was sopping wet. Desperation made her start to walk down the road. If a car came she would try to stop it and pray that it wasn't Carl. Or she might find a house that was inhabited.

She walked on, the rain running down her face. After only a few minutes she spied the outline of another building. She hurried towards it. As she came closer she realised in disappointment that it was a barn, standing a little distance off the road. It turned out to be quite large, with a wide, open doorway. She peered inside. In the gloom she discovered that it was full of straw and hay. The dry interior was inviting. Jane staggered in. She was exhausted as well as being soaked to the skin. She was now feeling the full effects of the cold or whatever it was. She would just rest for ten minutes and then she would continue walking. She sank gratefully onto the straw. She noticed that she was still clutching one shoe. She discarded it on the straw beside her. As she lay there listening to the rain steadily pouring down outside, the weariness enveloped her. Just for a second she let her eyes close…

It was the sound of a voice that woke her. Alarmed, she sat up. It was broad daylight, and Carl was standing in the doorway of the barn looking at her.

Chapter 44

For a split second they stared at each other, and then both sprang into action. Jane was already on her feet when Carl lunged at her. A scream burst from her lips as he attempted to grab her.

'You bitch!' he shouted.

She evaded his grasping hand and bolted for the door of the barn.

In a flash he was upon her. She fell to the ground with an impact that almost winded her. Even so, she struggled to her knees and attempted to escape from him.

He grabbed her ankle as she crawled away, but he slipped on the floor and she managed to evade him. But he recovered quickly. He grabbed her with both hands.

Jane found herself shrieking, 'No, no, no!'

'Shut up!' he snarled. His order was accompanied by a blow to the side of her face, followed by a second, which made her lose her balance and crash heavily to the floor.

The next instant he was forcing her face down on the rough floor of the barn. She felt the weight of his body pressing down on her, and then her arms were roughly pulled behind her back. He tied her hands tightly with something as she struggled.

Jane found herself shouting at the top of her voice in a frantic attempt to summon outside intervention. 'HELP! PLEASE, SOMEBODY HELP ME! HELP ME!'

Her efforts infuriated Carl. 'Shut your mouth,' he threatened.

Another 'HELP' escaped from Jane's lips.

'I'll shut it for you then,' growled Carl.

He grasped her hair from behind, yanking her head back as he forced something into her mouth to stop her cries. The next second he was tying a cord round her ankles.

Jane lay there shaking. If only somebody had heard her screams... She heard Carl get up and leave the barn. The next minute there was the sound of a vehicle reversing up to the barn door and stopping. Hearing Carl approaching her again, she made frenzied whimpering sounds, all she could muster, gagged as she was. The next instant he picked her up as if she were a sack of potatoes and slung her over his shoulder. He carried her to the door of the barn, where she caught a glimpse of open van doors before he deposited her none too gently on the floor of the vehicle and slammed the doors shut. She heard the driver's door close and the van began to move off.

Unable to move, Jane was jerked and bumped every second of the ten-minute journey. Not only did she feel utterly defeated, but she was also angry with herself for falling asleep. She guessed it was still quite early in the day, but if she hadn't allowed sleep to overtake her she might have been somewhere safe now. Instead, she was once again in the hands of her captors. She knew they would keep a close eye on her, and today they had something else planned for her. She lay there feeling every jolt of the vehicle, an occasional whimper escaping from her, the only bit of comfort she could muster.

She felt the van make a turn and draw to a halt, and then Carl call out, 'I've got her.'

The next moment the van doors were opened, and Carl stood leering down at her. He grabbed her and pulled her roughly out of the van. Somehow she found herself standing up. She was conscious of Mel, grim-faced, standing close by, and she realised that she was back at the farmhouse where she had been a prisoner most of the week.

'Welcome home, darling,' smirked Carl.

Jane said nothing. She stood, her eyes cast down, thoroughly beaten.

Mel bent down and started to untie the cord around Jane's ankles. 'Where did you find her?' she asked Carl.

'In Johnson's barn. She'd been kipping in there.'

Mel took Jane's arm and led her into the house. Carl followed, grinning. They took her up the stairs again and back into the room she had occupied previously. Jane noticed that the window was now closed, but the screws and the nail file were still lying on the windowsill where she had left them. Mel pushed her down onto the bed.

Jane made frantic sounds to have the gag removed, but she was ignored.

'Leave her like that,' growled Carl. 'She's had me up all night searching for her.'

Mel made no comment and she and Carl left the room, leaving Jane lying where she was. Once again, there was the sound of the door being locked.

Jane was face down on the bed. Her wrists hurt. The gag tasted awful, and she was beginning to feel ill again. On top of that her right foot was smarting. She remembered the sharp pain she had felt while she was crossing the field in the dark. A mass of complete misery, perhaps to comfort herself she found herself uttering low whimpers from time to time.

How long it was before Mel returned she had no idea. This time she remained silent when Mel appeared. She heard her put something down and then she was gently turned over.

Mel removed the gag from Jane's mouth and looked down at her. 'You little fool, trying to escape. You got Carl mad. He's dangerous when he's like that.'

Her remark stirred the little bit of defiance left in Jane. 'What do you expect me to do? There was an opportunity and I took it. I'm being held against my will.'

Mel made no reply. She started to untie Jane's wrists. She struggled with Carl's knots and in the end had to go downstairs to fetch a knife.

When she returned she also carried the handcuffs. 'You'll have to wear these,' she said coldly.

Even that was a relief. Carl had tied Jane's hands so tightly that she had begun to lose feeling in them. She held them out obediently for Mel to secure them. There were more angry red marks on her wrists. Her ankles also showed similar signs of her ordeal.

'I'll fetch you something to put on them,' said Mel, seeing her trying to rub the affected areas.

Jane murmured a thank you. But she had a more pressing need. 'Can I have a bath?' she asked miserably. 'I'm filthy all over.'

'You brought it on yourself,' snapped Mel.

Jane said nothing.

Mel seemed to relent. 'OK, but you'll have to wait until later, and I want your promise that you won't try anything.'

'I promise,' Jane replied softly. Her need to be clean would have to temporarily overrule her desire to escape.

Mel made no reply and quickly left the room.

Left on her own, Jane drank a little of the tea Mel had brought. She picked at the breakfast, but it had gone cold, and in any case she had no appetite. The soaking she had received the previous night, and the clamminess of her clothes drying on her had aggravated the cold or flu that had been bugging her on and off the previous day, and now it appeared to be gathering momentum. She had a general feeling of being unwell, her throat was sore, and she was feeling hot and cold by turns. She lay back on the bed and tried to recoup her strength.

It was quite some time before Mel returned. She regarded Jane sternly. 'OK. You can have a bath now, but remember your promise. No tricks, and Carl is only a call away downstairs.'

She led Jane to the bathroom. Jane was surprised to see that the bath was already filled with water. After Mel released her hands, she lost no time in stripping off her clothes. She no longer cared that Mel was watching her. Once in the bath, she began to realise how dirty she was. The soles of her feet were black, and it took a good deal of scrubbing to clean them up. As she did so, she examined the sole of her right foot. It looked red and inflamed, but she couldn't see what the problem was. The palms of her hands had been punctured by the barbed wire on the gate and the blood had dried on her hands, which were now painful. She took her time over everything, oblivious to Mel watching her from the corner by the bathroom door. She even managed to wash her hair after a fashion. When she looked into the mirror she received a shock. One eye was bloodshot where Carl had hit her. The surrounding area was red and there was every indication of a black eye developing.

'I'll get you something for that,' said Mel from her perch on the bathroom stool.

When Jane had finished, Mel waited for her to dress and then replaced the handcuffs. Jane walked back to her prison cell feeling a little better despite the fact that she was still wearing the filthy, torn clothes. She was surprised to find Carl there replacing the screws in the window. She hurriedly lay back on the bed and pulled the blanket over herself. Much to her dismay Mel disappeared, leaving her alone with Carl.

Carl appeared to make a big effort to tighten the screws. At last he had finished and he turned to Jane. 'You won't get those out with a nail file, darling,' he sneered.

Jane made no comment. She closed her eyes.

She heard him collect his tools and then to her horror he sat down on the bed close to her.

'We need to get acquainted,' he said quietly.

Jane snapped her eyes open. She held her hand to her damaged eye. 'I think we have, thank you.'

Carl wasn't put off. He spoke again, more softly still. 'You've got a good body. You need to exercise it more. Experience a good man.'

Fear struck into Jane. She knew what Carl was about. 'If you come near me I'll scratch your eyes out,' she replied coldly.

He grinned. 'I like women with a bit of fire in them.'

He made a move to grab her, but his action was brought to an abrupt halt.

'Leave her alone, damn you.'

Mel stood in the doorway, a tray in her hands. She turned angrily on Carl. 'Keep away from her. I'm not going to have you messing things up at this stage.'

Carl had already jumped up from the bed. 'She'll have worse where she's going,' he growled.

'Get back downstairs. If you'd done your job properly in the first place, she wouldn't have got away. It's only by luck we don't have a bullet in our backs.'

Carl muttered something under his breath, but quickly disappeared.

Mel put the tray down on the bedside table. She held a hand to Jane's forehead and looked down at her. 'You're a bit feverish. I've brought you some stronger tablets. We need to get you fit to travel.'

'What did Carl mean? Where are you taking me?' asked Jane.

Mel made no answer. She unlocked the handcuffs.

'Please tell me,' pleaded Jane.

'I don't know. We weren't told,' Mel replied curtly.

'Carl knows,' insisted Jane.

'Don't listen to his rubbish.'

Mel poured some water into a glass and handed it to Jane with two tablets. 'Take these. They'll help.'

'What are they?'

Mel smiled. 'Don't worry. They won't harm you. They'll just get rid of the fever. I used to be a nurse.'

Reassured, Jane swallowed the tablets. It was quite clear that Mel was a closed book as far as her future was concerned.

'Here's some cream for your wrists, and I've brought you an ice pack for that eye.'

Jane started to rub the cream on her wrists and ankles. Mel watched her for a second and then, with a 'See you later', left her alone and locked the door again.

Jane lay back on the bed, the ice pack over her bruised eye. Carl's remark had once again rekindled her fear. It was abundantly clear that if Mel did know anything, she wasn't going to tell her.

Misery started to envelop her and with it a feeling of despair. While there had been a chance of escape, it had kept her hopes alive. That chance had gone, thanks to her falling asleep in the barn. Nobody even knew she was still alive. She felt abandoned to her fate.

The tablets made her drowsy. The day seemed to pass her by. Around lunchtime Mel appeared with some soup, which Jane managed to eat. Later in the afternoon she came back with a mug of tea and a sandwich. She insisted on giving Jane two more tablets. Jane accepted them meekly. Suddenly she seemed to be losing her willpower.

Jane nibbled the sandwich and sipped half the tea, and then lay back on the bed. Within a few minutes she was asleep again.

She awoke from a muddled dream hours later. The room was in darkness. She could hear voices downstairs. She lay there with no inclination to stir any further. She felt decidedly unwell, but at the same time there was a strange feeling of dreaminess.

She heard steps outside in the corridor, and the next instant the door was unlocked.

Light flooded the room as Mel entered. She looked at Jane. 'Time to go,' she announced. 'They're waiting for you.'

Chapter 45

'I don't want to go. I don't feel well,' murmured Jane. She continued to lie where she was.

'Come on,' encouraged Mel. 'You'll be all right. I've brought you some clean clothes.'

Jane raised herself into a sitting position. Her body ached, her throat was sore, and she was feeling shivery.

'Where am I going?' she asked yet again.

'Never mind that now. Hurry up and get ready.'

Her body did not feel like the one she was used to. Reluctantly, Jane made an effort and stood up.

Mel slung the clothes she was carrying onto the bed. 'Come on now. Quickly. Get these on. You can't go in those. They're covered in mud.'

Almost in a dream, Jane started to fumble with the buttons on the blouse she was wearing.

'You'd better use the toilet. It's a long journey.'

Like a zombie, Jane allowed herself to be led to the toilet. Once again she had to use it watched by Mel. She pleaded to be allowed to nip into the bathroom and splash her face in an effort to regain her motivation, but the cold water seemed to make little difference.

Back in the bedroom Mel became impatient. 'Hurry up,' she urged. 'We've wasted too much time.'

Jane changed into the blouse and skirt Mel had provided. Again they were too big for her, but it made her feel better to be rid of the muddy and torn garments she had been wearing.

She was shocked and dismayed when Mel produced the handcuffs again.

'You'll have to have these on,' remarked Mel curtly.

'Must I?' asked Jane, her voice subdued. 'They hurt.'

Mel made no comment but snapped the handcuffs onto Jane's wrists. Jane was thankful that at least her hands were in front of her.

Mel produced two more tablets and a glass of water. 'Take these,' she ordered.

'I don't want them,' murmured Jane feebly.

'Take them, damn you,' snapped Mel.

Her willpower seemingly snuffed out, Jane obliged. All was lost now. They could do what they wanted with her. No one was going to come to her aid.

In silence Mel led her down the stairs towards the voices. Jane's foot was now quite painful when she put weight on it. Somehow, though, that seemed to be only a small part of her problems.

Mel guided her into a large kitchen, where Carl was sitting at the table with Babs, who had held Jane at gunpoint at the cottage, and a man Jane recognised as the fourth member of the group who had captured her. They all jumped up as Mel and Jane entered the room.

'Is she ready?' asked Babs, staring at Jane.

'Oh, we're all ready,' Mel replied cheerfully, with a glance at Jane who stood silent, dejected and defeated.

'Let's get going, then,' said Babs. 'She'll have to go in the boot,' she announced casually.

Panic overtook Jane and made her find her voice. 'No, please,' she begged. 'Not in the boot.'

'You'll have to be gagged then.' Babs was adamant.

'No. No. Please.'

Mel came to Jane's aid. 'You won't have any trouble with her. She's well sedated.'

This appeared to satisfy Babs. Jane tried to force her muddled brain into action. So that was why she felt so dreamy. Mel had been drugging her.

Babs pushed her almost aggressively towards the door. Outside

Jane could see a large car parked next to Carl's van. Babs propelled her towards it. It had been raining and the ground was wet and cold under Jane's feet. Mel had not provided her with any shoes, and she no longer cared how she was dressed.

Babs turned to her. 'I don't want to hear a word out of you,' she warned. 'One squeak, and you're gagged.'

Jane obediently stayed silent. Babs bundled her into the back of the car.

'You can lie down on the seat if you want,' suggested Mel, not unkindly.

Jane curled up and Mel covered her with a blanket, for which she was grateful. She was now feeling hot and cold by turns. She was vaguely aware of a parting conversation between the four, and then she felt the car move off.

She had no clear recollection of the journey. All she could remember was sleeping most of the time and occasionally waking up.

She was jerked into alertness by the car door being opened and Babs talking to her. 'You can get out now.'

Jane stirred into action. It was an effort. She wanted to continue lying there.

'Hurry up. Get out,' Babs ordered impatiently.

Somehow Jane found herself standing beside the car. It was still dark. She tried to look around, but could see very little. They seemed to be somewhere near the sea, because she could hear gulls crying. She did not anticipate the next thing that happened. Somebody was blindfolding her.

She heard a man's voice. 'Hurry up and get her on board.'

Somebody grasped her arm and she was forced to walk. Her foot was quite painful now. She was led a short distance over hard ground, and then she felt a sloping wooden plank beneath her feet. She was manhandled through what seemed to be a door. She heard the same man's voice order, 'Down here,' and she was helped down some steps. The next instant she found herself lying somewhere soft. The people and the voices disappeared.

She lay there waiting, but nothing happened. Somewhere in the distance she could hear men's voices, but all was quiet around her. She could feel the bed or whatever she was lying on gently moving up and down. Where was she?

She managed to pull off the blindfold. Peering around in the gloom, she realised that she was in the cabin of a boat. The bunks on each side and the portholes partly concealed by drawn curtains confirmed it. She raised herself up and tried to look through one of the portholes, but it was still dark outside and all she could see was a bit of water and the shapes of other boats.

She lay back in the gloom. She was feeling quite ill now. The flu, or whatever it was, seemed to be gathering momentum. She ached all over, her throat was sore, her chest hurt and she felt sick intermittently. She knew she was running a temperature. One minute sweat poured from her, and the next she was shivering. On top of everything her foot now throbbed relentlessly.

She felt utterly miserable. Where were they going to take her? A grim thought penetrated her clouded thinking. Perhaps they were going to drown her. Dump her overboard somewhere. The thought made her panic for a second, and then logic took over. No. These people were going to too much trouble with her for that. Something more sinister was planned for her. Carl had more or less confirmed that, and Mel had refused to enlighten her.

Nothing happened for a long time. She watched the daylight creep in and the cabin become brighter. Occasionally she could hear footsteps overhead and muffled conversation. It was not uncomfortable lying on the bunk, in spite of her confined hands. Shivering, she spied a blanket on the opposite bunk and managed to wrap herself in it. She wondered whether there was a toilet somewhere. Desperation made her leave her comfortable position and investigate. She tried several slim doors, but they revealed cupboards crammed with sea-going equipment. She ventured through a narrow opening and found two more doors. One led to a shower, but the other revealed a toilet. It was difficult with the handcuffs, but she managed. She had no idea how to flush the appliance at first. Then she spied a red lever. She pulled it and to her relief the contents of the toilet disappeared.

Back in the cabin she resumed her position on the bunk, pulling the comfort of the blanket around her.

Her solitude was interrupted by the sound of feet descending the short flight of steps leading into the cabin. A surly-looking young man holding a large mug approached her.

He stared at her. 'Cup of tea,' he announced roughly.

Jane raised her head. 'Where are you taking me?' she asked weakly.

'You'll find out soon enough.' He smirked at her briefly and left the cabin.

Jane looked at the mug of tea. It was swamped in milk. Her mouth felt dry and she tried awkwardly to drink a little, but the tea had an odd taste and the milk and the sugar that had been added nauseated her.

She fell back on the bunk again. She knew she was quite ill now, but who was going to help her? In her wretchedness, she wondered if she would die before they got to wherever they were going. She had reached the point where the combination of her isolation and her illness was beginning to make her feel that she no longer cared what happened to her. It was as if her willpower and determination were slowly being sucked out of her. She had no sense of time. The day just seemed to slip by. At one point the young man appeared again and in silence left her a sandwich and more tea, but she had no interest in food.

It must have been well towards evening that Jane heard the rumble of an engine being started, quickly followed by a second. Lying on the bunk, she could feel the vibration. The sound of the engines altered and she could feel that the vessel she was in was under way. For a while she felt gentle movement, and then the boat seemed to be bumping up and down much more. She guessed they must be out at sea now. She drifted in and out of sleep, lulled by the movement of the boat.

It was the sound of voices that woke her. It was now completely dark. The throb of the engines ceased. She felt a bump somewhere alongside. Then there was the sound of footsteps overhead, accompanied by louder voices. After that, there was silence for a considerable period. Jane dozed again.

She was woken up by the sound of someone climbing down into the cabin. She heard the visitor shout to somebody else.

'There's somebody down here.'

The cabin was plunged into light and a very tall figure approached the bunk. Jane could see that he was wearing a uniform under a yellow high-visibility jacket.

The stranger addressed her. 'It's all right, miss. You're safe now. My name's Greg Johnson. I'm a coastguard officer.'

In her muddled state, the words Jane had wanted to hear for days did not quite register.

The officer stooped over her. 'Are you all right, miss?' he asked.

'I feel ill. I think I've got flu or something,' murmured Jane.

'We'll get you fixed up soon,' replied the officer kindly. 'Can you tell me your name, miss?'

'Jane,' she almost whispered.

'And what's your surname?'

'Hawkins.' In her fevered state, Jane was completely unaware that she had given her married name. Her eyes half closed, she did not see the officer's puzzled look.

'I see. We're going to head into Portsmouth now. Once we're there the police will want to talk to you.'

Jane did not reply. She felt too awful. Even talking was an effort now.

The officer gave her a quick glance. 'It won't be long before we're in port. I'll be back shortly.' He hurried away back up the steps.

Jane could hardly believe what was happening. She had been rescued. Who had arranged it? She would be able to get on with her life. She would see Bob again. If only she didn't feel so ill...

There was the rumble of engines again, and she could feel the motion of the boat. At least when they got to land she could rest up somewhere warm and get rid of this wretched flu.

She dozed off again, and awoke to the realisation that the boat was no longer moving. She heard voices, and Greg Johnson appeared in the doorway.

'We've arrived, Jane. I can take you ashore now,' he announced kindly.

Jane made a big effort. The sooner she was on dry land, the sooner she would receive help and medical attention. She threw back the blanket.

For the first time the officer noticed the handcuffs. 'Who's got the key to those?' he asked, clearly concerned.

'I don't know,' Jane replied miserably.

'We'll get them off you as soon as we're on dry land,' he announced confidently.

Jane struggled to a standing position. She fought for something to hold on to. Her head was swimming.

He grabbed her arm. 'Let me give you a hand.' He glanced down at her bare feet. 'Where are your shoes?'

'I haven't got any,' Jane replied wretchedly.

She found the officer's strong arm supporting her as he helped her up the steps, through another cabin and into the wheelhouse of the vessel with its shiny dials and levers.

He put a bright yellow rain-jacket round her shoulders. 'It's raining outside,' he explained.

Outside on deck Jane found the comment to be accurate. Fine rain was wetting everything. It was still dark, but she could see that the boat was moored alongside a wooden jetty. It was only a short distance to dry land, where she could see people moving about and blue lights flashing.

The surface of the gangplank was slippery from the rain and Jane would have tumbled had not the officer's strong arm saved her. When they reached the jetty, a young woman police officer in a reflective jacket emerged from the shadows. She looked at Jane for an instant and then introduced herself.

'I'm WPC Henry, Jane. I'll be looking after you for a while.

You're quite safe now,' she announced pleasantly. She glanced at the handcuffs. 'First thing we'll do is get those off you.' She produced a key and released Jane's hands.

Jane managed to whisper, 'Thank you.'

'Will you come with me please, Jane?' The officer took her arm and gently led her along the jetty. The wooden planking was wet and cold under Jane's feet, and her right foot now hurt considerably when she put weight on it. She shivered, even with the jacket round her shoulders.

When they reached the end of the jetty the officer walked her towards a waiting police car. She opened one of the rear passenger doors and waited for her to get in.

Jane stood there shivering noticeably.

'Are you all right?' the officer asked, looking at her with concern.

Jane heard the question, but the voice asking it seemed a long way off. She was unable to answer. Suddenly she keeled over and crashed to the ground.

She lay there unconscious on the wet ground, a tiny figure spattered by rain, the police officer bending over her and talking into her radio.

Chapter 46

It was the telephone ringing that woke Bob. He struggled to emerge from a disturbed sleep. He had dozed off in a chair. Stirring into action, he made a dash for the hall, glancing at his watch as he went. Its hands showed half past ten. Somebody must want him urgently to call so late in the evening. He grabbed the handset and held it to his ear.

'Hello. Bob Harker.'

'Devon and Cornwall Police here, sir. Would it be possible to see you urgently?'

Bob was suddenly alert with expectation, his thoughts turning to Jane. 'What's happened?' he asked anxiously.

'Nothing significant, sir, but we have some additional items of evidence we would like you to look at and perhaps identify.'

'What sort of items?'

'They are items of a female nature, sir, but we do need you to identify them.'

'You mean they could be Jane's?'

'We are not sure at this stage, sir. That's why we need your help.'

Bob put his brain into gear. It was clear that whatever the police had found, they weren't going to give any further information over the telephone. He would just have to go down to Cornwall again. But how? He struggled to think. Train would be best, and quicker than driving.

He spoke into the telephone again. 'I could get there tomorrow, probably by early afternoon. I'd have to use the train.'

'That would be excellent, sir. Detective Sergeant Brogan is

dealing with this case. Just ask for him when you arrive. You'll be able to get a taxi from Truro station.'

Bob scribbled the officer's directions down, said goodbye and put the telephone down. He tried to think things out. The best plan would be to take the first possible train to London and sort things out from there.

It had been a difficult time for Bob. When he had left the police station after his mysterious ordeal, it had been quite clear to him that as far as the police were concerned Jane's disappearance and his own predicament had been the outcome of a midnight escapade and a tragic accident.

For him the situation was more disturbing. He kept asking himself what had happened after he had fallen asleep in the car. It seemed ridiculous to suggest that he and Jane had gone for a swim. Yet where was she? He clung to the thought that she was alive somewhere, yet as the days passed he became more and more despondent. There were times when he thought that perhaps he and Jane had indulged in a midnight swim, and then logic blotted out that possibility, but it all seemed too unreal to think about. Instead he just had to hope that somehow an explanation would materialise.

After Miles Ashington had collected him from the police station, the ordeal of dealing with the situation had begun. Miles and Gail had been extremely supportive. They had both wanted him to come and stay with them in their home for a few days, but he had declined their offer. He wanted to be at Barn Cottage. It was just a tiny bit nearer Jane. Once he was back there, Maggie had fussed over him and cooked him a meal that he had no appetite for. The most upsetting thing for him had been going into the bedroom and seeing Jane's things lying where she had left them. Instead of sleeping in the bed they had shared, he had spent a restless night in a chair, drinking cups of tea and racking his brain for an explanation.

The next day he had packed up his things and returned home. The police did not appear to want him any more and announced that they would contact him if there were any developments. When it came to sorting out Jane's possessions, he had accepted Maggie's offer to do so for him.

He had refused Miles Ashington's offer of a car to take him home and instead had taken a taxi to Truro and then the train back to London.

Back in Tatting Green he had been faced with the daunting task of telling everybody what had happened. He had been surprised to learn that news of Jane's disappearance had reached the national papers. The press had caught onto the story of a guest of Miles Ashington being lost while swimming, and had even named Jane. When Bob phoned Gerald and Anna he discovered that they already knew. They were shocked and distressed and it had been a difficult conversation. It occurred to him that he should get in touch with *Discerning Woman* magazine. He managed to speak to Annette, and he learned that Miles Ashington had already told her the news. It was quite clear from speaking with Annette that all the staff at the magazine were in a state of shock. It was the same when he spoke to his parents. His mother had wanted him to come and spend some time with them, but he had refused. He and Jeff were still in the process of setting up their new business venture, and Jeff needed his help. Work had been his salvation. He had thrown himself into it, spending long days in the studio rather than being at home. He lost track of the days. His time consisted of work by day and disturbed sleep at night.

Bob's reminiscing was brought to a halt when he came to the question of work. He would have to call Jeff and tell him he wouldn't be at the studio the next day.

As the train jerked into movement, Bob settled back in his seat. He sipped the coffee he had purchased at the station and nibbled the pasty he had bought to accompany it. He had been up at the crack of dawn and taken the first available train to London. Once there, he had dashed over to Paddington and arrived there to discover that the next train for Penzance was due to leave in fifteen minutes and he still had to buy a ticket. In spite of the queue at the desk, he had managed to buy both a ticket and a cup of coffee before being one of the last passengers to board the train.

Leaving the train at Truro he quickly found a taxi. At the police station he was ushered into a small interview room and brought a cup of tea. He did not have to wait long before a man carrying a briefcase entered the room.

The man held out his hand. 'Detective Sergeant Brogan.'

Bob shook hands with him and confirmed his name.

'Thank you for coming so quickly, Mr Harker.'

They faced each other across the table. Sergeant Brogan opened his briefcase and extracted some papers and a small polythene bag. He turned his attention to Bob. 'We've asked you to come along today to see if you can identify these items,' he explained. He placed the bag on the table in front of Bob.

Bob picked it up and saw the fine gold chain it contained. He suddenly found his heart beating fast. He turned it over. Yes. There was the tiny tag attached, and on it he could read one word: 'Jane'.

He looked up at the officer. 'It's the anklet my fiancée was wearing the night she disappeared.'

'You're quite sure of that?'

'Positive.' Bob's mind was full of questions, but the officer dipped into his briefcase again and pulled out another polythene bag. This time it was larger and contained one item: a woman's shoe.

'Recognise this?'

Bob looked at the shoe. It was old and had seen better days. There was even a hole in the sole. It certainly wasn't one of Jane's.

He shook his head. 'It's not Jane's,' he replied simply.

Sergeant Brogan nodded. He pulled a photograph out of his bag. 'It appears that Miss Carroll was not wearing shoes at the time,' he remarked, handing Bob the photograph.

Bob studied it. It showed the print of a naked foot in what looked like mud. He looked at the officer for an explanation.

It was not long in coming. 'The photograph was taken by our

team in the same area that the gold chain and the shoe were found. Experts believe that the owner of the foot was female and took a size five shoe.'

'Jane takes a size five shoe!' exclaimed Bob.

The officer nodded in agreement. 'Yes, we know. We have a pair of Miss Carroll's shoes here from the items found in her car at Dolby Cove.'

Bob could no longer contain his excitement. 'Where were these things found?' he asked anxiously.

Sergeant Brogan regarded him closely as he replied. 'They were found by a farmer in a barn. He had read about a missing woman called Jane Carroll. He thought they might be important and he took the items to his local police station.'

Bob was already assimilating the information he had just been given. It was exciting. He turned to the police officer. 'But that must mean that Jane could still be alive somewhere.'

Sergeant Brogan remained calm. 'It's a possibility we are looking into,' he advised.

'But how could it be anything else?' Bob persisted. He added. 'If the items were found away from the beach where the car was found, it must mean that Jane was still alive when she left Dolby Cove.'

The police officer smiled at Bob for the first time. His reply was guarded.

'You may be correct. What we have to do is try and establish where Miss Carroll is now. We are following up several possible leads. '

'Can you tell me more?' asked Bob.

Sergeant Brogan shook his head. 'Not for the moment. The investigation has reached a critical stage. We needed to ask you to come here today to see if you could identify these items, so that we can proceed with further enquiries. You have been of great help to us.'

'I see,' replied Bob. He could tell that Sergeant Brogan knew more but was not going to divulge any more details. He had many questions, but before he could raise any of them, the police officer spoke again.

'Mr Harker, I know this is a difficult time for you and that you would like to ask more questions, but I must ask you to be patient with us. You will be contacted immediately anything of importance happens. In the meantime we would appreciate it if you would keep today's interview to yourself for the time being.'

So that was it as far as the police were concerned. Bob could see that he wasn't going to get any more information. Sergeant Brogan took his leave and arranged for someone to escort Bob back to the reception area. Clearly that was the end of the interview.

On the train back to London, Bob went over and over the interview in his mind. On the one hand, he was elated. There was now substantial evidence that Jane could still be alive. His own suspicions were confirmed. On the other hand, he still felt deep concern at not knowing where she was. Clearly she was unable to make contact with him or anybody else. But why? It almost looked like a kidnap or something similar. How had she come to lose the anklet, and why was she wandering around barefoot? The interview had raised more questions than it solved. It had also been abundantly clear to Bob that the police knew more than they were prepared to divulge. It seemed they had now dropped the drowning theory. He had noticed the change in attitude to him throughout his visit. Asking him to keep quiet about today's meeting also underscored his suspicion that the police knew more than they were giving away. He realised that he had no alternative other than to be patient and wait for developments, whenever they might occur.

It was several days before Bob heard anything. One morning at about half past six, having spent another restless night, he was in the shower when he heard the shrilling of the telephone. Without stopping to grab a towel, he dashed dripping wet into the bedroom. A call at this time in the morning must be important. He grabbed the phone.

'Hello. Bob Harker.'

'Mr Harker, it's Hampshire Constabulary here. Miss Carroll has been found.'

The news hit Bob like a battering ram. He sank down onto the bed. He had waited days for this information and now here it was. He struggled to get his brain into gear and pose the question he was almost afraid to ask.

'Is… Is she alive?'

'Yes, sir. But she's in hospital in Portsmouth at the moment.'

'What happened to her?' Bob asked anxiously. 'Why is she in Portsmouth?'

'I don't have the full details, sir, but my understanding is that her condition is improving.'

It was a deliberately vague answer. He had to know what had happened to Jane. Phoning the hospital would be his best bet.

'Can you give me the name and phone number of the hospital?' he asked.

'Yes, sir. Do you have a pen?'

Bob managed to find a pencil and a scrap of paper. He scribbled down the details the police officer gave him. Thanking him, he put the phone down.

He paused for a few seconds to let the news he had just received sink in. He knew he should be elated, and in a way he was, but hearing that Jane was in hospital was worrying. What was wrong with her?

He just had to call the hospital. Grabbing a towel from the airing cupboard, he returned to the bedroom and dialled the number. It took a few minutes to get through to somebody in authority. A controlled female voice asked him who he was and what relation he was to the patient. He gave his name and explained that he was Jane's fiancé and that he had been contacted by the police. The same controlled voice advised him that they had an inpatient named Jane Carroll and that she had spent a comfortable night. He asked if Jane could receive visitors and was told that only selected people could see her and that they would have to check with reception first.

More mystified still, and even more worried, he thanked the person at the other end and replaced the telephone. He snapped into action. He had to get to the hospital at once.

The church clock at the end of the street was just striking eight as Bob stood outside the office of the only car-rental firm in Tatting Cross. It was closed and he waited impatiently, hoping that it would open soon. He had taken the first bus over from his home, having decided to hire a car rather than trusting his old banger. Once again he scolded himself for not buying a newer and more reliable model.

It was a good five or six minutes before the first of the staff turned up and he was allowed into the building. Half an hour later he was on his way. He realised that he had no idea where the hospital was, not knowing Portsmouth very well, so he quickly phoned for directions. Then he had to get hold of Jeff and explain that he would not be available for work. He had volunteered to handle the work in the studio while Jeff started converting the rooms above into an office. Now those plans had been blown apart. Jeff was quite understanding and wanted to know more, but Bob was unable to enlighten him further.

It was late morning when Bob arrived at the hospital. He had difficulty at first in finding a parking space, but he eventually succeeded when another car moved out. He made his way to the reception desk and explained his mission, and a rather sombre-looking woman asked him if he had any identification. He produced his driving licence and was asked to take a nearby seat and wait. After about five minutes another woman appeared and asked him to accompany her. She led him into a lift and then through a series of corridors. Bob was surprised to see her halt in front of a door guarded by a police officer sitting on a chair. The officer was immediately alert and asked for Bob's identification. Once again Bob again handed over his driving licence. He was puzzled by the security he was encountering. The police officer thanked him with a hint of a smile and gave him back the licence.

Bob was ushered into a small room. A figure lay on the bed. It was Jane. She was resting with her eyes closed, but she became alert to the sound of people entering.

Bob rushed over to her. 'Jane, it's Bob. What's happened? Can you talk?'

For the first time for days, Jane's face broke into a smile. 'Oh, Bob, darling! It's fantastic to see you.' She held out her arms.

Bob was alarmed at the sight of his fiancée, her face a mass of bruises and her hands covered in scratches. He kissed her gently. 'How are you?' he asked. 'What happened to you?'

'Darling, I've so much to tell you, and now you're here I feel a thousand times better.'

'But how are you?' insisted Bob.

She managed a grin. 'I'm battered and bruised, but I'm still in one piece. They brought me here because I was going down with pneumonia. But once the antibiotic clicked in, it helped a lot.'

Bob glanced down at the bed. 'But your hands – and your foot…' Her bandaged foot was clearly visible.

Jane made a face. 'I trod on something and it went into my foot. It turned nasty. The first thing they did was whip me down to the operating theatre and remove it. They told me if they hadn't done that there and then it could have been a big problem.'

'But what happened? Where were you? Why the police guard?' Bob was still worried.

Jane became more serious. 'Bob, it's scary. Somebody wanted to get rid of me.'

'But why? And who?'

Jane shook her head. 'I don't know, and the police won't tell me yet.'

Bob thought for a second. 'That's pretty much what I've been experiencing,' he replied.

'But…'

'What…?'

They both started to ask a question at the same time. Jane giggled. 'You first,' she prompted.

'What happened to you?' asked Bob anxiously.

Jane thought for a few seconds, and then she spoke, her face quite serious. 'That evening, after we'd been to dinner with the Ashingtons, you fell asleep in the car, and when I went into the cottage I was held up by a woman with a gun. There were more of them in the gang. They made me drive to the coast and then I had to take off my clothes. After that they put me in the boot of a car and drove me somewhere else and I was held captive on some sort of farm for days.'

She paused, remembering the traumatic events. Then she continued, speaking softly. 'I managed to escape, but they caught me again. Then I was going to be taken somewhere on a boat. That's when I was rescued.'

'Gosh!' Bob exclaimed. 'That sounds pretty horrendous.'

Jane nodded. 'It was.'

Bob started to ask another question, but Jane had more to relate. 'I got wet the night I escaped and it aggravated some sort of flu I'd picked up. I collapsed almost as soon as I was rescued, and they brought me here.'

'Phew. That was a pretty rotten ordeal.'

Compassion for Jane welled up inside Bob. She had had an awful time and he guessed he hadn't heard all the details. No doubt he would in time, but now she needed all the care he could give her. He had been shocked when he first saw her. Her eye was bloodshot and the side of her face was black and blue. Somebody must have hit her pretty hard. Her wrists and the one ankle he could see had red marks on them and he wondered how those had come about. He could guess. Yet in spite of everything she was smiling and cheerful.

His thoughts were interrupted by Jane. 'But what about you?' she asked. 'What happened to you?'

Bob smiled at her. 'My escapade was pretty tame compared to yours. I woke up the morning after almost naked, and the police thought I was a drunk.'

For the first time Jane gave a little laugh. 'I would have liked to see that,' she remarked gaily.

Bob grinned at her. Then his expression changed to one of seriousness. 'But the police guard… They must suspect some danger.'

Jane too was serious again. She looked at Bob, her face full of worry. 'That's my big concern. The police know something and they won't tell me what it is. The cold facts seem to be that somebody out there wants to get rid of me, and I don't know who it is.'

Chapter 47

Bob stared at Jane for a few seconds, his brain working overtime. Her comment about somebody wanting to get rid of her worried him. He had even been coming to the same conclusion himself. 'What did the police actually say?' he asked.

Jane's face became even more serious. 'Well, when I was first picked up, I must have given my married name by mistake, so for a while there was some confusion over who I was. Then I was pretty groggy for a few days.'

'But the police did eventually come to talk to you,' Bob prompted.

Jane nodded confirmation. 'Yes. Two of them. Both plain-clothes. They had been waiting to interview me. They asked me a mass of questions and then told me that their investigation was ongoing and they would contact me as soon as there were any developments.'

'That's exactly what they told me,' remarked Bob. 'And the police officer outside?'

'Oh, yes – they told me that after what had happened to me they were concerned about my safety and as a precaution they would provide protection.'

Before Bob could respond, Jane continued, her face full of worry. She looked at Bob intently as she spoke. 'You know, Bob, after what happened, I really feel scared. What's it all about? I've never done anything to anybody.'

Even though Bob was concerned himself, he did his best to reassure her. 'I think there's a lot more to it than we know and I think the police know a great deal they aren't telling us. Hopefully in a few days we'll find out what's happening and what it's all about.'

'I do hope so,' replied Jane gloomily.

A brief silence stirred Bob to ask the question that was burning inside him. 'Didn't you have any indication of where they were taking you on that boat?'

Jane shook her head. 'No. They wouldn't tell me – but the police here told me the boat I was rescued from was heading for France.'

'France?' queried Bob, puzzled.

Jane nodded. She continued talking softly. 'It's frightening when I start to think about it. If I hadn't been rescued I could be anywhere by now – or even dead. I was feeling pretty ill. I don't remember much about the time on the boat. I felt rotten, and I was handcuffed all the time.'

'All the time?' Bob asked, shocked.

Jane nodded again. She was silent for a few seconds, remembering. Then she spoke again. 'They tied me up as well – several times.' She glanced at her wrists and then at Bob. There were tears in her eyes.

'Bastards!' exclaimed Bob angrily.

'They tell me the marks will go eventually,' replied Jane quietly, glancing at them again briefly.

'How did you get rescued?'

Jane took a few seconds to recall events. 'All I remember is lying there in the cabin feeling dreadful and then the boat stopped. Everything went quiet, and then a bit later this man appeared. He said he was a coastguard officer. I don't know if the police were on the boat as well. They may have been.'

'And then they brought you here,' Bob prompted again.

Jane nodded. 'Yes. I remember being helped off the boat. A policewoman looked after me. It was wet and cold and I had no shoes. I must have fainted, because I remember waking up on the ground and she was trying to reassure me that help was on the way. Then an ambulance brought me here.'

Bob thought for a minute. Jane's ordeal had been pretty horrendous, but of one thing he was certain: it was a good thing she had been rescued then. If not, the outcome could have been unthinkable.

It was Jane who broke the brief silence between them. She looked at Bob pensively. 'There's one thing that's been puzzling me, and that is what made the police start looking for me after they'd concluded that I'd drowned.'

Bob's answer came without any hesitation. 'I think I know the answer to that,' he said. 'Some items of yours were found in a barn. The police called me back to Cornwall to identify them.'

'I spent the night in a barn after I escaped,' replied Jane.

Bob smiled at her for the first time since his arrival. 'You lost the anklet with your name on it,' he explained. 'I had to identify it.'

Jane's face suddenly lit up. Things were beginning to make sense.

'Of course! The anklet. I knew I'd lost it, but I didn't know where. Now it all makes sense.'

Her face took on a look of sadness. But she continued before Bob could say anything else.

'The night I escaped I walked for hours. It was raining quite heavily and I was soaked to the skin. I took shelter in the barn and like a little fool I fell asleep. Carl, one of the people who had held me prisoner, discovered me in the early morning.'

'That was pretty bad luck.'

Jane spoke more softly, her voice almost a whisper. 'I tried to escape from him, but he hit me hard, very hard, and sent me flying onto the floor. I tried to crawl away from him, but he grabbed my ankle and pulled me back.'

She paused for a moment, and then with a little forced smile remarked, 'That must have been when I lost the anklet.'

Bob got up from his chair and gently kissed her. 'I'm glad you did lose the anklet, poppet. I think it has been your salvation,' he said gently.

Jane looked at him and forced another smile. 'I must look pretty awful,' she remarked, turning her injured face towards him.

Bob shook his head. 'No, poppet. You being safe, that's what matters. The marks will go in time.'

Jane held his hand for a second. Having him close to her had been a tonic. Now she could really concentrate on getting her strength back.

She squeezed his hand.

'Darling,' she said, 'thank you for saying that. I'll be back to my old self in no time. You'll see. Just give me a couple of days.'

Bob remembered something else. 'The police had a shoe as well, but I don't think it was yours.'

Jane smiled again briefly. 'It wasn't,' she replied. 'The people who held me captive gave me a tatty old pair of shoes to wear, but they were too big for me. When I was escaping over the roof I dropped one of them and it fell out of my reach. The crazy thing was that I still carried the other shoe until I put it down in that barn. The other one is most likely where it landed after I dropped it.'

'And you trod on something,' Bob remarked, looking at Jane's bandaged foot.

She nodded briefly. 'Yes, I did. When I was running across a field in the dark. I don't know what it was, but it really hurt.'

'Does it hurt now?'

'It's getting better, but it's still a bit painful when I walk on it.' She thought for a few seconds. 'I was lucky,' she remarked. 'It could have been worse. I might even have lost my foot.'

Jane had been a bit subdued as she related the details of what had happened to her. Suddenly she gave Bob one of her old smiles. 'But I'm determined to get back to normal as soon as possible. I'll be full of beans soon. You'll see,' she announced more cheerfully.

Her brighter mood did not last long, however. She looked at Bob, her face full of concern again. 'It's just this not knowing what's happening – the police guard and everything. Somebody's got it in for me, and I don't know who it is.'

The whole situation puzzled Bob, but he was determined not

to let Jane see his concern. She had shown courage and tenacity. At least now she was safe. Now he wanted to support her as much as he could through the days ahead.

He tried his best to reassure her. 'I'm sure we'll be told what's happening fairly soon. The police must have made some arrests by now.'

Jane absorbed his comment. She tended to agree. She said, 'I've just had a thought. Once you'd identified my little anklet, the police must have moved pretty fast to grab somebody and get enough information to intercept that boat I was on – and they must have been pretty sure that I was on board as well.' She studied Bob for his reaction.

He responded immediately. 'I see what you mean. If you ask me, the police already know who's behind all this.'

'The couple who held me prisoner admitted that they were working for somebody else. I think they were afraid of whoever it was.'

Bob agreed. 'It all fits. The police must be after the person who organised everything.'

'I wish I knew who it was,' Jane remarked glumly.

Bob decided to change the subject. Looking around the room, he asked, 'Is there anything you need? Can I get anything for you?'

His questions suddenly made Jane aware of practicalities and her lack of essentials. 'You couldn't get me a nightdress, could you?' She looked down at the hospital gown she was wearing and made a face. 'I'm absolutely fed up with wearing this thing.'

Bob jumped into action. 'Of course I can,' he announced cheerfully. 'Anything else?'

Jane took up the opportunity and gave him a short list of things she would like, including a few cosmetics, and Bob made a careful note of her requests. She couldn't help adding with a chuckle, 'You'll have to trust me to pay you back. I haven't a penny to my name at the moment.'

'Your credit rating's good,' Bob replied with a grin. Then, with a kiss on her cheek and 'see you soon,' he left the room.

It took him a few minutes to find his way to the ground floor and the hospital entrance. He enquired at the reception desk where the nearest shops were and was given directions. A brisk walk brought him to a good selection of shops. With the help of a sales assistant in a clothes shop he purchased two pretty nightdresses and a light dressing gown and, as an afterthought, a pair of slippers, which were not on his list but he thought might be useful. The other things Jane had asked for were a bit trickier, but he managed to find a pharmacy and someone to help him. With everything ticked off, he felt quite pleased with himself. Before setting off to walk back to the hospital he purchased a beautiful bouquet of flowers and a selection of fruit for Jane.

It was while he was passing a phone shop that an idea struck him. Jane had no means of communicating with him. Her mobile was hundreds of miles away with the police in Cornwall, together with all her other personal possessions. He dived into the shop, bought a cheap phone and topped it up with funds. He explained that he was taking it to his fiancée in hospital, and the assistant set it up for him and let him leave all the packing in the shop.

Back in the hospital he had to go through the process of checking in at the reception desk again and be escorted to Jane's room. The police officer on guard wanted to take a closer look at his packages.

Jane was delighted with his purchases. 'Darling, what beautiful flowers!' She held up one of the nightdresses. 'Thank you – this is perfect. I'll feel much more human now.'

Bob delved into his pocket. 'A present to enable us to keep in touch,' he announced, handing Jane the phone with a smile.

'Darling, that's absolutely marvellous! You think of everything,' she exclaimed excitedly.

She leaned forward to kiss him on the lips. 'I'm sure I'm not infectious now,' she remarked cheerfully.

Bob spent another hour with her. She was glad of his company and she wanted to know more about what had happened to him since she had left him sleeping in her car. Late in the afternoon he left the hospital and drove back to Tatting Green. He felt much more comfortable now than he had on the journey down, but hearing Jane talk about her imprisonment caused him concern. Those people who had held her captive had made it clear that they meant business. He was glad that at least for the present she was in hospital with a police guard.

Chapter 48

Jane was in hospital for a further three days. She was beginning to feel much more like her old self, though she found the confines of the small hospital room frustrating to her progress. The bandage on her foot was removed and replaced with a small dressing. She valued greatly the phone Bob had bought for her. It made her feel less isolated. She had already called him several times, and she made a point of ringing Lucy, who was staggered at what had happened to her and asked her a host of questions, many of which she was unable to answer. She also spoke to Gerald and Anna. They were greatly relieved to hear that she was safe, but understandably shocked and concerned by what she had been forced to endure.

The day after she saw Bob she received an unexpected visit. A nurse came in to tell her that two police officers had arrived and wanted to talk to her. Jane expected to see the two men who had originally interviewed her, but she had not seen the plain-clothes officers who entered the room before. They approached her bed.

The older of the two held out his hand and introduced himself. 'I'm Detective Inspector Boyd, Metropolitan Police, and this is Detective Constable Penlow.' He asked Jane how she was feeling and how her recovery was progressing.

Jane answered as cheerfully as she could. 'I'm feeling much better now, thank you – and I'm making really good progress. But you're from the Metropolitan Police,' she added, puzzled.

Inspector Boyd gave a slight smile. 'The investigation into your abduction has expanded a lot in the last few days. We have now taken it over. The Devon and Cornwall and Hampshire forces are assisting us.'

'Can you tell me what's happening?' asked Jane.

The inspector shook his head. 'The investigation has reached a critical stage and I can't give you any details. What I can tell you, though, is that seven people have been questioned and five people detained over your abduction.'

He must have noticed the disappointment on Jane's face, because he immediately strove to reassure her. 'Miss Carroll, I realise you must feel you're being kept in the dark, and that must be particularly frustrating in view of what you've been through. However, I assure you that very soon you will be told what is happening.'

Jane did her best to smile. She felt she had to say something in return. 'Thank you. I'd really appreciate that.'

Realising that she perhaps needed to add a bit more, she thought for a second and then continued, almost speaking her thoughts. 'You see, after what I had to go through, not knowing what's happening and who tried to get rid of me is a bit scary. And it seems that I'm still in danger from somebody or something.'

Inspector Boyd hastened to reassure her. 'I think we can safely say that the danger is diminishing fairly quickly.'

Jane was determined to extract as much information as she could from the two police officers. She asked another question. 'Were the two people who held me at the farmhouse arrested? They were called Carl and Mel.'

It was DC Penlow who answered. He glanced at the documents he carried. 'Carl Brody and Melony Braymar?' he queried.

'Yes, I think that might be them,' said Jane, 'although of course I never knew their surnames.'

'They are in custody,' announced Inspector Boyd.

'What about Babs?' asked Jane.

'We have a Barbara Mooney in custody,' answered DC Penlow. He added, 'There is also a charge of illegal possession of a firearm.'

Jane was silent for a few seconds. In a way she had felt that Mel was not all bad. At times she had shown some compassion. Mel had had a bad start in life and now she was in trouble again. Perhaps another prison sentence. In spite of what Jane had experienced, she felt a little sad for her.

'What will happen to them?' she asked.

DC Penlow shrugged his shoulders. 'No doubt in time they'll be tried in court and convicted. Most likely end up in jail,' he remarked casually.

Inspector Boyd must have cottoned on to Jane's thinking about Mel. 'Don't feel sorry for these people,' he advised her. 'All of them have previous convictions. Carl Brody and Peter Grant are pretty violent characters. As you've found out,' he added, indicating Jane's eye.

Jane did not answer. Carl's treatment of her had been one of the worst parts of her ordeal. And she would have a constant reminder for a while every time she looked in the mirror.

Inspector Boyd changed the subject. 'Miss Carroll...' he began. He paused and studied her closely. 'Miss Carroll, I'd like to go over again one or two parts of the original statement you gave to the police here in Portsmouth.'

'Yes, of course,' replied Jane.

PC Penlow glanced through his paperwork and handed a sheet to Inspector Boyd. His colleague studied it for a second and then addressed Jane again.

'You say your name is Jane Carroll, but you also claim to be Ruth Ashington. Can you just explain again how that came about?'

Jane thought for a second about how best to explain everything.

'Well,' she began. 'It was when I started to research my family history...'

She described how she had gone to the churchyard and had been dismayed to learn that she had the name of a dead child. 'It wasn't until I went to the orphanage where I spent my early life,' she explained, 'that I discovered that I had entered that establishment under the name of Ruth Ashington. There seems to have been a mix-up over the names somewhere on the records.'

'Did you know anything about the Ashington family before you started your research?' asked Inspector Boyd.

Jane shook her head. 'Absolutely nothing,' she replied.

DC Penlow looked at her in surprise. 'Miles Ashington is a well-known public figure. He is frequently in the news.'

Jane hastened to set the record straight.

'I had heard of Miles Ashington, of course, but at the start I had no idea I was related to his family,' she explained.

'How did you find out that you were this particular Ruth Ashington?' asked Inspector Boyd.

'I made contact with the woman who had looked after me when I was a baby and had taken me to the orphanage,' replied Jane.

DC Penlow looked at his notes. 'Elizabeth Barton?' he asked.

'Yes, that's right.'

Jane suddenly thought of something else.

'When I met Miles Ashington, he confirmed that I must be the daughter of his late wife, Ann,' she explained.

Inspector Boyd smiled at her. 'How did you feel about that?' he asked.

'It came as a bit of a shock. You see, I'd always thought I was Jane Carroll.'

'And now you are part of a very old and illustrious family. And a very wealthy one.' It was DC Penlow who spoke, his eyes fixed on Jane.

Jane was a bit pensive. 'I've never thought about it that way. At the moment I'm just a bit confused and overwhelmed by the whole thing,' she said truthfully.

'Is it the case that you were staying at a cottage belonging to Mr Ashington at the time of your abduction?' asked DC Penlow.

'Yes.' Jane felt she had to add, 'Miles and Gail Ashington have been extremely kind and helpful to me, and when I disappeared they were very supportive towards my fiancé.'

The senior officer nodded. 'Yes. We have interviewed the Ashingtons and they confirm everything you have told us.'

Jane was determined to try to find out more about her abduction. She thought out her next question carefully.

'When I was being held by Mel and Carl, Mel admitted to me that they were working for somebody else. Somebody important – somebody they were afraid of. Have you any idea who that might be?'

Both officers seemed to be taken aback by her question. After a short silence, Inspector Boyd gave her a carefully worded answer. 'Yes, we have. But we can't tell you who it is at present.'

Jane could see that once again she was up against a brick wall. All she could say was, 'I see.'

Inspector Boyd seemed to understand her reaction. 'Look, I know it's tough not knowing what's happening, but I promise you you won't be kept in the dark much longer. As soon as something important happens we'll fill you in immediately. You are being of great assistance to us today by helping us to clarify things.'

Jane smiled at him. 'Thank you. I'm happy to do what I can, but somehow I don't think I am being much help to you. I know so little.'

'Sometimes the tiniest bit of evidence can lead to an arrest,' replied Inspector Boyd with a grin.

The officers continued to go over Jane's statement. Some of their questions she thought seemed quite trivial, but she answered all of them as best she could. The two men spent over an hour with her. At last they thanked her and told her she had been of great help to them in their enquiries. As he shook her hand, Inspector Boyd asked her if she had any idea how long she was going to remain in hospital.

'Not long now, I hope,' she replied.

'Let us know as soon as you are discharged,' he stressed. 'Ring me or DC Penlow. I'll give you a number where you can reach us. And if you could just let us have your mobile number...'

Jane put the details carefully into her mobile phone and then they made a note of her number.

After the two police officers had left, Jane went over the

interview in her mind. She had got over her initial surprise on discovering that they were from the Metropolitan Police. Clearly in the last few days the investigation had been extended considerably. She was convinced the police knew a great deal more than they were telling her, and this puzzled her. Even though they had assured her that she would be put in the picture soon, it was an odd situation, considering that she was the victim of the abduction. She guessed that all she could do was wait, but that was frustrating and worrying.

That evening she phoned Bob and told him about the visit. His reaction was one of mild surprise. 'Gosh!' he exclaimed. 'That means they must be after somebody in London.'

'Yes, but who? They won't tell me anything, and until they do I just have to sit and wait.'

'I'm sure it won't be long now,' replied Bob, trying to reassure her.

Jane suddenly thought of something important to tell him. 'Oh! There is just one thing. They told me today they thought the immediate danger to me was past.'

Bob was pensive. 'Hmm. That must mean they know who's behind it.' He laughed. 'I was wondering how they were going to give you protection at your apartment.'

'I'd never thought about that,' chuckled Jane. She tried to imagine her neighbours' reaction to the presence of a police officer at the entrance to the building, and what Gerald and Anna would say if they saw a guard outside her door.

She was still thinking about the scenario when Bob spoke again. 'Anyway, poppet, how are you feeling now?' he asked.

'I'm getting better by the hour. Seeing you yesterday was the turning point. I fully intend to be out of here soon,' Jane replied cheerfully.

'Good for you,' laughed Bob.

Something else crept into Jane's thinking. 'Darling, I can't stay on the phone very long. I'm eating up my credit, and I want to phone Lucy to warn her that the police might want to interview her. The poor girl will wonder what's happening if they turn up unannounced on her doorstep – or worse still appear at the children's home with that dragon of a boss around.'

Bob's reaction was more practical. 'Damn. I meant to leave some money with you to top up the mobile, and I forgot. Can you borrow some cash from someone? I'll reimburse them.'

Jane reacted swiftly. 'Darling, I'm fine. I have enough credit, but I just have to be careful.' She gave a little laugh. 'It'll teach me not to spend so much time on the phone.'

The following evening the young police officer outside the door came to see Jane and told her it was his last day and he had been instructed to return to normal duties. When Jane asked him if her police protection had been terminated, he told her that was the case.

The morning after that, Jane was transferred to a normal ward. She found herself in a four-bedded bay. Her two companions, both middle-aged women, were hardly the kind of people she would have chosen as close associates. One grumbled all the time about everything from the food to the hospital staff. The other talked incessantly. Within an hour of her arrival Jane had had a complete rundown of the woman's family and their activities as well as precise details of her operation. Somehow the woman had learnt what had happened to Jane. She kept up a barrage of questions. What did her captors give her to eat? How long had they kept her tied up? What had she done about the toilet? By lunchtime Jane felt exhausted. During the afternoon she spent as much time as she could in the dayroom at the end of the ward, flicking through the tatty magazines she found there and trying to absorb herself in a jigsaw. The circumstances she found herself in made her all the more determined to be discharged from the hospital.

Things did not move as quickly as she had anticipated. She had been hoping to speak to the consultant quickly and secure an early discharge, but it was late in the afternoon before he came to see her. Jane made a good case for leaving his care. She explained that she felt much better and was quite up to looking after herself now. At first he was reluctant, stressing that she should have a few more days' rest and supervision, but in the end he agreed that she could leave the next morning as soon as the ward doctor had examined her.

The outcome of their conversation pleased Jane on the one hand and frustrated her on the other. She would have to spend the night on that ward with her two companions.

That evening Jane called Bob and announced that, all being well, she would be out of hospital the following day. Her announcement fitted in perfectly with Bob's plans. The following day being a Saturday, he was planning to visit her again and had already hired a car for the weekend.

There was only one minor problem as far as he could see. He expressed his concern. 'What about some clothes for you?'

Jane had discarded the clothing she had arrived at the hospital in and had already worked out what to do.

'Can you come via Kew?' she asked.

'Of course I can.'

'Gerald and Anna have a key to my apartment. I'll phone Anna now and ask her to go up and dig out some things for me to wear.'

'It's fixed, then,' replied Bob. 'I'll pick them up from her tomorrow morning.'

They did not talk much longer as Jane was worried her credit would run out, and she still needed to phone Anna.

She spent a restless night. One of her companions snored continually and kept her awake. By the time morning came she was determined to leave the hospital, whatever the doctor had to say.

Fortunately, the harassed medic readily agreed that she was well enough to leave. A quick check of her injured foot and a word of advice to take things easy for a while and not try to do too much, and that was it. By the time Bob arrived Jane was waiting patiently in the dayroom.

She immediately embraced him, much to the amusement of the two other occupants of the room.

'Darling, it's marvellous to see you,' she whispered in his ear. 'I just want to get out of here as quickly as possible.'

Bob grinned at her and glanced down at the small suitcase he was carrying. 'Mission completed,' he remarked gaily. 'Here's what Anna sorted out for you.'

Jane grabbed the suitcase. 'Give me five minutes,' she called over her shoulder as she hobbled away as fast as she could.

She was anxious to know whether Anna had sent her the things she had asked for. Opening the suitcase, she was relieved to see that everything was in order. Anna had followed her instructions exactly. There was a set of underwear, a blouse, a skirt and a short jacket. Anna had even popped in a packet of tights she hadn't asked for. The only downside was footwear. Anna had packed a pair of high-heeled shoes, unaware of Jane's current difficulty. Jane upbraided herself for failing to tell her about her foot. Oh well. If the worst came to the worst she would have to wear the slippers.

It was a good ten minutes before she reappeared, the suitcase now packed with all the things she had collected while in hospital. For the first time since being admitted she wore the gold locket Bob had given her on the night of her abduction. She had managed to get into the shoes Anna had sent, though logic told her that flat heels would have been better. Despite her foot still hurting a bit, she was able to walk slowly in them.

She smiled cheerfully at Bob. 'Here I am, darling. I'm sorry I took so long.'

Bob grinned at her. 'How's the foot for walking on?' he asked.

Jane made a face as she glanced down at her foot. 'It hurts a bit, but it's fine really – and it's healing all the time.' She looked at Bob again, her face serious. 'But you don't know how good it feels to be dressed again and heading home with you.'

Bob led her down to the foyer. As they walked out through the automatic doors, Jane threw her head in the air and sniffed the cool, fresh morning.

'Fresh air!' she exclaimed. 'I feel so good. I haven't smelt it since that awful night I was rescued.'

Bob smiled at her and took her hand. 'It's not far to the car,' he announced.

As they walked, he suddenly remembered something. He stopped for a moment and turned to look at her.

'Oh, before I forget, there's something I need to tell you. When I collected your clothes from Anna, I spoke to Gerald while I was waiting. He told me he'd heard from Eric again, and Eric had told him he had some new information for you.'

'What could it be?' asked Jane, with a puzzled look.

Bob shook his head. 'He didn't tell Gerald, it seems, but apparently he said it was information that was vitally important to you.'

Chapter 49

Jane was glad to be back home in familiar surroundings. She had phoned Anna on Bob's mobile from the car to announce their impending arrival, but nevertheless she was surprised to be greeted by Anna in her apartment. Anna immediately started to fuss over her.

'Now, young woman,' she declared, 'you've just come out of hospital. Into bed this minute! You need to rest.'

That was the last thing Jane expected or wanted. She had been worried that she might feel a bit woozy coming almost straight from a hospital bed, but she had been surprised how well she had coped. True, she felt slightly light-headed and her foot still hurt a bit when she put weight on it, but she knew she would soon be back to her old self. Lying in bed was certainly not on her agenda.

She gave Anna a reassuring smile. 'I'm quite all right – really I am. I just need to take it easy for a few days.'

Anna was not convinced. 'But you've been very ill. And after the horrible time you've had you need a good rest.'

Jane shook her head. She suddenly thought of a solution. 'I tell you what I would like,' she announced. Pausing to receive Anna's enquiring look, she announced, 'I would love a nice cup of tea.'

Her strategy worked. Anna immediately changed tack and stirred into action. 'Let me make you one,' she urged.

Jane had another idea. 'Why don't Bob and I make the tea, and you go and ask Gerald to join us?' she suggested.

Anna hurried downstairs to prise Gerald away from the television.

There was another angle to Jane's thinking. In the car, she and

Bob had discussed Gerald's announcement that Eric had found some important information that he wanted to pass on to her. She hoped Gerald might now know more.

As soon as Anna had left them, Bob turned to Jane and grinned. 'That was a near miss,' he remarked.

Jane made one of her faces. 'Anna can be quite insistent at times. I'll have to watch I don't end up an invalid in bed.' She laughed.

Suddenly Bob moved towards her and put his arms around her. He looked at her admiringly. 'Poppet, you handled her marvellously,' he said softly.

Jane snuggled up to him. 'Oh, it's so nice to be home again.' She spoke quietly, almost to herself. 'There was a low point when I thought I might never see it or you ever again.'

'I'd have found you somehow,' whispered Bob.

Jane suddenly held him close and kissed him. 'Now I can really kiss you properly without anybody watching us,' she murmured.

They embraced and kissed for several minutes.

It was Jane who broke away. 'Hey! We're supposed to be getting some tea ready,' she giggled.

'I'll make a start,' announced Bob, heading for the kitchen.

Jane took the opportunity to pop into the bathroom and then her bedroom, where she exchanged the high heels for a comfortable pair of flip-flops.

She had just sat down in the lounge when Anna returned carrying a homemade cake and with Gerald in tow. Anna disappeared into the kitchen to help Bob, and Gerald sat down opposite Jane. He seemed most concerned about her, asking her how she felt now and whether she could manage now she was home. Jane answered his questions politely, but all the time she was burning to ask him what Eric had found out.

It wasn't until Bob and Anna reappeared and Anna had fussed over everybody, distributing cups of tea and plates of cake, that Jane had the opportunity to broach her question.

Taking a sip of her tea, she addressed Gerald. 'Bob tells me that

Eric has been in touch with you again and has some interesting information.'

Gerald put down his cup and saucer. 'Yes. That is correct. Unfortunately, we had no idea at the time that you had been kidnapped.' He gave Jane a slight smile.

'What did he say?'

Gerald thought for a second, clearly recalling the conversation with Eric. 'He was a bit vague at the time, but my understanding is that he had found some information about a will that he thought was important to you.'

Jane was mystified. 'But whose will can it be?' she asked.

Gerald shook his head. 'As usual Eric didn't go into details over the telephone. He was planning to come and see you, but then unfortunately you disappeared.'

'Perhaps we can contact him now,' suggested Jane.

'I tried yesterday evening,' replied Gerald, 'but unfortunately he is out of the country at present.'

Jane felt subdued. Life at the moment seemed to be made up of waiting. First, waiting for more information from the police, and now she would have to wait again to hear what Eric had found out.

'Have you any idea what it might be about?' asked Bob, who had been listening quietly.

Gerald turned to him, at the same time refusing more cake from Anna. 'It would seem, given the importance Eric attaches to it, that it must be something to do with the Ashington family.'

'But if that was so, surely Miles would know about it,' Jane pointed out.

Gerald looked from Bob to Jane. 'It's a bit of a mystery at present, but no doubt we'll find out as soon as Eric reappears.'

'I know what it's all about,' Anna suddenly chipped in.

The other three looked at her, waiting for her to elaborate.

'Somebody somewhere has left you a lot of money in their will,' she announced, directing her statement to Jane.

Jane laughed. The thought had occurred to her, but the idea

was so preposterous that she had not voiced it. 'That would be nice,' she replied gaily.

It was Anna who switched the subject of their conversation. She looked down at Jane's ankles. 'How did you get those marks?'

Jane explained what had happened, and from then on there was a constant flow of questions from Anna, interspersed with occasional comments from Gerald. Jane answered as patiently and as briefly as she could.

Gerald and Anna stayed for over an hour. Eventually Anna announced that they would have to go, but first she wanted to do the washing-up. Bob stressed that he had better do it – to earn his keep, he joked. To Jane's relief Anna seemed to accept this.

Once they were on their own, Bob turned his attention to Jane, who had now stretched full length on the settee.

'How are you feeling now, darling?' he asked, a bit concerned.

Jane smiled at him. 'I'm fine really, but I'm just a little bit tired now. This is my first real effort to be up and about all day.'

Bob suggested that she rest while he did the washing-up, and she gladly accepted. When he had finished, he offered to go out to buy them some food, and Jane gave him directions to the nearest supermarket.

While he was out, she lay back on the settee and closed her eyes. It was pleasant to just lie there in her own home and reflect on all that had happened since she had left its security. It had been only a matter of days since she had embarked with such happiness on her trip to Cornwall with Bob, but so much had happened to her since then that it felt like weeks and weeks. It all seemed unreal now, but she had the marks on her body to prove that all those dreadful things had taken place. She felt that she was being kept in the dark, not knowing who was behind her abduction. That was the worst bit now – not being told anything. And now there was this added mystery about a will. It was all completely baffling.

Bob returned with two bags of groceries. Together they made an omelette and some salad. After they had eaten, they sat together in the lounge, talking quietly over the events of the previous few days. During a lull in their conversation, Jane felt tiredness beginning to overtake her again. Several times she found her eyes slowly closing. They retreated to the bedroom and she fell asleep in Bob's arms.

Over the next week Jane made good progress. She began to feel stronger and much more like her old self, and her injured foot became less painful to walk on. Bob had to leave her the day after he collected her from the hospital, but he phoned her frequently after he returned to Tatting Green to find out how her recovery was going. Anna kept popping in and seemed to need a lot of convincing that Jane was not an invalid. Jane took it all in her stride, accepting the odd cup of coffee but drawing boundaries when necessary.

As requested, she phoned the number Inspector Boyd had given her to tell the police she was now back home. She was unable to speak to either him or DC Penlow, but the man who answered the telephone explained that he was part of the team and would ensure that the inspector was informed. Jane took the opportunity of asking if there was any news for her, but was politely told that the investigation was still ongoing and that she would be contacted as soon as there were any developments. She asked whether it was wise from a security point of view for her to go out alone. She was advised that the investigation team considered that there was no longer any immediate threat to her safety.

This reassurance spurred Jane on to venture outside. First she just walked round the block, and then she ventured further and did some shopping. She visited the hairdresser and was relieved to be able to have her hair attended to after its neglect over the previous few weeks. She had noticed a few passers-by glancing at the marks on her ankles, which were still quite noticeable. In the hairdressing salon she noticed a stand with packets of tights for sale. This prompted her to buy two dark pairs to wear until the marks faded, despite the fact that she abhorred wearing tights in summer.

She made a lot of telephone calls, including one to Annette, who was quite sympathetic but ended up by asking her when she thought she would be returning to work. When she talked to Amy she found out the reason.

'She had to be in the office more and do some work,' Amy grumbled.

Jane grinned to herself. There was no doubt Amy had been having a bad time while she was away.

This was confirmed by Amy's next remark. 'She's nearly driving me mad. First she wants this, and then she wants that. On top of that she keeps changing things. I don't know where I am.'

Jane sympathised as best she could and promised that she would not be away for much longer. She was sincere in this. Her recovery had been quicker than she had expected, and already signs of boredom were creeping in. She was considering the possibility of returning to the office the following week.

One highlight was a telephone call from the police in Cornwall to tell her that they no longer required her car and that she could collect it when it was convenient for her. She immediately rang Bob and they arranged to travel down to Cornwall a few days later to pick up the car and her other things.

It turned out to be a long day. First they had to travel to Truro by train and then take a taxi to the police station. When Jane saw the car, she was dismayed to discover that it had been parked in the yard at the rear of the police station and was now covered with a fine layer of white dust from a nearby building site. Bob suggested that they call in at a filling station, top up the car with petrol and put it through the car wash.

Next they drove over to Barn Cottage to retrieve the rest of Jane's holiday luggage. Visiting the cottage again brought mixed feelings for them both. They had spent several enjoyable days there, but Jane could not help but relive the evening when she had been held there at gunpoint. The lovely old building no longer felt the same. There were too many bad memories associated with it.

Maggie greeted them and tried to fuss over them, clearly keen to ask Jane about her ordeal. Conscious of the long drive ahead of them, they were polite but did not dally long.

They shared the driving on the return trip, stopping once for a meal and a rest. Jane was delighted to be behind the wheel of her car again, but she had to admit that she was beginning to feel tired by the time they were back in Kew and had carried all her belongings from the car up to her apartment. Despite this, she wanted to drive Bob home. He absolutely refused, saying that it would be too much for her, and she had to admit that he was right.

After Bob left, Jane briefly flung herself into the process of sorting out all the items they had collected from Cornwall. It was a mixed experience. While she was delighted to be reunited with such personal items as her cosmetic bag and mobile phone, when it came to removing from the plastic bag the clothes and watch she had been forced to take off at gunpoint, the trauma of that evening came vividly back to her. One high point was retrieving her engagement ring from the inner pocket of her suitcase, where she had placed it for safety on the night of the Ashingtons' dinner party. It was almost ten when she made herself a drink and took it to bed with her. Only one thing still bothered her, and that was not hearing from the Metropolitan Police. Surely, she reasoned, they must contact her soon and tell her what was happening. More than anything else now, she needed answers to the questions she constantly asked herself: who had ordered her brutal capture and confinement? What had they intended to do with her? And what was the reason behind her kidnap?

Chapter 50

Jane's return to work did not go exactly as she had planned. On the Monday morning she took her time getting ready and walking to the railway station. She had expected to arrive at the office later than usual but to her surprise she caught an earlier train and arrived at the same time as Margaret. Margaret fussed over her a bit and brought her a cup of tea while she sat at her desk and tried to make sense of the stack of paperwork that had piled up.

Once the rest of the staff arrived, that was the end of Jane's efforts to get any work done. Everybody crowded round her asking question after question. It was Annette's arrival that broke up the inquisition. Jane turned her attention back to the papers on her desk, but within five minutes the internal telephone buzzed, and as she expected she heard Annette's voice at the other end.

'Jane, it's nice to see you back. How are you now?'

'Oh, I seem to have made a quick recovery,' replied Jane breezily.

There was a slight pause. 'That's excellent. Are you free for a chat now?'

'Yes, of course. I'll come straight up.'

Annette was clearly extremely pleased to see her. 'It's really good to have you back, Jane,' she announced. She studied her with a concerned look. 'Now be careful you don't try and do too much, after all you've been through. I suggest you finish early for a few days.'

This was something Jane had already considered. 'I might do that,' she replied. 'I'll see how things go.'

It was inevitable that Annette, like the rest of the staff, would want to know everything that had happened to Jane while she was away from work. Jane gave as brief an account as she could.

When she had finished, Annette asked, 'Do the police know yet who did all this to you?'

Jane shook her head. 'I'm still waiting to hear. They keep telling me the investigation is ongoing and they will contact me as soon as anything changes.'

Her reply did not impress Annette. 'That's appalling. You should have heard something by now.'

Annette suddenly thought of something else. 'What about your safety?' she asked, concern in her voice. 'These people might try to kidnap you again.'

Jane smiled. 'The police tell me there's no immediate danger to me now.'

'Well, I suppose that's a relief,' Annette remarked thoughtfully.

The next instant she had changed the subject and started to give Jane a résumé of what had taken place at *Discerning Woman* during her absence.

Jane sat and listened patiently, making a note here and there where required. She had been with Annette for a good twenty minutes when the phone rang.

Annette lifted the receiver. 'Yes, Margaret.'

Annette listened for a few seconds. Jane wondered whether this might be an opportunity for her to leave. Annette's long telephone calls were renowned.

Before she could make a move, Annette turned to her. 'It's for you, Jane. It's the police.'

Jane leapt up, her heart thumping. Was this the long-awaited call?

'Take it here,' urged Annette, handing her the receiver.

'Miss Carroll?' It was a male voice.

'Yes. Jane Carroll speaking.'

'Detective Inspector Boyd here, Jane. I am sorry we haven't been in contact with you, but this investigation has been quite complex. How are you now? The last time we spoke you were in hospital.'

'I made a speedy recovery once I was home,' replied Jane. 'This is my first day back at work.'

She did not wait for a response. Anxiously, she asked, 'Have you got any news for me?'

'Yes. A lot has happened in the last twenty-four hours. I need to see you to talk about it. Can you come here today?'

'Can I just check?' Jane placed her hand over the mouthpiece and turned to Annette, who was taking a keen interest in the call. 'The police want to see me urgently.'

Annette responded immediately. 'Oh, but you must go. This is important.'

Quickly Jane turned her attention to the telephone again. 'Yes, that will be fine. Where, and at what time?'

Inspector Boyd gave her the address, which she was relieved to note was not far from the *Discerning Woman* offices. She scribbled it on her notepad.

'Can you get here for half past eleven this morning?' he asked.

'Yes, I can.' She could not help adding, 'I'm desperate to know what's happened.'

'We'll be happy to bring you up to date.'

As soon as Jane had finished the call she turned to Annette, who was now looking inquisitively at her. 'They want me there this morning,' she announced.

'Would you like me to come with you?' There was optimism in Annette's voice.

Jane shook her head. The last thing she wanted was to have Annette at her elbow at such a meeting. She intended to give Bob a ring as soon as she was back at her desk. 'No, thank you. I'll be fine,' she replied, pleasantly but firmly.

Annette appeared to accept her refusal, making some sort of comment that she had an appointment anyway.

Jane had difficulty getting hold of Bob. She tried first his house and then his office. Eventually she tried his mobile and managed to reach him. He was on the train travelling up to London.

'Hi. It's me.'

'Hi, me.'

Jane plunged straight in. 'I've heard from the police. Something has happened. They want to see me at half past eleven this morning. Can you come as well?'

There was a pause from Bob. 'I can't, but I will. Where are you meeting them?'

Jane told him the location.

'I know it. I'll see you there.'

With a quick 'Bye', he was gone.

Jane arrived a few minutes early at the offices where Inspector Boyd was based. Bob was already waiting outside for her, and together they entered the large modern building. They enquired at the reception desk, and DC Penlow appeared shortly afterwards. Formal greetings exchanged, he led them into a lift. Several floors above, he guided them along a busy corridor and opened the door into a spacious carpeted office, where Inspector Boyd and another man were seated at a large desk. Both men rose as DC Penlow showed Jane and Bob into the room.

Inspector Boyd greeted them. 'Thank you for coming. I'd like to introduce you to Neil Cotterill. He's a lawyer who has been assisting us on this case.'

Jane and Bob shook hands with the lawyer and then sat down opposite him and Inspector Boyd.

The inspector smiled at his two visitors. 'Would you like a cup of tea, Jane?' he asked. He turned to Bob. 'And you, sir?'

Jane and Bob politely accepted and DC Penlow disappeared to fetch the refreshments.

Formalities over, Inspector Boyd addressed Jane again. 'Thank you for being so patient. It must have been an anxious time for you, not knowing what was happening, particularly after all you've been through. However, I must say that this has been a most complex case to unravel.'

He paused, and Jane had the opportunity to ask the question that was uppermost in her mind. 'But I understand from what you said on the telephone this morning that there have been some developments now.'

The inspector nodded. He studied Jane closely. 'Ray Ashington has been arrested and charged with ordering your abduction and imprisonment.'

Jane was aghast. She could scarcely find the words to reply. 'But... But I hardly know him. I've only met him once,' she managed to get out.

'But you know his father.'

'Yes, and Miles has always been kind and helpful to me,' she responded quickly.

Inspector Boyd smiled at her briefly. 'Beware of the wolf in sheep's clothing.' He became serious again as he continued. 'Miles Ashington has also been arrested, questioned and released on bail pending further investigation. He has also had to surrender his passport.'

Jane was desperately trying to assimilate the information she had just received. What she had just heard was the last thing she had expected. It seemed almost impossible to comprehend, but it had happened and somehow she had to come to terms with it. Inspector Boyd was studying her, watching her reaction.

'But why?' she asked. 'Why? I have never done anything to the Ashington family.' She looked in despair at him.

The police officer was quick to reply. He glanced at the papers on his desk and then looked back at Jane. 'I think the root cause of the problem is the fact that you are a member of the Ashington family.' He hesitated for a second. 'You are the daughter of Ann Ashington, and Ann Ashington was Miles Ashington's second wife.'

'But how does that make me a target for abduction?' asked Jane anxiously.

Inspector Boyd gave another quick glance at the paperwork on his desk. He cleared his throat. 'We have reliable information that Ann Ashington made a will and named you as her beneficiary.'

This was another shock to Jane. 'But I was told my mother didn't want anything to do with me,' she replied.

441

The inspector gave her a brief smile. 'Perhaps that idea is open to question as well,' he remarked.

It was Bob who asked the next question. 'How was the will discovered?'

Inspector Boyd quickly turned to Neil Cotterill, who so far had sat quietly listening to the conversation. 'Perhaps you would like to elaborate on this one, Neil.'

The lawyer nodded in agreement. Adjusting his spectacles, which seemed to be continually slipping down his nose, he addressed Jane and Bob. 'You know Eric Alcott, I believe. I understand he has been assisting you with your research relating to the Ashington family.'

'Yes, he has,' replied Jane.

'I have known Eric for many years,' he continued. 'We are very good friends.'

He stopped talking for an instant and scrutinised Jane and Bob through the half-frame spectacles that balanced precariously on the end of his nose, as if to ensure that he had their full attention. Seemingly satisfied, he continued. 'It seems Eric has been working hard on your behalf. In the process he discovered that Ann Ashington had made a will prior to her marriage to Miles Ashington.'

After another pause, during which he looked closely at Jane again, the lawyer continued. 'The will was prepared for Ann Ashington by Miles Carlton, who later changed his name to Ashington.'

'How did Eric find that out?' asked Bob.

Neil Cotterill gave a little smile. 'Rather unofficial, I'm afraid. He knew the solicitors where Miles Carlton had been a partner before he married Ann. The will seems to have disappeared, but, being the detective he is, Eric traced a woman who had been a secretary at the solicitors' at the time the will was written. She had long retired, but she still had her shorthand pad with the details. In fact, she could remember typing the will.'

'Was this the new information Eric wanted to give me?' asked Jane.

'That is correct.'

'But you say the will has disappeared.'

Neil Cotterill nodded. 'Exactly,' he replied.

'Do you think it was destroyed deliberately?' asked Bob.

The lawyer adjusted his spectacles again. 'It certainly looks odd, given the circumstances,' he replied. 'Eric told me about his find and we discussed it at some length. I considered the matter serious enough, considering your disappearance at the time, to talk to my contacts in the police.'

Inspector Boyd suddenly broke his silence. 'I have to tell you, Jane, that we are treating this matter as serious. An investigation is under way.'

Jane was desperately trying to readjust her thinking to this new information. It all seemed unbelievable. 'You mean... Miles Ashington is also involved in all this?' she asked.

Inspector Boyd nodded. 'I'm afraid so. I also have to tell you in confidence that Ann Ashington's death is now being treated as suspicious.' He paused. 'Further investigations are taking place to establish the cause of death.'

Jane was silent for a few seconds, finding it hard to believe what she was hearing. When she spoke it was in a quiet voice. 'It all seems so unreal. Miles and Gail were so kind and helpful to me.'

The inspector smiled briefly. 'It's like that sometimes,' he replied.

Jane was still trying to make sense of everything. It seemed incredible that anyone would go to so much trouble to eliminate her just because she was a member of a certain family. 'You mean my mother may have been poisoned or something like that?' she asked.

'That is a possibility.'

Jane spoke her thoughts as she tried to analyse everything. 'But who would do such a thing? The maid would have nothing to gain. That would only leave Miles Ashington, and he and Ann were in love...'

'Were they?' interjected Inspector Boyd. He leaned across the desk towards Jane. 'Look at it this way. Ann Ashington makes a will leaving everything to you. That will is drawn up for her by Miles Carlton, who later marries her. Ann starts to become ill immediately after her marriage. You disappear into an orphanage and apparently acquire a different name, and then Ann dies, leaving everything to her husband, Miles Ashington.'

There was a long silence after the inspector finished speaking. When Jane's reply came it was almost a whisper. 'I just can't believe it. It's too horrible to even think that anyone would go to so much trouble for money.'

Bob had been silent, taking in and thinking about what he had just heard. He was prompted to add his thoughts to the discussion. 'I was under the impression that a will made before marriage was invalidated if the person making the will married afterwards.'

'Wills can be contested in court if there is sufficient justification,' replied Neil Cotterill.

The conversation was halted briefly by the reappearance of DC Penlow with a tray of tea. Once everybody had been served, Inspector Boyd continued.

'There's even more to it than you've just heard,' he said to Jane. He turned to the lawyer. 'Neil?'

Neil Cotterill took up the prompting. With a quick glance at his paperwork, he addressed Jane. 'Have you ever heard of the Ashington legacy?' he asked.

Jane shook her head. 'No,' she replied.

Neil Cotterill smiled at her. 'I would have been surprised if you had,' he remarked. 'Your grandfather, Edward Ashington, was a shrewd man, particularly with money, but he had a thing about women handling money. He left your mother sufficient to live on, but he had huge investments abroad and he set up a kind of trust to handle them. The income could be drawn but not the capital – that is, not until a certain period of time had elapsed.'

He paused to let Jane and Bob absorb the information. Then, with a slight smile, he announced, 'That period of time has now ended and Miles Ashington has spent the last two years trying to claim the inheritance. It is a large amount of money. At the last count it was around nineteen million pounds.'

'Phew,' broke in Bob. 'It's all beginning to make sense. Everything was going fine for Miles Ashington until Jane turned up – Ann Ashington's daughter – and could make a claim to her inheritance.'

'That's exactly it,' remarked Neil quietly.

There was several seconds' silence.

Inspector Boyd looked at Jane. 'I'm sorry if you find this rather upsetting,' he said sympathetically.

Jane took her time to answer. The realisation that Miles Ashington, who had always treated her in such a caring and friendly way, could be the very person responsible for her recent ordeal was hard to accept, yet she knew the police must be confident of their facts.

When she replied, she spoke slowly, her eyes cast down, almost as if she were speaking aloud her thoughts. 'It seems so odd. Somebody who has treated you with such courtesy and friendliness is actually at the same time plotting to have you abducted. To eliminate you, in fact. It's quite scary.' She looked up at Inspector Boyd as she finished speaking, as if seeking confirmation.

The inspector nodded. 'It must be quite a shock,' he agreed.

'What were they going to do with me?' asked Jane quietly.

'You really want to know?'

She nodded.

'You would probably have been taken somewhere and filled so full of drugs that you wouldn't care where you were or what you did as long as your desire for them was satisfied. Putting it bluntly, you would most likely have ended up in some low-grade brothel somewhere abroad. Ray Ashington has some rather unpleasant friends.'

Jane shuddered. 'It's too horrible to think about,' she replied softly.

Inspector Boyd spoke again. 'We believe the boat you were found on has been involved in suspicious trips to the continent before. We have also had our eyes on Ray Ashington's activities for some time. Not all of these people are what they appear to be. Your case has brought other investigations nearer to completion.'

'How was I actually found?' This was a question Jane had wanted to know the answer to for a long time.

'You lost your anklet in a barn. The farmer who owned the barn found it and took it to the local police. He had also noticed some unusual activity in the area. After the anklet was identified as being yours, our colleagues in Cornwall moved very fast, raided the farm where you had been held and arrested the occupants. You were far away by that time, but fortunately one of the suspects spilled the beans about where you were.'

'Was it Mel?' asked Jane.

'Yes, it was. She had been badly knocked about by that partner of hers. She had to be taken to hospital. But her action certainly helped you to be found before you disappeared out of our reach.'

Jane thought about what she had just heard. She was glad Mel had decided to risk telling the police what she knew. Somehow, despite Mel's rough exterior, she had always felt that underneath she was basically a good person. 'I'm glad it was her,' she replied.

Inspector Boyd smiled. 'It will go in her favour when she gets to court.'

'What will happen now?' asked Bob.

'As you can guess,' replied the inspector, 'both Miles Ashington and his son are in a pretty sticky situation on a number of issues. Investigations are continuing and I am fairly confident that when it comes to court they will both receive pretty stiff prison sentences. It will also mean discredit for both of them in the business world.' He turned to Jane with a smile. 'And you, Jane, will have to become accustomed to a new title and role in life as Ruth Ashington.'

Chapter 51

Jane gave a little forced smile in response to Inspector Boyd's suggestion. 'That's going to be the difficult bit,' she replied simply.

It was clear that the interview was drawing to an end. Jane and Bob thanked Inspector Boyd and Neil Cotterill for all their help. The inspector told Jane that he would be in touch again as soon as there were any developments, and DC Penlow then escorted them out of the building.

Once they were outside, the full impact of what she had just heard struck Jane. She turned to Bob, her face full of anxiety and concern. 'Oh, Bob, I feel so overwhelmed by everything. It almost feels as if I've been hit by a battering ram. I can't go back to work right away. I've got to think and get everything straight in my mind.'

Bob put his arm around her. 'Let's go somewhere for a drink,' he suggested.

They found a coffee shop close by. Jane sought out a quiet table in a corner while Bob went to the counter to get two coffees. He could see Jane from where he stood. She looked quite sad. Compassion for her welled up inside him. She had come through a pretty tough ordeal and just as she was getting over that she had to take in this new aspect of everything. Who would have thought the Ashingtons were behind her abduction? He paid for the coffee and carried it over to the table. Jane simply uttered a brief 'Thanks' as he pushed a cup towards her.

For a few minutes they drank their coffee in silence.

It was Bob who spoke first. 'Would you rather not go back to work?' he asked.

His question jerked Jane out of her silence.

She gave a bit of a smile as she replied. 'No, I'll be fine.' She hesitated for a moment and then continued speaking slowly. 'It's just that everything still seems a bit unreal. I mean, the Ashingtons were so friendly – and all the time Miles and his son must have been planning to eliminate me.'

Bob nodded in agreement. 'I know. I've been thinking the same thing myself,' he replied.

Jane spoke again. 'That evening when we all went out to dinner they had it all planned. They were completely relaxed and friendly, yet they knew what was going to happen to me.'

'I've thought a lot about that as well,' replied Bob. 'They must have put something in my drink to make me fall asleep like that, so you were left completely vulnerable.'

Jane took another sip of coffee. 'They thought of everything,' she replied, her voice subdued.

There was a brief silence between them. Jane was deep in thought. The revelation of the fate the Ashingtons had intended for her had been hard to comprehend. She knew now what Carl had meant when he said, 'She'll have worse where she's going.' Even Mel must have known what was going to happen to her.

When Jane spoke again her voice was quiet and a bit emotional. 'I keep thinking about what might have happened to me if I hadn't been rescued. It's almost too awful to contemplate.'

Bob smiled at her briefly. 'Thank goodness you lost your anklet in the barn. It was the key to finding you.'

Jane was deep in thought as she responded to his comment. 'That's the odd thing about it all. I never intended to wear it that night. It was an afterthought, because what I'd planned to wear didn't work out.'

Bob was about to reply, but Jane suddenly thought of something else. 'And I keep thinking of Mel. It must have been her telling the police where I'd been taken that enabled them to find me so quickly.'

'I'm glad she did,' Bob remarked, smiling. 'Otherwise I'd have had to search for you.'

'Even in a brothel?' Jane gave a brief smile as she asked the question. To Bob it was the first sign of the old Jane.

'Of course,' he replied, with a grin.

Jane was serious again. 'I hope Mel sorts her life out after all this. I am convinced that underneath she's OK; it's just that she didn't have the same chances in life as most of us.'

'As the inspector said, her co-operation with the police will no doubt be taken into consideration when she gets to court,' Bob commented.

'I hope so.'

Jane returned to her thoughts for a few seconds. Bob waited, guessing that she wanted to talk and get everything out of her system.

When she spoke again, her face was full of concern. 'Then there is all this business of the Ashington legacy – and being Ruth Ashington.'

She was talking slowly. She stopped. Suddenly she came out with her deeper thoughts. Looking at Bob intently, she continued. 'You know, Bob, the Ashingtons went to great lengths to get rid of me, I imagine with the thought that I was going to make a claim on the money. But in reality they went to a lot of trouble for nothing. The fact is that I don't want it. I don't want to be Ruth Ashington. I just want to be me – plain Jane Carroll.'

Bob could see that there were almost tears in her eyes. He placed his hand on hers as he spoke quietly. 'Poppet, you don't have to do anything you don't want to. You don't have to be Ruth Ashington. You can change your name officially. You can give the money to charity. You can just be you.'

Jane forced a smile. Hearing Bob using his pet name for her was a turning point in her misery. The mist began to clear. After all that, she thought, I don't have to do anything I don't want to. She leaned over the table and gave Bob a quick peck on the cheek.

As she sat back again, she tried her best to be more cheerful. 'Thank you for that. You're quite right. Everything can be sorted out. Thank you for hearing me out.' She drained the last of her coffee and grinned at Bob.

They stayed chatting for a little longer and then Jane saw Bob glance at the clock on the wall. It was a reminder that she should be making her way back to work. Bob walked her to her office and left her at the entrance before hurrying away to an appointment.

Back in the office Jane was bombarded with questions by the rest of the staff. She did her best to answer as briefly as possible. She had already planned a suitable explanation of events to satisfy their curiosity.

No sooner had she managed to get back to her desk than Annette called her in to see her. For the second time that day Jane made her way up the stairs. Annette already had two cups of coffee on the desk. She ushered Jane to a seat and pushed one of the cups towards her.

'Now. Tell me what's happened. What did the police have to say?'

Jane picked up the cup of coffee, which she did not really want, and gave her a résumé of events. Unlike the rest of the staff, Annette was not content with the explanation she had prepared. She wanted to know every detail and kept interrupting to ask questions.

When Annette heard about Miles Ashington's involvement, she almost went into a state of shock. 'I can't believe it,' she kept repeating.

In the end Jane was with Annette for well over an hour. When she managed to end the interview, she left Annette staring at her desk and murmuring, 'Miles Ashington. I just can't believe it.'

The day was now well advanced. Jane glanced through one or two items on her desk, sorted Amy out on a project she was doing, and then decided to call it a day. After all the trauma of the morning's revelations, she felt rather tired. Tomorrow she would return with more vigour and deal with everything.

As she left the office she was in for another shock. Several reporters were hanging about outside. It was clear that the news had got out. Inspector Boyd had warned her that the evening papers would carry the story of Miles and Ray Ashington's arrest, as well as reports of her own ordeal. Jane managed to shake off the reporters and their eager questioning. That was the last thing she wanted to encounter. Fortunately, they appeared to accept her 'Nothing to say' response as final and did not attempt to follow her.

She was relieved when she reached the calm of her own apartment and was able to relax at last. It had been a long and tiring day, and so much had happened. She had left the security of her home only a few hours previously, completely unaware of what she would learn that day. It was all new, and she needed time to adjust to it.

She had just changed out of her business suit into jeans and a blouse and was padding about barefoot in the kitchen wondering what sort of meal to make for herself when the telephone rang. It was Anna asking her how she had got on at work. She and Gerald had already seen the evening paper and she wanted to talk about that as well. Jane was as polite and patient as she could be, but an afternoon of talking about the morning's events to so many other people had exhausted her, and she felt in need of peace and quiet. Anna ended up by asking her to come to supper with her and Gerald. She declined, explaining that she felt too tired. Anna promptly offered to come up and prepare a meal for her. It took all Jane's strategy to wriggle out of that prospect.

By the time she had finished with Anna she felt too tired to make herself a proper meal. She ate a boiled egg and some fruit she had bought in a mini-market on her way home. She made herself a mug of tea and took it into the lounge and relaxed on the settee. She was going over the events of the day again when Bob telephoned. They chatted for half an hour or so and then she returned to the settee and her pondering.

She woke with a start some time later to find the room deep in darkness. Half asleep, she crawled into the bathroom and then her bed.

451

The following day Jane woke up feeling refreshed and ready to deal with things. She set off for work early and had her first shock of the day when she arrived at the station. She was headline news – or rather Miles Ashington and his son Ray were. The newspapers were full of the story, including a few somewhat exaggerated accounts of Jane's captivity. Some of the other details were also incorrect. Some newspapers referred to her as Ruth Ashington and others as Jane Carroll. She smiled briefly at one article that incorrectly described her as the editor of *Discerning Woman*. She wondered what Annette would think of that.

Outside the office she encountered the reporters again, their ranks now swelled to four. Questions were fired at her. 'How are you feeling now, Jane?' 'Have you talked with Miles Ashington since his arrest?' 'What will you do with the legacy?' Jane managed to evade their persistence and reach the security of her office. The rest of the staff came in armed with newspapers and crowded round her, anxious to discuss this new angle. They too had been bombarded by the reporters, who were hoping that one of them might disclose some titbit of information that so far had not reached the media.

Jane was interrupted several times during the day by telephone calls from eager newspapers that wanted to buy her story and have an exclusive account of her abduction and imprisonment. She managed to discourage the offers with an explanation that she had no plans to do this at present. Meanwhile she had to work through the pile of papers on her desk. Annette only contacted her once, and that was first thing, to enquire how she felt now, but for the rest of the day she appeared to be busy with visitors and Jane was able to get through some of her work without interruption. By the end of the day she was tired but she was pleased with her efforts.

The rest of the working week passed fairly smoothly. Though for the first few days she was glad when it was time to go home, she was now feeling much more like her old self. She had heard no more from the police and after a few days the newspapers had other stories to occupy their front pages. The throng of reporters started to reduce as it became apparent that there was nothing more to be gleaned from Jane. She still got the odd telephone call out of the blue from a newspaper or magazine seeking an interview, but these too eventually dwindled to nothing.

It was on the Thursday of that first week, as Jane was leaving to go home, that she received a very different telephone call. She was just walking past the reception desk on her way out of the office, when Margaret stopped her. 'Jane, I've got that Mrs Barton on the phone asking for you. She seems very agitated. She keeps saying she must speak to you.' She looked at Jane, seeking instruction.

Jane smiled at her. 'OK, Margaret. I'll take the call in my office.'

She returned to her desk and picked up the phone. A second or two later there was the sound of Margaret's voice. 'You're through.'

Jane answered the call. 'Jane Carroll speaking.'

There was a flustered voice at the other end of the line. 'This is Elizabeth Barton.'

'Hello, Elizabeth. It's nice to hear from you.'

'I need to see you. I want to tell you something.'

'I'd love to see you again,' replied Jane cheerfully.

'I must see you as soon as possible. Can you come tomorrow?' Elizabeth sounded very anxious.

Jane thought quickly. She didn't want to take any more time off work. She and Bob had nothing fixed for Saturday. She didn't know if Bob would be working Saturday morning. He spent a lot of time in London now as he and Jeff got their new business under way. But if necessary she could go on her own.

'How about Saturday morning at about half past ten?'

'Yes, yes, any time. I've got to see you.' Elizabeth's distress was now quite evident.

Jane felt concerned. 'Can you tell me now?' she asked kindly.

'No, no. I've got to see you.' Elizabeth's voice was quite firm.

'OK. I'll come and see you on Saturday, then,' Jane replied softly.

'Thank you, Jane.' Elizabeth sounded a bit happier. She suddenly asked. 'I can call you Jane, can't I?'

'Of course you can,' said Jane immediately. She added cheerfully, 'Although of course, considering recent events, perhaps you should be calling me Ruth.'

There was silence for a few seconds at the other end of the telephone. Then Elizabeth spoke again, her voice full of misery. 'But that's just the problem,' she almost whimpered. There was another pause, and then she announced more clearly, 'You are not Ruth Ashington.'

Chapter 52

Jane tried to take in what Elizabeth had just said. After almost a week of trying to accept the idea that she was Ruth Ashington, in just a few seconds here was somebody telling her something different.

She struggled to find words to reply with. 'But... but if I am not Ruth Ashington, who am I?'

Elizabeth was clearly in a very anxious state. 'I've got to see you. I have to tell you something I should have told you before,' she gabbled.

Jane took a deep breath. She knew she would have to tread carefully to glean anything.

'Can't you tell me over the telephone?' she asked softly.

'I've got to see you and tell you things.' Elizabeth's voice was quite agitated now.

Jane was about to try another tack, but Elizabeth spoke again. 'The police have been here asking questions. I should have told them, but I didn't. I don't know what to do, but I must see you and tell you.' Her voice trailed off to almost a whimper.

Jane could see that she wasn't going to make any further headway over the telephone. She would have to go and see Elizabeth.

She tried to adopt a soothing voice. 'It's OK, Elizabeth. We can talk about it on Saturday.'

Elizabeth seemed to accept the renewed suggestion immediately. 'Yes, yes. Please come.'

Jane breathed a sigh of relief. 'That's fine, then. I'll come and see you on Saturday at about half past ten and we can have a nice chat, and in the meantime don't worry. I'm sure everything can be sorted out.'

'Oh, yes. Thank you.' Elizabeth's reply was more positive.

'So I'll see you on Saturday at about half past ten,' reiterated Jane.

'Half past ten. Yes. Goodbye, Jane…' Elizabeth's voice trailed off.

'Bye for now, and don't worry,' Jane called out. But Elizabeth had gone.

Jane replaced the handset. Elizabeth's call worried her. Surely there couldn't be another twist in events, but Elizabeth was certainly in a stressed state over something important. No doubt she would find out on Saturday what it was all about. In the meantime all she could do was wait and wonder.

She made her way home, still deep in thought. As she neared her apartment block, she encountered Gerald going the same way, and they walked back together. She was still so preoccupied with Elizabeth's telephone call that she felt she had to tell Gerald what had happened. As usual he was interested in this new development, but he was unable to suggest what it might be all about. He insisted that Jane let him know the details after she had been to see Elizabeth.

Jane left him outside his and Anna's apartment and climbed the last flight of stairs to her own. She had hardly had time to change when her phone rang. It was Anna inviting her to supper. For once Jane caved in. She was a bit tired and was not relishing the thought of having to prepare a meal. She joined her neighbours for a meal of spaghetti bolognese. They chatted about Elizabeth's phone call in between Anna fussing over Jane, telling her not to do too much and asking about her injuries.

The time was heading for nine before Jane managed to return to her own apartment, explaining that she wanted to phone Bob and tell him the latest news.

Bob answered his phone immediately, and Jane couldn't wait to relate the day's events. Bob was unable to throw any new light on the subject of Elizabeth's announcement. He promised to join Jane early on the Saturday morning to accompany her to Elizabeth's house.

Friday turned out to be a particularly busy day at work, and on top of that, realising that she would not have time on the Saturday morning, Jane had booked a Friday evening appointment at the hairdresser's. Immediately after leaving the salon, she visited the supermarket to do some shopping, and it was well after eight by the time she returned to her apartment. Preparing a meal and doing a few household jobs took up the rest of the evening, and it had turned eleven before she finally got to bed.

The next morning she woke up with a shock to find it was nearly eight o'clock. Bob had said he would be there around nine! She flew out of bed and into the bathroom. Despite the rush, she was ready and waiting, neatly dressed in a pink blouse and casual trousers, when the outside buzzer sounded to announce Bob's arrival.

As soon as he entered her hallway Jane threw her arms round him and kissed him.

'Darling, it's marvellous you're here.' She planted another kiss on his lips.

They eventually released each other and Jane headed for the kitchen. 'I'm getting us some coffee,' she announced over her shoulder.

Bob followed her. 'Good. Just what the doctor ordered.' He grinned as he sat down at the table.

Jane was busy with two mugs. She made a face at him. 'I actually overslept,' she confessed.

'How did your first week back at work really go?' asked Bob.

Jane paused, the kettle in her hand. She smiled at him. 'Not bad at all. Much better than I expected, despite it being a bit busy at times.' She swiftly thought of something else to say. 'And the bruising has improved a hundred per cent.' She turned her injured cheek towards him.

'I've seen that,' he replied. 'It's looking much better than when I saw you on Monday.'

'And the marks on my wrists and ankles are fading as well,' Jane announced cheerfully.

'Good. I don't like to see you marked.' Bob gave her another grin.

'How's your week been?' asked Jane over her shoulder as she poured the coffee.

'The new project has really taken off. It looks as if we'll have to employ some extra help.'

'Oh, that's great!' exclaimed Jane, placing a mug of coffee in front of him. She sat down at the table. She suddenly thought of something else to add to her news. 'I think that new role for me at work is going to come off. You know – me being assistant editor.'

Bob took a sip of coffee. 'Good for you. Go for it,' he enthused.

They chatted over their coffee, talking about their work activities. At one point, during a brief lull in the conversation, Bob stifled a yarn. 'Sorry,' he said.

Jane grinned. 'You were up early. I was up late. That means I do the driving. No arguments,' she responded, laughing.

Jane kept her word and drove the car to Elizabeth's house. At the start of the journey she was quite cheerful and chatted endlessly about a host of things while Bob listened and commented here and there. As they drew near to their destination she became less buoyant, and anxiety started to cloud over her.

She voiced her concern to Bob. 'I'm getting a bit worried. I'm just wondering what Elizabeth wants to tell me.'

Bob did his best to reassure her. 'I feel pretty confident that after all you've been through in the last few months, you'll be able to deal with whatever it is.'

Jane gave a chuckle. 'I do hope so,' she replied.

It was almost half past ten when she turned the BMW into Tipton Street. She managed to find a parking space almost outside Elizabeth's house. Bob was out of the car immediately. Jane followed more slowly. Now they had arrived, pangs of anxiety were starting to stab at her again.

They walked up the tiled garden path, Bob in front of Jane. He gave several raps on the door knocker. It seemed a long time before anything happened. He was just about to try again when the door opened.

It was Beth Browne, Elizabeth's neighbour, who stood there. She smiled at them. 'Hello. Come in.'

Jane greeted her and shook hands and then introduced Bob.

'Elizabeth's waiting for you in the sitting room,' explained Beth, leading the way. She halted briefly and whispered to Jane, 'She's in an awful state about something. It was me who persuaded her to telephone you.'

Jane had no time to reply before Beth opened the door of the sitting room.

Elizabeth Barton rose to greet them as they entered. She held out her hand to Jane. 'It's nice to see you again. I'm so glad you've come.'

On the spur of the moment Jane gave her a hug. 'I'm happy to be here,' she replied cheerfully. She quickly introduced Bob, and Elizabeth gave him a limp handshake.

'Do sit down. I must get you a cup of tea,' said Elizabeth, but clearly her mind was on something else.

'I'll get it,' Beth was already turning to leave the room.

'No, no. I must help you,' Elizabeth insisted.

Jane and Bob were left alone in the old-fashioned room. They sat together on the settee, silently looking round at all the trimmings from a past age. It was a good four or five minutes before Elizabeth and Beth returned bearing tea and cakes. It took a further few minutes for everybody to be served.

It was at this point that Jane raised the matter in hand. Holding her cup and saucer on her lap, she addressed their host. 'Elizabeth, you said on the phone that you wanted to see me and that it was something to do with my not being Ruth Ashington. Could you explain a bit more?'

Elizabeth was clearly extremely stressed. Her tea rested on a side table untouched. She clasped a handkerchief in her hand, toying with it constantly as she responded to Jane's question. There was a pause before she spoke. 'Yes, I have to tell you about it. I should have done so when you were here before. Now I feel so bad about everything. It's all my sister's fault...' Her voice trailed off as if that was all she was going to say.

Jane tried to help her. In a soft voice she asked, 'Do you mean Mrs Marshall, who was in charge of Goodmanton Orphanage when I was there?'

Elizabeth shook her head. 'No. Susan became part of it later. It was Evelyn who started it all.'

'That's your sister in Australia?' Jane asked gently.

'Yes,' was all Elizabeth replied. She was still playing with her handkerchief and she looked completely miserable.

Jane could see that she was going to have to prompt her all the way. 'Can you tell us a little bit more about Evelyn?' she asked, hoping that what she wanted to know would come out in the process.

Her strategy appeared to work. Elizabeth suddenly seemed to be a bit more ready to talk. She looked at Jane and Bob as she spoke. 'Evelyn was the cleverest of all of us three girls. She trained as a dentist and was very good at her job. She got a good position with a practice in Bristol.' She paused yet again.

'And what happened then?' Jane asked softly.

Elizabeth took a sip of her tea for the first time. 'She went to Australia for a holiday. While she was there she met Danny, who was apparently quite high up in politics. Evelyn told me she was very attracted to him and got on very well with him.'

'So she stayed in Australia?'

Elizabeth shook her head. 'No. She came back here and went back to work, but she kept in touch with Danny. She planned to go back to Australia and marry him. That's when it happened.'

'What happened?'

'She was still seeing an old boyfriend of hers. And then she became pregnant.' Elizabeth paused for a second as if to let this sink in, and then she continued, her voice stronger now. 'I never liked the man. He was a rogue if ever there was one, but at the time Evelyn was stupid and careless. I tried to tell her not to see him, but she was very stubborn. She wouldn't listen to me.'

'What did Evelyn say when she found out she was pregnant?' asked Beth.

Elizabeth looked first at Beth, and then at Jane. She seemed happier to talk now. 'She was devastated. She didn't know what to do. At one stage she was going to have an abortion, but then she decided to have the baby.'

'What about the fellah who got her pregnant?' asked Beth.

Elizabeth sniffed in disgust. 'He refused to have anything to do with it. He always claimed the child wasn't his, which wasn't true. Eventually he disappeared, and later on he ended up in prison.'

The truth was beginning to glimmer for Jane. 'Was I that baby?' she asked.

Elizabeth tried to smile at her. 'Yes, dear. You were.'

Jane was silent for a few seconds. She was doing her best to take in what she had just heard. At long last she had the truth. But she knew there must be more, and now she was determined to find out whatever that might be. 'So Evelyn is my mother, but how did I become Ruth Ashington?'

The question seemed to upset Elizabeth again. She clutched her handkerchief as if for comfort. She looked up at Jane with tears in her eyes. 'It was all my fault. I should never have done it...' Her voice trailed off in misery.

Jane suddenly got up and moved over to her. She bent over and put her arm round her. 'It's all right, Elizabeth,' she said softly. She waited a few seconds and then asked soothingly, 'Can you tell me what happened then?'

Elizabeth stifled a sob. She wiped her eyes with the handkerchief and started to talk slowly. All the time she gazed at the floor in front of her. 'It was when the Ashingtons employed me to look after Ann's baby. One evening I discovered the baby dead. I knew it was a cot death.'

She stopped talking for a second and then turned to look at Jane. 'Evelyn and I changed the babies over,' she said simply.

There was silence in the room for what seemed to be a long time. Jane knew that everybody was expecting her to make some sort of response to Elizabeth's revelation, but she found that she needed a short time to fully comprehend what she had just heard. At long last she knew the story of her past. Things were starting to make sense now. There were just the loose ends to tie up.

At last she ventured another question. Looking at Elizabeth she asked, 'Did nobody ever suspect anything?'

Elizabeth shook her head. 'It was quite easy. Ann Ashington never came near her baby. She seemed to be always ill. Miles Ashington wasn't interested, and I had the baby to myself day and night.'

'Whose idea was it to swap the babies – yours or Evelyn's?' Jane asked gently.

Elizabeth appeared to be more relaxed as she explained. 'Evelyn never wanted you. She wanted to go to Australia and marry Danny. She knew he wouldn't marry her with somebody else's baby around. She'd have done anything to achieve her goal. When Ann Ashington's baby died, I could see it was an opportunity. I contacted Evelyn and we exchanged the babies that night.'

'And Evelyn never had any regrets?'

Elizabeth shook her head. 'She thought it was a good idea. She thought you would grow up in a well-to-do family and have all the privileges.'

Jane hesitated as she waited to see if Elizabeth would reveal more. When nothing came she smiled ruefully and spoke her thoughts. 'Instead of that I ended up in an orphanage.'

'That was Miles Ashington,' Elizabeth responded quickly.

'But I went there as Ruth Ashington and ended up being Jane Carroll. How did that happen? It was the question to which Jane had sought the answer for a long time.

This seemed to catch Elizabeth unprepared. She looked miserable as she replied. 'That was the work of my sister Susan.

Miles Ashington paid her quite a lot of money to change your name on the orphanage records.'

Jane was aghast. 'You knew about this?'

'Susan made me promise never to tell a living soul. She told me both of us would be in danger if I told anybody.'

Jane did not respond immediately. She could hardly believe what she had just heard. When she had set out to find the truth about her past, she had had no idea that it would all end up like this and that she would find herself to be the object of intrigue and greed.

It was Beth who brought the conversation to life again. 'So what happened to Evelyn after all this? Did she marry Danny?'

Elizabeth looked directly at her. 'Yes. She went to Australia and married him, but it wasn't a happy marriage. He died about twelve years ago.'

'Did they have any children?' asked Bob.

'Only one, and the baby died at about twelve months old. Evelyn couldn't have any more children after that.'

'Did she never want to come back to England?' asked Beth.

Elizabeth was still looking miserable. Her voice was scarcely audible at times, almost as if she was talking to herself. 'She did talk about it a few years ago. I wish she'd make the effort. Her health isn't too good now and she's getting forgetful.'

'It would be nice if you could be together,' remarked Beth.

Elizabeth did not reply. She seemed lost in her thoughts.

Jane quietly returned to her seat beside Bob. She was trying to get everything into perspective. There was one big question that she still had to ask Elizabeth. She took advantage of the lull in the conversation. 'Elizabeth, when a friend and I were looking through the birth, marriage and death records, we never found my birth listed. We only found the one for the Jane Carroll who is buried in Great Wishington. I don't appear to exist in the records.'

Jane's comment stirred Elizabeth from her thinking. She stared at her for a second as if in disbelief. 'Oh, but you must be. I have your birth certificate here somewhere.' She reached over to a side

463

table and retrieved a bundle of old envelopes tied with a ribbon. She started to look through them, studying each envelope in turn. 'Evelyn left it with me when she went to Australia. She was fearful Danny might see it,' she added.

The others waited as Elizabeth searched the bundle. Suddenly she exclaimed, 'Ah, here it is! I knew I had it.'

She got up and handed Jane a rather tatty envelope that was yellowed with age.

With almost trembling fingers Jane opened the envelope and pulled out a familiar red certificate. She started to read aloud, slowly, then abruptly stopped. She looked with astonishment at her three waiting listeners. Then her gaze fixed on Bob.

'But this is a different name,' she announced.

Chapter 53

Jane was silent for a few moments. She looked at the document she was holding once more, then at Bob as she spoke again. 'The name on this certificate is Correll, not Carroll.'

There were murmurs of surprise from Bob and Beth.

'That explains a lot,' remarked Bob, looking over Jane's shoulder at the certificate.

Jane started to read aloud again. 'Mother, Evelyn Correll.'

'I don't think Evelyn could ever have looked at it,' remarked Elizabeth. 'I never looked at it either.'

Jane continued her examination of the certificate. 'It was Evelyn who registered the birth,' she remarked. She looked at Bob. 'No wonder Gerald and I never found any record of my birth.'

'Everything certainly fits together now,' he replied.

There was another silence. It was Jane who eventually broke it. She spoke softly as she addressed Elizabeth. 'Did Evelyn... my mother never enquire about me after she exchanged me for a dead baby?'

Elizabeth did not respond straight away. She looked utterly miserable and anxious as she formulated an answer. When she did speak her voice was hardly more than a whisper. 'Evelyn wanted to build a new life for herself without you. She thought it was the best thing for both her and you.'

Elizabeth's words hit Jane like a battering ram. Her own mother had abandoned her to fate.

'It seems so callous.' Jane almost choked on the words. Her tears were not far away.

Bob quickly put his arm round her. 'It's all right, poppet,' he whispered.

Jane made a big effort to regain control. She tried her best to absorb the information she had just received and put everything into perspective. As far as she was concerned she was still the same person she had always been. She had grown up believing that she had no mother, she reasoned, so what was the difference now?

Partly to divert attention from herself, Jane glanced again at the certificate. She suddenly noticed something else. She turned to Bob, a glimmer of surprise showing. 'Look at the date. I'm younger than I thought I was. Over six months younger.'

Bob grinned. 'That's one bonus!' he exclaimed.

Jane turned to Elizabeth again. Observing her obvious distress, she tried to make her voice sound as kind as possible. 'Why didn't you tell me about this when I came to see you the first time?' she asked.

Elizabeth clutched desperately at her handkerchief for some comfort and looked at Jane. She was almost in tears, her voice almost a whimper.

'I should have. I know I should have, but somehow I couldn't bring myself to tell you. It all happened so long ago. Then there was Miles Ashington. He made me promise not to tell you.'

Jane interrupted. 'You told Miles Ashington I'd been to see you?' she asked.

Elizabeth nodded. She paused for a short time and then continued talking. She was looking down at the floor now, and at times it was almost as if she were talking to herself. 'He told me not to tell you anything – and that if I did things would be bad for me.'

'Phew. Nice guy to have around,' remarked Bob.

Elizabeth continued. 'He can be a nasty man at times.'

'So it would seem,' commented Jane, remembering her own ordeal. She prompted Elizabeth again. 'What made you change your mind and contact me?' she asked.

'It was after I read in the paper that Miles and his son had been arrested, and all the horrible things that had happened to you. If I'd told you everything before, all that might not have happened. Then the police came to see me. I didn't know what to do. I should have told them about all this, but I didn't... Now I'm so confused. I don't know what you must think of me.'

As she finished speaking, Elizabeth's tears began to flow. She dabbed desperately at her eyes with the handkerchief.

Compassion welled up inside Jane. She moved over to Elizabeth again and put her arm round her as she spoke softly and calmly. 'It's all right, Elizabeth. Really it is. I'm not angry with you. You did what you thought was best at the time.'

Elizabeth looked at her, tears in her eyes. 'The police... What will I do about the police? I should have told them everything when they came.'

Before Jane could say anything, Elizabeth became quite agitated. 'Do you think they'll send me to prison? I couldn't bear that,' she whimpered.

Jane thought quickly. The police would not be very pleased about Elizabeth withholding information from them, but in a way it was understandable, given Miles Ashington's threat of retribution hanging over her. She still had her arm round Elizabeth. She continued to address her quietly. 'I think you need to tell the police everything you know and explain why you couldn't tell them before – that Miles Ashington threatened you.'

Elizabeth was clearly not too happy with the idea. 'But they might arrest me for withholding information or something like that.'

Jane shook her head. 'I doubt it, but you have evidence they'll be interested in that relates to the case against Miles Ashington,' she explained.

'But what about me exchanging the babies?' asked Elizabeth. 'They might arrest me for that.'

Again Jane shook her head. Her reply was slow and considered. 'Well, as I am the person who was chiefly affected and I don't intend to do anything about it, I should think that would go a long way to influencing whether any action is taken.'

Beth swiftly turned to Bob. 'What do you think, sir?' she asked.

Bob thought for a second. 'I think I agree with Jane. The police need to know because of the involvement of Miles Ashington. I think it is unlikely that they would take any further action, though,' he added.

'Oh, I do hope you're right,' replied Elizabeth.

Out of the blue Jane had an idea. 'Was it an Inspector Boyd who came to see you?' she asked Elizabeth.

'Yes, I think that was his name. There was another policeman as well,' Elizabeth replied vaguely.

Jane launched her suggestion. Speaking in a kindly voice, she asked, 'Would you like me to explain everything to Inspector Boyd before they come to see you?'

'Oh, would you, dear? I would so much appreciate you doing that.' Elizabeth sounded a bit more cheerful.

'I'll get in touch with him and let you know what he says,' replied Jane. Then, gently she asked, 'How are you feeling now?'

For the first time since they arrived, a glimmer of a smile reached Elizabeth's face. 'I feel much better now that I've told you,' she admitted. 'I don't feel so upset about everything,' she added thoughtfully.

Jane and Bob exchanged glances, in silent agreement that it was time to take their leave of Elizabeth. She seemed to have calmed down a lot and appeared to be happy to let them go, now that Jane had reassured her by promising to contact her when she had spoken to Inspector Boyd.

It was Beth who showed them to the front door. As she shook hands with them, she whispered to Jane, 'I'll keep an eye on Elizabeth.'

It was early afternoon when they returned from Elizabeth's, and the rest of the day flew past. Bob had insisted on driving back from Charlton, and Jane had not objected. She wanted to think about all that had been revealed to her in the last few hours. Bob seemed to understand how she felt. He concentrated on his driving and let her sit back with her eyes closed and relax.

By the time they were back in the apartment, Jane was feeling brighter. Bob suggested that they dine out in the evening, and on the spur of the moment Jane decided to telephone Mario and see if she could book a table at such short notice. She was lucky. After Mario had flirted with her as usual, he announced that as she was his special client he would find her a table.

Jane decided to tell Gerald immediately what had come out of their visit to Elizabeth. Of course Anna insisted that they stay for a cup of tea while Jane related all the details. It took some time because Gerald and Anna kept asking questions.

Anna seemed quite disappointed that Jane was not Ruth Ashington after all. 'Oh, I think it's so sad that you aren't going to inherit all that money,' she remarked. 'Are you quite sure you aren't Ruth Ashington?'

Jane gave a little smile. 'Quite sure,' she replied. 'I'm just plain Jane Carroll.'

'Well, at least now you won't need to change your name,' Gerald remarked, at the same time giving Jane a grin.

Jane suddenly thought of something. 'Of course! All my personal documents will have incorrect information. I hadn't thought of that until now. How do I deal wlth that situation?'

Gerald thought for a second or two. 'I think Elizabeth and perhaps even Evelyn will eventually have to sign an affidavit so that changes can be made,' he remarked.

Jane was more concerned now. 'Do you think it will be difficult?' she asked, adding quickly, 'I mean, changing the details on my documents.'

Gerald shook his head. 'I would think not if you obtain the right information.'

'It's something for the future. We'll tackle it together,' declared Bob, smiling and putting his arm round Jane.

It was inevitable that Anna would want them to come for a meal in the evening, but Bob quickly chipped in, explaining that he and Jane had arranged to eat out.

The first thing Jane did when they were back in her apartment was to look at her watch. An exclamation burst from her lips. 'Gosh! Just look at the time. Six already. We've got to be at Mario's at seven.'

'We'll make it OK,' replied Bob.

'But I've got to get ready,' she wailed.

Bob grinned at her. 'Off you go, then.'

Jane sped away, calling over her shoulder, 'I'll be as quick as I can.'

'OK. Take your time,' Bob called back, as she disappeared into the bathroom.

He grinned to himself. He was pleased to have observed that since their return to the apartment Jane had brightened up considerably. She was back to her old self again. He was glad that he had been able to go with her to see Elizabeth. At least he had been there to give support. His admiration for her had increased when he saw how she had received Elizabeth's story, and the compassion she had shown her. Many people would have been angry and even spiteful over the whole thing, but she had accepted everything with great dignity.

It was a good fifteen minutes before Jane reappeared. She had chosen a simple outfit of a flared floral skirt with a wide belt, teamed with a white blouse. Her favourite necklace with the deep blue stone appeared in the vee left by the lapels of the blouse. She carried her white high-heeled shoes in her hand.

'Here I am,' she announced, smiling. She gave a quick glance at her watch and looked anxiously at Bob. 'Darling, I wasn't too long, was I?' she asked.

Bob grinned at her. 'No. You're fine.' He was already getting up from the settee to have a wash and brush up.

When he returned ten minutes later he had changed into a fresh shirt and a lightweight jacket. Jane was standing by the window looking out as he entered the lounge. She turned to face him.

'Darling, do you notice anything different about me?' she asked breezily.

Bob moved towards her and scrutinised her for a second. 'You're wearing our engagement ring,' he replied with a smile.

'I said I'd wear it on my finger as soon as I knew who I was,' remarked Jane, holding up her ring finger in full view.

Bob moved to kiss her, but she backed away. She gave him one of her coy looks. 'Save it for later,' she whispered. She added with a grin, 'Besides, you'll get my lipstick all over you.' She smiled at him. 'What else do you notice about me?'

Bob put his hand to his face and pretended to be thinking as he continued looking her up and down. 'You're wearing the anklet,' he announced triumphantly.

Jane was serious for a second. 'I had it repaired during the week. It's my lucky charm. I shudder to think where I might have been but for it.'

'Don't lose it again,' Bob urged.

Jane was smiling again. 'I won't,' she replied gaily.

Bob was going to say something, but she chipped in again quickly. 'And what else do you notice? There's a third thing.'

Bob was ready with the answer. He had noticed that Jane's legs were encased in sheer nylon immediately she had appeared. 'You're wearing a lighter shade of tights,' he replied confidently.

'Am I?' Jane asked with a mischievous grin.

Before Bob could even think of an answer, Jane slowly gripped each side of her skirt and raised it just high enough to reveal what she was wearing underneath. She let the skirt go immediately. 'Now you know,' she remarked, almost casually.

Jane had made some split-second decisions while she was getting ready for the evening. Suddenly a little bit of wickedness had come over her. She had always intended to celebrate the conclusion of her family history, and tonight was as good as any other. True, the outcome of her search was not what she had originally imagined, but at long last she knew where her roots lay. Bob had been a brick throughout the whole process. He had stuck by her and supported her through everything. Her decision to wear the anklet and stockings for the evening was just a little token of her appreciation and love for him.

Sitting in Mario's that evening, they talked about a host of subjects, but so far not the events of the day. It was almost as if they wanted to keep those until last.

It was only when coffee had been brought to their table that

Bob brought up the subject of Jane's past. 'How do you feel about things now?' he asked, looking at her intently.

Jane played with her spoon in her cup for a few seconds, thinking, staring down at the cup. She looked up at Bob. 'Now that I've had time to take it all in, I am beginning to feel fine about everything.' She sipped her coffee. 'It was a bit of a shock when Elizabeth first told me – I mean, the bit about me being exchanged for a dead baby. It all seemed so callous and a strange thing to do.'

'And now?' Bob prompted.

'I think I've accepted it. I had a mother who didn't want me and is still of the same mind by all accounts. I've considered myself an orphan all my life, so nothing has changed really.'

'So Elizabeth is really your aunt,' Bob pointed out.

Jane responded to his suggestion quickly. 'That's another odd thing. I don't regard her as my aunt. Somehow, I don't think I ever would.'

Bob nodded in agreement. 'I know what you mean,' he replied.

Jane took another drink of her coffee. She was deep in thought. It stimulated her next comment. 'There is one thing that I still do find hard to comprehend.' She paused for a second, looking at Bob for a reaction, but when he continued to wait for whatever else she had to say, she continued speaking. 'I just can't understand how anybody could be as charming as Miles and Gail Ashington, yet at the same time plan to do what they did to me.'

Bob's reaction was prompt. 'It's very hard to understand. Miles comes over as such a nice guy. I doubt if Gail knew anything about what was being planned. I don't think Miles or his son would have discussed their intentions with her.'

Jane nodded. Then her face took on a serious look. 'I still can't help wondering what they had in mind to get me out of the way…' She stared thoughtfully into her cup, and could not help adding, 'And they would have succeeded but for one little bit of luck.'

'Thank goodness you lost your anklet in that barn. That was the clue that convinced the police that you might not have drowned and could still be alive.' Bob smiled at her as he finished speaking.

'And Mel apparently telling them where I was,' she added.

It was Bob who spoke first again. 'It seems quite ironic now that Miles Ashington went to all that trouble to get rid of you and get his hands on more money, when all the time you weren't Ann Ashington's daughter at all.'

Jane was still in a pensive mood. She looked at Bob, her face still serious. 'You know, Bob, that's one of the things I'm really glad about after visiting Elizabeth. Somehow it never felt right to me being Ruth Ashington, and I'm pleased now that I am who I am.'

'Well, I think you can say that you have completed your family history research,' Bob responded with a smile.

Jane smiled briefly as she remembered something. 'You know, I think Gerald was quite annoyed with himself for not picking up my birth. I could see it in his reaction when I was telling him about the incorrect name on the certificate.'

'It was an easy thing to miss.'

'Well, I certainly did.'

'And now you'll have to change your birthday,' laughed Bob.

'And, yippee! I'm six months younger!' recalled Jane. She was immediately serious again. 'Well, I know one thing. I'm rather glad it's all over. I don't think I'd want to go through everything again,' she remarked.

There was a short silence between them. It was Jane who broke the spell. She was smiling broadly as she regarded Bob. 'Guess what? I had a card from Angus Pike during the week. He sent it to the office wishing me well.'

Bob was amused. 'Good for him,' he replied.

'He most likely still wants me to model nude for him,' Jane remarked, almost casually.

'Hey! I've got first option on that.' Bob feigned indignation, but he was grinning.

'You'll have to marry me first,' replied Jane, with a mischievous smile.